The

MW01141586

By the same author

THE PERILOUS ART OF FORGETTING

THE BRIDE'S VEIL

GOODBYES, THEY OFTEN COME IN WAVES

First Edition 2015

This book is a work of fiction. Names and characters are the product of the author's imagination and any resemblance to actual persons, living or dead, is entirely coincidental.

ISBN 978-1-329-75600-7
©Marisa Livet 2015

Visit the author's website at
www.marisalivetbooks.com

MARISA LIVET

GOODBYES, THEY OFTEN COME IN WAVES

To Thomas Vivian Mahon

CHAPTER ONE

The Arno River had risen as a consequence of the torrential autumn rain, which had fallen relentlessly for nearly a week. In Firenze they were already waiting for the flood in a kind of distressed resignation. But in Capacciano there was no serious risk the river might burst its banks. When the Arno crossed the village it was just an average stream, still close to its source on mount Falterona. Even the growing flow would remain in the riverbed of the hilly Casentino area, dragging its ruinous power down to the plain.

Notwithstanding the lack of immediate danger, several villagers, sheltered by large old-fashioned umbrellas–oddly all black–stood on the top of the banks, scanning the churning muddy water with distrust. They looked doubtful and slightly ill at ease, like a casual visitor stopping on the threshold of a hospital ward to give a quick glance at the patients.

Amelio Sanchini, the mayor of Capacciano, called 'Riccioli d'Oro' (Golden Locks) because of his untimely and premature baldness, leaned carefully over the railings and cast a sidelong glance to the right, toward the Alpe di Catonaia buried in a dark shroud of heavy, leaden clouds.

"Humph! The rain won't stop falling, at least for today..."

Sanchini was a stately man in his forties, whose face–as if balancing the bald head–was adorned by a staggering dark beard and an equally impressive drooping moustache. His rather disquieting appearance made him look like a pirate or a cutthroat, at least at the very first sight, because it was immediately clear that the mayor of Capacciano was as meek as a lamb.

"Good morning, mayor!" A tall man, endowed with a thick head of grizzled hair, which luckily excited no envy in 'Riccioli d'Oro', greeted him heartily. "It's still bucketing down, isn't it? How about coffee? At least we might have a chat without the nuisance of these open, dripping umbrellas

"Oh, Mr Reginald, good to see you! Actually I need to speak to you about something...Let's have a coffee, but my treat, I insist! What about Mrs Ellie? Isn't she with you today?"
Reginald McKenzie shook his head and shrugged his shoulders. "With such miserable weather...I suggested she stay at home. I didn't want her to catch a cold. But I already miss her. I know it will make you smile, and it probably sounds quite silly, mostly coming from a man of my age..." He smiled earnestly to justify himself. He had been living in an incredible dimension of total serenity and happiness for more than a year and he still could not fully believe his luck.

The two men hastened to the coffee bar, nestled in a slightly de-crepit old house of a bright shade of ochre, tucked away in a corner of the small main square. Over the door an old fashioned sign, shining with raindrops, read: 'RaBARbaro' (RhuBARb), in an intentional but mysterious botanic pun. They closed their dripping umbrellas and propped them against the wall, where other umbrellas were already waiting for their owners, surely holed up in the comforting dry warmth of the 'RaBARbaro'. Inside the café a small troop of patrons were drink-ing cups of espresso, standing by the counter, as Italians do. The bar-keeper, a certain Lapo Tramontina, gave a slight, sober nod of greeting to Reginald and the mayor. Saying that Lapo was not loquacious would be a euphemism. He was very tall and lanky, with a melancholy, ab-sent-minded look unlike the traditional stereotype of a perfect bartend-er. But he was a master in his field and his cappuccino was renowned. They said that people even came from Arezzo to taste it. Besides that, Lapo's wife, Rosalba, could bake the most delicious 'sfogliatelle' one might dream of. Nobody knew how he met her or how he persuaded her to leave her native island of Ischia, in the gulf of Napoli, to follow him to Capacciano. They had been married for several years by now and were probably happy together. Rosalba had never lost her Neapoli-tan accent and the patrons of the 'RaBARbaro' had become used to hearing her sing in the back of the café, while she kneaded her sfoglia-telle and her baba, which so perfectly accompanied her husband's spe-cialty coffee beverages.

"Two cappuccinos, please, Lapo!" The mayor asked. Lapo seemed indifferent to the order, but his hands started immediately working skilfully with the professional coffee machine which made a fine show behind the counter. He adjusted the pressure of the steam to infuse the milk with air, transforming it in soft foam. Then he poured it carefully over the surface of the coffee and added the master's touch, rotating cleverly the cups. Finally he put the cappuccinos in front of the mayor Sanchini and Reginald, who, even though it was not the first time, couldn't help feeling childishly pleased to see his initial sketched elegantly on the foam. The personalized cappuccinos were one of the surprising creations of the RaBARbaro owner. Reginald reached out gluttonously for one sfogliatella, while the mayor chose an almond croissant. Then he whispered in Reginald's ear: "I'd like to speak to you about something a little confidential. If it's okay with you, it would be better to sit at that table in the corner, we might have a more private conversation..."

Reginald, a bit puzzled, nodded in assent and they took their cups and pastries to move to a more discrete place, while the other patrons remained at the counter.

Then he looked interrogatively at the mayor, biting into the sfogliatella, wonderfully crispy outside and filled with a soft mixture of ricotta cheese, cinnamon and candied citrus.

"I know it will sound silly to you," said Sanchini, "but my wife is tormenting me and I cannot persuade her to let it be. She claims I have to do something to reopen the investigation on a case already completely closed and solved. You'll wonder why I'm telling you all this..." Sanchini hesitated, trying to find the right words. "You see, Mr Reginald, this is a small village, people talk, there are rumours... In short, apart from the official version of facts, people say that you and the other owners of the farm 'L'Oliveto', how to say? Uhm, that you all are really the ones who solved the crime; you know what I mean, that awful story about the murdered girl, for which our fellow citizen, Giorgio Cini the photographer, was groundlessly charged. Of course you were right to stay out of all that, but, well, people say that Mr Peter was a police detective once and Mr William knows life well and he has a real investigative talent. My wife is aware of all this, so if you were so kind to listen to her and then reassure her that there is no reason to suspect anything fishy, she'd probably listen to you and leave me in peace..." He stopped, waiting for his interlocutor's reaction, to guess what direction he might take to continue.

Reginald was taken by surprise, but also felt intrigued.

"Please, Mr Sanchini, if you think we might be useful, don't hesitate. But frankly, I don't see what we might do for your wife..."

"Oh, let me explain a bit more. Then you'll decide. Maybe you can speak to your friends at the farm and then perhaps meet my wife.

She doesn't listen to me, but I think she would listen to you. She holds all of you in high esteem."

Amelio Sanchini sighed like a furnace and gulped down half his cappuccino. "My wife had a very close, dear friend, Iris Ciancaleoni. They had been schoolmates. Iris was the only daughter of a magnate, the owner of the most important ceramics and pottery factory in the region. She got married a few months before us. Obviously we attended the wedding, an extraordinary party. My wife was the bride's maid. A few years later Settimio Ciancaleoni, Iris' father, suddenly died. A heart attack. But Iris had always been intelligent and strong willed; she took over the reins of the factory and made it flourish and prosper even more than before.

My wife and Iris could not meet each other as often as before, since she was extremely busy with her management tasks, but they had always remained in touch. She told me that, in the last months, Iris seemed to be worried or maybe nervous, but she never told her about any particular problem. At least I don't think so. Just to make a long story short, about two years ago, Iris' husband, one Sabatino Alunni, persuaded her to take a break for a holiday cruise. Unfortunately it appears poor Iris suffered with a serious form of depression—surely due to the work pressure. While the cruise ship was on the open sea, she committed suicide. Her body was never found.

"Of course the police investigation was long, careful and accurate. All suspicions were against the husband at the beginning, but he had an unassailable alibi, since he was never alone when his wife disappeared and he was the first one to ask for a search of the whole cruise ship. He could prove his absolute innocence and really was devastated by the loss of his wife.

"He was investigated and observed for a long time, but the evidence never favoured him as a suspect. The case was finally dismissed as suicide.

"But recently my wife has heard that Iris' widower is going to get married again and has gotten it into her head that there's something very suspicious and that Iris didn't commit suicide, but was killed. I don't know what to do. She insists I must go to the police and persuade them to reopen the case, but...Oh well, you can see what I mean!"

Reginald sipped the rest of his cappuccino with renewed pleasure, taking the time to think over what the mayor had just told him. In a corner of his mind a warning bell started ringing, suggesting to him that maybe Mrs Sanchini wasn't talking through her hat. But how could he take an assignment in the name of his friends? Besides, the whole matter seemed quite delicate.

Amelio Sanchini was staring at him with the look of a child expecting to be reassured of his rights in a quarrel with schoolmates. The stocky mayor really resembled an actor dressed up for a Disney's film, something like "Blackbeard The Pirate" or who-knows-what-else. Reginald had never had much chance to go to the cinema in his life and by now people went even less often to theatres to see films, but since he had the incredible luck of marrying his wonderful Ellie–he could not help smiling with infinite tenderness thinking of her–like many middle-aged couple they had taken the habit of watching several films on TV and he'd somehow recouped his former lack of familiarity with cinema production. There was nothing menacing in Sanchini's expression. He reminded Reginald of a rather childish, but frankly amusing, character from a phantasmagorical film he had watched with Ellie some time ago. So also the mayor's strange story sounded to him like an improbable film plot. But Sanchini was obviously waiting for an answer, which Reginald couldn't deny him. Reginald had never been able to disappoint people.

"I see, Mr Sanchini. I can understand your situation. Very often women trust their apparently irrational perceptions more than the logic of facts, but it doesn't mean that their way of approaching a topic is necessarily wrong. Anyway I'm sure your wife was questioned by the police at the time of that, uhm, sad episode and she expressed her doubts, if she had any and clearly the detectives took everything into due consideration..."

Sanchini shook his big, bald head with resigned fatalism.

"That's just it, Mr Reginald. When the inquiry was in progress my wife didn't seem to find anything suspicious in poor Iris' suicide. Of course she was deeply saddened and shocked by her dear friend's death, but she accepted it. We tried to give our moral support and sympathy to Sabatino, even though we had never been his personal friends. He appeared to be really devastated by his grief and he refused our invitations saying he had to save his mental energy to keep running the factory, because it was what Iris would have wanted. Then he got really absorbed by work and we hadn't heard from him very often. It's only when my wife heard he was going to get married again that she started thinking these inane thoughts about Iris's death. I think it's only because inside herself, maybe unconsciously, she can't accept that Sabatino loves another woman, she thinks he's betraying Iris' memory. But it's absurd. Sabatino Alunni is more or less in his forties. I think he's as old as me, and I'm forty-five. Of course I'd be devastated if I lost my Loredana, God forbid, but if I did I couldn't exclude to make a new life for myself one day...after that."

The mayor stopped speaking and passed his hand over his eyes, as if the simple thought of losing his wife could move him to tears. Reginald suddenly realized he could not remember the features of the woman who was obviously dearly loved by her husband, even though he was sure he had met Mrs Sanchini several times. Still he felt the need to reassure Sanchini that he would pay attention to his trouble.

"Well, if you really think our advice might help your wife calm down, I suppose you two could come to our restaurant for dinner one of these days, as our welcome guests, of course. Mrs Sanchini could clarify her concerns and then we might try to..."

The mayor didn't let him finish and grabbed with both hands Reginald's hand which disappeared inside them, like a thin slice of ham between two generous slices of bread.

"Oh, thank you, thank you. Just tell me when and we'll come with infinite pleasure. Please, let me order you another cappuccino or maybe would you like something else?"

"Oh, no, thanks, I'm fine. I have to go to the farm before I get home to see my wife and it's already a bit late. But I'll call you in the afternoon, after I talk to Peter and William."

Reginald freed himself with difficulty from the mayor's powerful hold and went to recover his umbrella, which was faithfully awaiting him by the coffee bar entry. He was aware of the inquisitive and curious looks of the other patrons, who had not been able to hear his conversation with Sanchini, but had guessed it might be something interesting enough to enliven the monotonous daily routine of the village.

The dogged rain kept falling and Reginald smelled something in the air that reminded him of the Irish weather from his former life.

He drove carefully up to the farm; he had never been a passionate driver and still found a bit hard to drive on the right. Luckily the country road was empty so he felt no need to hurry.

There wasn't that much work at the Bed & Breakfast these weeks. It was low season and the bad weather didn't make people want to book a holiday in a country farm, even if it did sit atop a Tuscany hill.

But William's small and smart restaurant was, as always, very busy. There was no low season for the fashionable and by now well appreciated 'Mr W.'s Seven Tables'.

The tables were always booked, even months in advance. They accepted the reservations in the order they received them, without making any exception for so called 'VIP's', who often thought that their pseudo-fame would be enough to give them privileged access. But William always kept the seventh table free for anyone who might arrive at the last moment, often just ordinary people.

Reginald parked in the main courtyard of the farm. He still felt relieved when he reached his destination safely and could leave his car. However, he didn't dare reveal his unreasonable fear to his wife, who was an excellent, self-confident driver instead.

Gulliver, Peter's big hairy dog of indeterminate breed with an inexplicable liking for rain, greeted him with a totally unbidden enthusiasm as soon as he got out of the car. Fortunately Peter appeared to call off that remarkably huge ball of wet fur.

In the cosy warmth of his studio, where Peter had followed him, Reginald briefly informed his friend about his meeting with mayor Sanchini. Peter, still miraculously and naturally suntanned even in the rainy late autumn, was pensive listening to Reginald, as if the petty episode had stirred something deeper in his mind. Finally he spoke with his usual calm and firm tone of voice, just veiled with a slight unease.

"Maybe this is the perfect opportunity to seize. I intended to speak to you about a confused feeling creeping about my mind for a while, but maybe it only needed the right moment to crystalize." Immediately Reginald felt alarmed, even though he had no idea about what Peter was talking about. Simply it was painful for him to imagine his friends having sorrows.

"I...I didn't realize there was something wrong..."

"No, no, take it easy." Peter immediately tried to calm him down, since he well knew how empathic Reginald was. "There's no problem, at least I hope not. You see, it's William. You know how restless he is. You and I, Reginald, we're less complicated souls." He grinned lightly. "William is different. People like us are happy living in peace and we get uneasy with change. We're creatures of habit. But William needs stimulating challenges; he's not comfortable with routine, even if it's as enjoyable as our daily life here.

"Of course he likes living with people he loves, and he enjoys playing in his restaurant. But that's not enough for him. He needs intellectual stimulation to feel alive. Lately, I get the impression he's bored. Of course, everything is fine between us. It's not that. But odd as it may seem to you and me, everything goes almost too smoothly here for him."

With a melancholy smile, Peter continued. "Even those of us most close and dear to William don't know much about his life before we met him. Shreds of his past resurface now and then, giving me the troubling impression that he endured much more than he's allowed me to guess. I know, more or less, that he suffered with depression for a while, although it may have been a long time ago.

"I'm worried, Reginald. I'm worried William might slide into some form of manic-depression if there's nothing to break the repetitive rhythms of his life. Of course it's not happening yet, but I'm afraid of this risk. So, to make a long story short, I do think the potentially intriguing case of Mrs Sanchini's suspicions—whether well founded or not—might be a speculative diversion for him. For sure, William will be amused to hear her story."

Reginald nodded. "So it's settled, then. If you think it's okay, I'll call Sanchini to invite him and his wife to our restaurant tomorrow evening. Of course I know in advance that Ellie would like to be present, too. She so enjoyed her role in our inquiry to clear Giorgio of the murder charge, and I think she turned out to have the makings of an amateur detective!"

"Who has the makings of an amateur detective?" William Collins, wearing jeans and a black jumper which made him look even taller, winked cheerfully at his friends, who couldn't tell if he'd heard more of their conversation or not. But after all, one never knew anything exactly about William Collins.

CHAPTER TWO

Mrs Sanchini's main feature was her total lack of features. Unlike her extroverted husband, whose distinct facial hair meant his presence, Loredana Sanchini had no physical trait, no peculiarity, which might remain impressed in others' memory. She was a completely bland person, impossible to describe. She was in her early forties, of average height, average build, average everything... She was neither beautiful nor ugly. Her nose was neither too long nor too short, without any slight hump or capricious top. Her eyes were neither too large nor too narrow and their too common light brown colour didn't contribute to make them unforgettable. Her voice was neither shrill nor deep. Her hair-style, even though tidy and accurate, didn't add any special feature to her face, which only a very compassionate observer might label as "moderately pretty".

She had enjoyed the excellent and refined dinner. She participated modestly in conversations, without competing for attention with table companions, and surely said nothing silly or misplaced, though nobody would remember anything she said.

Ellie, who was nearly 15 years older and had slightly irregular lineaments, shone like a newborn star in comparison with the plain Mrs Sanchini. Nobody could easily forget Ellie, after meeting her; she received many glances, not only from her besotted husband.

'What did I do to deserve such a marvellous gift from life?' Reginald kept wondering with moved gratitude every time he looked at his wife *'She's the sunshine of my old years.'*

As if she'd read her husband's mind, Ellie reached out to caress his hand, then winked ironically at Peter. "I know, it's definitely sloppy and even rather kitschy that two old people like Reginald and I indulge in so many sentimental ridiculous gestures, but although my beloved husband here was not my first love, he will be my last beyond a doubt. I feel free to enjoy my love."

"Oh, Mrs Ellie, I could not agree more deeply! My beautiful wife will be my last love too. There is no one else like her." The piratical mayor nodded touched at his featureless wife, leaving the others under the impression of the mysterious effects of love.

It was late and most clients had already left the restaurant. Only two well-known television anchor-men and their charming even though a bit too flashy partners were still sipping a digestive liqueur at a table in a corner.

William and Themba came out from the kitchen and, pretending to not notice the wave of one of the two showgirls from the anchor-men's table, pushed two chairs between Reginald and mayor Sanchini and joined them.

William looked as fresh as a daisy and Peter caught himself thinking that he could not remember ever having seen William really tired.

After listening patiently to the usual thanks and congratulations on the quality of his culinary art ("That roasted duck was really delicious, Mr William. I've never tasted anything better..."), William turned directly to Mrs Sanchini.

"My friend Reginald has already reported the main points of what your husband told him about this matter that's troubling you. But I'd like to know your version and your impressions..."

Mayor Sanchini squirmed on his chair and loosened his shirt collar, hidden under his beard.

"Loredana, darling, maybe it's not necessary to tell the entire story right now. Mr William and Mr Themba must be exhausted and there is really nothing they can do. They can only repeat what I have kept on repeating during the last few weeks. Iris unfortunately committed suicide and nobody is to blame for that. There's no shame if Sabatino feels like turning the page after two year. You would do the same and..."

But Loredana seemed quite determined and she detected in the silent attention of the onlookers an encouragement to continue. With a gentle, apologetic smile at her husband she started her accurate and detailed report.

Everybody listened without interruption. Only Themba had to leave for a moment when the anchor-men and the showgirls decided to finally pay the bill and leave, but he hurried to come back, reluctant to miss any part of Mrs Sanchini's story.

At last Loredana laid both hands on the table, punctuating the evocative gesticulating which had accompanied her speech. She once again smiled ruefully at her husband, as if to make clear she didn't like contradicting him, but couldn't do anything else under the present circumstances.

"I know my husband hoped you would persuade me to change my mind and to accept Iris' death, but I cannot. He will object to my apparently delayed doubts. It's true, when Iris died two years ago, at first I accepted the idea of her suicide, but I was too shocked to think rationally at the time. I didn't have the mental energy to think about the judicial inquiry. Then, my daily life overtook my grief. We didn't keep in touch with Sabatino. We've never been very close to him; for me he was Iris's husband, not a personal friend.

"Things have changed since I heard he was going to get married again. Don't get me wrong. He has every right to do it; Iris died two years ago and he's still young. But, even against my will, a small warning signal started flashing in my mind. I believe Iris was killed, or maybe kidnapped...her body, as I told you, was never found."

"Loredana, honey, Iris threw herself out of their cabin balcony into the Atlantic Ocean. How could they find her body?"

Ignoring Sanchini's faint attempt to rebut, Peter asked Loredana directly. "Mrs Sanchini, according to what you told us, your friend's husband was questioned carefully in great detail by the police and he was under investigation for several months, but they couldn't find the slightest evidence to prosecute him. He had an alibi for the night his wife committed suicide, because he was always with other passengers when she disappeared..."

But Mayor Sanchini insisted.

"Yes, yes and then there was that handwritten message by Iris. Tell them about that, Loredana!"

Mrs Sanchini looked hesitant. She started drawing little circles on the table surface with her forefinger, then she said plainly, "It's true, actually, they found a note, written by Iris, on the cabin bedside table..."

Peter watched William out of the corner of his eye and noticed that he looked deep in thought. He had not said a single word since Mrs Sanchini had started speaking. Suddenly he took out from a pocket a small notebook which he usually kept in the kitchen to write down a sudden inspiration for a recipe change or a fancy ingredient he needed to buy. Reginald captured his glance and handed him a ballpoint pen.

Reginald, oddly, always had several pens with him. '*Each of us'*, thought Peter, '*has his own oddities and peculiarities. Who can claim what is normal and what is not in all that?*' William jotted something down and then looked at Mrs Sanchini with his incredible green-grey eyes, which never went unnoticed. His voice sounded neutral, but Peter realized immediately that something had aroused his interest.

"Mrs Sanchini, do you by any chance remember the exact wording of that note Iris wrote?"

Loredana Sanchini nodded in assent with a triumphant expression.

"I brought it all with me, here...just a second!" She bent partially under the table and resurfaced with a briefcase nobody had noticed before, protected by that strange spell which made everything related to the woman practically unnoticeable. "I have collected all the press-cuttings which were published at the time of the inquiry. For several days the news made the headlines of local newspapers and also national television coverage. I couldn't record videos, but I wrote down the main information given, and here you can see all the articles I cut from magazines too. There are also photos of Iris' last message, look!" She thumbed through the papers and took one out, which she handed directly to William.

As if they were members of a jury, William passed it from hand to hand, after scanning it carefully. Only the mayor gave it immediately to the person on his right, Ellie, without examining it. He was coming to the unhappy conclusion that it hadn't been the best idea to try to eliminate his wife's absurd obsession about Iris 'death.

The photo was very clear. The newspaper cutting had been carefully preserved. It showed a note that looked like a quarter page, partially torn, of what might have been an exercise book or writing pad. The message was written in clear handwriting.

'*My dear Sabatino,*

I know I'm going to upset you and, believe me, I'm sorry for that. But I cannot see any other way out. I'm tired of this kind of life and my decision is made'

That was all. There was no signature.

"It was undoubtedly Iris' handwriting. I can recognize it myself. But handwriting experts have examined it carefully and it's an absolute certainty that it was Iris who wrote these words." Mrs Sanchini admitted honestly.

"In spite of that, you are still persuaded that Iris didn't commit suicide..." William said with a wry smile. Then he raised his voice a little and asked, "Why, then?"

"I cannot justify it rationally," Mrs Sanchini shook her head with a humble expression, "but I know Iris would never have killed herself. She was not really depressed either. Of course I had not seen her often in the last years before her death and I must admit she sounded nervous or worried about something the last time I spoke to her. But I think it was a matter connected with her business. She had all the responsibilities of the factory on her shoulders, you see."

"And these responsibilities are now all on her widower, aren't they?" William grinned lightly. "By the way, Mrs Sanchini, you started having doubts when you heard that he was getting married again. Do you know who the lucky fiancée is?"

Loredana's face was suddenly lit up by a confident smile which made her look almost pretty.

"Of course I know and it's exactly what pushed me to think this over again. I knew I was right in trusting your flair. You and your friends are all so clever and we are well aware of what you did to help Ilaria and Giorgio. Thank you for listening to me in such an unbiased way, in spite of my husband's preconceived ideas." She cast another apologetic glance at the mayor who had remained speechless. "Sabatino is going to marry a woman he met on the cruise ship, when Iris disappeared, one from Milan. I don't know anything else about her, besides her name, wait, I made a note of it." She sorted through all the papers she had taken out from her briefcase that were now spread over the table. "Jessica, Jessica Mandelli. She should own a kind of beauty centre or hair salon in Milan. I don't know exactly. I haven't seen her in person yet. But she was on that ship; they met there."

"I see. What do you expect from us, Mrs Sanchini? How can we help you?" It was Peter's turn to talk, while William, Themba and Reginald had begun reading all the old articles she'd carefully collected from newspapers and magazines.

"I don't know exactly. I'd simply like you to help me to understand if my doubts are completely baseless. If they are, I promise I won't insist anymore and will resign myself to it; but if you think there is actually something strange in this whole story, then, please help me to persuade my husband to use his influence to ask the police to reopen the case." She opened her arms to show she had nothing else to say and waited hopefully for an answer.

Peter and William exchanged a knowing look, and then Peter said "Mrs Sanchini, can you leave all these documents and press-cuttings here until tomorrow? We'd like to read them more carefully, then tomorrow we'll return them to you and give you our sincere opinion."

"Oh, certainly, you can keep them. Thank you, thank you so much!" Mrs Sanchini smiled with an intent expression. "Now it's time to go back home, darling, it's very late." She added, turning to her husband, who appeared lost in a rather goofy situation he couldn't master as he had expected. He mumbled, "Yes, yes, darling, it's time to leave now." And then he nodded to the others. "Thank you so much for the delicious dinner and for your patience."

After the Sanchini's departure Themba, Caterina and the small kitchen staff went to tidy up the kitchen and to do the usual routine to close the restaurant until the next evening. Reginald, Ellie and Peter remained sitting at the table with William perusing all the notes and clippings which Loredana Sanchini had entrusted to them.

"I like when everything seems to be clear and solved in a case like this. That's exactly when you can be sure that an imponderable element is hidden somewhere, ready to emerge and to shake up all certainties." William looked full of energy as if he had just awakened from a perfectly restful sleep instead of carrying the weight of a long day's work on his shoulders. "I wonder why the suicide's note was written so banally and plainly on a torn piece of paper", he said.

Reginald, who had not spoken much during the evening, emerged from his silence to add his opinion to the discussion.

"I'm no expert at cruises, well, to tell you the truth, I've never been on a cruise, but I've seen these big cruise ships on many TV documentary films. I think that, like in hotels, they have complimentary stationery on the cabin desks, notepads with the cruise company logo, pens and so on. It would be the first sheet of paper one would find within reach, in case an emotionally troubled person would feel like leaving a last message, before..uhm before..."

"Exactly!" Peter smiled at his friend. "But Iris...Iris—what's her name? Ah yes—Iris Ciancaleoni wrote her last goodbye on a plain, half torn piece of paper, coming from we don't know where..."

"Oh but we do know!" Ellie, who had continued to carefully read a couple of long articles, intervened. "It's written here that during the investigation the police found a notepad in a drawer that corresponded to the sheet of paper where Iris wrote her note..."

"Did they say whether the other piece of the torn page was found in the cabin too?" William asked.

"No, it's not mentioned. Probably it wasn't considered an interesting detail by the journalist who wrote this article, but we can't exclude the possibility the police found it somewhere. Surely they controlled the wastepaper basket." Ellie shook her head, unable to add further information to that apparently marginal detail.

"Very, very amusing. An intriguing challenge we have here, my friends. We haven't tackled a 'cold case' yet. It's time we members of the great 'Improbable Kitchen Detectives' Club' start fighting against crime once again!" William was jubilant. "It's decided then. We'll accept the case!"

"But, William, wait a minute, we don't have any official authority to act as private detectives..." Peter sounded quite amused and also relieved to see the bubbling enthusiasm of his partner.

"Ah, Italian bureaucracy...I know, I know." William humorously pretended to be worried. "But I didn't mean we necessarily have to add an elegant brass nameplate at the entry gate: ' L'Oliveto – B&B – Gastronomic Restaurant – Private Investigation Bureau'. If we don't ask our clients for money and if we don't look for any privilege, as private citizens we're free to allow our little grey cells to work. I hope you are in, because I really feel like accepting the case. Tomorrow I'll go to Capacciano to meet Mrs Sanchini and...yes, I'll go to the hair dresser too, because I need to get my hair cut!"

His last statement took everyone's breath away. Nobody could imagine William without his long ponytail, which danced on his shoulder every time he laughed in his typical ways, like he was at this very moment.

CHAPTER THREE

The soft and expert fingers of Annina threaded their way through William's thick, dark hair as if she was unravelling a skein of precious silk. He closed his eyes with a pleased groan. The scalp massage was not only nicely relaxing, but it seemed to also stimulate his concentration.

William had gone into that small hairdresser's at random. Capacciano was a small village, but possessed–apparently incongruously–six hairdressing salons. Peter and Reginald had become clients of the same barber shop, the one by the photographic studio. It was run by a rather old barber who was considered an institution in Capacciano, but William had never felt the need to get his hair professionally cut, since he kept it in a long ponytail. He had chosen this place by chance, maybe attracted by the vaguely Chekhovian name of the parlour 'The Three Sisters – Unisex Hairstyle'. Actually there wasn't an intentional tribute to Russian literature in that, just a simple statement that it was a family business, run by three sisters, and one of them, William learnt with amused surprise, was actually called Olga. The similarities stopped there.

"Your hair is marvellous." Annina spoke with a soft voice that matched well the delicacy of her movements. "But it's really time to cut it and change your style. A handsome man like you should adopt a more modern and fashionable haircut." She sighed. No illusions. Everybody knew by now in Capacciano that the two owners of 'L'Oliveto' were a gay couple. But she had never seen two men more attractive than them. What a waste. And Annina sighed again deeply.

William roused himself from his thoughts and smiled at her captivatingly.

"Fashion is a form of ugliness so intolerable that we have to alter it every six months."

Annina was baffled, unable to neither recognize a Wilde's quote nor fully understand what it might mean. But she didn't lose her professional aplomb and asked gently "Do you already have an idea about the haircut you'd like? I might suggest you a popular modern style for you. Very short cut on the sides and the back of the head and much longer hair on top, softly fixed with spray after giving it volume with a good brushing..."

William didn't answer immediately, trying to find the most suitable words to decline, without hurting Annina's feelings. Only one year earlier the great majority of men under forty proudly flaunted the same hair style with erect gel-stiffened spikes on top of their heads. Now they've replaced the spikes with the same style Annina was suggesting to him. Shaved heads with a bush of hair on the top left untouched, but carefully arranged in a kind of up-to-date version of the Elvis Presley's pompadour style. William grinned imagining himself decked out like that in an Elvis' costume. It would definitely be a great way to celebrate his forty-second birthday, if he'd ever celebrated birthdays.

"One of my fellow countrymen once said that everything popular is wrong. He didn't follow fashion, he created it. Personally I have no interest in creating fashion, but I'm too old to follow them. I think, Miss Annina, that I'd be perfectly happy if you give me a normal haircut to the middle of my ears and let it be, but I'd be pleased to try your special herbal balsam and any other treatment you might suggest. "

The only other client present on that gloomy autumn morning in 'The Three Sisters', whose hair was carefully trimmed by Olga, turned amiably to William.

"So you are Irish. I'd heard in the village the owners of that so beautiful big farm were Britons. You speak Italian perfectly, by the way."

The man who'd spoken was partly hidden under a pink cape to protect his shoulders from cut hair, a cape left from days when the shop was a woman's parlour exclusively. He was well-built with a broad, sincere smile and dark eyes. He withdrew his right hand from the cape and held it out to William.

"My name is Emilio Ciricola and I'm warrant officer of Carabinieri, Maresciallo, as we say. I have just been transferred here to be in command of the local Carabinieri station. My predecessor retired. But I've already heard of you. It's my job, after all." He smiled again apologetically.

William vaguely remembered the former officer commanding the Carabinieri station, a stern, bony man he'd never had any contact with. Maresciallo Ciricola, on the other hand, had an open, friendly attitude and William thought he might be about his own age. At his turn reached out to shake hands, while Annina warned him with a little shriek,

"Oh, please, don't move, I'm cutting your hair!"

William grinned and kept on speaking without turning his head, but looking at Maresciallo Ciricola reflected in the mirror in front of them.

"Nice to meet you. I'm William Collins and, yes, as you rightly guessed, I'm Irish, exactly as my two friends who run the farm with me are. I'm used to people here getting confused when they see us speaking English to each other."

"Oh but you quoted Oscar Wilde twice, saying he was your fellow countryman..."

William thought this Maresciallo Ciricola definitely sounded like a nice person, but the surprises in store were not over yet.

"I have been to Ireland." The Maresciallo kept on. "It will make you smile probably, because it might sound quite unusual for a Southern man like me, but I'm passionate about Irish traditional music. Of course I'm not a real musician; I'm an average enthusiastic amateur. My wife and I went to Ireland on honeymoon. She lovingly indulged my longing to see Ireland for our first trip together, a place I'd always dreamed of visiting. Though you'll forgive my saying the Irish weather isn't exactly the best for tourists from warm and sunny climates." He paused for a moment. William realized that Ciricola was a very extroverted and spontaneous man. They'd known each other barely five minutes and he was already telling him everything about his life.

"I have always been intrigued by serendipity." William shook his head, provoking another outraged squeak of alarm from Annina. "I'm an amateur musician too. What instrument do you play?"

"Of course it will be familiar to you. I can play bodhrán, uhm, I'm afraid I can't pronounce it properly, and violin."

William laughed openly. Luckily Annina had just finished the most perilous part of her work with scissors.

"I play bodhrán too! I'm not very skilled with violin, but I can manage with banjo and guitar, then I sing..."

Ciricola fidgeted in jubilant surprise with the arm of his chair, but Olga didn't protest, since she had almost finished with him.

"It's fantastic to accidentally find someone in this small village I can talk with about one of my main passions, Mr Collins!"

"Please, call me William. I think we're more or less the same age, too. I'd be glad to show you my musical instrument, maybe we could play together once, just for fun. We have a restaurant which is open only in the evening, but I'd be happy if you came to visit us for lunch, when it's convenient for you. We'll have time to compare our musical experiences. Of course my invitation is heartily extended to your wife, as well..."

Maresciallo Ciricola suddenly showed a strangely melancholy expression.

"Thank you, William and you, please call me Emilio. I'll be more than happy to accept your kind invitation. As for my wife..." He paused. "My beautiful Rosaria, she died one year ago. All of a sudden, you see. A fulminating cancer. There was nothing to do. In three months she was gone." And, at William's great embarrassment, he burst into tears, silently. Big tears rolled from his eyes down his cheeks, through an indelible shadow of dark beard, even though the man shaved twice a day. The Carabinieri were allowed to have beard and moustache by now, but very few of them seemed to enjoy the opportunity. The majority of them remained faithful to the traditional look as originally established: accurately shaved face, well-trimmed short hair, nothing unique which might not match the perfect uniform they proudly wore.

Annina and Olga didn't seem to be surprised by the emotional reaction of Maresciallo Ciricola. In fact both of them immediately started comforting him with sincere and vaguely motherly cares. Olga brought him a glass of water, while Annina handed him a box of tissues, encouraging him in a chanting voice, as if she were cheering up a child.

"There, there, don't cry, Maresciallo. Your wife would not like to see you suffer like that. She's surely looking at you from heaven now..."

Oddly Emilio Ciricola calmed down immediately at these words and smiled with gratitude, without feeling uncomfortable at all. He drank a sip of water and gently refused the box of tissues, taking out from his pocket a perfectly ironed and well folded white handkerchief. In order to do that, he had to remove the pink cape and William noticed he was wearing an impeccable black uniform with red bands on the trousers' sides.

"I'm sorry, William, but it's still so hard for me living without her. I'll never get used to that. Are you married?" Then suddenly the Maresciallo remembered something someone had told him and blushed a little for the gaffe. William, frankly amused, reassured him.

"I'm not married, I live with my partner, we have been together for several years and, yes, I'd be totally devastated if I lost him as tragically and suddenly as you lost your wife. You have all my sympathy and understanding."

Annina gave the last touch to William's new haircut. His head felt unusually light. Without the weight of the long ponytail that kept his hair relatively straight, his natural curls took shape again and framed his forehead and cheekbones.

Olga also looked satisfied. She joined her hands and naively expressed her approval.

"Holy Virgin Mary! You look so gorgeous and young. I have never seen hair as beautiful as yours." Then she cast a glance at Maresciallo Ciricola, who was standing in his elegant uniform. While his average height seemed rather short next to William, he looked quite good, and she quickly added, "You are a handsome man, too, Maresciallo. I hope both of you will become our regular clients."

William and Emilio left the hairdresser's together and William proposed they have a cup of coffee. Ciricola nodded vigorously in assent.

"I was going to suggest the same thing. You beat me to it because I needed a second to put on my cap. You know we can't be without it on the street when we're in uniform. Since you invited me first I'll let you pay for our coffees. Then I'll have the pleasure of taking my turn next time."

William had begun finding this open and spontaneous man very pleasant. He liked his direct but kind way of speaking.

They walked to the 'RaBARbaro', which was only a few metres away. Lapo Tramontina, the silent barkeeper, emitted a little grunt, which was his usual way of greeting his patrons, but then he realized that the Maresciallo had arrived to Capacciano only recently and probably it could be good to make an effort to show him a sign of welcome. So Lapo, full of good will, rubbed his hands on his apron, as if to encourage himself, and spoke:

"What might I serve you?"

All present in the café were flabbergasted, like the audience in 1930, when, for the first time, it was possible to hear the peculiar Greta Garbo's low voice in the film "Anna Christie" which was promoted with the slogan 'Garbo talks'.

Unaware of all that, Maresciallo Ciricola asked politely for two cups of espresso.

CHAPTER FOUR

"Come for lunch to meet my family!" William had told him. Emilio Ciricola confessed to himself it was one of the most appealing invitations he had had for a few years. Accepting the reassignment to this Tuscan village seemed to be a good decision, at least so far. It looked like a very quiet place and his subordinates at the Carabinieri station had impressed him positively, but he had a feeling the daily routine would be a bit flat. What could happen in a place like this? Car thefts, burglaries, maybe a few altercations among villagers. Of course there was the recent case that resonated across the country, the murder of that politician's daughter, a dirty story of paedophilia. But Capacciano was not the Bronx. According to probability theory, nothing like that would happen again in the village for a very, very long time.

Fate had brought him–quite unexpectedly–to a place where he'd never have imagined finding shared interest in his great passion for Irish music and culture. He was determined not to miss the chance. So as soon as he could manage to have half of a day free from work, he called the farm to ask if the invitation could be considered still valid. The man who answered greeted him heartily, even though Emilio was sure he'd never spoken to him before. Then William was on the phone, who soon confirmed he would be welcome at any time. "Today? Of course. When I say anytime, it means exactly that. Come over whenever you are free. We are quite informal. If you arrive early we'll take an aperitif, waiting for lunch."

Ciricola wore plain, civilian clothes. It would unwise to land at the farm in high uniform. Nevertheless he didn't feel completely at ease without his uniform, which he had been used to wear most of time.

He knew where the farm was, on the top of a hill, a few kilometres north of Capacciano, but he had never been there. In spite of the gloomy weather and the veiled horizons, covered with a light mist, he realized that the view from there was breathtaking. The rain had stopped falling so relentlessly, but kept on reminding everyone of its presence with a few showers a day. When the Maresciallo parked his car in the farm courtyard, the clouds parted briefly, allowing him to enjoy the landscape which faded in bluish uniformity over the last line of poplars downhill.

His contemplative mood was abruptly interrupted by the advance of an enormous, hairy dog, completely wet and a rather worrisome little squad of fluttering geese. As a peasant's son, he was familiar with all domestic animals, so this unexpected welcome committee didn't trouble him at all. The dog and the geese seemed to realize that and stopped their defensive assault to remain there, staring curiously at the stranger.

Four men emerged from the farmhouse and Ciricola's first thought was that they were all amazingly tall. Then he recognized William's broad smile as he held out his hand to him and made brief introductions.

"Hello, Emilio! You have already met Gulliver, our dog, and my geese. Here is Peter, my partner." He pointed at the youngest of the tall men, a very handsome and sun tanned fair-haired fellow, with sincere and childlike clear blue eyes which oddly fit his strong-willed face.

"And here are Themba, our associate and dear friend, and Reginald, the most precious of our friends and a manager of our farm too."

The aforementioned Themba, a slender and very tall black man, curiously dressed in a rainbow-like outfit, wrung his hands and greeted him in perfect Italian, veined with a slight Tuscan accent. The last man, equally tall, was older, with a very distinguished look; he greeted Ciricola with very kind words in fluid, understandable Italian marked by a heavy English accent.

"Let's go inside, it's humid and cold today. The ladies are waiting for us by the fireplace," said William leading the guest to the main door.

One minute later Emilio Ciricola found himself comfortably installed in an armchair and surrounded by smiling people, without realizing exactly who had put a stem glass full of Prosecco in his hand. The room was large and looked very cosy, even though the furniture was not at all pretentious. A large stone fireplace, where big logs were crackling and spitting, made him feel a sense of homely warmth which he hadn't felt for too long a time.

"It's good you came a bit early, so I have time before lunch to introduce my family to you." William smiled in a humorous way. "I suppose we might seem like an anomalous and dissimilar bunch of people, and some might find it difficult to consider us a family. But that's what we feel ourselves to be. Schiller said that it's not flesh and blood but the heart which makes us fathers and sons.

"Reginald, Peter and I are Irish. We were all born in County Galway, in a village called Ballybeg. We have in common the fact we have never had any real family. Reginald and I never had supportive parents, while Peter was luckier from this point of view, since he had a wonderful stepmother, an exceptional lady, who was a great friend for Reginald and me. Unfortunately she died five years ago. It was a terrible loss, but it led to a fundamental change in our lives. Peter," William winked, ready to one of his favourite coups de theatre, "Peter was a police officer, a very good one, and he would probably have continued his professional careers if we hadn't meet. I know I needn't make you a sketch, but it would be quite hard to make the villagers accept a chief of local police living in a couple with another man. At the same time we were really fed up with the obligation of keeping our relationship hidden as if we had to be ashamed of it. When Julia, Peter's stepmother, who of course was informed of everything and thought there was nothing to be ashamed of, she was a special lady, as I told you, well, when Julia died, we took a decision and...just to make a long story short, we have been living here happily for nearly five years.

"As for Reginald," William looked absolutely delighted reading certain amazement in the eyes of the Maresciallo, "Reginald had been a Catholic priest for uhm...how long? Don't know exactly, thirty-five years? So to our great regret we had to leave him in Ballybeg, when we left. But, being a man of intelligence and integrity, he'd already started his, I would say, philosophical evolution. He had been in a great spiritual crisis, but as he described it, he'd come to believe that while he would never lose his faith in God, he had totally lost faith in the church. It was difficult for him, but he was very brave and consistent and left the priesthood. After a very difficult year, he joined us here. We are a family you see.

"Themba, Italian Citizen, born English, professor of Philosophy and happy husband of that smiling Italian beauty you see there," William pointed at Caterina, who blushed, "And the proud father of the twins, who keep disturbing us taking photos, is a lifelong friend and valued collaborator."

The aforesaid twins, a girl and a boy obviously both eighteen, who actually had spent most of their time with cameras in their hands, bowed graciously and ironically.

At that point a nice lady with curly hair, who was sitting on the sofa by Reginald and hadn't yet spoken, could not help interrupting William's long description to introduce herself directly.

"I'm Ellie. I'm not Irish, and maybe for this reason William neglected me." She laughed affectionately at him. "I'm English, even though I have been living here in Tuscany for many, many years and last, but absolutely not least, I'm Reginald's wife. We got married less than six months ago, so we can be considered newlyweds, which is rather humorous at our age, but life often is an amusing tragedy isn't it?"

Emilio Ciricola, overwhelmed by all this unexpected information and by the peculiarity of the people he was meeting, realized he had not taken a single sip from the glass he kept in his hand. He did. The sparkling wine was delicious. The girl, one of the twins, handed him a tray covered with little spoons of white china, each filled with a mouthful of something different. He tasted one at random and then, nearly against his will, he took another one captured by the gorgeous flavour.

Suddenly he felt relaxed and perfectly at ease in that uncommon company. He decided it was his turn to introduce himself.

"I'm happy to have accepted your invitation and I hope we'll have a chance to develop a friendship. You know probably already, that I arrived to Capacciano only few weeks ago to be in charge of the local Carabinieri station, after my predecessor retired; but I don't think it's a good idea speaking of official charges now. I prefer to let you know something about me on personal level, since you have been so kind to do so with me. I'm Apulian; I'm a widower, unfortunately. My wife and I had no children. Nevertheless I come from a huge family, still based in my native Apulia and I'd tell a lie if I claimed all my relatives are as close to each other as you appear to be. My parents made me study at University at great economic sacrifice. I got a degree in Political Science. I joined the Carabinieri because for us it's a family tradition and I'm very proud of my choice. My life had always gone smoothly until my wife's illness. She left me too early, after fighting bravely for three months. I don't see how I can overcome that...." His eyes suddenly filled with tears and he was unable to speak.

A general feeling of embarrassment chilled the atmosphere, but Caterina, Themba's wife, reacted immediately. She went closer to the Maresciallo and hugged him tight, nearly cradling him gently, whispering to him.

"Poor, poor soul. But she's always with you; you feel that. She doesn't want to see you suffer. Be brave, cheer up, drink a little wine, it will help you. You are among friends."

Emilio Ciricola looked relieved and smiled sadly. William was absolutely sure that Caterina had never met him before, but she had approached him to relieve his sorrow quite naturally, exactly like the two hairdressers had done in their parlour a couple of days earlier, in similar circumstances. William thought it over and realized that Caterina and the Maresciallo were the only two really Italian people in the room. Maybe there was something in their alchemy that he'd not fully grasped yet.

"Please, feel all free to call me just Emilio," requested the already emotionally recovered Maresciallo. Then he added pensively, "Perhaps when we meet in official situations, we might be more formal, but..."

There are so many different ways to express grief and it's never certain that he who cries louder is the one who suffers more; but nobody doubted that the extroverted Maresciallo was not totally genuine in his displays of emotions, which followed each other like on a roller-coaster.

During the meal the conversation was lively and relaxing and there were many the questions about Ireland and its traditional folklore.

"I'm so pleasantly excited." Repeated Ciricola sipping his coffee. "It's one of my dreams which comes unexpectedly true. I can learn so much from real Irish musicians..."

"Well, in reality William is the only Irish musician here." Peter couldn't help smiling at that burst of enthusiasm. "Reginald and I are Irish, but we haven't any talent for musical instruments; we might just sing along a little. Gianna and Malusi can play, but they are not Irish... Maybe next time you visit us—because we do hope you will— you might bring your instrument with you and we'll have the joy to imagine being back at one of our authentic Irish pubs."

"No need to wait for next time." William pretended to be serious. "Emilio brought his violin with him; it's in his car boot. Isn't it, Emilio?"

"How can you know that?" Ciricola was a bit puzzled.

"It's not difficult to deduce that at all. You would ask me to see my musical instruments and if I proposed we play together, you would have taken out the violin. You didn't show it earlier because you are a very polite person and you didn't want to impose an unrequested music-session on us. On the other hand, you might not have necessarily brought the bodhrán with you, because when we met for the first time I told you I played it too, so you might have rightly presumed I have surely one or two here at my home."

"Hell's bells! I thought that it was Peter who was the former police detective." Ciricola laughed, genuinely impressed. "So, if you agree, I can go to get my violin, which really is into my car boot."

"Eh, I was a regular cop and I followed traditional means of enquiry. But William, uhm, he's a kind of mentalist, even though he keeps on denying it. He's teasing and playful and he adores surprising others playing the role of a literary detective. Nonetheless I have to say he does have a certain intuition..." Peter grinned.

"A certain intuition?????" William pretended to be offended. "Is that all you can say? A certain intuition?"

The afternoon of music was a success. Reginald, for the first time in many months felt a slight pang of homesickness listening to William singing 'Mna Na H-Eireann' (Women of Ireland). But a glance at his wife made him feel that he was at home right here.

Emilio turned out to be a quite good amateur violinist. Pushed by popular acclaim, Reginald consented to sing 'The Rare Ould Times', after shying away, claiming that he had not sung for ages. He was gifted with a fine baritone voice and could sing along in tune. At the end of the ballade, Ellie hugged him enthusiastically.

"My husband! Do you see how talented my husband is?"

Several hours later when they were lying in bed, already close to sleep, Peter asked William what he thought of Maresciallo Ciricola, knowing in advance what he would answer.

"He's a rather gifted violinist, a pleasant, good-natured man, maybe a bit too emotional. I like him. Then it's always good to have friends among the investigating authorities. Ah, by the way, I do think we need fashionable new floor tiles for the restaurant. I've heard of a very good artistic ceramic factory in Umbertide... I might give them a ring."

Peter was not surprised at all.

"I bet you're talking about a certain Ciancaleoni Factory..."

"Ah, yes maybe..."

Both grinned silently in the dark.

CHAPTER FIVE

September 2012

To be honest, it was big indeed. Even bigger than that he expected. Notwithstanding there was something disappointing, even deceiving; he didn't know exactly why, trying to collect his thoughts. He always tried to understand the logical reasons of his first impressions. He found that reassuring, easier to accept.

The waiting hall was large and very crowded; in front of him a huge glass wall allowed people to see the side of the...the thing which stood up at its full height, so close. It didn't look like a ship. It reminded him of a building, a block of small flats. It didn't look like a ship. Ships, in his mind, should have a slender stem, a solid stern and be as tapering as a big, fast fish to ply the oceans lightly and securely.

He had never been on a big ship before. He had never been on a small one either. His experience as seafarer was limited to the small fishing boat he shared occasionally with a friend, and to the little rubber dinghy which had been his son's main joy during summer holidays at the seaside. But that was so many years ago.

Here was his only beloved son, handing him coffee in a paper cup. "I'm sure it's average, Dad. But it's better than nothing. Everybody crowds around the counter. It's a miracle I didn't spill it. I already added sugar, two spoons, as you like."

His son, Michele. A man now. But in Michele's bright eyes he still saw a little boy he'd had fun with in the inflatable dinghy those past summers ago.

Michele was forty and he was seventy. They were born on the same day and had always celebrated their birthdays together, usually in a warm, simple way, in their small family. But this time the women had decided to do things differently. They had thought it would be fantastic to do something altogether extraordinary to mark the jubilee. He had tried to protest feebly.

"But also when I was sixty and Michele thirty there was a jubilee, and the same when I was fifty and he was twenty...We did just fine at home as usual, a good meal and..."

Carla, his wife, had been unshakable. Carla was a very determined woman, and he admitted her temperament had been of great help and support in their married life and in the good state of their little business too.

Carla was the living proof of the relative truth of stereotypes about mothers-in-law and daughters-in-law. Not only had she never quarrelled with Valentina, Michele's wife, but from the very beginning she had found perfect harmony with her. They had a special relationship, as if they were mother and daughter instead of in-laws. He and Michele had even felt a little excluded from that privileged small feminine universe, where in some cases, like this one, decisions were made which involved them, as well.

The women had planned the cruise, claiming it would be a perfect opportunity to spend time all together in a different way from the usual, simple family celebrations and would also be a second honeymoon for all of them.

When he had realized that his only grandchild wouldn't be one of the party, but would be entrusted to Valentina's parents' care, his remonstrance had grown more vigorous, but Carla had made him feel selfish, saying that Valentina and Michele also needed a respite from dedicating their lives only to their son and their work.

So it was settled.

They had arrived to Savona, the departure port, early that morning and had left the car in the reserved parking.

"Everything is already perfectly organized." Carla had explained. And it seemed once again that she was right. They received a ticket with their parking number and handed their baggage to the clerks in charge. Then a mini-van took them to the harbour station. Here a large group of kind hostesses bustled about explaining patiently to everyone what they had to do. Basically they had to wait to be called, according to a colour code, and then to board the ship. He supposed it was necessary to follow this procedure to allow all the people to find their way to the ship in an orderly manner, since the number of awaiting passengers seemed to be really huge. Nevertheless all this reminded him of the queue at the post office, when everyone has to take a small ticket with a number at the automatic machine by the entry.

The small crowd of their fellows in colour started tottering and heading for the gate, which had finally been opened.

Valentina sounded thrilled; she dragged Michele by his arm and urged her parents-in-law.

"Hurry up, let's board. We need to find our cabins and..."

He isolated himself mentally, as he had learned to do to create a relaxing vacuum when he was in the middle of a noisy crowd. He became less receptive to sounds, but enjoyed looking over people, as if he were watching a silent movie. He promptly and dutifully followed his relatives, who preceded him along the boarding walkway, at the end of which two curvy hostesses, dressed up like improbable sailors, put a colourful lifebelt in front of every couple of passengers while a photographer took pictures of the scene.

He felt somehow sorry for the two girls, who had to repeat the same welcome phrase with the same standard smile to more than a thousand people. Or maybe there were even more. He remembered Carla mentioning the cruise was full up.

There was only one couple ahead of Michele and Valentina, who tidied her hair quickly with her hand, after noticing the photographer.

He could see them clearly, since they were in a slightly higher position than him; the walkway was on a gradient.

They were apparently about the same age as Michele and Valentina. The man was tall and well-built, dressed with a casual elegance (He had never paid attention to fashion, it's for young people. Rather he preferred to wear sober and proper clothes and he would have never put on one of those horrible, flashy fancy shirts he saw on many other mature passengers-to-be). The woman was also tall, with long blond hair. She wore dark sunglasses and stumbled imperceptibly, but her companion held her up promptly. She leant against him and he embraced her fondly. When the photographer took the routine photo of them, they didn't look at the camera but at each other, her head nearly hidden on his shoulder.

Michele and Valentina smiled when they all entered the stomach of the metallic whale, after the quick stop in front of the lifebelt, and he made an effort to smile warmly too, when one of the two sailor-girls put her aseptic and perfectly manicured hand, on his shoulder. Carla was more interested in hastening to their cabins.

They had booked two luxury cabins on the top deck. "We are entitled to get a 20% discount, because we are over sixty-five!" Carla had enthusiastically informed him. "But even if we had to pay the full price and even if it were more expensive...well, we deserve to afford it once in our lives after always working so hard."

He had to admit that the organization on board seemed efficient; they were directed to their cabins easily, even though the whole interior of the ship looked like a worrisome labyrinth. There was no time right now to explore the new environment more carefully, but he would have several days to do that at his leisure.

While they were trying to open their cabin doors, he noticed that the couple he had seen during embarkation were doing the same, one cabin away. Michele, who had recognized them, nodded friendly, and the man smiled broadly and said,

"Oh, you are Italians, too! There are so many foreigners on this cruise; I've heard a real babel of languages. I'm glad we are neighbours. I'm Sabatino Alunni and this is my wife Iris." Iris, the charming, tall blond woman, smiled too, silently.

"Nice to meet you. I'm Michele De Paoli and here are my wife, Valentina, my father Ernesto and my mother Carla. We are from Torino." They all shook hands with each other and then hesitated, a little ill at ease, as it happens when one is closed in a lift with strangers. Sabatino Alunni seemed to be the most self-assured in the circumstance.

"I've heard it's better to book a table at the restaurant as soon as possible to get a good one. Since the ship is full, there's likely to be a big rush trying to do the same thing as soon as it occurs to them", said Mr. Alunni. He then said to his wife, "Iris, darling, you might wait in the cabin to check whether they've already delivered our baggage, if you prefer. I can find the restaurant and arrange a table with the maître."

"Do you have any idea about the type of tables?" Carla realized that Mr Alunni had a certain experience with cruises.

"Well, as far as I know the majority of tables are for six people and several tables are for two as well. But I'm sure the maître can change the disposition to suit the passengers' preferences too. By the way, if you don't mind, since there are four of you and two of us, we might take a table together. I'm sure we are in the same restaurant, since we have the same type of cabin, on the same deck."

They quickly exchanged a glance, and then they decided there was no reason to refuse.

Carla and Valentina said they'd check their baggage first, but they wanted to go to see the restaurant, as well.

"Knock on our door when you are ready." Sabatino Alunni said amiably and disappeared into his cabin with his wife.

After tinkering a little with the plastic card that served as key, he managed to open the door and Carla, who had started showing signs of impatience ("Ernesto, can you manage or should we ask Michele for help?"), cheered up at once when she saw the size and furnishings of their cabin.

"Ernesto, look at this! It's as big as a hotel room, and the balcony... look!" Carla fluttered around opening all the doors. "The bathroom, look at the bathroom, look at the towels, they are so nicely folded like swans, look, look!"

He felt happy for her. Maybe it was really a good idea to take this cruise. Carla deserved something different as a holiday, and it was not a big problem that she'd insisted on bringing all those bags and suitcases for only twelve days. After all she was right about it; they didn't have to carry them on board. Someone had already done that for them. He went out to the balcony; he could see other passengers embarking. How many, he could not say. There were still hundreds of people. It reminded him of a melancholy procession, and he immediately reproached himself for this negative thought. Maybe it was because their cabin was so high, on the top deck, and everything looked small from there. He also wondered if the sea would look any less impressive when contemplated from the top of this enormous floating building.

CHAPTER SIX

Peter was driving calmly and safely, concentrating on the road, glossy from rain. The distance between Capacciano and Umbertide was about sixty kilometres, but the conditions of the road climbing up the Apennines were not optimal. The sweetness of the Tuscany hills had been replaced by the more severe and wild mountainous Umbrian reliefs. Several articulated lorries cluttered up the road. They climbed up slowly, like a procession of caterpillars on a twisted branch.

"We'll never arrive at this rate!" William snorted, fidgeting on the passenger seat. "There isn't any motorway restaurant either. I need a coffee!"

Peter grinned. He knew that William was not really so impatient; he was simply playing a role, like that, just for fun. It was William...

"It's not a motorway, so there can't be a motorway restaurant, by definition. But we're almost there and we can have a good espresso in Umbertide, before looking for the Ciancaleoni factory. We didn't fix any precise hour for the meeting and they told us we'd be welcome any time in the morning." Peter said, without need to stress that driving in the rain on this narrow and busy road was annoying him as well.

After the umpteenth bend, suddenly they could see an imposing fortress dominating a built-up area and the skyline of several bell towers and other apparently ancient buildings.

"Ah, here is Umbertide, at long last!" William sat up properly, while he had nearly curled up on the seat when he was pretending to be bored and sleepy for the too long trip. "It looks quite interesting. I've never been here. I wonder if it's possible to find a good restaurant. I think so. An interesting town indeed..."

Peter laughed heartily. "I can't believe it! A place you don't already know, William Collins! A first for both of us. Listen, I have an idea. I'm sure you'll survive awhile without an espresso, and I know they'll offer us one at the factory. So maybe we should go to the factory and then afterwards we can explore old Umbertide and find an appealing trattoria... As they say, business before pleasure."

William had called the factory two days before, introducing himself and feeling proudly surprised realizing that the person he had on the phone knew his restaurant. This fact had made everything even easier. William had explained that he intended to have all the tiles replaced with custom ones and he also wanted some artistic ceramics made especially for his restaurant. After that he had been asked to hold for a minute and was almost immediately put through to a man who had introduced himself as the director and owner of the company.

Following the directions of the TomTom navigator, Peter could reach the factory without problem. William hated GPS. He claimed that getting lost in an unknown place was one of the most enjoyable and sophisticated experiences to learn the dimension of travelling. But he didn't protest this time, since he was very curious to meet Sabatino Alunni in person.

The factory looked efficient and modern, even though it was set in a rather old fashioned building. A large ceramic plate by the entry door read: 'Settimio Ciancaleoni – Artistic ceramics and pottery'.

A slightly plump receptionist, soberly dressed, gawped at Peter and William when they went into the hall. She was very sensitive to male beauty and those two specimens of charm were for her like the apparition of holy saints for a churchwoman. Anyway she recovered from her sudden, delighted amazement and professionally welcomed them to sit on a comfortable leather sofa while she spoke quickly with someone by interphone.

A few minutes later a slender and tall young secretary, wearing smart glasses and a classy suit arrived to fetch them. She exchanged a quick glance with the receptionist, who, sure to not been seen by the two visitors, answered silently with a knowing smile.

Peter and William followed the secretary along a clean, well-lit corridor. "Please, this side." The secretary whispered politely. "Mr Alunni is waiting for you." When she pushed the door of an office a tall man got up from his desk armchair and jovially went to meet them holding out his hand.

"Good morning! I'm Sabatino Alunni. We spoke on the phone. It's a pleasure to meet you. Thank you for coming. As I told you, it would be much better for you not only to see our catalogues, but to visit our atelier and to see your production directly. Please take a seat. Would you like a drink? A coffee? A cup of tea?"

"Oh yes, thank you! I've been dreaming of an espresso during the entire trip from Arezzo." William grinned gluttonously.

"I'd like an espresso too, thank you." Peter said, giving a circular look at the office. A large and elegant room, well-furnished, without any flashy or superfluous element.

"Angela, would you bring us three espressos and maybe also a few croissants? I didn't find time for breakfast yet and maybe also these gentlemen didn't."

Sabatino Alunni was tall and well-built, without being necessarily considered overweight. He was exactly on the dangerous edge between having a sturdy constitution and the menacing beginning of obesity. His height helped him to remain on the safe side. He was perfectly shaved and emanated a light scent of expensive aftershave lotion. He wore a well-tailored, dark grey suit, a bit too classic maybe, which might suit an older man, while Mr Alunni was in his mid-forties and might look even younger.

Angela brought the espresso cups and a basket full of croissants. She asked briefly if they needed anything else and, after accepting her boss' thanks with a modest smile, she left casting a last, long glance at Peter, who was actually the one who most matched her tastes. Such a handsome man! The other visitor was also attractive, but she preferred a less original kind of male elegance, and she had always had a weak spot for fair-haired men.

The espresso tasted good, as if it came from a real coffee machine, with that special flavour which was impossible to find in coffee from a canteen. The croissants were decent, nothing more. Peter and William each ate one of them, feeling suddenly hungry after the first sip of espresso.

Mr Alunni seemed to be passionately fond of his work and he proudly showed them many catalogues of the items produced in his factory. William had to admit to himself that, besides the real reasons for coming here, he started feeling really interested in choosing ceramic decoration for his restaurant.

Alunni grasped his attention and made clear that, still being an artisanal factory, in spite of its dimensions and the international renown, they could make all kinds of tiles and pottery according to customers' wishes.

"Our designers are highly qualified and marvellously creative," he said gesticulating a little more than was necessary.

Peter had already noticed this peculiar habit of the man and he was sure William had observed that as well. Alunni practically mimed with his hands the things he was speaking of. He reminded a sign language specialist who translated the TV news to deaf-mutes.

They visited the workshop, always guided by a gesticulating Alunni. William hardly refrained from firmly blocking his hands, when he mimed with all details the work of the talented craftsmen. One of the designers, a real artist, found a common language with William and fascinated him by promptly intuiting just what William imagined for the new tiles. When they reached Sabatino Alunni's office again William and Peter were determined to finalize their conspicuous order. *'In any case we didn't come to Umbertide for nothing,'* thought Peter, nearly touched by the sincere enthusiasm William was showing for the ceramics. They agreed upon a first estimate and Mr Alunni guaranteed his total flexibility and availability. He mimed, probably quite unconsciously, the gestures of a man signing a contract and of other characters—who knows who and why—packing something.

Then he added "I'm particularly happy you decided to come over today, so we could discuss all the main points of the deal personally. Of course my valued collaborators will be at your disposal to fulfil all your requests, but unfortunately I won't be present for a while, and I would have regretted missing the chance to meet you and to show you our work. The matter is that I'm getting married next Saturday, and then my wife and I will leave on honeymoon for a couple of weeks."

William grinned, but Peter was quick to distract Mr Alunni's attention from that facial expression, which might be read in not too positive a way.

"Our congratulations! We appreciate the time you dedicated to us today even more."

At that very moment the office door opened and a woman came in, but immediately froze when she saw that there were two unknown visitors.

"I'm sorry, I thought you were alone. I don't want to disturb you, darling. I'll come back later."

"Oh no, please, honey, don't leave. These gentlemen and I have already finished our business and we were just chatting a little." Then he turned to Peter and William who had risen politely on their feet when the woman appeared. "Lupus in fabula! Here is my fiancée, Jessica Mandelli."

Miss Mandelli was a fresh-faced brunette, apparently in in her thirties. Her hair was cut very short, a style which enhanced her gracious features where the beautiful and lively brown-green eyes stood out together with a delicate and capriciously pointed little nose. She was not too tall, but well-proportioned and pleasantly slim. She looked tiny by her stout and tall fiancé, but her height was not below average either. She was wearing elegant grey trousers which the accurate eyes of William identified as real vicuna, a colourful jumper created by a well-known stylist and flat dolly shoes of soft leather. On her thin wrist she wore an incongruous, expensive men's watch. No jewels, except a big solitaire ring.

They shook hands and after few other phrases out of politeness Peter and William said goodbye to the fiancés and left.

It was practically lunch time when they managed to find a parking place in what looked like the historical centre of Umbertide, by a wonderful medieval church which immediately attracted their attention.

"It's better to feed the body before the soul." William stated with a semi-serious expression. "But after lunch I'd like to explore this church a bit more." Then he started roaming about with the same concentrated expression of a truffle-dog doing its job in a holm-oak grove. Peter followed him silently and trustfully. Finally William detected a small trattoria in a narrow cobbled alley. He approached and studied carefully the door and a little menu posted there.

"Here!" He cried, passing his final resolution. And Peter felt sure they would enjoy a gorgeous lunch.

The place was unpretentious, but cosy. A few tables were occupied by local regular customers. A ruddy-faced man in his forties cast a questioning glance at the two elegant and tall strangers. "Would you like to eat?"

Peter would have liked to answer that no, they didn't intend to eat, since they were in a trattoria at lunch time just by mistake, but they wanted to dance tango on the table. But he restrained himself, realizing with astonishment he was becoming more and more like William in these absurd reactions. William on the opposite paraded all his charm and answered the man that they intended to taste his 'Strangozzi' and they had come from a distance just for the fame of the dish.

The man was tamed and pointed at a table for two.

"Does it suit you?"

"Perfect, just perfect!" William gave a friendly smile; then he asked, "Is it still your mother who runs the kitchen? I was told that her Strangozzi are incomparable."

The man looked puzzled, but automatically replied, "Yes she's still our cook, and I'm glad you know her specialty. How do I serve Strangozzi to you?"

"Oh, we fully trust the cook. Please let your mother decide the best sauce. We are sure it will be delicious. We like all food cooked with love and mastery. We'd also enjoy a little wine, but it depends on the sauce your mother will suggest to us. So please, be so kind to bring us the wine you consider most suitable to the dish. "

The man nodded and disappeared into the kitchen. Peter laughed and spoke to William in English. "What in the world are Strangozzi and how could you know that the cook is the waiter's mother? You have never been here before, at least you told me so..."

William shook his head; since he cut his hair shining dark curls danced freely around his head when he did that.

"Strangozzi noodles are a slightly thicker version of spaghetti. The word Strangozzi is derived from the verb 'strangolare' which means to strangle in Italian. Legend has it that this was the pasta served to the parish priests when they dined at the homes of the parishioners. They would serve the priests large quantities of Strangozzi to strangle not only their appetite. This dish is one of the oldest in Umbrian cooking. It's made with 'poor' dough, without the use of eggs. It takes much more strength to make this type of pasta: without eggs as a binder for the flour, the dough has to be very stiff, almost hard. You are absolutely right. I have never been here before, so I look forward to tasting this home-made pasta in its original region.

"As for the lady cook, well it wasn't difficult to guess. Usually small restaurants like this one are a family business and if the owner/waiter is a man, it means that women are in the kitchen. Our man is not married, no wedding ring. So with good approximation I might deduce that it's his mother in the kitchen, not an eventual wife."

A short and plump woman with mighty forearms, which made a fine show out of her short-sleeved blouse, came to bring them two steaming plates of pasta. William smelled carefully then he sighed. "Just great! Black truffle and...let me guess...maybe fillets of trout? What a clever and creative sauce. You are an artist, my dear lady!"

The cook seemed to be beside herself with joy.

"Trout from lake Trasimeno and black truffle, right you are. I hope you'll like it. It's one of my specialities." And she called out loudly to her son, even though he was just a few metres way. "Arnaldo, bring the wine. Our Orvieto."

William nodded in assent. "Orvieto white with a fish and truffle sauce. A praiseworthy choice."

Obviously the dishes were delicious and the fresh wine, served in a modest pitcher, was greenish-yellow with pleasant floral and fruity scents. Peter regretted he could not drink more than a glass of it, since he had the task of driving back.

"So what do you think about the owner of Ciancaleoni factory?" He asked William, who kept on refilling his glass instead.

"Uhm, it's an interesting case indeed, and we'll have to work on it. Mr Alunni is a big man, but he's not strong-tempered at all. There are many details which intrigue me. Now that I have met him and his fiancée, I'd like knowing what exactly happened on that cruise ship..."

"But Alunni doesn't seem to be a murderer to me. At least not from my first impression today." Peter hesitated.

"I don't know yet; I don't know." William was pondering something he could not fully define. "If only we could question some of the witnesses. I mean people who were on that cruise ship together with Sabatino Alunni and Iris..."

They paid the bill which was ridiculously cheap, and William insisted on going to the kitchen to thank the cook.

Peter remained in the dining room so he could not hear exactly what the lady and William said to each other, but she insisted on accompanying them to the door, where on the threshold she suddenly hugged William, who cheerfully lifted her up.

"Good bye, Lucia. Thank you for all. We'll come back for sure."

CHAPTER SEVEN

September 2012

The ship was full up and the restaurants served the meals in two shifts. They had been asked to choose their shift, which apparently would have to be the same for the entire cruise. They hesitated, considering the possible pros and cons, but Sabatino Alunni suggested that taking the second shift would be better. The first series of meals would be served at 12 and 19:30 and the second one at 13:30 and 21.

He didn't feel much persuaded at the beginning. He was used to eating rather early and waiting until nine in the evening seemed a bit too late. But then Mr Alunni explained that the people who chose the first shift would be under pressure. They could not take the time to have a fully relaxed meal, since the waiters had to clean the tables and to lay them for the next shift guests. At least, if they chose to eat later, they would have time to relax at the table, chat, sip their coffee at their pace, since nobody else would be expected in the restaurant after them.

"Mr Alunni is right, Ernesto..." Carla started saying.

"Please, please call me simply Sabatino...."

"Of course, so I was saying that Sabatino is right. It's also a good idea for lunch. I don't feel like getting up early in the morning at least on holiday, and if we take a late breakfast we won't feel hungry again at noon!"

And so it was settled. To the ladies' great delight they reserved their table by the glass wall overlooking the sea, even though he realized that sitting at the table they would see only the sky, since the sea was down there, many floors below.

He noticed that Sabatino gesticulated a great deal when he spoke; he wondered if he worked in showbiz, if he was an entertainer, an illusionist maybe. Then he reproached himself for such silly thoughts. The women seemed to be determined to have a rest in their cabins, even though they hadn't done anything special which might justify their tiredness. Michele told him that just the changing rhythm of life might have a tiring effect.

"But do you feel tired, Michele?" He asked his son.

"Not at all, Dad. Let's go to explore the ship a little, you and I!"

He felt happy with this proposal. He missed some privileged time for just the two of them. Luckily Sabatino didn't offer to go with them; rather he claimed that he had to help his wife to unpack.

They walked at random along a series of huge halls set in circles and galleries over different levels and connected with each other by shining glass lifts. He absurdly thought of a science fiction television series, which his grandson particularly liked; he felt a pang and realized he missed the child so much. He watched those films mostly to please the boy; in reality he found it quite hard to follow the plot and to remember who was who, except for one of the characters who had peculiar pointed ears and a name easy to remember, something like Spuck or Spock. In the series nearly all the people wore a kind of sweat suit or pyjamas, which served as uniforms, and they lived in a huge spaceship with glass, steel and lights everywhere, definitely similar to the place where he was at that very moment. One remarkable difference was that the people who crowded these shining halls didn't wear intergalactic uniforms, but fancy vacationers' dress which didn't suit the ship's environment that much.

On their way back they had some problems finding their deck and cabins once again, after this first rather dazing wandering. Every corridor looked the same, but finally they found themselves in the right spot. They stepped aside chivalrously to give way to a young lady who came out from a cabin door. She greeted them in Italian and smiled. She was slender and not too tall, with short, very dark hair. He noticed that her beautiful brown-green eyes looked slightly reddish, as if she had been crying.

The first dinner aboard was a thrilling event for the women. Carla and Valentina had a sort of summit to decide what to wear.

"In the guide about life on board they say there is no strict dress-code and the passengers can wear casual clothes also in the evening," Valentina said with a note of regret in her voice.

"Never mind. We can feel free to dress decently and elegantly. I'm sure that also Mrs Alunni will be reasonably elegant, too. We are responsible for our table; the other passengers can do what they want." Carla had, as always, the last word. And actually she was

right, because when Sabatino and Iris Alunni came out from their cabin, after Michele's polite little knock on their door, Iris wore an elegant cocktail dress which suited her very well. Her long, blond hair was nicely combed and veiled her cheek and forehead with soft curls. She wore accurate make-up, and her large, blue eyes were enhanced by a suitable eye-shadow. She clung to her husband's arm; Sabatino looked very protective. When they arrived at the restaurant it was already 21:15. He realized he felt hungry. All the tables seemed to be occupied by now. A waiter in a perfect uniform welcomed them saying something he could not understand, but he guessed them to be polite and warm words. Soon he realized that the waiter could not speak Italian very well and could understand it even less. They chose from the appealing menu. The service seemed quite slow, but he was ready to forgive that, thinking that the staff had just finished with the first shift of guests and probably had still to arrange something in the kitchen. Moreover feeding that crowd was not such a simple matter to organize.

The refined names of the dishes masked a rather average level of food. It was impossible to say that it was of bad quality or doubtful freshness, on the contrary. However every dish was a bit standard and overcooked for his tastes. There was the general impression of a showy display of rich food, while the substance was basically at the standard of a good canteen, nothing more. He knew what he was speaking about, because the family business was a smart delicatessen, one of the most appreciated in Torino, for generations. It was his grandfather who had started with a small shop where he sold cheese, salami and cold pork. Then, little by little, working very hard, they expanded their business and began serving refined cooked dishes, which had become their main features. They could manage to supply their clients with everything, from appetizers to dessert, through a series of main courses. Their prices were expensive, but their clients didn't complain, because such quality has no price.

He remained with his fork in mid-air, lost in a whirl of old memories of his childhood, when after school Dad and Granddad sent him to deliver boxes of delicacies to the rich clients living in old residences on the hills.

Michele and Sabatino seemed to get on well with each other, and they bolted down their dinner, without paying much attention to it. They were completely involved in a friendly conversation, as if it were compulsory to get acquainted immediately.

He noticed that Iris barely nibbled at her dishes. Perhaps he was not the only one to feel moderate enthusiasm for the ship's cooking.

"What time are we supposed to get to Marseilles tomorrow?" Michele looked interrogatively at his wife.

"At eight in the morning." Valentina was always very methodical and read all information carefully. "Then the ship will sail away at five in the afternoon. We'll have the time to take an excursion to visit the town; we have already booked it at the cruise director's desk. Will you join us?" She asked Iris directly, but it was Sabatino who answered.

"It's very kind of you, but I think my wife prefers a more relaxed, individual excursion. We'll take a taxi from the port, and we'll stroll a little through the centre of the town. I've been told that there is a lively fish market on the pier of the old port. We'll meet again for dinner, and it will be amusing to exchange our different impressions and experiences."

The following day, when he was sitting in a crowded coach together with Carla, Michele, Valentina and about other fifty passengers from the ship, all labelled with the same colour code ("Don't forget your colour and your coach number," repeated the hostesses. " You must not take a different bus to go back; it must be always the same..."), he started thinking that maybe Mr and Mrs Alunni had taken a wiser decision. But then he forgot his criticism, trying to enjoy the touristic tour.

They all felt tired when they returned to the ship, which was waiting for them like a patient beached whale. After a shower he felt better and was grateful to Carla for pushing them to choose the later shift for dinner. At least they had time to relax after a rather frantic day of excursion...and it was only the first stop of the cruise.

They again met their table companions. Sabatino seemed to be in great mood. Iris was not very talkative, as always, but she seemed to be at ease. Actually it was Iris who informed them briefly that she and her husband had taken with them a lady they had met by chance, a lady who had her cabin in the same corridor and who was travelling on her own.

"A very fine lady," explained Sabatino, with a sympathetic smile. "She started speaking to my wife and...oh, well, we felt sorry for her. I think we cannot be considered gossipy if we merely summarize her misfortune. She had booked this cruise with her fiancé, but a few days before the departure she discovered that he had an affair with another woman, and they broke up. She decided to take the cruise on her own, rather than remaining at home crying over her lost love. But of course she's a bit depressed and feels lonely."

Iris intervened. "Jessica is a very pleasant, lovely young lady. Her fiancé must be a real idiot. We had a nice day in her company, even though she was not exactly bursting with joy and enthusiasm."

"Oh, but we might invite her to our table." Carla felt immediately supportive; men can really be incredibly cruel and unfair. She looked sternly at her husband, whose only fault in that circumstance was belonging to the male race.

"We thought of that," said Sabatino. "But the tables are for six at most, and then she told us that she prefers the first shift of meals. You'll meet her later anyway. We asked her to join us at the theatre. It seems that tonight's show should be very entertaining."

When they were finishing their dessert, a quite banal pudding, Iris whispered that she felt really very tired and didn't feel like staying up late at the theatre. Sabatino immediately suggested going with her to their cabin, but she refused with a thankful smile, caressing his hand. "It's not necessary, darling. You are so sweet. I need a good sleep, that's all. But if you are not tired, go and enjoy yourself."

They waited for few minutes by the theatre door, since the lady was not there yet. Soon she arrived and he recognized the woman with the greenish eyes whom he had met in the corridor when he returned from his exploration of the ship with Michele. He noticed once again that her eyes looked reddish and glistening with tears. But since he knew the entire story about her by now, he was not surprised. Poor girl! She had to feel really lonely and disheartened.

The magician's show was the best thing he had experienced so far on that cruise. He was amazed at all those incredible tricks, which made the unreal appear to be totally real. The dance number that followed left him a little less enthusiastic. Perhaps it was because he felt sleepy, after that long day. The young woman with the short dark hair was sitting between him and Sabatino, and she seemed to be in a much better mood now. She also vigorously applauded the magician. What was her name, ah, yes, Jessica? He felt sorry for her; how could it be possible to cheat on such a nice person? Sometimes he felt ashamed, as a man, of what other men could do.

Since he had met Carla, he had never thought of another woman in 'that' way, even though he was sensitive to feminine charm. One of the dancers, by the way, was really attractive. Oh my, she could be his granddaughter...

The younger ones, Michele, Valentina, Sabatino and this Jessica, considered whether to have another drink after the show and maybe a walk on the upper deck. Sabatino hesitated.

"I'd like to go and see if Iris is well..."

"I need to look for a shawl in my cabin, because it must be cool outdoors on the deck." Jessica said." I could check if Iris is still up, maybe she'd like to join us."

The two younger men and Valentina decided to wait for Jessica in one of the bars and he returned to their cabins together with Carla and Jessica.

Jessica knocked gently on the door of Iris' cabin, but didn't get an answer.

"She is sleeping. I don't want to impose and to wake her up." Jessica greeted them warmly and quickly went into her cabin. A minute later he heard her door being opened again. Surely she had found her shawl.

CHAPTER EIGHT

The sky was still murky and overcast, but the sulky clouds had turned off their water taps. The rain had stopped for two days, but a deep sense of moisture had soaked everything, creating a general feeling of cold, one of those creeping sensations which are quick to come and very slow to leave.

William could already smell winter in the air. He knew that winter could be very harsh on the Casentino hills. He wouldn't be too surprised if what remained of the rain, still stored somewhere in the clouds, could change into the first snow of the season. Peter had something to do at the Post Office in Capacciano, and William had decided to go with him to the village because he had projects in mind. His first was having one sublime cappuccino at 'RaBARbaro' and the second was paying a quick visit to mayor Sanchini, even though the person he needed to meet was Mrs Sanchini. He knew that Mr Sanchini didn't cope serenely with his wife's interest in the presumed mysteries about Iris Ciancaleoni's suicide. It would definitely be too hard for him to accept being bypassed if William went directly to speak to Loredana.

William wrapped his shearling coat around him. It was an old, heavy jacket that he liked in a special way and had worn for many years. It was one of those garments which periodically come back into fashion again—like a broken clock which marks the right hour twice a day– if one cared for that, one only had to wait patiently. For the rest of the time it could be considered pleasantly 'vintage'.

Peter had said that they would meet at the café, and William wondered for a short moment whether it wouldn't be more thoughtful to wait for his partner, and to have a cappuccino together. Finally he decided he could take a first cappuccino immediately and a second one when Peter arrived.

The usual patrons gathered by the counter, but William had the impression that the café was more crowded than usual. Conversations were in full swing and nobody seemed to notice William's arrival, except Lapo, the barkeeper, who was, as always, totally silent. He nodded at William who ordered his cappuccino. But soon there was an exchange of glances and greetings with the other clients.

"Oh, William, have you heard what happened? The old Ripamonti is missing. He's nowhere to be found. His sons went to report his disappearance to the Carabinieri station." Giorgio, the photographer, informed him briefly about the subject of the general discussion. As if summoned by these words, Maresciallo Ciricola walked into the café, shivering with cold in his uniform. The temperature was definitely dropping.

"William, what a pleasure to see you! It's so cold. I should have worn a coat, but I thought I wouldn't need it on such a short walk."

"Maresciallo, do you have any news about Ripamonti?" A tall, slim man with an incongruous tartan cap played spokesman for the general curiosity.

"Unfortunately we haven't found him yet." Maresciallo Ciricola looked really sorry and sympathetic. "We're afraid he might have had an accident, since his Ape car[1] is also missing. We checked out the area, all along the road from the village to the farm of the Ripamonti family, but we haven't yet found any trace of an accident."

William recalled the missing man very well. He had met him many times, even though they had never had any real personal conversation. Ripamonti was an old man, lean and strong as a wire. He had lost his wife many years before and nobody could remember her, but everybody knew Ripamonti and his three sons, who ran a farm, west of Capacciano. Ripamonti still worked in the fields and gave his practical contribution, even though he might be more than eighty years old by now. He lived together with his sons and their families and all the grandchildren. Proper and sensible people, the Ripamontis were, hard workers. William had never seen him without a hat. He wore a straw hat in summer and a dark brown hat in the other seasons. The old Ripamonti went back and forth with his Ape car from the family farm to the village nearly every day, and he was always ready to do little errands and odd jobs for the villagers.

"May I buy you an espresso, Emilio? You look frozen. Lapo, please, could you serve a drink to everyone? It's my treat." William's offer was warmly welcomed by a grateful hum. The villagers had be-

[1] A three-wheeled light commercial vehicle produced since 1948 by Piaggio.

come used to the 'Englishmen' of the farm, as they insisted on labelling Peter and William, and they had accepted them on equal terms. They were considered a bit eccentric, but proper people, and they took actively part in the village life.

Emilio Ciricola put his hands around the hot cup, trying to warm them up. "What disgusting weather!"

"Wait and see, Emilio." William didn't encourage him. "Wintertime is hard here. I won't be surprised to see snow in few weeks. On the other hand our summers are tropical. You'll get used to our weather. What's the story about the old Ripamonti, by the way?"

"Oh, poor chap. His family is so worried about him; his three sons look distressed. When they didn't see him at home for dinner, they went to look for him, thinking he might have a mechanical problem with his vehicle. Ripamonti has always refused to have a mobile phone. But they could not find anything. So they came to the Carabinieri station. It's as if Ripamonti and his Ape car vanished into thin air." Maresciallo Ciricola lowered his voice, "You see, William, I think he had a sudden indisposition and fainted somewhere, in a field and with this cold, at his age..."

William could not help retorting. "But what about the Ape car?"

"Right you are, it's a mystery..."

"Listen, Emilio, the last thing I wish is to get my intention misunderstood. I know that you are skilled, intelligent and you can do your job exceptionally well, but..."

Ciricola smiled; definitely he liked William and had already learnt to appreciate him, not only because of his musical talents.

"You don't need to justify anything, William. These dull autumn days are boring, and Ripamonti's disappearance is the only new event here in the village. If you feel like becoming my external consultant for this case, you are welcome. You know the inhabitants of Capacciano much better than me; I've just arrived here...You might pop round to my office after we finish our coffee. The brothers Ripamonti should pass by to ask for news and if you have a sudden inspiration to ask them any further questions...The only important thing is that we manage to find the old Ripamonti safe and sound, even though I'm not too optimistic at this stage."

William seemed to be slightly absent-minded. He cast a circular glance and then fixed his eyes on the barkeeper.

"Lapo, you know Ripamonti well, don't you? You know everyone..."

The laconic Lapo nodded in assent. But William was not yet satisfied. "Lapo, please make an effort. We'll be all grateful to you. Is there any specific detail you can tell us about the habits of Ripamonti in your bar?"

Lapo sighed like a man asked to do something extremely difficult, nearly painful, then he spoke, "Ripamonti comes on Saturday, every Saturday."

"Thank you, Lapo. And what does he do in general?"

"He takes a Crodino[2]."

"C'mon, Lapo, you can do it! Tell me something more. What does he do besides drinking a Crodino?"

The barkeeper wrinkled his forehead for the evident effort. "He buys one instant scratch-it."

It was too much for Lapo and one of the patrons intervened to help.

"It's exactly like that. I see Ripamonti here at RaBARbaro every Saturday. He checks his scratchcard while he drinks his Crodino, then he greets everyone and goes back home for lunch."

"Does he win often?"

The man who had confirmed the scarce information supplied by the barkeeper grinned.

"I think that once he won 150 euros. But I don't remember exactly. Nobody wins, Mr William, but illusions help."

William smiled sympathetically in return, and then added "Let me see. Today it's Friday. The brothers Ripamonti reported their father missing yesterday evening. Does anyone remember if last Saturday Ripamonti came here to take his aperitif as usual?"

The clients of the bar started humming together, but nobody was sure. Routine creates confusion in memories.

The calm voice of Lapo Tramontina made its way through the noise. "He was not here last Saturday." Succinct and final.

Maresciallo Ciricola pricked up his ears. His new Irish friend was an inspiration, not only for matters related to the folk music of the Emerald Isle. But he had no intention of delegating his power completely, so he took his own turn questioning the bystanders.

"But Ripamonti was not missing yet; someone of you has surely met him during the last few days."

---

[2] A non-alcoholic bitter aperitif

The various answers confirmed that old Ripamonti had behaved as usual and many people had seen him; simply, for whatever unknown reason he had skipped his usual Saturday visit to the RaBARbaro.

Ciricola shook his head casting a sidelong glance at William, who looked absorbed in thoughts, but then suddenly smiled.

"Emilio, I'm late, and I have to see the mayor. Peter seems to be late too. We had a meeting here, but I have to rush. We might join you at the Carabinieri station as soon as it's possible, if it's fine for you, but now I must really go..." He addressed Lapo and the clients present in the bar. "Would you be so kind to let Peter know that I'm waiting for him at the Carabinieri, when he arrives, unless the Maresciallo is still here as well?" He waved goodbye and walked away with a spring in his step.

A few minutes later William went into the town hall and asked the multifunctional secretary–a plump man of indefinable age–if the mayor was in his office. The man, happy to have something to do on that boring and lazy morning, tried to protract the event and started to say that he would go to have a look, and if the mayor were not too busy then...but he was pitilessly interrupted by the mayor himself, who had heard the brief conversation and came out from his office to welcome William.

"Dear Mr Collins, to what do I owe this pleasure?"

And, to the greatest disappointment of the secretary, they disappeared into the mayor's office.

William was aware that mayor Sanchini had not been that happy about the turn that the entire story of his wife's suspicions had taken, but he loved and esteemed his Loredana so much, that he had even started changing his original mind-set. For this reason William wanted to be extremely diplomatic with him, even though he knew that what he was going to ask him for was unconventional.

He tried to find the mildest words to make the mayor feel comfortable with the idea, but at the same time he was direct and explained to him that after the first informal investigations he and Peter thought that Mrs Sanchini was right. There was really something fishy in the whole affair.

"But so far it's just an instinctive feeling; unfortunately we don't have any concrete evidence. I do think it would be extremely useful to speak to the eyewitnesses of Iris Ciancaleoni's last days. From the newspaper articles your wife supplied me with, I could get the names of the people who were with Iris and her husband the day of the accident–

if we can call it that– a family from Torino. It seems they also had contiguous cabins. Anyway, there is a problem. I don't think they would feel like speaking to me, a stranger, a foreigner, more than two years after the fact. But if Iris' best friend were with me, and if she were seen as the motivator for this further private investigation, maybe..."

Mayor Sanchini was perhaps a little naïve and too optimistic, due to his innate goodness of heart, but he was not dumb at all.

"So you'd like to take my Loredana to Torino to investigate with you, wouldn't you?"

"Uhm, that would be my idea..." William started improvising a strategy which might reassure the mayor. "Of course, if you had time, it would be fantastic if you could join us for the short trip. But if your work and official tasks prevented you from taking a few days off, don't worry. Mrs Sanchini won't be in the embarrassing position of travelling alone with me. Mrs Ellie McKenzie will accompany us." William was bluffing, because in reality he had never spoken to Ellie about this. It was a sudden excuse which instantaneously crossed his mind when he noticed the mayor's slight scowl. He had a liking for Ellie. It was mayor Sanchini who officiated her wedding. But then everybody had a liking for Ellie. Sanchini looked calmer after hearing Ellie's name and William decided to take advantage of this chance and continued.

"In little more than a month it will be Christmas, and I'm sure the ladies will enjoy doing a little shopping in Torino, which is, by the way, a very beautiful town. I'll be happy to take care of them and they'll be, obviously, my guests."

The mayor still hesitated.

"Have you already discussed this with Loredana?"

"Of course I haven't, mayor! It wouldn't be proper to do that before informing you. If you think it might be unpleasant for your wife, I won't disturb her."

It was the winning strategy. The mayor forgot his concerns and felt reassured by such a display of thoughtful tact.

"I'm afraid I won't be able to come with you, but if Loredana likes the idea of taking a short trip with Mrs Ellie and you...Well it would be a recreation for her. She needs some relaxation."

"Maybe we could call her right now..." William suggested.

If mayor Sanchini still had a hope that his wife would refuse the invitation, it was immediately wiped away by the enthusiastic tone of Loredana's voice, as soon as she heard the proposal. Then he handed his cell to William, who spoke directly with an excited Mrs Sanchini to organize the details of their sudden trip.

When he left the town hall William laughed inside, thinking that now he had to call the totally unaware Ellie to persuade her to go to Torino with them. He dialled her number while he crossed the square walking to the Carabinieri station.

CHAPTER NINE

Describing Maresciallo Ciricola's office as sober would be a euphemism. It was a plain, small room, with beige walls. There was an old, basic desk covered with papers and a laptop in a corner. A few melancholy wooden chairs and a couple of small armchairs, which had known better days, completed the furniture, together with a massive, antediluvian filing cabinet and a crammed bookcase. The President of the Italian Republic sadly contemplated the room from a photo hung on the wall behind the desk. A tricolour flag in a corner strove to give a colourful note to the room. Peter was already sitting on one of the armchairs chatting with Emilio, when William arrived. Nearly simultaneously a carabiniere came over to inform the Maresciallo that the brothers Ripamonti were there too.

"Let them come in, Maccaluso," the Maresciallo told his subordinate.

The three brothers Ripamonti were strikingly alike, hefty men in their sixties. They looked saddened and anxious. They nodded at Peter and William, whom they knew by sight. They didn't seem surprised to see them on friendly terms with the Maresciallo.

Ciricola took out a copy of the report and handed it to Peter and William; then with reassuring words suitable for the occasion he tried to comfort the men, telling them that the fact they hadn't yet found their father might still be considered partially positive, since there remained considerable hope that he could be alive and well.

William read the short report attentively. Then he kindly asked the brother Ripamonti closest to him, "So your father's first name is Abelardo, I read here."

"Yes, sir. Abelardo Ripamonti, born in Capacciano on the seventh of July 1932." It was the brother sitting in the middle who answered, while the other two merely nodded in assent.

Peter couldn't help asking, "Forgive my curiosity, but are the three of you triplets?"

The same Ripamonti answered also this time. "Oh no, we aren't triplets. I'm the eldest and my name is Primo. Here is my brother Secondo, who is one year younger than me and the youngest, Luigi, who is two years younger than Secondo."

William was delighted by the serendipitous meeting. He knew that Primo (first) and Secondo (second) were relatively common male names in Italy, even though out of fashion by now, but he wondered why their parents decided to give such a banal name as Luigi to the third offspring. Maybe it was because Terzo (third) was not an accepted Italian name. But he realized that this was not the most suitable moment for joking, because the three men were so worried about their father's uncertain fate. Luigi unexpectedly guessed the silent question and explained shyly, "I was called Luigi after my mother, whose name was Luisa. I never met her, because unfortunately she died giving birth to me..."

Maresciallo Ciricola immediately expressed his sympathy in a moved and sincere way, even though the mournful event happened at least sixty years before.

"You can understand, Maresciallo, why we are so worried about losing our dad now, too."

William suddenly recalled an Oscar Wilde' quote '*To lose one parent may be regarded as a misfortune; to lose both looks like carelessness.*' But luckily kept this thought only for himself.

He tried to dispel the tragic atmosphere with a superficial remark.

"Your father has a very original name, taken after an illustrious and wise savant of the middle ages..."

"Our great-grandfather." Primo explained. "I don't know if he was so cultivated, he was a peasant, as far as I was told. He was called Abelardo too."

"I'm sorry your mother passed away when she was still so young. I'm sure it was very hard for your father and for all of you." Peter added his contribution.

"Right you are! It was sad for us growing up without our mother, but our father has always done his best for us. He loved our mother so deeply that, even though he was still young when she died, he never thought to marry again. He simply could not imagine having another woman at his side. Poor dad...They were so poor when they got married. You see it was only a few years after the end of the war; it was a hard time...They could not afford any celebration for their wedding. Our father told us many times that mother would have dreamt of a honeymoon trip, but there was no money for that. Nonetheless they were content, because they hoped to have time for that later." Primo sighed, and all three big men sniffed.

William seemed to be absorbed in his thoughts and apparently didn't pay attention to what the Maresciallo and Peter were telling the three Ripamonti to encourage them. Then he suddenly smiled.

"Don't worry. I'm sure your father is well, and you can expect only good news very soon. I think someone told me that your father doesn't have a cell phone as he's a bit old-fashioned about 'modern' devices. I do think this is the reason for his silence. Please, don't get annoyed with him for the worries he has caused you since yesterday, when he didn't come home for dinner. You told me he has been an excellent father, and that he never did anything for himself. At his age he deserves something extraordinary just for himself. But it's not a final goodbye. Trust me; very soon you'll get news from him. Now go home with peace of mind. Maresciallo Ciricola will keep you up to date. Ah, just a last question...Do you know where your parents would like to have gone on honeymoon, if they could have afforded the trip when they got married? Well, let me guess...to Paris, maybe?"

Primo, Secondo and Luigi stared at William quite mesmerized. It was quite true what people said in the village; the Englishman was really something...

"Yes, it's true. Paris has always been my father's dream, because mother had always idealized it." Primo nearly stammered with astonishment, then he peeped at Maresciallo Ciricola to get a clue. Emilio Ciricola was nearly as astonished as all the brothers Ripamonti, but he tried to show a dose of assurance.

"You can go home, now. I'll soon bring you good news."

Primo, Secondo and Luigi in order of age left walking backwards, their eyes staring at the three men who seemed so sure that everything was fine. They felt quite puzzled but trustful.

As soon as they closed the door of his office, Maresciallo Ciricola gave up the confident expression he had reserved for the brothers Ripamonti and addressed William vehemently.

"Now you must tell me what in the world made you so sure of everything you told those chaps. This is not a damned joke! I didn't want to contradict you in front of them, but..."

William looked indifferent to the Maresciallo's worries, and remained silent with a seraphic expression. Peter laughed and tried to calm Maresciallo Ciricola down.

"This is William, Emilio. Now you can understand how annoying he can be sometimes. Imagine what it means living with him..." Then he spoke directly to William. "Enough is enough. Emilio is upset, so stop playing and tell him all that you know. Because I'm sure you've figured out exactly what's happened to old Abelardo Ripamonti!"

William got on his feet and started striding around the office. He spoke more to himself than to the other two.

"Well, our Abelardo disappeared yesterday, with his Ape car. He cannot have gone too far with that funny vehicle. He's not allowed to take a motorway driving it either, and we are practically sure he was not involved in any accident, or else our valid Carabinieri would have found him by now. Emilio, if I were you, I'd check if there is an Ape car corresponding to the description of Ripamonti's one, left somewhere in a parking lot near the railway station of Arezzo. I think you can get confirmation of that rather easily. Then I also think that if you identify the clerk who was on duty at the ticket window of the railway station, let me say, early yesterday afternoon, you might ask him if by chance he remembers a very old man with a hat who asked him how to get a train ticket to ...Paris. If so, then we can really be reassured about our good, old man. If you can check that, you'll see everything will be clear. Peter and I have some errands to do, but we can come back here in one hour and then we can settle this matter all together."

William winked at Ciricola and gestured to Peter, inviting him to leave the office too. The Maresciallo roused himself quickly from his amazement, cried out loudly "Maccaaaluuuso!" and even before the young carabiniere appeared, he was already on the phone.

CHAPTER TEN

A chilly wind was driving grey clouds east in the sky like dirty sheep toward their fold. Peter and William again crossed the main square of Capacciano, shivering in spite of their warm clothes. Peter realized that William was heading back for the RaBARbaro café and interrogated him with a puzzled look.

"You don't intend to wait for an hour outdoors in this icy weather, do you?" William grinned wryly.

"We don't have any errands to do, obviously. I did understand that, and I backed you because it was clear you wanted to give Emilio time for his investigation, which will surely confirm your statements. Probably you collected some clues about the old Ripamonti while you were waiting for me at the bar and then you put them together with the information offered by the three sturdy brothers. But now your greatest pleasure will be surprising our poor Emilio with your mental conjuring tricks, and you look forward to seeing his face when someone in Arezzo confirms everything you had predicted." Although Peter was actually amused, he pretended to reproach William a little.

William shrugged his shoulders and energetically pushed the café door.

"Lapo, it's too late for another cappuccino. It's aperitif time, now. Please give us two Crodino in honour of Abelardo Ripamonti!"

Lapo looked at him doubtfully, but without a word carried out the order.

William took a sip carefully, then grimaced slightly.

"I hope that in Paris Abelardo will drink something better today..."

"Are you quite sure he's in Paris?" Peter tasted the Crodino too.

"I can't be completely sure that he's arrived yet, but he's definitely on his way." William took out his smart phone and quickly started entering something. "Let me check the possible timetable..."

"Wait, William, wait a minute." Peter put down his glass of Crodino on the counter. "Paris to Arezzo is more than 1200 km. It's too far to go reasonably by train. One would do best to take a flight from Pisa to Paris and...How can you be so sure he took a train destined specifically to Paris? Uhm, I do understand Paris is where he wished to go with his dear wife for a honeymoon...You may be right about that..."

"Nomen omen, the presage is in the name. A man called Abelardo with a wife called Luisa–which sounds so similar in Italian to Heloise–are destined to Paris. As for the train, well, our Abelardo has never travelled abroad, and he has never once been in an airport his entire life; he's likely to feel much more comfortable with trains and railway stations. As for all elderly people, time and patience are on his side. Great, I have found it!" William handed the smartphone to Peter. "I guess he took this one. He was surely in Arezzo at the railway station yesterday afternoon, even though his family only noticed him missing when he didn't arrive home for dinner. He needed time to gather information and reassure himself he could reach his destination. He could not come back to Capacciano once his decision was taken, and he had to spend the night somewhere. I think taking a night train seemed a good choice to him. I bet he took this train from Arezzo to Bologna, look!"

Peter read on the phone display that a train from Arezzo to Bologna was scheduled very early that morning at 00.47 and then, taking a connection in Milan and another one in Switzerland, one could arrive to Paris at four pm.

"If you are right–and even though it drives me crazy, I'm sure you are— our adventurous old traveller should be in Lausanne now, ready to take his final train."

"Indeed!" William nodded in assent. "I have started to like old Abelardo, and I regret I didn't spend more time chattering with him, but I'll make up for lost time when he gets back. A very intriguing and interesting man he is. I suppose he will look for an accommodation, and then will immediately call his family to reassure them. He cares dearly for them, but couldn't reveal his intention earlier, because surely they would have tried to prevent him from taking his trip. But they'll be so happy to know not only that he's well, but also that he won all that money, that the worries and the distress over his disappearance will fade quickly away. So let's give him the necessary time for everything. I could predict to good approximation that the telephone will ring at Ripamonti's farm around six pm."

"But what did you mean by referring to the money he should have won?"

"Oh, Peter, don't ask me about the sum. I'm not a magician." William looked to be in a great mood. "But he won with his last scratch-it card. It must be a rather huge sum, because he didn't ask for immediate, direct cashing from the barkeeper, as usually happens with small sums one usually wins in this type of lotteries. When you've won a larger sum, you must draw it through a bank and that takes a few days. This explains why Abelardo Ripamonti didn't go buy another scratchy the following Saturday. He had already won. Well, it's time to join Emilio once again now." William chuckled.

They barely had the time to cross the threshold of the Carabinieri station when carabiniere Maccaluso greeted them again waving his hands frantically. "Maresciallo Ciricola is waiting for you!"

When Peter pushed the door of the office, Ciricola jumped up from his desk chair as if he had been bitten by a tarantula.

"Doggone it! William Collins, damn you! The colleagues of the Carabinieri station—in front of Arezzo railway station—found the Ape car immediately and I've just spoken to the ticket window clerk of the railway station, who by chance is the same one who was on duty yesterday afternoon. Damn!" Maresciallo Ciricola slapped the heap of papers on his desk, scattering them in all directions, while the President of the Republic seemed to reproach him from his framed picture. "Damn! The clerk remembers perfectly the old man with a brown hat, who quite corresponds to the description of Ripamonti. He said he could not forget him, because the man, who looked perfectly reasonable and normal, asked him how to get to Paris, as if he might have asked how to get by train to San Giovanni Val d'Arno. He checked the possible connections and explained to the old man that it would be a very long trip, but Ripamonti was calm and determined. So he sold him the tickets and made the seat reservations; he printed the schedule for him and explained some practical details. The old man paid cash. Then, since there were still several hours to wait before his train—he had decided to take a night train to Bologna first— he told the clerk that he would buy some useful items, and then he would wait in one of the cafés in the station hall. He didn't see the man again, because his shift ended at 8pm." Ciricola took a deep breath. "And now you must tell me how you could have known all that!"

William repeated to Ciricola what he had already explained to Peter and when he mentioned the conspicuous win in the lottery the Maresciallo interrupted him.

"No! This is too much. You are the devil incarnate!" But he was not that surprised anymore, totally captivated by the intellectual talents of his new friend.

William smiled modestly. "Oh, just a matter of logical concatenations and a pinch of luck."

"Shut up, William! In reality you are quite proud of yourself, and you adore performing, surprising people like that." Peter menaced him with a finger, while he helped the Maresciallo to pick up his official papers from the floor.

"The case is solved, it seems. It was not a final good-bye, but just a deserved holiday for a very pleasant, old hard worker. Abelardo Ripamonti will call his family as soon as someone helps him with the international code to phone from France to Italy. Surely the receptionist of his hotel will be happy do it for him. He's a pleasant old man, and everybody will give him suggestions to make his short stay safe and enjoyable. Maybe you could give the reassuring news to the Ripamonti, so they'll be calmer when their father calls them. But tell them it won't be earlier than six pm or they'll get anxious again waiting. Ah, by the way, I'd be glad if the one of them who answers Abelardo's call from Paris could give him a message from me. Please, let him know that once upon a time there was a very wise and cultivated scholar in Paris who was called Abelardo like him and he loved immensely a woman called Heloise, which is a little like Luisa. Life cruelly parted them—better not go too deep into details mentioning the emasculation—but they kept on loving each other forever and are now they resting together in the same tomb, in a very romantic cemetery, called Père Lachaise, in Paris. Maybe he would like to go and visit it."

"You are amazing, William, you can be caustic, sarcastic and then suddenly thoughtful and compassionate." Ciricola shook his head, but he was happy, as they could see on his honest and demonstrative face.

"Would you join us for lunch, Emilio?"

"Unfortunately I have no time for that today, with all these matters to coordinate."

"Then come to dinner, so you can tell us about the developments of our old runaway's case."

"With pleasure!" The Maresciallo accepted, remembering his first and so enjoyable visit to the big farmhouse.

While driving back to 'L'Oliveto' William looked both relaxed and lively. Peter couldn't help thinking that solving mysteries with his logical skills was exactly what William needed to feel well with himself, even though he knew that William would never be completely free from his personal ghosts until he could manage to come to terms with them.

CHAPTER ELEVEN

September 2012

After a full day of navigation Ernesto had begun to feel that the cruise ship, despite its massive size, didn't fit him well. A little like those cheap 'one size fits all' shirts that never fit anyone very well. It will always be a poor fit for everyone. Even though he was a rather simple man, without need for extravagant and luxurious environments, he couldn't help noticing that the interiors of the ship were flashy with only a superficial razzmatazz, but not really elegant and comfortable. The whole staff, particularly the team of the cruise director and the entertainers, showed a cursory friendly and merry attitude, which barely concealed their bored indifference toward the passengers.

"They treat us as if we were all in our dotage," he told Carla one night after briefly watching a kind of game organized to entertain the passengers in one of the bars.

Carla was too intellectually honest to deny what was evident, but since she was the one who had planned the cruise, it was logical for her to find all possible justifications.

"You see, Ernesto, the ship is crammed with passengers. It's normal that the members of the staff are tired under such continuous pressure."

Michele and Valentina seemed to enjoy the experience and he was relieved that at least they could fully relax and have fun. They spent a lot of time together with Sabatino Alunni and his wife, Iris. They went together to visit Malaga, giving up the organized tour, but taking a taxi on their own. But at dinner they all looked a bit over-tired, maybe because it was very warm on the mainland, while all of them had become used to the ship's air conditioning. Iris spoke even less than usual and left practically all the food on here plate.

Of course there were also nice moments. He felt quite enthusiastic when the ship crossed the strait of Gibraltar and left the Mediterranean Sea to enter into the Atlantic Ocean. He had the mystical feeling of being an ancient explorer who had left the known world to venture into the unknown. Actually there was nothing much unknown left to discover. He found the Canary Islands very touristic; the forced stops at the souvenir shops that had an agreement with the coach drivers and the local guides annoyed him. Sabatino Alunni had taken the tour with them and he looked a bit worried because Iris had decided to remain aboard, claiming she felt too tired for a day excursion on a crowded coach. Sabatino often repeated that he should have remained with her, but she had insisted he shouldn't miss the excursion. Jessica, the slim brunette who had her cabin by theirs, had come over too. She looked more serene than the first time he had met her. Maybe taking the cruise had really been a morale boost for her. She had become more talkative and seemingly open. She chattered in a lively fashion with all of them, and took many photos.

Two entire days of navigation awaited them after leaving the Atlantic Islands. Ernesto summoned up his patience to cope, imagining two days of terrible boredom.

As usual they met Sabatino and Iris for dinner. That night was scheduled to be the great Captain's banquet with entertainment and attractions. The ladies had worn elegant cocktail dresses and he and Michele had been kindly but firmly requested to wear a suit with a smart tie. Actually their expectations were partially disappointed because the food was of the usual mediocre level. The great entertainment consisted of the noisy entry of all the waiters, a majority from various South American countries, singing slightly off key though full of good will, and inviting all those present to twirl their napkins over their heads. The Captain, a middle-aged Italian with lots of auburn hair plastered down with an overdose of brilliantine, made a short tour among the tables, quickly greeting most of the passengers, manifestly eager to return, as soon as possible, to his secluded table with his officers and some young ladies.

Before the dessert—he couldn't remember exactly what they served, probably one of the usual huge portions of a rather chalky chocolate mousse—Iris suddenly whispered something to her husband; then she smiled apologetically to everyone.

"I'm really sorry. I have headache, and all this confusion doesn't help me. I feel sick. I prefer to go back to our cabin to lie down for a while."

Sabatino immediately pushed his chair and offered to go with her, but Iris calmed him down.

"It's not the case, darling, indeed. My stomach is just a bit upset and I can't tolerate seeing and smelling food. But I'll be well soon and join you later at the theatre. Keep a place for me. I read on the program that this evening there is another show by that magician, who is the best attraction of the cruise. Take it easy. Everything is fine with me."

She kissed her husband's forehead and started walking toward the lift, stumbling lightly on her high heels. But after a couple of steps, she stopped and turned again toward her husband and told him

"Don't forget; I love you deeply." Then she left.

Before going to the theatre, they all decided to take a cup of espresso. They also found Jessica, who said she had arranged to meet Iris.

Sabatino explained to her that Iris was tired, but she would join them later. Then they all rushed to the theatre, which was already nearly full.

Once again the magician's show was excellent and Ernesto nearly forgot his gloomy thoughts about the two days of navigation without stop ahead of them. They decided to leave the theatre while the tango dancers were still performing on stage. The nearly hieratic poses and evolutions of Antonio and Milagros on the recorded notes of a bandoneon might have been evocative the first time one saw them, but they had already seen the same show a few days earlier. Instead they decided to take a walk on the outdoor decks, because the night was starry and it was rare treat for them to see a dark sky unobscured by light pollution from the towns. Carla remarked that she needed a shawl because the night air in open sea could be quite cool. Since the other ladies, Valentina and Jessica, agreed, they decided to go back to their cabins briefly, just to get their coats. Sabatino commented that Iris had probably fallen asleep, but that surely she would like to join them for a drink and a short walk.

Ernesto would never forget what happened after that. They took the lift to their deck all together. Jessica went quickly to her cabin, leaving the door open and reappeared with a jacket on her arm.

Valentina took a moment to decide if she should also bring a coat for Michele. He opened their door and Carla went into the cabin while he remained in the corridor. Sabatino knocked at his door, but didn't get an answer. He looked slightly embarrassed and said that he *hadn't brought the key card; it had to be inside Iris's handbag. Then he tried knocking harder.*

"Surely she's fallen asleep..."

Michele, Valentina, Carla and the other lady, Jessica, all gathered in front of the closed door of the Alunni's cabin.

"Let's look for a maid. There's always one around the corridors. Surely she has a master-key," Carla suggested, always pragmatic.

"Oh yes, please, I'm worried, maybe Iris doesn't feel well..." Sabatino started to look anxious.

Jessica and Valentina moved along the corridor and came back immediately followed by a dark haired maid, who looked unsure what to do. The woman didn't understand Italian. Luckily Jessica seemed to be able to speak a little Spanish and the maid, probably South American, smiled broadly when finally she could grasp what that group of passengers needed from her.

She opened the door of the cabin. All the lights were on; the glass door to the balcony was open, and the cold night air had chilled the temperature of the room.

"Iris, darling, are you well?" Sabatino spoke loudly in front of the bathroom door, since Iris could only be in there. Then, he pushed the door, which was not locked, and realized that the small bathroom was also quite empty.

"Iris, Iris..." He started shouting. The others had stopped on the threshold, but instinctively Carla and Valentina entered, as if they could help Sabatino find Iris hidden somewhere.

Michele tried to calm everybody down saying that probably Iris had decided to join them at the theatre a little too late and was now surely looking for them somewhere on the ship. But Carla stumbled over something left in the middle of the cabin floor—Iris' smart stiletto shoes. Valentina looked around, trying hard to find a reassuring sign proving that all was fine and that Iris was definitely waiting for them somewhere else. Then she smiled with a small sigh of relief. She had noticed a written note on the bedside table.

"Here, Sabatino, look. Iris left a message to you." Either Valentina was too polite to read the note or she simply was not wearing, for a sort of coquettishness, her reading glasses. She handed the small piece of paper to Sabatino, who read it and then broke down shouting, "Iris, Iris, my love, what did you do?"

The Peruvian (or was she Bolivian) maid looked astonished and scared, as if this entire sudden bustle were her fault.

Ernesto picked up the paper that Sabatino had left to fall on the floor and read,

'My dear Sabatino,
I know I'm going to upset you and, believe me, I'm sorry for that. But I cannot see any other way out. I'm tired of this kind of life and my decision is made'

Then everything became quite frantic and Ernesto had the impression that events followed one upon the other at great speed. Michele went to the small balcony and found that the white plastic table had been pushed against the railings and a chair had been likewise put by it, as to create two stairs leading... oh my, leading to a tragic jump. It was obvious by now.

Jessica rushed to call for help and to find an officer in charge. Sabatino looked lost in despair, unable to react in any reasonable way. Very soon two officers and the cruise director arrived and ordered the maid to leave and to not speak to anyone about this. Then they tried to comfort Sabatino saying that it must be a misunderstanding and that his wife was safe and sound somewhere on the ship. However they appeared unpersuaded by their own words. They asked everyone to leave the cabin; they locked the door, then led all the members of the scanty and shocked party to a private parlour by the cruise director's office. While they were there they could hear the announcement by loudspeakers inviting Mrs Iris Alunni to come meet her husband at the cruise director's desk.

They waited for an indeterminate time. A waiter brought them coffee and light drinks, but no one paid attention to that. Iris didn't appear.

Later the Captain himself arrived. He assured Sabatino that he would ransack the whole ship and if his wife was aboard they would find her without doubt. Ernesto noticed that the Captain, even though he spoke in a firm and kind way, looked slightly annoyed. How could anyone blame him, after all? It was a fine kettle of fish...

The Captain also stated that until Mrs Alunni was found, it was better to lock the cabin and to leave all as it was. Obviously the Captain had already concluded that they would never find Iris on the ship. The cruise director, with an expression suitable to the circum-

stance, informed the distressed Sabatino that, to his great regret, since the ship was full up, it would be a bit complicated to find an alternative accommodation for Mr Alunni, but they would do their best and... At that point, Jessica Mandelli, that so compassionate brunette, and Valentina took a generous decision. Valentina whispered with Michele, who nodded in assent. Then they told the cruise director that Sabatino could share the cabin with Michele, and Valentina would move to Jessica's cabin, since both were suites and they would be comfortable even in this unexpected situation.

Sabatino seemed unable to understand what was happening, as if he had been trapped in an invisible cocoon, which prevented him from hearing and seeing what was happening around him.

One of the officers said that a cabin assistant would move part of the baggage to the new accommodations. Valentina insisted that she would leave most of her things in the cabin with Michele and would take with her only what was necessary for the night plus some basic toilet items.

They all felt worn out, and he realized that it was already so late at night, or so early in the morning, that soon the first light of dawn would emerge from the horizon. Michele told him in a low voice

"We can't leave Sabatino alone. He might commit a rash, insane gesture. He's totally in shock, as you can see."

When he was finally in bed, with Carla on his side, Ernesto felt too tired to comment on what had happened. After all there wasn't any need. They were both sure that no one would ever find Iris. He had a restless sleep and awoke feeling like he hadn't slept at all. In fact he was surprised to see from his watch that in reality he had slept for five hours, even though he felt more tired than before.

"When are we supposed to arrive to Barcelona?" He asked Carla with a gloomy voice, while he shaved automatically.

"The day after tomorrow, in the morning. What do you have in mind, Ernesto?"

"Nothing. Nothing besides the fact that I don't want to remain on this ship any longer. Let's land there and all go immediately back home by plane." As soon as he said that he felt sorry for Carla, who looked at him sheepishly. Poor Carla, the cruise was her dream and she could never have expected that the family holiday would turn into a nightmare. He caressed her on her check and added, before she could answer, "I'm sorry, darling. I'm a stupid, grumpy old man. I

forgot our car is parked in Savona. In any case we have to get it. It's just a matter of a few more days. Then, when everything is over, we'll take another holiday, you and I, wherever you'd like."

She smiled, touched by his sincere wish to cheer her up.

That afternoon the Captain asked them to join him in his office and told them that he had contacted Interpol and the Italian police of Savona. Then he informed them that sadly it was certain by now that Mrs Alunni was no longer on the ship. He asked them to cooperate and to be so kind as not speak about the...uhm, accident with other passengers. He added that the police had said explicitly they should not leave the ship and that they were also kindly requested to remain at the authorities' disposal once the ship landed at Savona, because they were the most important witnesses.

"What does that mean exactly?" He asked. "We have nothing to do with this tragedy. We don't know Sabatino Alunni and his family. We met them for the first time, by chance, here on the ship..."

"I know, Mr De Paoli. You are right. But please, try to under-stand. It's a very delicate circumstance. You and your family, like Miss Mandelli, will be fundamental in helping the police clear up this unfortunate event. As far as I know, Mr Alunni had been in your con-stant company since the last time any of you saw Mrs Alunni. There will be an investigation; you know how these matters are (No, he did-n't know and didn't want to know either, but what could he do?) You'll be requested to give a full report. I'm afraid it will take some time..."

And actually that was what happened, when at long last they landed at Savona.

CHAPTER TWELVE

Maresciallo Ciricola gaily whistled a tune he could not clearly identify, while he drove carefully along the dark country road. He would never like the idea of going out in such cold and unfriendly weather, in the darkness of a late autumn, already fading into winter. But the opportunity to spend some hours with his interesting new friends and to possibly make music with them was enough to put him in an extraordinarily good mood. He looked forward to informing them about the developments in the case of the missing old man–with the Ape car. He had already come to understand that William Collins had a special analytic talent. But he was still pleasantly surprised by the incredibly exact explanation he had formulated in this circumstance. Primo Ripamonti had phoned to the Carabinieri station, it was about half past six pm. Young carabiniere Maccaluso had redirected the call to his superior, as he had been asked to do, if any of the Ripamonti family had called. Ciricola had been blessed by the relieved gratitude of the eldest of Ripamonti brothers, who had thanked him for reassuring them about the missing father, who was not missing at all, since he had just called from Paris ("Exactly as you told us he would, Maresciallo!").

Emilio Ciricola was surprised when he found the main courtyard of the farm partially occupied by parked cars. He felt slightly disappointed by the idea of a more formal dinner with several other unknown guests, but then he slapped his forehead and told himself, '*Emilio, what a fool you are! They're surely the clients of the restaurant.*' Actually the restaurant of the farm was always busy, even during the so-called low season, which emptied most of others.

An icy wind attacked him as soon as he got out of his car, but the warm lights which lit the farmhouse windows from inside steered him reassuringly to the door, like a lighthouse showing the right direction to a small boat.

Peter welcomed him, as soon as he pushed the door.

"Emilio, here you are! Come in, come in. There is a foul weather indeed tonight. William and Themba are busy in the restaurant, but they'll join us when they can. We'll have the same menu they serve there, anyway. William will send us the dishes." He gave a friendly wink.

There were only four other people gathered in the cosy, large kitchen when Peter led him there. Mr Reginald, his wife Ellie and the mulatto twins, Themba's teenage children. Emilio was sorry that William wasn't present, because he wished to inform him immediately about the news concerning the elderly runaway. But it was clear the others also knew everything about the story, because Reginald greeted him with one of his very warm smiles and asked,

"Did the Ripamonti receive a phone call from their father, as William had predicted?"

One of the twins, the pretty girl, took his anorak to hang it on the coat rack in the corridor and looked at him with expectation.

Emilio grinned and looked forward to telling them all what had happened. He sat comfortably in one of the armchairs which created a sitting-room corner in the big kitchen and when he was sure the general attention was focused on him he started,

"What can I tell you? William was right. I think I won't doubt his conclusions anymore, even when he tells me something apparently quite improbable. William has perceived things we human people wouldn't believe." He grinned again, realizing that his paraphrase of the famous quote from 'Blade Runner' was a bit misplaced. "I'm afraid I'll take advantage of William's talents, even if involuntarily, because now the Brothers Ripamonti are convinced I was able to guess what their father decided to do. I suppose they'll spread flattering rumours over the village..." He savoured the curiosity of those present for a moment, and then decided it was time to satisfy it.

"Abelardo Ripamonti phoned his sons from Paris. He's perfectly well and he apologized for not informing them in advance, but he claimed they would have prevented him from taking such a trip. The Ripamonti brothers had to admit he was right on that point. They would have been terribly worried for him, if they had known that he intended to take a trip abroad on his own, at his age...The old Ripamonti had never been further than Rome before, and even that short trip out of Tuscany dated back at least forty years. But it seems the elderly man managed perfectly–only God knows how– and he told his sons that he's having a great time and he will be back home in few days and will bring them good news."

The old Ripamonti's amazing story had put everyone in good mood. "I hope I get a chance to meet him and hear his version when he's back to Capacciano." Peter said, helping Ellie to lay the table. "It will be extremely interesting to learn his impressions of Paris."

Caterina arrived from the restaurant, bringing a tray covered with dishes. Her children rushed to help her and to free her from the heavy, bulky load. "Let's eat, while everything is still warm," she invited. "I've got to go back, and William apologizes, but he's still quite busy. He will join you for the coffee, he hopes. He just wants me to ask the Maresciallo if the phone call arrived at the expected time. I don't know exactly what he was talking about..."

Maresciallo Ciricola felt serenely at ease in this place, among these people. Life holds so many surprises in store for us. He would have never expected to find such an unusual group of people when he arrived in Capacciano. But now that he felt more self-confident about his fate, his loneliness and grief for his beloved wife could be alleviated at least a little by these unexpected new friendships.

"You can tell William that everything happened as he had imagined and old Mr Ripamonti is safe and sound in Paris. Ah, by the way, his son gave him William's rather cryptic message about the cemetery where Abelard and Heloise are buried and it seems that old Ripamonti asked twice for the name of the cemetery and wrote it down." The Maresciallo was amused by reading surprise in Reginald's and Ellie's eyes, while it was obvious that Peter already knew about that.

It could be at any time, in any place. People didn't change their natures. They might appear different at times, but only superficially so, due to circumstances, cultures or other factors that always looked more important than they really were. Emilio Ciricola was sure that this peaceful, intimate atmosphere was the same that others had perceived centuries before or perceived right now in totally different corners of the planet. The reassuring pleasure of an empathic relaxation with a few trusted friends after sharing a meal.

Peter stretched his long legs, scratching his dog's head. The hairy, sturdy animal had remained crouched at his feet nearly motionless, like a big, soft footstool, but he suddenly got up when the door was flung open and William entered with his usual long strides. As always, he didn't look tired at all, even though he had just finished his kitchen chores. He shook his dark curls.

"I don't know if you have already taken your coffee. In that case let me make another one for all of you. I hate to drink coffee by myself when I'm with company. Hello, Emilio. Caterina has already told me about our dear Ripamonti. A very pleasant character, I must say. I must try to get to know him when he's back." He spoke quickly, bustling about with his coffee percolator. Another of William's fixations was his absolute refusal of all capsule coffee machines.

"Ah, Emilio, I do need your advice and experience. Peter and probably also Reginald would be too worried about infringing the law. They are archetypes of honesty and justice, while Ellie and I are—how to say?—more flexible, aren't we, my beautiful English rose?" He pirouetted elegantly to kiss quickly Ellie on her forehead. "You see, Emilio, we have fully accepted you into our rather exclusive circle of amateur detectives, even though you are a professional. So it's time to confess the truth, hoping to find in you a tolerant and sympathetic listener." He pretended to feel anxious and uncomfortable, while he poured the fresh coffee into small cups. Emilio still hesitated, not being completely sure about William's histrionics. As he noticed that all the others were smiling, he allowed himself to slip into the play too.

"You know I'm a representative of law and order, William, so if you confess any crime you might have committed against the Italian rules, it will be my duty to proceed against you."

"Oh, I'm aware you won't hesitate for a second. But this is a preventive strategy. I didn't commit any crime yet; I simply want to know in advance in case I do it inadvertently. If a private citizen, without receiving any emolument for the action, decides to inquire about a case, cautiously avoiding violating any law during this procedure, does this private citizen commit anything illegal?"

Ciricola felt intrigued and slightly worried at once.

"No, I do not think this theoretically indefinite private citizen would commit any crime. Of course he might run the risk of getting himself in trouble, but that's not a crime. And now, William, would you be so kind to tell me what in the hell you and Mrs Ellie and the others have in mind?"

Unexpectedly William refused the leading role and stepped down in favour of Peter, who calmly and precisely informed the Maresciallo about the case of Iris Ciancaleoni and the role of the mayor's wife in all of it.

Emilio Ciricola listened silently, looking absorbed. Finally he drew his conclusions.

"So all of you agree there is something unclear in this case, even though all the investigations had been carefully done and concluded. How can I help you? I cannot get the records of the inquiry either and I cannot study the official papers. The case, according to what you told me, depended on the police of another region. I belong to Carabinieri and, as you know, there is not always a good collaboration between us and the police. Unfortunately in some cases we even appear to be in competition."

"Oh, but we didn't expect anything like that from you, Emilio!" Peter reassured him.

"We'd like simply to know if it might create problems if we try to go over everything that happened two years ago on that ship." William intervened and handed to Emilio a small plate with a slice of cake on it. "Taste my version of the Linzer Torte. The Linzer Torte is said to be the oldest cake in the world. Mrs Sanchini, Ellie and I are going to Torino to meet the witnesses of those tragic events that happened on a cruise ship over two years ago. After that, if we find them and if they agree to speak to us, I hope we'll have a more precise idea about the facts. Your role would only become essential after these first phases. The matter is that, if we can find evidence that Iris Ciancaleoni didn't commit suicide, you might help us with the necessary steps to get the case officially reopened."

The twins, who had remained in silence, eating their portions of dessert, suddenly spoke with a vibrant tone, practically in unison.

"William, William, please take us with you as well. Please, say yes! Decide before our parents arrive, or else they'll object for sure." Malusi tried hard to be convincing. "We can help you in many ways. We've already done it."

"I can take photos, without being noticed." Gianna suggested, as if it could be possible that a beautiful mulatto girl with a big tele-lens could easily pass unnoticed.

William laughed. "You are both of age by now. So you don't need any authorization or permission if you feel like going to Torino.

"But we want to come with you and Ellie and take part to the inquiry..."

Before William could answer it was Reginald's turn, who harrumphed and took off his glasses.

"By the way, William, well I thought, if it's no trouble...I spoke with Ellie about this...I have never been to Torino and I know there is a fantastic Egyptian Museum there and...I don't want to put all the burden on Peter, Caterina and Themba, but we are in low season and there is no work with the B&B and it will be only for a few days, I suppose and..."

William looked incredibly amused, even pretending to be annoyed and frowned a little.

"Is there anyone else ready to join the organized tour? Should I rent a coach? Maybe we could wait for Ripamonti's return and to take him and his sons with us and I'm sure you want to come over as well, Emilio, together with Maccaluso and the other Carabinieri..."

Then with a funny grimace he opened his arms.

"I surrender. This will be the most ridiculous bunch of amateur detectives ever put together. Let it be. We'll all go– the six of us– to Torino, but I won't accept any more participants."

Maresciallo Ciricola told himself that he would have liked to be one of the party too, but his rigorous professional conscience obliged him to remain silent.

CHAPTER THIRTEEN

It was a gloomy and foggy morning when old Abelardo Ripamonti crossed the threshold of the Carabinieri station with purposeful strides. He respectfully took off his brown hat, revealing a frail birdie-like head covered with scant hair, like wet light feathers. Maresciallo Ciricola thought about how often elderly people become similar to birds, flimsy and thin, with a sharp nose dominating the middle of their faces like a beak. Maybe when their lives reach the final point they fly away silently and mysteriously, as if blown in the wind. But he roused himself from poetic speculations and shook hands with the old man.

"Good morning, Maresciallo. I came to apologize for all the bother I created for you," he started.

"What are you saying, Mr Ripamonti? You didn't disturb me at all, but your family was concerned. Luckily all's well that ends well. But, please, come to my office and take a seat. There's no reason to speak standing up here in the corridor."

The Maresciallo invited Ripamonti to make himself comfortable; then he couldn't help asking the old man what most of villagers would,

"How was Paris, Mr Ripamonti?"

"Ah, you see, Maresciallo, Paris is really very big. There is only one hill there and when you are on top of it you can see how endless the town is, much bigger than even Firenze. But it's very beautiful, different from any other place I had seen in my life. Now I can fully understand why my Luisa so wished to visit there. I did it for her, Maresciallo, not for me. I'm reaching the end of my life, and I'm the only one who still keeps the memories of my Luisa alive. Our children can't remember her; she left us when they were too young. All her relatives are dead by now. I'm the only one who keeps her alive. Because I think we keep our dear ones alive as long as we remember them clearly."

Ciricola felt moved; the thin old man had just spoken a great truth in the simplest way. We can keep our beloved ones alive thinking of them as they were when they lived with us. He realised he needn't fear the memories of his wife; but only had to preserve them carefully and serenely, while life goes on.

"We were all a little worried about you, Mr Ripamonti, because we knew you had no experience travelling abroad and we wondered how you could manage."

A child's smile lit up the old man's lined face.

"Oh, it wasn't so hard. I bought all the train tickets in Arezzo and had a printed timetable. When I arrived in Paris—such an enormous and busy railway station, Maresciallo, you cannot imagine it!—I looked for a policeman. They have a different uniform there, but a uniform is always a uniform. The policeman, a very kind chap, could not understand a word, but he led me to an office where they give assistance and information. There was a young lady who spoke Italian. She helped me find a suitable hotel and gave me helpful advice. I told her why I had come to Paris. I explained that it was the last chance to show it to my wife through my eyes and my heart. She printed the hotel address for me and showed me where I could take a taxi. I was thrilled, Maresciallo, such terrible traffic, and the taxi driver was an African who liked high speed. But he knew his job, and I arrived safely to the hotel. A man at reception could speak Italian. He was so kind to me that even my sons wouldn't be more thoughtful. He suggested I take an organized tour with a guide speaking Italian. And I did that the following day.

"I took my meals at the hotel. It was expensive but good; even though they had different food from what I'm used at home, I liked it. I called my sons on the phone as soon as I could. I was sorry to hear they had been worried about me, but luckily you had reassured them. I'll always be grateful to you for that. Primo told me that the pleasant Englishman of 'L'Oliveto' left a message for me about a man called Abelardo like me, who was buried in Paris with his beloved Luisa. I asked the receptionist and, guess what, Maresciallo, he offered to take me there the following day, when he had his break from work. It was the most beautiful cemetery I had ever seen. When we found the tomb, the receptionist took a photo of me in front of it. What an impressive tomb! It looks like a little temple of lace, with slim marble columns. Suddenly an idea struck me, and I knew what I had to do once back home. I'll redecorate our family tomb exactly like that. I'll build a small elegant temple with polished columns and I'll put my Luisa there and then, when my time comes, I'll rest forever by her side like the other Abelardo of Paris and his Luisa." He stopped with an ecstatic smile, as if he could already see the new tomb before his eyes.

Maresciallo Ciricola prodded him to continue, saying,

"Mr Ripamonti, it's a splendid idea indeed, very romantic, I'd say. But it must be very expensive..."

The old man lowered his voice a little and continued.

"I also intended to speak to you about that, Maresciallo. I need your advice. But money is not a problem. I won one million euros. They are in my bank account in Arezzo. I was obliged to open a bank account, because I couldn't draw my winnings directly. I have three sons, three good sons. My idea would be to give three hundred thousand euros to each of them and to use one hundred thousand euros to build the tomb monument for me and my wife. Do you think it would be enough? I've already paid all the tax, the notary told me that. What do you think?"

"I think, Mr Ripamonti, that you are a good husband and father, and you definitely took the right decision." Maresciallo Ciricola felt comforting warmth inside. There are people who have the natural talent to spread positive vibrations around and this little old man was surely one of them.

While Ripamonti and the Maresciallo were having their conversation, Themba and Peter were driving a party of six, with a hodgepodge of baggage, to the railway station of Arezzo.

CHAPTER FOURTEEN

"Excuse me, I don't mean to sound meddlesome, but I'm sure you're going to the fashion week of Milan too, aren't you?"

The young man had cast more than a few covert sidelong glances at the six people who occupied three rows of seats in the first class carriage of the "Freccia Rossa" train. He had whispered his excited impression in his travelling companion's ear. She was a tall and pouting girl, riskily poised between elegant slenderness and incipient anorexia. She had nodded in partial assent and then scanned the small group of passengers, hidden behind the protective screen of her very dark "Dolce & Gabbana" sunglasses.

"Uhm, I think I've seen some of them somewhere. Two of them are British stylists for sure. I think I have met the woman with Vivienne Westwood once. The two young models should be those I have heard of, two new faces with a future, they said. But the girl is definitely too plump..."

He grinned, smoothing down his pale pink pullover and fiddling compulsively with his smartphone at the same time.

"Amaranta, you're just worried and envious, my dear. After years of starvation to always stay at the top, now you're not ready for the triumphant charge of the curvy models."

He grinned again with a malicious, little hiss. But Amaranta paid no attention to him, because suddenly the relative silence of the carriage was broken by notes from "Shut up and Dance", which made the younger of the stylists raise an eyebrow. Amaranta hastened to answer her cell phone and, unexpectedly, left her seat to go to speak outside the carriage. The eyebrow of the handsome stylist recovered its usual form again.

The young man was absolutely sure that they were well-known stylists and models. He was in the same business, after all, even though he had to admit honestly–only to himself– that they had to be at a higher level than Amaranta and himself. But still he could not put names to their faces. One of the women was dull, but she had to be the personal secretary of the younger stylist, since they were sitting side by side. All the others were elegant and remarkable. The two young models worried him, because they looked so different from the usual trend, but so appealing and full of personality. He wondered if he had not committed a mistake adopting his hairstyle, so similar to what was fashionable for everyone. The stylists and the mulatto models, on the contrary, had rather long hair on the sides of their heads, without a tuft or forelock mummified with gel. One could call that awfully out of fashion, had they not made it look so elegant, personal and modern. And the mulatto girl didn't look too plump at all. The truth was that, compared with Amaranta, even a dragonfly would look obese.

He had to find a way to communicate with them; it could be useful for his career, so he asked:

"Excuse me, I don't intend to sound meddlesome, but I'm sure you are going to the fashion week of Milan too, aren't you?"

And immediately he felt uncomfortable, noticing the ironic little smile on the perfect lips of the younger stylist. But it was one of the older stylists who answered kindly and calmly, in Italian with strong English accent.

"No, we are going to Torino to visit the Egyptian Museum." Nevertheless there was something strange about that. The two mulatto models–or presumed ones– were giggling as if he had asked something very funny. Maybe, he thought, they had to present a new collection and couldn't tell anyone, to keep the specialized press off the scent.

William–because the small group of apparent fashion stars was in reality composed of our amateur detectives–had lent a careless ear to the chattering of Amaranta and her smart companion, being more interested in making Mrs Sanchini feel comfortable. She was wearing a drab outfit, not of bad taste, but that didn't stand out in any way. He was sure he wouldn't be able to remember its colour either. But she was so sincere and enthusiastic with her gratitude for the help which William and his friend had decided to offer to her, that he felt a spontaneous liking and sympathy for her. He had reserved the seat at his side for her. He was sure she wouldn't bother him with vain and useless superficial conversations. Actually, shortly after settling on the train, she removed a couple of paperbacks from her large handbag and put them on the little folding table in front of her seat.

William couldn't help peeping at the books. He'd always thought one could learn a lot about people by what they ate and what they read. He was sure in advance that Loredana Sanchini was not one of those women who might enjoy infamous best sellers like "Fifty Shades of Grey", just to mention one; but he was pleasantly surprised reading the titles of the two books she had brought with her. The thinner one was a copy of Dostoyevsky's short story "The White Nights", while the larger one was a good biography of the poet Giacomo Leopardi.

Loredana crossed his glance and shyly nearly justified herself.

"I love classical Russian literature. I have the habit of reading my favourite novels again and again and, oddly, every time I discover something new, something different in them." She smiled as if she felt like she'd apologized for having such old fashioned literary tastes, without realizing that she had just risen in William's esteem.

William was already anticipating the pleasure of an intelligent exchange about the characters of Nastenka and the nameless 'narrator' with this enjoyable woman, when his cell phone started vibrating imperiously in his trousers pocket—William always kept it in vibration mode. He got to his feet and walked through the aisle out of the carriage, passing by the pouting Amaranta, who was taking her seat again after a gossipy chat with a friend.

As soon as he read the name Lyubov Orlova on the phone display, the serendipity made him smile. He'd had no contact with Lyuba for more than a year. And now Miss Orlova showed up unexpectedly just as he had thought of Dostoyevsky. He postponed his memories and answered.

"Hi, Lyuba!"

Her voice sounded, as always, apparently emotionless. Lyuba was not very talkative.

"Hi, William!" She said. "I wonder if your invitation to taste your cooking is still valid. I'm in Firenze right now, but I can come to Arezzo in a couple of hours..." She hesitated. Surely she had heard the sound of the train running in the background. "But, well...I guess you're not at home right now..."

"Actually we're going to Torino, it's a long story. But I'll only be away for a couple of days. You might go to the farm anyway, if you have some free days at your disposal. Peter and Themba are there and it's very quiet this time of the year. I'll be happy to meet you when I return." As soon as he said this banal sentence William realized there was something wrong. Lyuba would never pop up so suddenly, leaving London without informing him in advance. Even though they had shared some vicissitudes connected to a dramatic event, they had never been in touch on a regular basis. Actually William had met Lyuba only three times in his life.

The wilful Russian businesswoman clouded over. William perceived it from the rhythm of her breathing. She didn't reply immediately. He could imagine a slight, vertical wrinkle of disappointment appearing on her forehead, between her pale eyebrows. Lyuba was not used to having obstacles to her plans. He was surprised to hear her heaving a sigh of distress. He thought he had misunderstood the sound. It didn't seem like Lyuba at all.

"I didn't come for a holiday, William." She sounded determined and serious. "It's Iraida. She left me. I don't know why, and I have no idea of what is going on with her."

William leaned against the window of the train, staring incongruously at the toilet door, as if the monotonous parade of flat fields and poplar groves which ran on behind him might prevent him from any mental activity. He had met Lyubov Orlova when he and his friends had managed to solve the mystery of Fiammetta Innocenti's murder and to prove the initial suspect innocent. Lyuba was Fiammetta's best friend, and she turned out to be the depositary of the key to the whole mystery.

Such an unusual and intriguing young lady, this Lyuba. William had mixed feelings, but he had to admit that he was not completely indifferent to her. She had something in common with him, unfortunately mostly with his dark side. Facing her was like facing himself in an inky, distressing mirror. Peter was his twin soul on the sunny side of the street. Lyuba was his dark memento, a reminder of his own contradictions and psychological conflicts.

William had guessed one of Lyuba's secrets, and he had sent her a copy of a Dostoyevsky's book to highlight that he knew it. It had created a deeper bond between them, even though they had had no further contact with each other since then.

And now here is Lyuba, after so many months. He knew he could not let her down. Iraida, her governess and confidant, was one of two people who had importance in Lyuba's life. The other one had been Fiammetta. Fiammetta was dead, and without Iraida Lyuba would be totally alone. No, he could not let her down.

"What's happened, Lyuba, and how can I be of help? You have more powerful means than me to find out what happens around you."

Lyuba was a well-off businesswoman; she lived in London and could easily make connections in many different social environments. William had guessed who had been behind the still unsolved murder of Fiammetta's killer, on the day of his trial. A professional hit man, still free, had assassinated him during transport to court. But the inquiry into that execution had been dismissed as a crime of patronage for an unnamed bigwig involved in a dirty paedophilia story, a story that led to poor Fiammetta's murder. But William had understood who had engaged the hit man... Lyuba was not someone who could easily forgive or forget.

"You have the means which I have not." He repeated.

Lyuba's voice seemed to come from a distant time; she sounded unusually frail.

"She would never have abandoned me; you know it. She didn't explain anything to me. She just left me a short, handwritten goodbye note..." Lyuba paused and William realized she was silently crying. He reflected upon how different people seemed to be leaving in one way or another without any logical explanation lately. Iris Ciancaleoni, the old Abelardo and now Iraida. But William knew that there is always an explanation for everything. Sometimes it's simply hidden, and not the one appearing to be the most logical at a first sight.

A tall, stout man arrived from the other carriage and looked at William in a puzzled and mistrustful way; then he pushed the toilet door.

"William..." Lyuba insisted, recovering her usual tone. "William, I've already done everything I could. I know when she left London, and I'm almost certain she flew directly to Switzerland, but I lost track of her. She's evaporated. I can't understand, and the uncertainty haunts me. Only you can help me."

He suddenly felt sorry for her.

"Lyuba, I cannot change my plans right now; this matter is also a serious one. I'll explain everything to you. I'll be at the farm in two days."

Lyuba understood and didn't insist. She knew when she couldn't change things, even though that rarely happened.

"Call me when you are back then. I won't be far from Arezzo."

They hung up without further word. It was not because of rudeness. It was simply because nothing more needed to be said. Everything was settled.

CHAPTER FIFTEEN

Torino was cold, rainy and busy. The central streets were made more cheerful by the first Christmas decorations, even though it was still November. William thought that soon they would start with Christmas immediately after stopping celebrating Easter; alternating chocolate eggs with candles and fir trees in a frantic commercial spiral.

He led his small group out of Porta Nuova railway station zig-zagging through a crowd composed of hectic passengers, resigned North-Africans of indefinable age looking for warmth and corpulent female gypsy beggars, who intoned a plaintive psalmody that became an annoyed hiss, if they were ignored. He had reserved rooms in a good hotel not far from the station, in the centre of the town. While they were walking quickly across the main hall, Gianna stopped him, taking his arm and showing him a solitary piano that seemed to float like an island amidst waves of walking people.

"Look, William. There's a sign; it says 'Play me'. What a great idea. Let's stop for a minute."

A few other people were apparently waiting, but nobody dared approach the piano. Only a little girl furtively pressed a key and then remained paralyzed as if the sound might accuse her of doing some-thing forbidden.

"Oh, William, let's do it, please." Gianna's eyes were shining, and her twin brother nearly pushed her toward the stool and took out his camera.

Music has always a salvific effect. William looked interrogatively at the others and saw only enthusiastic expressions on their faces.

"Let it be. But all together and something definitely pop, to please the audience. No Christmas carols, obviously. Mrs Sanchini ...(she menaced him with a finger, joking); yes, I'm sorry, I meant to say Loredana. So, Loredana, do you know the lyrics of 'Imagine'?"

Loredana said shyly that she knew them a little, but it was clear she felt glad to be included in the band. Ellie grinned, claiming she would have expected to have to perform 'Eleanor Rigby' again and Reginald hugged her fondly.

William took his place at the piano and tested the keyboard. It was not in perfect tune, but it could be worse. When he started playing the famous song people stopped by and others arrived from distance. William and Gianna sang together and the others improvised a rather acceptable chorus. Malusi turned around taking a volley of photos. A girl asked him if it was a flash-mob.

When the last note was still trembling in the air, a spontaneous applause rumbled under the vaults of the railway station. Many voices started shouting "Encore! More!"

William and Gianna were deciding what to play when they were distracted by another voice, a distressed female one, which shouted loudly in the general cacophony

"My wallet, someone has stolen my wallet. Help!"

Malusi, who was a bit outside the closer circle of audience, apparently concentrating on taking photos, made his way through the crowd pushing a gypsy girl who wriggled like a grass snake in front of him.

"Dirty black bastard, leave me alone, I didn't do anything. Help me, he's hurting me!"

Malusi smiled with a seraphic expression.

"To be precise, you might call me a dirty mulatto bastard. But it doesn't make any difference."

Then he turned to the distressed woman, who was now nearly crying because her wallet had disappeared and winked gently at her.

"All's well that ends well. This girl just told me she found your wallet on the ground, and was going to return it to you. Because it's what she told me, wasn't it?" And he shook the girl gently but firmly, as her flowered, long skirt danced around her thin legs, making her looks like a rag doll.

"Please, give back the wallet you picked up from the ground. Everybody will be grateful to you, and you'll be free to continue your walk."

The young gypsy shook her shoulders and tried to claim she didn't have a wallet, but a second glance around persuaded her that people were not considering her presence in a very friendly way. She angrily rummaged into her thick layers of colourful clothes and took out the wallet, which Malusi handed to the owner.

"Here you are, Ma'am. Please check that everything is in order."

The woman checked quickly. Nothing was missing. She thanked Malusi, who was still holding the gypsy girl. She had now stopped flailing about and looked hostile, but resigned. He nodded in a gentlemanly way. The people around clamoured. Somebody said to call the police; others seemed determined to scold the young gypsy with the support of a couple of slaps.

William intervened.

"As my friend the photographer rightly said, quoting Shakespeare–I hope knowingly– all's well that ends well. This girl is probably 11 or 12 years old. She would be released in one hour, if she were taken to a police station. There is nothing else we can do, besides showing we are all more civilized than her parents, who have given her so little in every sense. We cannot change the world by slapping a child."

Malusi loosened his hold, and the little girl disappeared like a wild little animal that had found an unexpected way out of a cage.

William and Gianna played and sang for another ten minutes to cheer everyone's spirits. People forget quickly. Music has a salvific effect. At least nearly always.

After their quick check-in at the hotel, Loredana Sanchini declared she was not tired at all; the train trip had been relaxing and enjoyable. William proposed they immediately go to see Ernesto De Paoli and his family, the main witnesses of what had happened to Iris and Sabatino during the tragic cruise. Loredana accepted.

The others were probably disappointed when they realized that William would only go with Loredana, but they didn't complain, because they all understood that arriving in group would have a negative effect.

William hadn't contacted Mr De Paoli yet, since they had no official authorization allowing them to question him. But William thought they might improvise, depending on how the man reacted. He intended to be frank and to tell him the truth. Loredana had brought an album with many photos of Iris and herself to prove they had really been very close friends. Then they could only hope to be lucky enough to gain the trust of the witnesses and to rely on their direct memories of those days.

Mr De Paoli owned one of the smartest delicatessens of Torino. The shop was not far, maybe ten minutes walking. William and Loredana walked quickly under the arcades of a large avenue lined by an endless series of shining shop windows. It was already dark; the days were becoming ever shorter. The lights stood out even more against the night background, and there were already signs of the excited and busy atmosphere which invaded the central streets at the beginning of the Christmas shopping season. They turned left, after walking through an elegant square. It was easy to find Mr De Paoli's delicatessen. It was exactly on the corner with an attractive, discreet, old-fashioned sign saying 'Premiata Salumeria De Paoli & Figli' in golden letters.

William couldn't help giving a quick, appreciative look at the display of food in the shop windows. He had the impression that the delicatessen owner–or any other on his behalf– knew his job well. He pushed the door and let Loredana in, following her. He recognized Ernesto De Paoli instantly from the photo he'd seen of him on one of the press-cuttings, which Loredana had carefully collected. The man had not changed in two years; he was wearing an immaculate white overall and a long, equally white apron. A white peakless cap was perched on top of his still thick grey hair. He had to be about seventy, maybe older, but he looked energetic and strong. He offered a spontaneous broad, friendly smile. William immediately took a liking to him. Without hesitation he spoke directly to the delicatessen owner.

"Good evening, Mr De Paoli. You'll probably be a bit surprised, because you've never met us before, but we'd appreciate it if you could give us a few minutes. My name is William Collins and this lady is Mrs Loredana Sanchini. We came from Arezzo to speak to you. It's about a tragedy that happened two years ago, on a cruise ship...We'd be grateful if you could answer a few questions..."

Ernesto De Paoli waved discretely to one of his shop assistants to make her take his place behind the counter and stepped in front of it. He shook hands with Loredana and William and kindly said,

"Let's go to speak in the back of the shop, please. But I'm surprised...I already told everything to the police detective two years ago, and since then it had all been over in my opinion. Ah, it was a terrible accident indeed, a tragedy..."

He led William and Loredana to a rather cluttered small office. One wall of the room was made of glass and allowed a peep into a perfectly clean and efficient kitchen where a couple of ladies were very busy. At a glance, William recognized the professionalism of their gestures.

Mr De Paoli looked at them, waiting with a puzzled expression. Loredana Sanchini seized the initiative.

"Forgive us, Mr De Paoli, for turning up suddenly, without warning. Let me explain. Iris Ciancaleoni Alunni was my best friend. Here, please, look at these photos. You'll recognize her, my poor Iris...We were younger then, but you can see us together. Here, here, these photos were taken at her wedding. She lived in Umbertide, I live near Arezzo, but we had always remained in touch. I knew Iris so well. She would never have committed suicide, believe me. Since I heard that her widower was going to get married again, I have not been able to sleep well anymore. There is something, something strange in it all. He's marrying a woman he met on that cruise as well. It's strange..." She stopped for a while, unable to speak, with her eyes full of tears. Ernesto was listening sympathetically to her. She found the strength to continue, even though she was overwhelmed by emotion.

"William, here, is a friend; he's very clever and honest and he has already helped many people to discover the truth in what happened to them. He's Irish, but he has been living in our village for several years. He's a great cook, you know, and he owns a restaurant..."

Loredana had done her best to introduce briefly William in a positive way and to provide the basics about his judgment to Mr De Paoli. Once again William appreciated the intelligence of that so self-effacing woman.

Ernesto De Paoli was digesting the information he had just received. He nodded in assent.

"It was a very bad story; my first time on a cruise...I would never take another again. Are you telling me that he, Sabatino, I think that was his name, that he's going to marry a lady he met on the ship? That's intriguing indeed. Don't tell me she's the little, slim, brunette..." He saw the positive answer in William's eyes and scratched his forehead.

"It really sounds strange. My daughter-in-law even shared the cabin with her, after the tragedy, and my son did the same with Sabatino, because the captain had sealed the couple's cabin, after the...the disappearance of Iris. I'll be glad to tell you what we remember of those days, if it can be of help. You seem like good people. After a long career in contact with the public I have learned to understand people. But unfortunately right now I can't give you the time the matter deserves. If you came all the way from Arezzo, it's important that you get to ask me everything you want with calm.

"I have an idea. If you are free and don't mind having dinner a little later, I'd be happy to invite you to my home. I'll inform my wife. My son and my daughter-in-law can join us. We close the shop at 19:30, then we need thirty minutes to tidy up everything. If you don't mind having dinner at nine in the evening..."

Definitely William liked this man. He felt the trip to Torino would have interesting repercussions.

"You are incredibly kind, Mr De Paoli, but we hate the idea of disturbing you and your family. Besides that, we are not alone, Loredana and I. We came to Torino with other four friends, who are waiting for us at the hotel. Maybe we should meet you again tomorrow and...."

Ernesto shook his head and smiled in a disarming way.

"But it wouldn't disturb us at all. I just need to tell my wife. We have a big house and, as you can guess, knowing my profession, we are never short of food. It will be my pleasure to meet your four friends. Let's all get together for dinner. You see, tomorrow we'd have the same problem; I'll be in the shop all day long, and it's impossible to have time enough to speak of such delicate matters here."

A lady in her late sixties with an impeccable perm, which made her blond hair look a little like a medieval helmet, poked her head through the door.

"Ernesto?"

"Ah, Carla, my darling, these two good people came here from Arezzo. This lady was poor Iris Alunni's best friend and...."

In a few moments he had informed his wife, and Carla agreed with her husband.

"Of course, of course, you are all heartily invited to our home. Oh my, I hoped that tragedy was over. But I have always thought there was something fishy. So you think Iris didn't commit suicide, but someone threw her into the sea, don't you? But who could do that and why? As far as I remember—and I can't forget that nightmare, believe me—he, Sabatino, was always with us. Then the police inquiry decided it was a case of suicide. Oh, I've always thought there was something suspicious about that story!" She looked interested and engrossed.

"Well, we don't know how to thank you. We feel a bit ill at ease. There are six of us..." William mumbled.

"No problem, it's our pleasure." Interrupted Ernesto. "Now Carla and I have to go back to look after our shop. Please don't consider us impolite. We'll meet later at our home. Let me write down the address for you."

CHAPTER SIXTEEN

They had been obliged to take two separate taxicabs to go to the De Paoli's home. And now the two cars were following each other along a road full of bends, which wound its way up on the hills, on the other side of the river. It didn't take a long time; it was only a few kilometres from downtown, but when they arrived at their destination they already felt like they were in the countryside. The air was cleaner, while the lights of the town barely sparkled down there, veiled by a rather thick fog. The house looked like an old country residence, with a certain elegance of lines, vaguely 'Art Deco', without any pompousness.

Even though William knew it was a breach of etiquette to bring flowers to the lady of the house when arriving for an invitation–one should always send a bouquet the following morning, with a thank you message elegantly handwritten on a card–he had decided to act in his own way. Reginald and Ellie–mainly Reginald– had showed a certain embarrassment at the idea of being invited for dinner by perfect strangers; so it would have been unimaginable to arrive without a small gift for the hostess at least. On their way back to the hotel William and Loredana had stopped to buy six bottles of excellent Italian champagne (William decided that offering a foreign wine to an expert of Italian cooking wouldn't be adequate) and a beautiful bouquet for Mrs De Paoli. Nothing too big, because enormous bunches of flowers are often troublesome for a hostess. One couldn't be sure she would have a suitable vase immediately at her disposal.

They had no time to ring the bell, for the door was already opened by a smiling young lady with a boy about 12 years old at her side who scanned the six guests with curious eyes.

"Welcome, I'm Valentina De Paoli and here is Marco, my son." She pushed the boy imperceptibly to remind him of good manners. Marco shook himself out of his delighted astonishment and greeted the guests at his turn. They looked like very intriguing and amusing people, it would be fun. The black boy winked at him and Marco merrily recip-rocated.

The interior decoration was not particularly refined; it reflected a solid middle-class taste. There was a moment of confused awkwardness when they had to introduce themselves to each other.

"This is my son Michele, you already know Carla, my wife..."

"Here is our dear friend Ellie McKenzie and her husband Reginald...."

"These are Gianna and Malusi Nkosi... No, they are both Italian, their father is of British origin, their mother is Italian. Their parents work with us at our farm. Yes, we have a farm with a B&B and a restaurant... yes on the hills near Arezzo. They all came with us because they intend to visit the Egyptian museum...yes, tomorrow morning..."

Ernesto accepted the bottles of champagne with a glance of deep approval for the choice, and Carla rushed to look for a vase to hold 'such an exquisite bouquet'.

"We have improvised the meal, but we trust you'll like it." Ernesto warned his extemporary guests. "All Piedmontese specialities. We brought many 'antipasti' from our shop and then we'll have agnolotti, but the typical ones, we call them 'agnolotti del plin'..."

William could not control his sincere enthusiasm.

"I look forward to tasting them!" Then he turned to his friends with a necessary explanation. Obviously he spoke Italian in respect of their hosts.

"Plin means a 'pinch' because you pinch with thumb and forefinger between each mound of filling to close and seal the little pasta packets. A delicacy, you'll see..."

Ernesto felt an increasing liking for this pleasant, handsome man, he had just met.

"Oh, I see you are really expert about cooking. You mentioned that you own a restaurant, I'd be pleased to discuss about that with you. We seem to have some interests in common. But now, please, let's go to the table. I think we are all hungry."

"I cannot speak for everyone else. But I'm starved!" Malusi showed his intention with one of his shining smiles. The atmosphere became immediately more relaxed, and all of them took places at random around the nicely laid table.

The women brought large trays from the kitchen. William was pleased as Punch.

"Yum-yum! Insalata russa, vitello tonnato, tomini elettrici, insalata di carne cruda, crespelle con la fonduta![3] I cannot believe it."

He thought everything had been much better than expected so far, and he felt that probably the very kind De Paoli family would help their investigation as well. But suddenly the thought of Lyuba and her distressing phone call pierced his mind, while he was generously helping himself from the dish of 'vitello tonnato'[4]. William decided to store the disquieting matter in a corner of his head and to not let it spoil the rest of that evening.

"I know you have taken this trip to ask us some questions about our memories of that unfortunate cruise, and I promise that we'll try to remember every detail which could be important for you. But I ask you for a favour. I'd prefer not to speak too much during the meal. I don't think it's a good habit. Conversations are pleasant either before or after a good meal. During it, the food deserves all our attention.

"Oh, Ernesto, if you allow me to call you like that, I could not agree more. We can talk all we want after enjoying your sublime dishes." William approved vehemently. The more he knew that old man, the more he liked him.

Carla and Valentina, the two ladies of the house, at first stood a little on ceremony, when Ellie and Gianna spontaneously offered their help to clear the table and to prepare the tray with the coffee cups. But the ice had already been largely broken during dinner, when all the guests had appreciated the dishes and had behaved in a friendly way, as if they had already been used to be in each other's company. So they accepted and all the four women started chattering in a very easy going way while they arranged the crockery in the large, slightly old fashioned kitchen. Loredana Sanchini would have liked to join them as well, but William suggested discretely that she could give a bit more of information to Ernesto and his son, who were ready to come to the main topic to consider after that unplanned dinner.

Loredana spoke briefly about her friend Iris, describing her as a determined business woman and a very pragmatic person.

"Iris fell suddenly in love with Sabatino, when she was still very young. She got married a few months before me; I was the bride's maid, of course. I was already engaged to the man who became my husband

---

[3] All typical cold and warm starters.
[4] Basically a carpaccio of veal meat with a rich tuna sauce.

then. I was deeply in love, too. The main difference is that my poor Iris passed away, and her husband has just married another woman, while my husband and I keep on loving each other like we did the very first day."

"Oh, I can understand you; it's the same for me and my Carla." Ernesto smiled, overflowing with tenderness. "She will always be the love of my life even though we have been married for nearly 45 years! It's a pity your husband didn't come over too. I'd have been happy to meet him."

Loredana was neither too talkative, nor inclined to special dialectic diplomacy. She was only able to tell things the way they were and in the simplest way.

"My husband didn't agree with my suspicions about Iris' death. If it had not been for William and the others here...well, I would never have found the courage and the determination to come to speak to you, Mr De Paoli. But my husband loves me very much and esteems me too, so he didn't oppose my coming and I'm sure he will support me. He wouldn't have been able to come with me in any case, because it's a very busy time for him, besides his professional engagements, he's also the mayor of our village, Capacciano..."

The other ladies arrived with a big coffee percolator and a tray of pastry.

"We might move to the living room to have a cup of coffee more comfortably." Carla invited them with a gesture. She could not wait any longer. She felt extremely thrilled and intrigued. The idea of a dark mystery behind the bad adventure of their unlucky cruise appealed to her. Carla passionately followed all the TV programs where unsolved crimes were analysed, and the idea of being an eye witness to one of those obscure cases excited her. In reality she had fully accepted the idea that Iris Alunni had committed suicide, as the police inquiry had stated. She had not thought about it for many months now. But the unexpected arrival of these six people had offered her a new perspective on what had happened two years before. By the way they were unusual, but very smart and proper people indeed, Carla thought. She had not had opportunity to get on more familiar terms with all the guests yet, but she had spoken a little more with the pleasant English lady, an art restorer, who was married to that reserved, tall gentleman with glasses. She told Carla that they had celebrated their marriage only six months earlier, but it had been a real love at first sight.

What Carla liked in a very special way, besides crime stories, was watching the most romantic soap operas. She also hoped to have a chance to learn a bit more about the love story of this mature and beautiful English couple as well. But one thing at a time...

When they were all comfortably installed on soft and cosy, slightly worn out sofas and armchairs, William nodded at Ernesto to encourage him to start.

"Please, Mr Ernesto, tell us everything that you remember about what happened on that cruise; all details can be important."

Everyone fell silent. The only sound was the clinking of the small spoons, which stirred the espresso in the cups.

He started,

"We were in Savona, ready to board that big cruise ship when I noticed them for the first time. There was only one couple ahead of Michele and Valentina. Carla and I came after them. The man was tall and well-built, dressed with a casual elegance. The woman was also tall, with long blond hair. She wore dark sunglasses and stumbled imperceptibly, but her companion held her up promptly...."

CHAPTER SEVENTEEN

Ernesto and his son Michele had insisted on driving back all the guests, with their two cars, directly to the hotel. The simple and spontaneous kindness of the family impressed Reginald and Ellie in a very special way, mostly because they were still surprised by their unexpected invitation. They had exchanged phone numbers, email addresses and had promised each other to keep in touch. It was already very late. The twins had dropped the idea of exploring Torino night life and decided to go to sleep, since the visit to the Egyptian museum was planned relatively early the following morning. Reginald stifled an attack of yawns, making a real effort to keep his eyes open. Ellie had not spoken that much, lost in her own thoughts. Loredana had listened with moved attention to everything that Ernesto De Paoli and his son had told them. She had asked a few detailed questions, and she had noted something on a small pad she had taken out from her handbag.

William also had taken many notes, as it was his habit, when he had to order various elements in his mind like pieces of a puzzle.

All the others had decided to go to sleep, but he couldn't. He called Peter, who was surely sleeping, even though he answered at the second ring. Their short conversation filled William of a sort of peace of mind, which only Peter could give him. William acquainted him with a brief, but quite informative report of their visit to De Paoli's home.

"Loredana was right to suspect something fishy about Iris' death. The only problem is that I'm not completely sure where the key to everything is hidden yet." William added as conclusion. Then he suddenly remembered something he had temporarily removed from his mind, and felt uncomfortable because of that.

"Wait, Peter, wait! I forgot to ask you something. Did you receive any phone call from Lyuba?"

"Lyuba?" Peter sounded completely awake and puzzled now. "Why the heck should she call me? As far as I know we have not heard from her anymore since we left London last year."

William detected a badly repressed, slightly annoyed note in Peter's voice and it made him feel even worse. He hated hiding anything from Peter, but he had been obliged to do it in the past. Fortunately this time he could share all with him.

"She's in Firenze now. She called me yesterday saying she was in trouble because her governess had disappeared. She wanted our help to find out what happened. I told her that she could go to the farm and wait there for my return and explain everything to you in the meanwhile…"

"Probably she didn't consider me up to that." Peter sounded sarcastic, a feature which usually didn't belong to him. "Besides that, I think she has her own means to find out practically all she needs to know."

Peter was right, of course.

"Never mind, I'll see to this matter when I'm home again. Tomorrow—or I might say today, since it's well past midnight now—we have planned to visit the Egyptian Museum and if we don't give Reginald all the necessary time to do that at his own pace, he will be terribly disappointed. He even managed to get Gianna and Malusi involved in his sudden passion for Egyptian culture, and they have been informed that, as students, they can get a special permission to take photos inside the museum and are now beside themselves with excitement. Then I hope we'll find a good restaurant to have a decent lunch and finally we'll take an afternoon train. We should arrive in Arezzo around nine in the evening…"

"Call me to confirm the timetable. I'll meet you at the railway station. Go to sleep now, William. Uhm, it's stupid of me telling you that. I know even too well that you won't sleep until your whole reasoning about what you have learned from the eye witnesses is clearer. I deeply regret now that I wasn't there with you. I'm getting very intrigued by the possible development of this story." Peter concluded. "Since I can't participate in any other way, I'll try to fall asleep again myself."

William considered with a mixture of relief and slight uneasiness that Peter knew him fairly well indeed.

It had to be bitterly cold outside, but he definitely felt like going out for a walk, hoping to find concentration. He knew there were some details which had struck his attention, but still unconsciously; he needed to find them out like the silhouettes of people walking in the fog, which become clearly visible only when one passes them more closely.

There was no one walking under the arcades–one of the main typical features of Torino central avenues. The fog was rather thick, made yellowish by the street lamps.

William tried to imagine how sumptuous and beautiful the arcades might look, before the apparition of a couple of generations of urban taggers without any specific artistic talent, but only gifted naturally for the perverted pleasure of smearing everything beautiful with their scribblings.

He had seen amazing examples of beautiful street art in many places, but these quick sprinkles of red or dark paint had absolutely nothing creative. They were destructive and useless signs of personal uneasiness, disguised under the frail alibi of a form of social protest.

The arcades were dirty and the shops, with all their rolling shutters down, added to the gloomy atmosphere. William surprised himself thinking of the young gypsy pickpocket girl whom Malusi had caught at the railway station. So young, but already morally poisoned by her life. How old could she be? Twelve or thirteen. Maybe she was gifted with unnoticed bright intelligence. Maybe if she had had a chance to study, to live in a different context... Diversity is richness. He was persuaded of that. Different cultures always have something positive to offer to each other. Discrimination is a cruel torture which he had experienced personally in his youth. But mutual respect is the only way to interconnect different cultures without destroying them. There should be a way to become integrated in the society, in which one lives, without necessarily exploiting it or, even worse, creating antagonisms of values. But what could save the little gypsy girl from all that? She would keep on pickpocketing absent-minded passengers without thinking for a second that it might be wrong. Then in one or two years she would marry another gypsy teenager and they would have soon children who will grow up who-knows-how.

"I'm getting older, a damned old moralist..." William told himself, without being completely sure if he should be sorry for that.

He tried to put together all the fragments of impressions that he had received listening to the De Paoli's narration. There was something he could not grasp yet, but he knew it could really be the fundamental clue to answer to all the questions. Iris had been killed. He was sure of that by now. Loredana Sanchini had been adamant in her certitude. Her friend Iris was not depressed, and she would have never committed suicide. It's true, they had not met each other often during the few years before her death, but they had spoken regularly and Iris had never showed any sign of psychological distress. She was under pressure from the responsibilities of her work, and she dedicated most of her energy to run the factory. Maybe her relationship with her husband was not as deep as it was when she married him. But that happens in all couples. Then Loredana had thought it over. There are couples, such as hers, whose love grows with the years instead. Iris had mentioned the cruise to her during their last phone conversation. Loredana had explained everything clearly to William. Iris didn't sound particularly enthusiastic about the idea, but it seemed her husband had insisted.

William thought of the reactions of Loredana, when Ernesto De Paoli had told them accurately all that he remembered about Iris and Sabatino and those awful days on the cruise ship. He tried to see them again like in a slow motion film. He was concentrating so hard that he didn't feel cold either, even though the night was freezing and humid.

On the corner of a street he took two steps forward and nearly collided with two girls who were standing on the edge of the sidewalk. One of them, maybe scared or taken by surprise by the sudden apparition of the passer-*by* from the fog, swung on her absurdly high wedge-heeled shoes and lost her balance. William grabbed her and held her up gently.

"I'm terribly sorry, I was totally thoughtless." William saw the heavily made up and tired face of a black girl, who stared at him. The other girl looked on defensively. She was shivering with cold. They both were wearing micro-skirts and were hardly protected from the chilly night by short synthetic fur jackets, one of an incongruous fluorescent pink and the other one of a dirty white. Two Nigerian prostitutes. They had little chance of finding clients in that place, at that hour. They both considered William's appearance, without nourishing any hope. He was too young, too handsome, and too wealthy to look for their company. But they tried an approach, even though with very little determination. His kind answer surprised them.

"Don't take it badly, but I prefer to decline your offer. If I were in your place, I'd stop working for tonight. There is nobody around, and it's cold and very late. Too foggy for drivers too. You are nearly invisible on this corner and then, you are frozen. Standing with such uncomfortable shoes for many hours must be awful." William smiled warmly. "Since we are, apparently, the only living souls outdoors, I'd be glad to offer you a warm drink, if only we could find an open café. I'm afraid everything is closed in this area..."

The second girl looked him up and down and, supported by her instincts and her professional experience on the street, decided he was not dangerous. Bizarre, very handsome, but not dangerous. She had not said a word yet. She couldn't speak Italian that much yet. She knew the name of various sexual services and how to ask for the relative prices. Her colleague was already much more fluent in the local language. But the gentle stranger surprised her once again, switching from Italian to English. A language she knew well.

"Maybe you know better than me if there is a kiosk where we can find a hot drink nearby. I'm not from Torino." He said.

"Well, actually there is a small club which is open all night long. It's just two minutes' walk from here. But...uhm, we can't go there now. The man we work for...You understand...He's waiting for us there and we are not allowed to get there until we earn what was planned for today. But it has been a bad night for work. Then I'm sure it wouldn't be a good idea for me and my friend to pop up there in your company. It would be dangerous for you and for us." She smiled apologetically and suddenly she looked very young.

"How much are you still missing to reach the planned... budget for this night?" William asked with calm, as if this conversation with two young prostitutes in an empty and foggy street were the most common display of a social gathering.

The girls talked together in an incomprehensible language. Then the one with the pink fur coat stared at him directly, lifting up her chin. In spite of the very high heels she was much shorter than William.

"You aren't a cop, are you?"

"Oh my, of course I'm not. I'm a cook."

"Fine. I believe you. You don't look like a cop, but you don't look like a cook either. I don't know why it interests you, but we still need at least two hundred Euros."

William was aware that she had increased the sum, but maybe not too much. It was not important. If he could prevent them from being beaten up, at least once, he wanted to do it. He fumbled in his pocket and took out his wallet. He handed four fifty-euro notes to the closest girl, the one who had nearly fallen down.

"So this night is over for you. Go home or wherever you intend to go. Keep warm..."

The girl made the money disappear probably into her bra, with such a quick gesture–like a conjuror–that William could not be sure of it.

"You must be a complete nut, sexy cook or whoever you are. But we were lucky to meet you. Are you sure you won't enjoy a quick blow-job? Just to thank you. We are very good at that." The second girl spoke in a playful way, as if she had already guessed the answer and she was just teasing him.

"I'm sure you are wonderfully gifted." William laughed without any scornful intention, just friendly. "Maybe another time, when it's less cold, less foggy and less late. Now hurry up to the club you mentioned and drink a double cappuccinos or something like that."

"Ah..." The first girl sighed with a beginning of relief. "Thank you then. I look forward to taking off these shoes. I'm not used to such high heels; they kill me. I'll never get used to them. You can't imagine how many times I have run the risk of a bad fall because of them. But, well, they say I'm too short and my legs are not slender enough, so I need to wear high-heels for my work, you see. When I still lived in my village, I was comfortable only barefoot or with flat sandals..."

William had the impression that the fog had suddenly faded away, even though it still surrounded the three of them with its cottony, fluffy coat. The clue he was looking for was finally there, right in front of him.

He interrupted the girls who were still adding a few words of thanks. Waved an imperceptible goodbye at them, and turned his back, walking quickly toward his hotel.

The girls saw him disappear into the waves of mist that infiltrated under the arcade, and they took the opposite direction, to reach a hopefully warm shelter, knowing that soon they would be blessed by needed sleep.

CHAPTER EIGHTEEN

The breakfast buffet was elegantly laid with a huge display of food and drinks. William, perfectly shaved and as fresh as a daisy, didn't look like someone who had slept only a couple of hours. He voluntarily ignored the heaps of small jars of various jams and marmalades and considered with benevolent mistrust the baskets full of croissants and rolls. A smiling waitress offered him to prepare his fresh drink, and he felt relieved to notice the absence of those awful dispensers of the pale, watery pretence of coffee, which were often the only alternative in average hotels. The waitress served him quite a good espresso and in that very moment Loredana and Reginald, who had met in the lift, entered the breakfast room together.

William waved at them.

"Good morning! Nice to see I'm not the only early bird. I recommend you have a good cup of espresso. This young lady can make delicious coffee." The waitress agreed modestly. She had arrived at work on that cold November morning when darkness still reigned over the awakening town. Days became shorter and shorter. She always tried to do her best at her job, but it didn't happen often that a client recognized her efforts so kindly. William brightened her morning up with another warm, shining smile, and she hastened to prepare the other coffees, putting even more attention than usual into her gestures.

"Ellie just woke up when I left our room," said Reginald, once all the three of them had taken their place at a corner table. "But I told her to take all her time, since we are not in a hurry, and I decided to come downstairs to see if any of us were already up. I didn't expect to meet the twins, obviously. It will be necessary to go to wake them up, I suppose. But I was nearly sure that you and Mrs Loredana might be here already. I think that, exactly like Ellie and myself, you have thought over what we learned yesterday evening from Mr De Paoli and his family. By the way, before leaving I hope we'll have time to go to tell them goodbye and to thank them again for their immense kindness ..."

Loredana nodded in assent.

"I was really very impressed and deeply touched by the narration of Iris' last days. I realized how deeply her death still affects me. Grief is sometimes well hidden under our daily routine, but it doesn't disappear easily and it's always ready to pop out when we leave it an opening to slip through. I'm very comforted by the fact that I'm not alone anymore in my suspicions. Your sympathy and support fill me with endless gratitude. I have tried to order my thoughts this night, but I have no real talent for synthesis and rational speculation, I'm afraid." Loredana shook her head with a slight resignation.

"Mr De Paoli and his relatives gave us such a detailed report, but still I'm not sure I can match the image of Iris they gave us with the Iris I remember. Maybe she was ill; maybe she had problems we cannot grasp. Iris was a determined woman, she was very strong tempered. She generally attracted attention wherever she was. But Mr De Paoli told us she was very dependent on Sabatino, and she kept a low profile. On the other hand, he well described her elegance and her way of always being impeccable, her accurate hair style and her passion for smart high-heels shoes." Loredana smiled briefly, lost in memories. "She had so many pairs of shoes; I once told her that she was becoming like that Eastern dictator's wife who had wardrobes full of a thousand pairs of shoes."

Reginald had listened to the brief conversation, casting sidelong glances at the door, looking for Ellie. He sipped his cappuccino—he hadn't managed to get fully used to Italian espresso yet—then he intervened calmly.

"I noticed that, during his so detailed description of the events they had witnessed during that tragic cruise, Mr Ernesto and his daughter-in-law both stated a few times that Iris stumbled. I didn't pay great attention to this detail, assuming it was a sign of Iris' weakness, both physical and psychological, even though for reasons which are not completely clear. But last night thoughts kept on whirling in my mind. I'm getting persuaded that there is something unconvincing; things don't match as they should. If Iris, as our dear Loredana has just confirmed to us, was so fond of high-heel shoes and so used to wearing them on every occasion, how is it possible that she couldn't walk easily with them on that ship? Maybe the sea was rough, but nobody mentioned that. Then I remember that Ernesto described her slight awkwardness in climbing up on board, the first time he noticed her, when they were still at Savona harbour..."

William didn't let him finish and, provoking a certain amazed concern in Loredana and the waitress, jumped up slapping Reginald on his forearm while putting the contents of his cup in serious trouble.

"I have always known you're a genius, Reginald, the best detective of our small amateur group! It took me a long walk in the fog and a meeting with two prostitutes to arrive to the same conclusion which you reached simply in your hotel room, all by yourself."

Loredana and Reginald didn't know whether to be more puzzled by the sudden, energetic movements of William, who only a minute before was calmly sipping his second espresso, with the same expression of a lazy, meditative feline, or by the unexpected revelation that he had met prostitutes the night before.

Ellie arrived, pushing ahead two sleepy twins, whom she had wisely decided to awaken.

"Oh, here we are, all together now...But, hum, what's happened? Did we miss something fundamental?"

"Ellie dear, your husband has practically started solving the case, even though we are still groping in the dark. But thanks to Reginald, down there, at the end of the dark corridor we can start perceiving a weak light...."

All traces of sleep disappeared from the twins' face.

"Why do interesting things always happen when we are not there?" Malusi complained while filling a plate from the buffet display.

"Tell us immediately everything you have learned," added Gianna, "The story of William and the prostitutes included. We are largely of age for that." And she grinned, without realizing how incredibly pretty she was.

"The shoes, you see, the contradiction is in the shoes. Iris was used to wearing stiletto-heel shoes all the time and she felt comfortable with them. It seems, to the contrary, that she had problems walking easily with her shoes when she was on the ship. There must be an explanation for that...I came to this conclusion only by chance, while Reginald followed his logical reasoning and was quicker than me." William explained briefly.

"What are we going to do now?" Gianna asked, spreading a generous dose of honey on a toast.

"We'll go to visit the Egyptian Museum!" Reginald concluded, feeling flattered by William's praising remarks. He tenderly caressed Ellie's hand. "Are you sure, darling, that you'll be warm enough with this light shirt? It seems bitterly cold today."

Ellie was proud of her husband. She kept on discovering new qualities of his, day after day. Like many people apparently distinguished only by an endemic exterior awkwardness, Reginald was gifted with a natural inclination to introspective reflection, which allowed him to go much deeper in mental speculation than others, apparently much more self-assured. He was generous, sympathetic, humorous and humble. These qualities had attracted her immediately. Later she had found out also the depth of his remarkable intellectual faculties, which he seemed to prefer to keep hidden behind the screen of his clumsy shyness. She was unable to picture her husband's life before their meeting. She knew, obviously, that he had been a Catholic priest for most of his adult life, but she had never asked him too many questions, because she realized that he preferred to turn that page completely. Ellie was aware, anyway, that it wouldn't be completely possible to erase all his past experiences and inner ideological troubles. They were part of him, like scars which are not painful anymore, but have drawn a different physiognomy.

"I'll wear my quilted jacket, honey. I suppose there is a good central heating in the museum, or else the Egyptian mummies would feel uncomfortable." Ellie reciprocated the loving caress taping softly on her husband's arm.

The Egyptian museum, recently restored, was considered the best in Europe and second in the world only to the Cairo museum. William couldn't help thinking again of a small school excursion, captained by an enthusiastic teacher, Reginald in this case, while they all walked under the arcades toward the museum, which was set in the heart of the centre. William brought up the rear of their small procession, completely absorbed by his thoughts. Without any apparent logical reason he suddenly stopped.

"Reginald, wait a moment. Listen to me. I have something urgent to do. Go on to the museum without me. I'll join you later. Either you'll find me at the Museum or, more probably, I'll wait for all of you at the hotel. I'm sure you'll have a wonderful time and the visit will be quite enjoyable, but I have to go now..."

The other five members of the small group were taken by surprise, even though they all knew William well enough to not be too amazed by his sudden changes of mood or mind. Before any of them could react or add a word, William had already taken a side street and had disappeared from their view.

Something had suddenly rung a bell in William's mind when he realized they were walking not too far from the De Paoli's delicatessen shop.

Five minutes later he pushed the glass door of the shop. They had probably just opened, and he saw Ernesto coming from the kitchen with a large tray full of delicacies to arrange in the refrigerated shop window.

"William, what lucky chance brings you here this morning? You arrived on time to have a cup of coffee with me, if you can wait until I arrange this stuff." Ernesto De Paoli greeted him warmly. Carla, his wife, was already sitting behind the cash desk, but it was a bit too early for the first clients. She smiled at William too, maybe a bit surprised to see him on his own.

"Good morning Ernesto, good morning Carla. I'd take another coffee with great pleasure and, of course I can wait. But I came to bother you again this morning because I need to ask you something very important."

"But you never bother us, William! On the contrary it's a pity your other friends didn't come too. It's a pleasure meeting you again. We thought you would leave Torino today..."

"Yes, we will, but only in the afternoon. By the way, Ernesto, I'd like if you could recommend a good little restaurant for our lunch, not too far from the railway station. But the reason for my visit isn't that trivial. I have thought over everything that you told us so accurately about Iris Alunni's disappearance and about the people you met during that cruise. I think you can help us again. I have an important question which can cast a different light over those events. The young lady who travelled on her own, Jessica Mandelli, who, by the way, is now Jessica Alunni, since as far as I know she got married to Iris' widower a few days ago, Jessica the brunette, as you call her, Ernesto, you met her several times as well, didn't you?"

William towered in the middle of the empty shop, while the shops assistants were arriving in dribs and drabs. The owners always arrived first to open the shop and were the last to leave in the evening at closing time.

Ernesto finished arranging his shop windows and looked up at William.

"Yes, of course, we met her often. She had started getting on well with poor Iris, then after the tragic accident, she shared the cabin with my daughter-in- law, while Sabatino slept in Michele's cabin for the rest of the cruise, you know that we have already explained all that happened in those days..."

"And you did it very accurately indeed. But I didn't ask you something very important; it was entirely my fault because I didn't think of it...Please, Ernesto, try to remember. As I have just told you, it's very important. Did you ever see Iris and Jessica together?"

Ernesto looked a bit confused.

"But I have told you that they went all together on excursion with Sabatino and then the two ladies spent time together several times...."

"I know, I know, Ernesto. But YOU, personally, I mean, had you ever seen them together?"

The delicatessen seller knitted his brows to concentrate, then said, with a slight hesitation,

"Well, I'm not sure, but I don't think I ever saw them together. I cannot remember exactly after two years, but since one was tall and blonde and the other one short and dark-haired, I suppose I would have noticed them together, as a contrast, you see. What about you, Carla?"

Ernesto's wife had left her seat behind the cash and approached.

"Oh, once we suggested having dinner all together, with Jessica too, but she had chosen the earlier shift in the restaurant and, besides that, there was only space for six people at our table. Now that you make me think over, I'm sure, I have never seen the two ladies together. Ernesto is right. I'd have surely noticed their difference in physical appearance and in the style of clothes. They looked so different from each other, that I'd have surely had a memory of that, seeing them side by side."

William hugged Carla.

"You have been precious; really precious...The light at the end of the corridor is getting brighter." William added quite mysteriously, at least for the two De Paoli. "And now, Ernesto I'd be happy to offer you and Carla a cup coffee. Your shop assistants are here, and they'll look after the shop even without you for a little while. Then you could be so kind as to help me to choose a good restaurant for lunch."

CHAPTER NINETEEN

The visit at the Museum had been a success. Gianna and Malusi had received authorization to take photos. While the display of historical treasures was really impressive, one of the main surprises was finding William in the papyrus room, completely absorbed in contemplation of the 'Royal Canon', a series of fragments of a long papyrus dating back to the reign of Pharaoh Ramesses II. The fact that William could already be there appeared nearly as mysterious as the content of the ancient list of kings.

Reginald was used to the unexpected talents of his friend, which revealed themselves in the less foreseeable circumstances, but there were limits... Nevertheless a slightly worried note trembled in his voce when he asked William if he could read Egyptian hieroglyphics.

"Unfortunately I cannot." William shook his head. "But I'm quiet fluent in reading Sumerian cuneiform script, mostly for the adapted version of Akkadian language." He smiled modestly.

Reginald was flabbergasted, but a second glance at William, who hardly managed to look grave, made him realize that it was just a joke.

"Oh, I feel relieved! It means you are human, after all, William Collins. Now I suppose you should tell us the real reasons for your disappearance and sudden reappearance."

"Reginald, I deeply hope you don't intend to spoil our visit to this splendid museum with useless chats. I was simply trying to find a good little restaurant where we could book a table for our lunch. But let's follow Gianna and Malusi, who have already started taking photos of the tomb of Kha...".

Reginald nodded, Ellie grinned, and Loredana considered it was really one of the most pleasant and intriguing groups of people she had ever met.

During the entire lunch William had been quite evasive about what he had done that morning before joining all of them at the museum. The small restaurant, of very unpretentious appearance, was a little gem of good, traditional local cooking. When they arrived, the owner welcome them saying, "Ah you are Mr De Paoli's friends! You are welcome, here is your table."

Reginald immediately made the link and he whispered to William,

"Did you go to meet Mr. De Paoli again this morning? Why? Don't pretend with me that it was because you needed a suggestion for a restaurant..." But his words bounced against the wall of William's imperturbability.

"Oh, Reginald, you know that I never speak about anything during a meal, except about the food I'm eating. Take it easy and enjoy your lunch."

Only later, when they were all installed comfortably on the train which would take them back to Arezzo, William took his cell phone out and called Peter, speaking to him in front of the others, since they were the only passengers in that carriage.

"Peter, yes, we are on the train. I could not wait to let you know what we have found out. I think we have taken very important steps forward. We have to deal with quite refined criminal minds, so we must try to be cleverer than them if we hope to find any evidence. I'm sure Iris was killed, but she was not killed on the cruise ship. Actually I'm persuaded she had never been on that cruise ship. Yes, a very Machiavellian plot. I'll explain it to you more accurately when I'm home again. We'll arrive in Arezzo on time according to the schedule. I look forward to meeting you again too."

Five pairs of eyes were staring at William with enormous curiosity now.

"William, don't try to outsmart me too much now. I'm not as tolerant as Reginald. If you don't tell me everything now, I won't be able to control myself, and I'm ready to extirpate the truth from you by all means!" Ellie menaced him waving her finger under his nose.

"I surrender!" William laughed throwing back his head in his typical way. "Everything started from the incongruence of the high-heels. One idea took shape in my mind little by little, but I needed to have a confirmation from De Paoli family. They were very precise, as always. None of them had ever seen Iris together with Jessica Mandelli.

I met, even though briefly, Jessica Mandelli, when I went to Umbertide with Peter. She's a rather short brunette, exactly like Ernesto and Carla described her and she was wearing flat shoes when I saw her. Our witnesses were adamant: she always wore flat shoes every time she met her on the ship. I know it might sound absurd but..."

"But she pretended to be Iris when they were on the cruise." It was Loredana who spoke like that. William was surprised once again. What a remarkably intelligent woman she was.

"This is exactly what I think. My idea is that Sabatino and Jessica already knew each other well. They are probably long time lovers, and now they are partners in crime. I wouldn't be too surprised if the mind behind this crime were Jessica's. We need to collect more information about her, but we already know she had a beauty salon or something like that; so she should have a certain experience with make-up techniques, wigs and so on. Iris was rather slender and as is Jessica. Of course Iris was much taller and had blond hair and blue eyes, while Jessica is greenish-brown-eyed. But coloured contact lenses are quite common and, besides that nobody on the cruise ship knew the real Iris, besides Sabatino. The witnesses would have spoken of a tall, slim, blond lady with blue eyes and Sabatino would have confirmed she was his wife.

"Jessica—I have met her—is not as short as people have described her, but with her flat shoes she might look shorter, since the majority of women prefer high-heeled shoes, particularly in formal circumstances. In order to pretend to be Iris, she wore very high-heels, to mark a clear difference between the two roles she played. But she's not used to walk with stiletto-heels; it's not something one can learn quickly and easily. It explains why the false Iris had so many difficulties of balance in walking around."

A pensive silence fell on the five listeners. It was Reginald who expressed everyone else's thought.

"It makes complete sense, but in reality it's just a series of suppositions. There is not the slightest concrete evidence. We might try to find the proofs that Sabatino already knew Jessica. But even if we were successful in that—and I have serious doubts about this chance— it could be difficult to find reasons sufficiently enough to reopen the file. Sabatino had a perfect alibi for that night. Then there is always the message handwritten by Iris herself..."

"I have thought of that." William tapped his fingertips on the small table between the seats, as if he were listening to a silent rhythm of reasoning. "There is also a small incongruence in that. The message was written on a partially ripped sheet of paper, which apparently didn't belong to the writing pad, sponsored by the Cruise Company, which was in the cabin. Then, the message itself is somehow vague. Iris wrote that she was sorry to upset her husband, but she was not happy with THAT kind of life. She didn't write that she was tired of life. She stated only that she had taken a decision, because she was tired of a certain situation in her life. We don't know why she wrote that or when she did it. Probably we'll never know. But that is not the main point. I think that Sabatino found that note–maybe the whole page–and thought it was a gift of the Fate to support his criminal plot, their criminal plot, I should say..."

"Cherchez la femme! With all due respect to the present ladies, of course. I don't mean to generalize." Reginald was carried away by his own speculation. "Jessica must be the evil plotter while Sabatino merely carried out her orders. It's not just a matter of love affair. If it had been only that, he could simply ask for divorce..."

Loredana, who had listened to every word with her eyes closed with concentration, gave the suitable answer.

"The factory. It belonged entirely to Iris. If he had asked for divorce, he would have lost it. He inherited it from Iris, after her death. She didn't have any other relatives. Then there are all the other real estate properties. I don't know exactly their value, but it means a lot of money."

"It's bitterly ironic." William looked half angry and half devastated. "We have practically solved the case. To a nearly prefect approximation we know what happened, but we haven't got a shred of evidence..."

The twins had remained silent with wide-open eyes.

"But they cannot get off like that, William!" Malusi nearly shouted. "We must do something; those two murderers cannot get off like that!"

"William, there must be a way..." Gianna insisted.

Unexpectedly it was Reginald who said the final words. He took off his glasses, put them on the small table and rubbed his eyes, as if he were overwhelmed by infinite tiredness. Then spoke firmly.

"There is only one thing to do. We must find Iris. Her body, I mean. After two years it's impossible to think that there is still much of her around, but her bones must be somewhere. We must find Iris. For sure she's not on the bottom of the ocean. I think she's much closer to her home, poor soul."

CHAPTER TWENTY

The wood was crackling and spitting happily in the fireplace. It filled the room with the fragrance of a comforting homey atmosphere. William flopped into his favourite armchairs with a delighted groan. He had a deep inner feeling that he really had a home, that he had really landed to a safe port and Peter had been the guiding light of his life. They had driven home all the others, and finally they were at the end of that long day.

Peter didn't ask William the question that everyone also would have. He didn't ask him if he was tired, if he wanted to go to sleep. He knew William too well, even though, in spite of all his love, he was not completely sure of fully understanding him in all circumstances. He didn't ask anything. He sat in front of William and looked at him with his trustful, intelligent blue eyes. There was no need to invite him to talk. William stretched like a satisfied cat and started.

"Loredana, Mrs Sanchini, is a very interesting, intelligent woman. I think there is logic in her being physically unnoticeable and apparently dull. A more remarkable physical appearance would have been an obstacle for her. She would have filled her life with useless and distracting people. Being protected from superfluous attention is a gift. She has the chance of being appreciated only by people who really deserve her. My esteem for mayor Sanchini has increased a great deal since I started to know his wife a little better. I can fully understand now why he loves her so deeply."

"Uhm, it's an intellectually elegant way to begin singing a paean in favour of nerds. You should be more objective; you cannot pretend not to know that you are intellectually rich, even too much, and, at the same time, you are very handsome, equally too much, I'd say..." Peter smiled at him with deep affection.

"Ah, Peter, darling, I'm knitted with contradictions, you know that. Would you like a stirrup cup, before going to sleep?"

Peter shook his head, he was happy to have William back home, even though he had been away only for two days.

"Not for me, I'm fine. But if you like a last glass, I'll keep you company. By the way, did you speak to Lyuba?"

"Augh! Lyuba, how could I forget her? I'll call her immediately." William felt guilty. He always felt slightly guilty when he thought of Lyuba; maybe it was the reason for removing her from his mind. He knew they were very similar, and it somehow slightly scared him. But he had good fortune in his life, after several difficult years. He was now surrounded by real, devoted friends, who had become his family, and he had Peter and his priceless, perfect love. Lyuba was alone; she had nobody in her life. Her only friend was killed, and now it seemed that also her governess, the closest person Lyuba had had in her whole life, left her.

Poor, poor rich girl, so lost in her secret inner world, so empty that she had to call him, practically a stranger, to share her distress. William felt even more uncomfortable. He knew that he could not be defined as a stranger to Lyuba. When you share secrets with someone, you are not a stranger anymore.

"I'll call her immediately!" He said, more to himself than to Peter, who protested feebly, without conviction.

"But it's very late, William..."

"I told her that I'd call as soon as I'm back home. She's very reliable, and she expects reliability from others."

Peter felt a warm flame of joy inside realizing that William would have called Lyuba in front of him. They had always been quite respectful of each other's privacy, and Peter would have understood if William had decided to speak to Lyuba privately, but he was happy he didn't. Peter had seen Lyuba only once. He had not fully analysed his feelings for her. She was a peculiar young lady with some dark sides that he could confusedly guess. But he was aware of having something in common with her. Only one thing, to be exact. Both of them were in love with William.

Lyuba answered at the first ring, as if she had been waiting for the call. Actually she was.

"Hello, Lyuba!" William said. He had never been keen of the traditional greeting formula on the phone. He often skipped the first 'hello' and always skipped the final parting words. When he finished what he had to say in a phone call, he simply broke off the communication. The majority of people would find that rude, maybe it was. But it was William...

"Hello Lyuba! I'm in Capacciano, at the farm..." He suddenly activated the hand-free mode of his phone and Peter could hear Lyuba's voice, with a slight embarrassment, as if he were peeping in her life.

Lyuba spoke perfect English, without any remaining Russian accent; she spoke slowly, with a plain tone.

"I'm in Arezzo. I didn't want to disturb your friends at the farm. I don't know any of them, except for Peter and..."

William caught Peter glance and interrupted her.

"Lyuba, Peter is here with me, do you mind if I put you on speaker?"

"Of course not, not at all." Lyuba's voice didn't change.

'But he has already put her on speakerphone' Peter could not help thinking; so William might be not completely sincere with Lyuba or maybe with others too...

"So, if you can hear me, hello Peter! It has been a long time since our last meeting." Then, as if she were satisfied to have quickly fulfilled her politeness duties, she kept on addressing William.

"I don't feel like going back to London, at least not for a few days. I think... I think it would be painful for me to find myself alone at home. I told you yesterday that Iraida had left me. I managed to find out why. Unfortunately she left not only me..." Her voice started cracking, as she tried to control her emotions. She remained silent for a few seconds, and then she kept on with her report. "I told you that I had found out that she was in Switzerland, but I didn't know where and why yet. I came to Italy because I felt a bit lost and I hoped you could help me to find an explanation. Only few hours ago, I got the explanation. It was Iraida herself who gave it to me. Not directly. I got a message that she had left for me. There is a legal society in Zurich, which is called 'Exit'. It's an organisation for living wills and physician-assisted suicide. Iraida suffered with a terminal cancer, but I didn't know it." Lyuba's voice started trembling. It was too much even for her granitic self-control. "She had pretended with me for months. She claimed to suffer with rheumatic arthritis, which provoked pain for her, but nothing really serious; she told me it was age, can you believe it? She told me lies for months, maybe for years. I don't know any more at this stage. She claimed she went to a clinic to treat her arthritis. I was so blind...I believed her. Sometimes she looked much better. I was so selfish. I didn't go deeper. She was there for me as she had always been, for all my life.

She neglected herself not to make me understand the seriousness of her illness. I don't know. When there wasn't the slightest hope left, she took her decision to leave silently, not to disturb me. I understand she wanted to spare me the distress of seeing her going little by little. I don't know if it was right.

"She's gone now. They told me that she had asked to inform me only when all would end. They told me she had contacted them several months ago and planned everything. They told me she was serene and all was painless. I'm sure about that. But I wanted to be there with her, to hold her hand..." Lyuba was crying now.

Peter felt ill at ease; it was such an intimate moment. He had the impression of being out of place, but, at the same time, he remembered the day when his beloved step mother died. He was there at her side, and he did keep hold of her hand until the end. He felt a deep sympathy for Lyuba, because she could not do the same.

"Lyuba, Lyuba. Listen to me." William voice surpassed her sobs. "Be totally sincere with yourself. If Iraida had told you the truth, would you have accepted her idea to pass away with dignity when she wanted or would you have tried to persuade her to keep on with all kinds of medical treatments?"

There was another silence, and then Lyuba spoke softly and more calmly once again.

"I would have obliged her to undergo all the most complicated medical treatments. I'd have put her in a clinic; I'd have spent all my time at her side...I'd have been terribly selfish just to have her some more months with me, without thinking of her ordeal, which would have become mine. You are right, William. This is what I'd have done. It would have been unfair. I'd have been unfair."

"I know it's hard for you to get used to living without Iraida, but she decided to protect you from the tormenting agony of a long good-bye without return." William spoke gently, as if he wanted to calm her down with the sound of his voice. "Now that you have understood that, it will be less hard. But you should really come to the farm, to see where we live, and then maybe you could help us. We are dealing with a very intriguing case. I'd like discussing it with you. Are you totally on your own in Arezzo?"

"Well, not exactly. There is Pasha with me, obviously." Lyuba had recovered from her emotional breakdown and now spoke again like the self-confident business woman that she was. "Are you working on a case? Of course I'd be glad to help you, if I can. And, yes, I confess I'm curious to meet your friends too. But it's a difficult time for me, and you know I'm not the sweetest and most sociable person. I hate to feel like a burden."

Peter spelled on his lips the name 'Pasha' in a silent question. Living in Italy had added an eloquent expressive feature to the two Irishmen. They had learnt to gesticulate spontaneously to show surprise, joy, astonishment and many other moods. William answered in the same way; he goggled and then mimed with a horizontal movement of a finger against his throat the gesture of a cutthroats. But in front of the worried and puzzled look of Peter, he mitigated the picture, pretending to drive a car with his two hands on an imaginary steering-wheel. Finally, realizing that he was not successful in his performance, he whirled round his right forefinger, meaning *'I'll tell you later'*.

"But we'll find a suitable activity also for Pasha here at the farm. Both of you are welcome. Now tell me in which hotel you are, and to-morrow morning I'll come to drive you here." He noted down quickly the address Lyuba gave him. Then, since everything necessary had been said, according to his habit, he broke off the call.

"Do you have just invited a cutthroat to our home?" Peter smiled, pretending to sound shocked.

"Pasha is Lyuba's chauffeur and body guard. Frankly speaking I don't know that much about him, and our first meeting was in a cemetery. I admit it sounds a bit lugubrious, but I have no proof he has ever killed anyone, even though I cannot exclude peremptorily that he has. In any case, as long as we are absolutely kind to Lyuba, we have nothing to fear from him." William grinned, absolutely amused. "What about going to sleep now?"

CHAPTER TWENTY-ONE

The scene could be directly from an old Italian Neorealism film. Four men sitting around a wooden table, on a winter day, playing cards, with the support an uncorked bottle of wine, four glasses and a plate of slices of salami. But a perceptive and subtle observer would have immediately noticed the incongruousness of the four players. One of them wore an impeccable black suit with a black tie and a white shirt; his hair was rather long, without any gel. Had it not been for the haircut, he would have looked like the prototype of a FBI agent in an American movie. The second man was older, with an open face and bright eyes framed by smart spectacles; he looked totally harmless and peaceful, even though in that very moment he was concentrating fiercely on the game, nearly menacing his team partner, sitting opposite him.

"Malusi, mind what you are doing, the seven of coins must pop up soon; I guess you didn't memorize the cards which have been already played..."

"Hey, Reginald, you shouldn't give any suggestions, it's unfair. It's not by chance that I have chosen to team with Pasha instead of with my son. Malusi cannot remember all the cards, but Pasha is excellent at that." Themba said, all wrapped on in an oversized, colourful, hand-knitted pullover, which made of him a kind of living rainbow of all the nuances of purple and orange. He winked at his partner who, at his turn, suddenly swept up all the cards present on the table at that moment gaining more points. "Well done, Pasha! I can hardly believe that you had never played 'Scopa'[5] before."

---

[5] It's one of the most popular card games in Italy. The name is an Italian noun meaning "broom", since taking a scopa means "to sweep" all the cards from the table

Pasha, the man in black, didn't say a word. Claiming that Pasha was not very talkative would be just a euphemism. But an imperceptible hint of a smile curled his upper lip.

Many people were present in the large living room of the farm that evening. Maresciallo Ciricola had also been invited for dinner, and he had accepted with enthusiasm, realizing suddenly how comforting the presence of the entire slightly extravagant group of the farm inhabitants could be for his endemic melancholy.

He was introduced to two "new entries". Two people he had never seen before, even casually in the streets of the village. Because of his professional habits, he had developed a real talent for remembering people's features, but even had he not had that skill, it would have been difficult to not notice two people of that kind together.

There was a young lady, nearly embarrassingly too tall for the none too remarkable height of the Maresciallo. She made him think immediately of a slender silver birch.

Many women, when they are quite tall, walk in a rather awkward way, as if they were hampered by their own height. They try hard to make it less noticeable by bending a little. But it was not the case of this Miss Orlova ("Please, call me Lyuba, like everyone else"). She did not look self-conscious at all and she moved in a very soft, elegant way, like a ballet dancer–he thought. She could not be considered beautiful in a very traditional way. Her eyes, although they were of a very charming amber colour, were definitely a little too small; her face was vaguely too flat, except that her cheekbones were nicely raised. She had her long silver-blond hair tightly plaited, but a few curly locks danced on her forehead like moon beams.

William had introduced her simply.

"This is Lyuba, a Russian friend. She cannot speak Italian, but she can understand it a little. On the contrary, her English is perfect, since she lives in London, so you can practise yours with her, Emilio."

But what Lyuba might be doing at the farm, was still a mystery in the Maresciallo's mind. Then there was the man. Maresciallo Ciricola was immediately on the lookout. His instinct of policeman made detect something in that Pasha who was introduced to him as 'Lyuba's collaborator', which meant all and nothing at once, but which stated clearly that they were not a couple.

Nevertheless this fellow, Pasha, seemed to be well-disposed and unable to hurt a fly. He had started playing cards with Reginald, Themba and Malusi and had barely uttered a few words. Ciricola wondered where in the world William and Peter had met those two Russians, but he had already learnt to be ready for all the oddities which might be connected with his recent friends from the farm. He had realized perfectly that they were generous and proper people and that was largely enough to make him accept their apparent nonconformism.

William and Peter had described in a very lively way all the further development of their investigation. Maresciallo Ciricola felt nearly involuntarily dragged into their story and he couldn't help thinking that there was really something strange about that case. Unfortunately there was very little he could do, and he felt vaguely guilty for his useless role. The theory which William and Reginald had formulated was quite plausible, but was pie in the sky so far, since there wasn't a scrap of evidence. The case had been handled and closed by the police. Carabinieri had not had any involvement in it. In any cases, it would have been the concern of the Umbrian police, not the Tuscan police. There simply was nothing he could do, aside from trying to protect his friends from infringing the law at their turn. He cast a sidewise glance at Lyuba. She looked serious and lost in thought as she curled up on the sofa by the fireplace where she seemed to look for warmth like an absent minded feline. She could not, however, be compared with a domestic cat. Lyuba had nothing of a domestic pet in her. She had a feline attitude, like a wild young tiger who had voluntarily decided to not attack anyone, at least not for a while. Emilio Ciricola admired her thighs with well trained, long muscles, as if he expected to see her pouncing upon someone. An Amazon–thought the Maresciallo–a haughty and daring Amazon. But on giving a more attentive second look he perceived a contrasting emotion radiating from her. A feeling he recognized with moved amazement, because he could not have expected to find in that young lady something in common with himself. Lyuba exuded a deep melancholy, a nearly devastating sadness, and he hardly could repress the impulse to take her hand to comfort her.

As if he had read in the Maresciallo's thoughts, William, apparently incongruously said,

"Lyuba will stay with us for a while; she has just lost a person who was very dear to her."

Emilio nodded with sympathy, realizing there was nothing else to add. Any question would be indelicate.

Lyuba rose to her feet graciously. Her eyes absently grazed Emilio and Peter and then fixed on William.

"I'd like taking a short walk, before going to sleep..."

"But it's bitterly cold tonight..."Ellie's voice sounded protective, but Lyuba seemed not to hear her words at all. William repeated her sentence.

"It's very cold outdoor, Lyuba, but if you really like walking a little, I'll come with you. Put on your coat while I get mine." One minute later they were both muffled up to their eyebrows.

"I have taken a flashlight, just in case. But we'll go only down to the Lombardic tower..." William had a slight apologetic note in his voice, which was not usual for him.

Lyuba impatiently pushed the door and both disappeared into the cold, dark arms of the night.

CHAPTER TWENTY-TWO

Only a few remote lights were visible in the compact texture of the night. However they failed to provide a comforting feeling, because they seemed to be suspended in nothingness, rather than serving as guiding lights to a protecting shelter.

William and Lyuba walked until the edge of the farm courtyard, feebly lit by the two post lights of the entry door.

They stopped on their way, remaining closely side by side, without grazing each other.

"Lyuba, why did you lie to me? When you called me, you already knew what had happened to Iraida..." William whispered, even though no one could hear their conversation.

"I knew that you'd guess. It was a partial omission, not a lie. I didn't feel like telling you about that, realizing you were on a train, busy with other people. It was stupid of me thinking even for a second, that you wouldn't immediately understand everything." Lyuba spoke calmly, with a plain, apparently indifferent tone.

"Actually I couldn't conjecture exactly the happenings, but I was immediately sure that you already knew everything, because I'm aware of the means at your disposal to collect all possible information which interests you." William had taken nearly the same voice tone as she had. He realized that and felt slightly annoyed by this involuntary similitude.

"It's true. I have my ways to find out many things, but unfortunately it's rare that I can prevent them from happening..."

It was too dark to allow William to see Lyuba's eyes, but he could perceive the change in her breathing and realized she was holding back her tears.

"I'm not a clairvoyant, Lyuba, but I have learnt to pay attention to all the little signs and clues which might help me to see through the surface which people decide to reveal." William spoke to her in the dark. "I sincerely hope that staying here with us can help you a little to recover from your grief, but I'm not completely sure now that it's the best idea. As you see, unlike you, I'm totally sincere. Don't misunderstand me. You are welcome here, if it can really make you feel better. The point is that you won't feel less lonely, because your expectations cannot be fulfilled. I know you can understand me, because we are very similar, you and I, Lyuba. Too similar, I'd say. You remind me constantly of a part of myself, which I have worked hard to repress or even to eliminate. Looking at you, Lyuba is like reflecting my own image in a dark mirror. We are different people in all that we have that is positive, but we are alike with respect to our obscure, negative side. I'm intrigued by your personality. If I were not perfectly happy with my sentimental life, I might even be attracted by you physically. You would not be the first woman in my life. But I don't feel for you anything, except a sincere sympathy and a well-balanced dose of friendly affection." William suddenly felt cruel; perhaps he should have been milder in expressing his resolution. He perceived the unpleasant feeling of selfishness which often haunts involuntarily people who are too happy in their life. He had love, friendship, and a serene, enjoyable life now. Lyuba had remained alone... with Pasha. Against his will, William grinned silently. The idea of having Pasha as an only confidant was not the most appealing for anyone.

Lyuba had not added a single word. William knew that she somehow approved of all that he was telling her, even though it was not what she would have liked to hear.

"I have gone through very hard and dark vicissitudes in my life, and I have always fought against them all by myself. This is another element we have in common, Lyuba. I wonder if being totally sincere, in all circumstances, can be really considered a fundamental proof of love for our dearest ones or if instead it's only a selfish way to rid ourselves of emotional burdens, putting them on others' shoulders.

"I have chosen to carry certain burdens on my own shoulders alone, to protect the people I love and, believe me, it's not always easy. I cannot carry your loads too, Lyuba. I have already shared one, a very heavy one with you; you know what I'm talking about. I cannot take any further one."

Unexpectedly he felt the firm yet gentle touch of Lyuba's hand on his forearm. He perceived her force through the thick layer of his coat.

"I have never repented of that, William. Never. It was the right thing. I'd do it again, without hesitating. That bastard deserved to pay. You know better than me that a good lawyer and his powerful family's connections would have freed him from jail in only few years." Lyuba's raised her voice a little.

Lyuba had been behind Flavio Tribulzi Aldrobrandi's killing. The man had been shot, after his arrest, while he was being taken to the court for his trial. Aldrobrandi was guilty of particularly sordid and heinous crimes and had also murdered Fiammetta, Lyuba's best friend. William had guessed she had hired a professional killer, probably one of the best on the market, and the police detectives still couldn't find an explanation to solve that case. They had put Fiammetta's father–a very well-known and powerful Italian politician–under investigation, but they could not find anything on him and had to drop the charges. On the contrary, William had guessed correctly and he had made clear to Lyuba that he knew, but that he would have never revealed her secret.

"Once, I'm sure I'd have reacted like you, Lyuba. But not now. I don't judge you. I just feel much better keeping my distance from personal revenges. This world is full of unfairness, but maybe playing the role of a revengeful god is not exactly the best solution." William suddenly felt cold and nearly shivered, wrapping his scarf more tightly around his neck. Surely the temperature had dropped below zero.

"You see what I mean. I have to carry your heavy secret too, but at least I'm not alone in that. Who knows it, besides you and I? I know that, I don't need your answer. Iraida knew, of course. Then Pasha, probably, and the professional killer, obviously. No one else?"

Lyuba graced him with an invisible smile and whispered again.

"You can answer also this question by yourself, William. It would be really stupid of me if I let others know about the, uhm, transaction I concluded with that professional..." She hesitated for a second, as if looking for a word..."That professional sniper. By the way I have never met him personally either. He's a real professional in every sense. Pasha managed to find the necessary contacts for me. That's all. I'm sorry you have to carry what you consider to be a burden, but on the other hand I'm glad you guessed right."

William softly, but firmly, put his hands on Lyuba's shoulder and made her turn to have her face slightly lit by the post lights of the courtyard, while his own face was hidden in the dark. He confusedly thought of the confessional booths in Catholic churches, even though he hadn't entered any of them since he was ten or eleven. The confessor was separated by a thick grating from the repentant who, in turn, was in a dim light, protected by a dark curtain.

"I knew an extraordinary woman, whom you surely would have liked, if you had had a chance to meet her. She died five years ago. She was Peter's step-mother. But she had been more than a real mother for him. Peter was the son of a girl from the household staff. He has never known who his father was; his mother died when he was ten. The woman I'm telling you about–her name was Julia Fitzpatrick–was a very rich widow; she had no children. She took care of Peter in the best possible way. She made of him the wonderful man he is. Intelligent, cultivated, generous, well-balanced, totally honest. She helped him to accept his sexual identity as a natural matter. I did not have the same luck, but it's another story.

"Julia was clever, humorous, pleasant and loving. We all adored her. Reginald–you have just met him–was her best friend; he was a Catholic priest at that time, but that is another story too. Julia reminds me a little of you, at least in certain reactions. But she was definitely serene and at ease with herself, surrounded by affection. Unfortunately we cannot say the same for you, Lyuba. I'd like to see you like that one day. Maybe time will help. I met Julia when she was already old. I don't know if, when she was as old as you are now, she had already found her inner dimension. You'll wonder why I'm telling you about this person in the middle of the courtyard in a freezing night of November. Well, Lyuba, it's because I'm too tired to carry all these heavy secrets all by myself. I must speak of them at least once, to renew my fortitude and to keep on protecting them in future. I can speak to you, because you cannot be hurt by what I'm telling you, because I know you are reserved, and I trust your discretion and finally because I know you will understand Julia's motivations."

Lyuba interrupted him. "Do you trust me?"

"Absolutely." There was not the slightest hesitation in William's voice.

"Thank you!" Lyuba said in an undertone.

And William started telling her all that he kept hidden inside himself, to protect Peter and Reginald and all the people who had loved Julia. He told Lyuba of the murders that had happened in their Irish village several years before and the guilty, evil lawyer who had killed two women and traded several teenage girls to a morbid Russian tycoon (Lyuba hissed scornfully. "Kurchin, damned bastard, of course I know who he is..."). Then he revealed that Julia had told him and only to him that she had pushed the killer down from a cliff and also that she had found out who was Peter's father: her own violent husband who had raped Peter's teenage mother for years. Julia had provoked voluntarily his death as well. Julia had confessed without any sense of guilt. She considered it simply an act of justice planning her husband's death, after realizing what he had done. Peter had always been persuaded that he was the result of a juvenile flirtation between teenagers and that his conception was, all in all, an act of love, even though fleeting. If he had known that his father was a brute and that his birth was a consequence of sexual violence, he would have been upset. He venerated his step mother, and his moral integrity would have troubled him in an unbearable way, if he had known that she had practically killed two people.

When William fell silent, for a moment no sound broke the night. Then Lyuba asked, with an apparently incongruous, lively note in her voice,

"Do you really mean that she, Julia, threw down from an Irish cliff a man in the strength of his age when she was over eighty?"

"Yes, she did. You should have listened to her when she told it to me, as calmly as if she reported a trivial domestic matter. She banged him on his head with her walking stick, then put him on a wheelbarrow and... By the way, she saved the life of a girl whom he would have probably killed too..."

"A wheelbarrow, her walking stick...ah!" Suddenly Lyuba broke into a laugh. William became conscious that he had never heard her laughing before. It was a liberating laugh, for both of them; Lyuba laughed with a light, crystalline sound, like a little girl.

She controlled herself again and added,

"You are right; I would have adored her too. Fantastic lady! I can understand you perfectly. Of course in cases like this one keeping the truth hidden is simply a great gesture of love. You have chosen to carry Peter's burden, to allow him to live a happier life. I'd like if one day someone could love me so much."

"Never say never, Lyuba. Believe me, not even in my most optimistic dreams (if I ever had optimistic dreams) would I have expected that one day my life would have been so joyful... and now it is...Let's go back indoors. I'll make you a coffee. Ah, by the way, I'm pleased to have you here with us."

Lyuba still smiled when they pushed the entry door of the farm.

CHAPTER TWENTY-THREE

William and Lyuba were surprised to find everyone exactly as they were when they had left. They had thought they had spent a quite long time outdoors in the courtyard, while in reality they had been absent only half an hour.

'We know by now that time is an illusion' William surprised himself thinking, *'Here we are, trapped in the amber of the moment. There is no why.'*

Maresciallo Ciricola got on his feet gallantly, giving his seat by the fireplace to Lyuba.

"Here, here, Miss Lyuba. You look so pale. What kind of an idea was it to go out on a night like that, while we are all so comfortable indoors?" Then he looked in a semi-serious way at William. "Unless you had secrets to tell each other, which were not suitable for our ears..." Immediately realized he had guessed right, even though involuntarily, and he felt embarrassed because he had stressed something which he should have pretended to ignore.

William had just managed to cope with his dose of secrets and omissions and really didn't feel to add others. He chose the straight but perilous way of sincerity.

"To be honest, Lyuba and I had to speak of something related to her life which would be unsuitable for her to display in front of others. It belongs to a chapter of her existence, which she prefers to close once and for all. I know I can rely on your understanding."

He spoke to everyone, but his look concentrated on Peter's eyes. Silently Peter reassured him that all was fine.

The card players had finished their last game. Reginald could hardly mask his disappointment because he and Malusi had lost again against Themba and the invincible Pasha, who seemed to be born to play 'Scopa'. They all came to sit by the others, except Pasha, who remained on his feet, by the door.

Lyuba told him quickly something in Russian and he shook imperceptibly his head. Then he came to sit on the edge of one of the sofas, by Ellie, who gratified him with one of her ever warm and communicative smiles.

"Pasha is not used to social gatherings, so you'll forgive his manners, which might appear a bit, ehm... rude." Lyuba justified him with a half-smile. "But I can assure you that he enjoys your company."

Pasha nodded in assent and unexpectedly spoke too.

"I'm a man of action; I'm not good at conversations. But I appreciate your welcome; Mr Themba, Mr Reginald and Mr Malusi have been very nice to me. I need to make myself useful, so tell me what I can do for you and I will." Then he looked at Lyuba for approval. He looked like a big watch-dog, totally devoted to his mistress. And probably it was exactly like that.

"We'll spend a few days here, Pasha. You'll have the opportunity to make yourself useful in many ways. You have heard about the problems our kind hosts are trying to solve. If you have any idea, your suggestions will be welcome too." After saying these words it was Lyuba who looked at William to be sure she had not done something inappropriate. Maresciallo Ciricola had noticed all that and his brain had started working at a whirlwind pace. This amazing young lady looked in better mood after the short walk she had taken with William. What there was between them? As far as he knew they were not very close friends; they had met only occasionally...But it was obvious that she had feelings for William, who played an important role for her, even though these feelings didn't appear to be mutual. Emilio Ciricola, all of a sudden, realized, to his troubled amazement, that since his Rosaria's death, it was absolutely the first time that he looked with interest at another woman.

"It's a very intriguing case and I'm grateful to all of you to share your investigation with me." Lyuba seemed to become very talkative. "I do think your suppositions are absolutely founded, but, as Emilio here rightly stressed, it's impossible to expect the police authorities to open the case again if we cannot support our theories with solid evidence. We must find the woman, Iris. According to a general logic, she was killed before the cruise and her body has to be somewhere not too far from her home. I know it's extremely difficult for us to have even a pale chance to find it, but we know that at least two people know where it's hidden. So working on them is the only option we have. You said that the man and his second wife are still on honeymoon. Perfect, we must not waste our time. If we inquire about them now, nobody will inform them until their return."

Everyone looked at Lyuba with astonishment. In few minutes she had naturally taken the leadership and even William didn't interrupt her speech. As if she was sitting behind her desk in her office in central London, Lyuba kept on with a determined tone.

"I hope you agree with my idea, I'd like to send Pasha to Milan– you told me that this Jessica is from Milan, isn't she?– to collect information on her. We can learn more about Alunni, because the mayor and his wife know him personally, but we don't know anything about his second wife yet. Pasha has many contacts and he's full of...hum...resources. Emilio, please, can you reassure us that we are not going to infringe any Italian law if we simply go around asking some questions about this woman of Milan?"

Maresciallo Ciricola was more and more impressed by Lyuba and her style. She had called him by his first name twice already and now she was asking for his direct advice.

"Well, Miss Orlova, ehm, Lyuba, if you don't commit anything illegal to collect your information, but simply ask around a little, there wouldn't be any problem. I can be of help too, because I might ask for official documents about Jessica Mandelli Alunni. It's something I can do without contravening the rules of my professional position."

William recovered his use of speech.

"Emilio, you are precious! This is the best path to follow right now. Lyuba I'm glad to see that our case engrosses you. Do you intend to go to Milan as well?

"Nope!" Lyuba exclaimed nearly cheerfully. "Pasha will go to reconnoitre on his own first. Is it fine for you, Pasha, leaving tomorrow to Milan? We'll give you all the limited data we have on the woman so far. I know you know what to do."

Pasha, the man of action, nodded imperceptibly. Definitely he knew what to do.

"Tomorrow morning I'll go to see Loredana and Mayor Sanchini. I'll bring them up to date, and I'll ask them to make an effort to remember every detail about Sabatino Alunni, also the apparently more insignificant. The key to a mystery is always hidden in insignificant, negligible details. The best way to hide something is to make it visible, but unnoticeable. I'm sure all of you remember the short story of Poe 'The Purloined Letter'. Auguste Dupin is an inspiration for all amateur detectives, at least for those of our calibre. I'm sure that what we are looking for, in this case the hiding place of poor Iris' body, is practically in front of our eyes, but we cannot see it, because we are trying to find something much more complicated. It would be useless to start digging in all the area around Umbertide, trying to discover a skeleton. But we know that Sabatino and Jessica know the exact place. We have just to ask them for it. Of course not directly...." William grinned.

"It's really time to go home for us now; it was a most enjoyable evening, as always with you, my friends." Reginald got up looking for Ellie's coat.

Ellie smiled with a pinch of irony. "Do you really think that Reginald will be able to let me sleep immediately at home or do you suspect, like I do, that he will keep me awake discussing all his ideas to solve the case?"

"I have to go too." Emilio Ciricola looked around at all those present in the cosy room and thought with a pang of his solitary, small flat in the village. "I was really happy to meet you Lyuba and also you, Pasha." Then he blushed, because in reality he had not any remarkable feeling for the slightly disquieting and silent Pasha.

CHAPTER TWENTY-FOUR

When Peter and William parked their car in front of the town hall of Capacciano they had to sidestep two communal employees, precariously balanced on their ladders. The inevitable ritual of Christmas decorations didn't spare villages like Capacciano either.

They had driven Pasha to the Arezzo railway station, even though he had tried to get out of their offer at the beginning, claiming he could manage by himself. Obviously Pasha didn't want to feel dependent on others, but he was obliged to accept the lift, since—unless he had decided to walk for more ten kilometres—there was no other way to get there. He had barely spoken during the short trip, that was not a surprising behaviour of his. Peter and William had watched him disappear into the railway station carrying only a small dark leather overnight bag.

"What in the hell do you think he might have inside it?" Asked Peter with an amused smile.

"Uhm, I prefer not to imagine..." William had grinned. "Are we going to get a coffee here or is it better to go back to the RaBARbaro in Capacciano?"

"What a question! You have already decided anyway." Peter laughed openly. They both knew that nobody could make a better coffee than Lapo Tramontina, the RaBARbaro owner.

Now they were rushing to the welcoming warmth of Lapo's café, greeting on their way the two men who were suspending to a cable a kind of big Christmas star.

"Good morning! Another very cold day, it seems. Do you know if the mayor is in his office?" Peter looked up at the two workers, while William preferred to stay aside, not exactly overflowing with trust in their skills for fixing the voluminous and probably heavy star.

"Good morning, Peter, good morning, William. He was in his office until five minutes ago, but he has just left to go for a coffee. You'll find him at RaBARbaro."

'Riccioli d'Oro' the mayor of Capacciano looked even more like the stereotype of a film pirate that morning, all wrapped up in a kind of heavy jacket with leather trims. His impressive, dark beard and drooping moustache shined as if they had been polished.

'Holy crap! Blow me down! For sure you glossed them with whale's grease. Ahoy, Matey!' William thought with an incontrollable burst of a comical mood. But he kept for himself this pirate-style language and greeted the unaware mayor in a more conventional way. He felt a sincere liking for the man.

"Amelio! Nice to find you here. We came to Capacciano mainly to meet you today." They had started calling each other by their first name recently.

The mayor let a shining smile make its way through the hair jungle, which covered the lower half of his jovial face.

"William, Peter, I'm at your disposal. Lapo, please..." He gave a glance to the silent bartender, who had already put two perfect cappuccinos in front of the newcomers. "It's on me."

"Thank you, Amelio." Peter took the first sip with relief. "It's bitterly cold today. How is Loredana?"

"Oh, but I'm really impolite!" The mayor smiled apologetically. "I didn't thank you properly yet, William. You really offered a very enjoyable trip to my Loredana. She was enthusiastic, mostly about the company, of course, but also because she had a confirmation about her suspicions; that was very important for her. I must admit I was wrong, while my splendid wife was quite right. I must admit it's not the first time it has happened..." The mayor didn't sound annoyed recognizing the superiority of his wife, quite the opposite. He seemed extremely proud of her. William thought that he had every the reason for that. Loredana Sanchini was a remarkable person

"It was my pleasure. You have a wonderful wife, Amelio. Of course we'll do all that is in our power to find all the necessary evidence to get the case of her friend's death open again. We need your help. Later I'll call Loredana to ask her to make an effort to remember more details, but right now I'd appreciate your trying to think over all that you remember about Sabatino Alunni. Anything could be important, mostly what might look irrelevant, believe me." William encouraged him with a wink.

"Well, as I have already told you, we have not met Sabatino many times, even though we were at his wedding. My Loredana was Iris' bridesmaid. He seemed to me a proper person, and Iris appeared to be deeply in love with him. I don't have many things in common with him. He likes, as far as I can remember, fashionable clothes and smart status symbols. I think he considered me like a kind of peasant, even though he has always been formally very kind to me.

"I remember he had the strange habit to gesticulate all the time, to stress what he was saying. Loredana told me many times that he was not at the same level of Iris intellectually, even though I think he had a diploma in accountancy. But Iris, like my Loredana also had a degree. I have a degree too, in pharmacy." He sheepishly justified himself. "But beyond my professional field, I have no deep culture, while Iris and Loredana...."

Peter intervened. "What else, Amelio? Can you remember a specific peculiarity, something which maybe could annoy Iris a little..."

The mayor concentrated for a moment, and then he said hesitating, "I'm not sure it is important. Surely Loredana can tell you something more about that, but I noticed many times that Sabatino was...oddly superstitious. Once I had the impression that Iris was frankly annoyed with him for that. But she was so deeply in love at that time. You know how things are, we are ready to forgive everything when we are in love."

"Uhm, superstitious...This is very interesting. Can you be more precise, Amelio?" William forgot to finish the last sips of his cappuccino, provoking Lapo's distressed surprise. It had never happened that someone didn't finish one of his cappuccinos. Usually the clients asked for a second one.

"I don't know exactly. He believed in horoscopes, but I know many people do the same. It was not only that; he believed that there were people or objects which might bring bad luck. Once he started speaking about spiritualism. Yes, I remember it was exactly on that occasion that Iris became annoyed with him. She was embarrassed and tried to push him to change subject. But he insisted on telling us about a medium he had heard of. I remember vaguely that he mentioned his visits to a psychic too...But it was just a short, casual conversation. I think he realized we were not inclined to follow those beliefs and he didn't want to disappoint Iris."

"Ah, my friend, you have just given us an immeasurable help!" William pushed away the cup where the leftover of his neglected cappuccino remained like a spot on the shining career of the bartender. He met the gloomy look of Lapo and immediately realized himself to be the source of Lapo's undeserved frustration.

"Lapo, I'm unforgivable. I forgot my own rule about never being distracted when I have the chance to taste something particularly delicious. It was an exceptional circumstance, and I beg you to pardon me. Would you be so generous and understanding to make me another of your extraordinary cappuccinos?"

Lapo, apparently imperturbable as always, quickly put a new fragrant cup of beverage in front of William. On the foam there was not 'W'–Lapo's speciality was serving his cappuccinos with the initial of the client's on the thick milky foam–but an enigmatic '?'.

Peter noticed it too and laughed.

"We promise to you, Lapo, that when this case is completely solved, we'll come here and tell you the whole story."

William drank his cappuccino until the last drop and only when it was finished, he spoke to the mayor again.

"Amelio, you have given us one of the needed keys. We have the lead now. We have our man!"

Peter nodded and smiled indulgently.

"I guess you have already a plan in your mind, William, but I'm afraid to ask you what it is...I suppose we have to wait for the return of our honeymooners and very probably, in the meanwhile, Pasha will bring us the most unexpected information. I have no doubts about his potentialities and his skills of sleuth, but I prefer not to know the details of that...

"We should go to see Emilio now. We must play fair with him, and we promised to him to inform him in advance about all our strategies."

"Yes, I suppose so." William sighed. They said goodbye to the rather puzzled mayor, asking him to report their conversation to his wife. When they pushed the door of the café, leading to the main square, a light snow, like a kind of bright icing sugar had started falling. A larger flake landed on William's nose, while he looked up at the Christmas star, which the two communal employees had finally managed to hang.

CHAPTER TWENTY-FIVE

A black Volvo station wagon climbed up the hill deftly. Obviously the driver could manage well with the muddy-snowy surface of the twisted road. Finally the car pulled over in the middle of the main courtyard of the farm, nearly in front of Themba, who was carrying a crate from the pantry to the restaurant kitchen.

"Nice car, Pasha!" He greeted the driver who was getting out of his smart vehicle.

"It's not mine. I rented it in Milan." Pasha wore a black trench coat. If he had worn also a fedora, he would have looked like a character of a detective film of the fifties. But he was bare-headed, as always, with his slightly too long hair tidy and well-trimmed. "Where is Miss Orlova?" He asked.

"She's in the kitchen, with all the others, I think they have just had breakfast. I bet you'd like to have something for breakfast too. I guess you drove straight on from Milan...I'm going to put this crate down, and then I'll join you to the kitchen. I have the impression you have brought interesting news to us." Themba hastened to the restaurant. When he went into the farmhouse, he found Peter, William, Lyuba and Pasha sitting around the table. Pasha was sipping a cup of tea and eating with apparent great pleasure a slice of cake (we can only guess his pleasure, because as usual his face had an imperturbable expression).

"Ellie and Reginald would be sorry to not be here now, and I'm also sure that Gianna and Malusi would like to be informed immediately of everything Pasha has to tell us. But we'll let them know about that as soon as it's possible." Peter said, drumming his fingers on the table, a clear sign that he was very curious too and couldn't wait.

Pasha glanced at Lyuba, as if he asked her for permission. Lyuba looked calm and relaxed; she wore an oversize pullover on a pair of leggings; probably she had just finished her daily training session. She looked very young.

"You can speak freely, Pasha. After all the results of your inquiry are more important for our friends than for us."

Pasha cleared lightly his throat. He was not used to speak that much, especially not in public.

"Maresciallo Ciricola sent me all the data he had gotten about the woman, Jessica Mandelli." Everyone, except Lyuba, was surprised to know that Pasha and Emilio were in contact, but nobody interrupted the narration. Pasha continued, "It was not difficult at all to find out more. She worked as beautician, but she has never been the owner of a beauty centre. It seems she had an affair with the husband of the beauty centre owner and she was fired. Then she worked, always as beautician in many other places, included a hair salon, and then she became make-up demonstrator. She took part in several fairs, household and furniture fairs, and things like that.

"I have some acquaintances in Milan; they went around a little, asking questions. Jessica is described as being an ambitious and very strong tempered woman. They said that she never spoke of her sentimental life, but one of her colleagues had the impression she had a steady relationship with someone. I wrote down all the details here in this document. You can read it. I feel more comfortable with written reports, you see." Pasha pushed a cardboard folder to the middle of the table. "But there is something I consider rather important here; let me show it to you."

Pasha opened the folder and, leafing through several pages, extracted a copy of a leaflet with a photo.

"Here, you see. This is a photo which was taken more than three years ago during a fair in Milan. It was a rather important fair at the national level. Something about home decoration, but, as it happens in fairs of that kind, there were also small gastronomic stands, or promotional offers of other services, which were supposed to interest female customers." Pasha handed the photo to William, who was sitting directly by him.

The picture showed a small group of people, all smiling, posing in front of a stand, decorated with big, green plants. In the second row there was a tall, well-built man, smartly dressed, who kept his arm around the shoulder of a young woman, much shorter than himself. A quite gracious brunette, as far as it was possible to see from the photo, which was not of excellent quality. But the image was clear enough to allow William to recognize immediately Sabatino Alunni and Jessica Mandelli.

"Blimey!" William could not repress the exclamation. Then he passed the photo to Peter.

"It's another tile which found its right place in our jigsaw puzzle. This is the proof that those two knew each other very well, at least one year before the famous, or infamous, cruise!"

"Pasha you are a genius!" Themba shouted full of sincere enthusiasm.

Pasha accepted all the congratulations as if he had not quite heard them. But then Lyuba said calmly and briefly,

"Well done, Pasha."

And incredibly he smiled, even though for less than a second.

"We must call Emilio, Reginald and Ellie." Added Peter.

"I suppose we'll have guests for lunch then." William grinned; he was deeply amused because he had other surprises in store.

"Gianna and Malusi will come back from the University lessons for lunch as well. I'm sure Caterina would like to be present too, even though for her is still a bit difficult to follow our conversation in English." Themba made clear, tactfully, that he didn't intend to exclude his family from the surprising developments of the case.

Reginald, Ellie and Emilio had been notified and they arrived excited and full of curiosity.

Nevertheless, everyone had to wait until the time when William, helped by Caterina, served coffee and small chocolates with a soft centre—a speciality of Caterina—because he refused to speak about anything except the food during a meal.

Finally all the table companions were informed about Pasha's exhaustive report, and they handed each other the old photo proving a long time relationship between Sabatino Alunni and Jessica Mandelli, who had always claimed to have met each other for the first time on the cruise ship.

Maresciallo Ciricola was particularly impressed, but wisely decided not to question Pasha about his contacts in Milan. Luckily he was not officially involved in that case yet, and his professional instincts suggested that he not to go too deep, to avoid the risk of facing certain rather ambiguous situations which would require his professional intervention.

"We are progressing fairly well." William sounded satisfied; he popped a square of delicate chocolate into his mouth and smiled, whether because of the scented filling which melted on his tongue or the satisfaction from the good results their investigation had already achieved.

"Pasha did excellent work in Milan, finding out so many things about Jessica." He continued after a short, tasteful pause. "But we found equally interesting characteristics of Sabatino Alunni, thanks to the habit of observation and the good memory of our dear mayor. Peter and I think that Jessica is the mind and Sabatino the executor. But Jessica is surely more strong-tempered than he is, so, as always happens, it's important to find the weakest link of the chain. In our case it's surely Sabatino." William couldn't help slowing the moment of his revelations to savour his friends' impatient curiosity.

Reginald, who was sitting by Pasha and had gone into a kind of little huddle with him when he had arrived before lunch, seemed to get on fairly well with Lyuba's rather enigmatic body guard. It happens that people, quite different from each other, with respect to cultural backgrounds, origin and personal stories, can find unexpectedly a common basis of dialogue, founded on who knows what impact of an experience of life or whatever else. After exchanging a knowing glance with the Russian, he intervened,

"Pasha told me that, even though Jessica looks much more pragmatic and rational than her...uhm husband–and she probably really is– he has discovered that she used to visit an astrologer every now and then, and she reads her horoscope daily. At least according to what her former colleagues have said. Of course a lot of people do the same and it doesn't mean they are all conditioned by superstition. On the other hand there is no proof that Jessica is interested in spiritualism.

"I think we all agree that in order to have a chance to get the case open again, we have to find Iris." He looked at Maresciallo Ciricola, who nodded in approval. "Now we are sure that Iris was not on that cruise ship; she was killed before the cruise departure. It's reasonable to deduce that her body has been hidden somewhere not too far from her home. Only Sabatino and, maybe Jessica, know exactly where. I'm persuaded Sabatino killed Iris, but when it happened, Jessica obviously was not present. They had to pretend that they met each other only on the ship, and she may have been with him in Savona, the port town, the night before the cruise departure. Actually Sabatino had to take some of his wife's clothes to Jessica, because she had to wear them when she boarded the ship as Iris, together with Sabatino. Very probably she boarded the ship twice, once as Iris and once as herself. Jessica has surely many resources and is a clever woman; she found a way to leave the boat with an excuse, and then she came back playing the role of a different passenger. For this reason I suppose she doesn't know exactly where Iris' body is hidden, even though Sabatino surely told her. But she's not too familiar with all the country area around Umbertide, since she had never lived there before getting married to Sabatino."

"You could not sum up the whole matter better than this, Reginald!" Peter smiled at him with admiration. Reginald shook his head modestly.

"It has been a team effort. I don't have any special merit..."

Maresciallo Ciricola had listened to everything silently. Every now and then he looked at Lyuba, who had remained equally silent, but then, immediately he averted his eyes, as if he were afraid to be caught doing something inappropriate. Finally he felt the need to express his concern and said,

"Your deductions are remarkably clever and probably completely correct, but I'm worried for you, my friends. I'm afraid you can be dragged into a dangerous situation, and I feel bad because I cannot help you at this stage....Of course if you can find a line of investigation that leads you to the place where the body of the late Mrs Alunni is buried...Well that would be the needed evidence and I'd have the possibility of taking the case in my hands officially and to contact the police authorities. But for the time being you have very few convincing facts; all the rest is only based on deductions...We know that Sabatino Alunni already knew Jessica before the cruise, and he told a lie to the investigators. But he might always claim that in reality he met her only by chance at that fair for the occasion of a group photo, but he didn't know her at all; he forgot her and on the cruise ship she was still a stranger for him. The evidence is too weak, you see... I beg you, my friends, be cautious and, please, inform me of all your next steps."

The sincere, affectionate concern of Emilio touched everyone in the room. They promised to him that, of course they would keep him completely informed, and all would be fine.

"The point is that we cannot go to Sabatino and ask him politely where he has put his wife's body, after killing her." William grinned. "But we can destabilize, him letting him know that someone already knows his secret. He might decide to go to check if everything is still in order in the place he knows; in that way he can lead us there..."

"It's easier said than done!" Ellie puffed impatiently.

"Sabatino's superstition and his trust in spiritualism, psychics and mediums will be our Trojan horse to penetrate into his dark secrets." William looked amused and excited. "So we need a plausible psychic... Peter and I are out of the game, because Sabatino knows us. Reginald is not very skilled with lying, besides that, forgive me, Reginald, you don't have the "Physique du rôle" for that. But we have the perfect actor for the role, here under our eyes, my friends..."

"Oh, no, no, tell me you don't mean that..." Themba tried to shy away from the designation which he felt hanging over him, but his son and his daughter, who had immediately grasped the future possibilities and found them extremely amusing, started immediately encouraging him.

"C'mon, dad! You'll be fantastic as an African Marabout. William is right; you are the only one who can do that. Think of poor Mrs Sanchini, who has fought so much to preserve her best friend's memory and to punish her killer. You have the moral obligation to offer your contribution and, William, if you need also a young Marabout as support, I'm ready! Gianna can play a witch; after all she's very gifted for that role." Gianna kicked her brother's ankle; then both looked hopefully at their father.

Unexpectedly Lyuba's voice rose over the widespread, surprised buzz which had instantly followed William's suggestion.

"I'd adore watching the rehearsal of Themba's great performance, but I'm afraid I have already taken advantage of your hospitality for too many days. Tomorrow I must absolutely go back to London. I received a couple of phone calls from my company, and my presence seems to be necessary." She nodded slightly, as if she had to justify that she was at the helm of an important export-import firm. She addressed Pasha directly. "You need to have a good night's sleep, but everything must be ready early tomorrow morning. I want to be at my office in the afternoon."

Nobody was particularly surprised by the notice, except Maresciallo Ciricola, who remained gaping for a moment, then scratched unconsciously his chin, already veiled by the dark shadow of the beard, even though he had shaved just before arriving at the farm for lunch.

"It's a pity that you are obliged to leave us, Miss Lyuba. I hope to have many other chances to meet you again in future..."

Lyuba smiled, maybe with a pinch of half-hidden irony and answered warmly.

"You are so nicely spontaneous in your kindness, Emilio. You see, I have to resolve many business matters before the Christmas period. Everything slows down around Christmas and New Year...Tuscany is a region I like in a very special way, so I think it will be my pleasure to visit it again in future. I'm glad everyone gathered at the farm for lunch today, so I could greet each of you before leaving. I would regret if I flew back to London without saying goodbye to the wonderful people I have had the good fortune to meet here." And she smiled with a charming spark of melancholy in her eyes, which now looked like those of a tamed tiger.

Reginald noticed that Pasha, at his side, seemed to be slightly less impassive than usual and, oddly, squirmed like one who has to say something without finding the needed words. He tried to encourage him with a knowing glance; maybe that was exactly what Pasha was waiting for. Actually he decided to speak,

"I, I imagined that we would leave soon...Ehm, when I was in Milan, I bought something for each of you. You have been all very kind to me. I have the parcels inside the car boot. If you agree, I'm going to get them..." And as usual he looked at Lyuba for approval, but this time Lyuba was taken by surprise exactly like all the others. She didn't nod at Pasha, as she would have done under normal condition. She remained speechless, and lightly scratched her chin in a spontaneous gesture, which, oddly, looked very much like Maresciallo Ciricola's habit.

She had the disconcerting feeling that the situation was beyond her control, at least as for the unexpected behaviour of Pasha, who, as far as she knew—and actually she knew a great deal about him—had never bought a souvenir gift for anyone; for whom should he have, after all?

Reginald was the one who reacted more coolly; he arose to his feet, asking Pasha if he needed some help and they walked out together.

A couple of minutes later, Pasha and Reginald reappeared carrying many shopping bags, which they put down on the large kitchen table.

Everybody stared at Pasha, who now looked rather uncomfortable, but determined in carrying out his project. He rummaged in a bag, took out two identical cardboard boxes, all nicely wrapped, and handed them to Gianna and Malusi, who remained clumsily motionless, without knowing what to do.

"You are twins...ehm. So you have twin gifts. Ehm...I hope you might like them...oh, well, I do hope so." Pasha's face became nearly red for the effort he had to make, pronouncing the sentence. The twins decided to relieve him of his embarrassment and quickly unpacked their boxes, but they remained frozen when they realized the contents. They found two sophisticated, professional digital cameras. Something they would never dare to dream of either.

"Pasha, it's not a joke, is it? Are these jewels really...for us?" Gianna recovered the use of speech a little before her brother. But Pasha didn't reply; the answer was obvious, and he was not a person who wasted words for something obvious. He was already giving other two parcels to Caterina and Themba, who discovered with touched surprise a tasteful amber necklace and an elegant ebony walking stick with a silver carved handle.

"I'm Russian," Pasha mumbled, "For us amber has a special meaning, it brings good luck and positive feelings..."

The general astonishment about the quite unforeseeable gift session was gradually fading into a slight self-consciousness. How was it possible that none of them had noticed before Pasha's deep thoughtfulness, which clearly showed itself in such a suitable choice of presents? They had considered him, in the best case, a bizarre although not necessarily very shady fellow; a Lyuba's employee, whose life was better not to investigate that much, whereas he had payed attention to each one's interests and likings and had surely spent a good amount of time to find something to please each of them.

Maresciallo Ciricola found in his parcel a collection of rare recordings of folk Celtic music, on vinyl records, of course, with the original covers in very good condition. How in the world could that presumed cutthroats have guessed that he cherished old vinyl records? He was sure—well, nearly sure—never to have mentioned that, or maybe only once, briefly. Ah, if all his Carabinieri had the same attention to detail as Pasha in their investigations...

William admired with a knowing smile his new huge series of the most exotic spices, nearly unobtainable in Italy, which came from the most famous and refined delicatessen shop of Milan; while Peter caressed with a connoisseur's touch his blue cashmere sweater, which perfectly matched his size and his tastes.

Pasha, who had not pronounced any further word, turned to Lyuba and shyly said,

"This is for you, Miss Orlova."

Lyuba reached out, slightly hesitant, and remained still with a flat, rectangular parcel in her hand, until the excited voices of the twins urged her to open it. She slowly unwrapped Pasha's gift and then could not hold back a pleased sigh when she discovered the content. There were two old photos, carefully and soberly framed. The twins, pushed by their genuine interest for photography nearly plucked them from Lyuba's hands to admire them more closely. One of the photos, an original beyond any doubt, showed a ballerina wearing a complicated and exotic costume; the girl had very delicate features and a rich, dark head of hair. At the bottom of the picture there was a short inscription which read in French:

'À Monsieur Latour.
Tamara Karsavina
Paris, 1910'

In the other photo there was the same girl, performing a 'pas de deux' with a male ballet dancer who looked at her with an intense expression. Even though the costumes looked rather old-fashioned, a vibrant elegance radiated from the two dancers, making them totally indifferent to the time.

Lyuba sighed again with a note of delight and whispered, probably only to herself,

"An autographed photo of Tamara Karsavina and here, this splendid photo of her, performing 'Giselle' with the divine Vaslav Nijinsky..."

Then she put her left hand on Pasha's and smiled silently at him.

Maresciallo Ciricola forgot his vinyl records for an instant and surprised himself thinking that it would be so nice, if it had been he who could offer those so appreciated old photos to the obviously touched Miss Orlova...

But now all the eyes turned to Reginald and Ellie, who were the only ones who had not yet opened a parcel. Reginald had helped Pasha to carry all the paper bags from the car, and now Ellie was folding carefully all the beautiful wrapping paper, as, a little absurdly, many women do, thinking that maybe one day they can be used it again.

Pasha took out from his black leather briefcase a last parcel and put it on the table in front of Ellie, adding with a slightly apologetic tone,

"This is for both of you, for your home..."

Ellie and Reginald looked at each other, undecided as to what to do. Finally Ellie handed it to her husband, inviting him to open it.

Protected by a solid box and layers of tissue-paper there was a padded envelope, from which Reginald extracted a small drawing of a devastating beauty. It showed the portrait of a long-haired young man, wearing a kind of soft cap. The drawing was made with black chalk and, even though only the face was finished, while the rest of the portrait was basically a sketch, the effects of light and shadow were remarkable.

Ellie's hands started trembling and she didn't even dare to touch the drawing, at which Reginald stared with mesmerized eyes.

"I cannot be completely sure, but it's my job. I have a certain experience..." Ellie felt a lump in her throat. She swallowed two sips of water from a providential glass which was still on the table and added,

"I cannot be sure, as I said, but I do think it looks...it is authentic..."

In the general silence, William's voice was perfectly audible, although he had barely whispered.

"Raffaello! A drawing by Raffaello..."

Reginald recovered from his catatonic status and spoke directly to Pasha.

"Oh, but we cannot accept it..."

Pasha this time misunderstood completely and tried to reassure Reginald's presumed concern.

"Don't worry, Reginald, I'd never put you and Mrs Ellie in a risky situation. The drawing is not of any suspicious origin. I assure you it was not stolen. It simply...uhm, it doesn't exist in any official record, it's not classified, because its existence is unknown. So you can keep it. Maresciallo Ciricola can confirm my words. If the drawing is not listed in any catalogue and has never had any registered owner, it's perfectly legal to have it. It will be your decision whether to make its existence public or not."

Pasha breathed deeply, it had been an unusually long speech for him.

Emilio Ciricola felt to be in shock. One could never expect to get bored in his new friends' company...He tried to find the right words in English to be sure that Pasha could understand him.

"You realize perfectly, Pasha, that I'd be obliged to act if the drawing had illegal provenience ... But if things are as you told us, then there is nothing against the law. I don't doubt about you, but maybe about the way you have got it...I should enquire, you must understand my position."

Pasha realized everything; he had the suitable answer.

"I know, Maresciallo. You are right. You are not obliged to believe me. But I assure you that I told you the truth. This drawing had belonged for centuries to the same family. They had never considered the possibility of making its existence public. The last member of this family – when he was still alive–owed me a favour and gave me the drawing. I have kept it for a few years, but I'm alone. I wanted to be sure to leave it to the right person who could appreciate it. Mr Reginald and Mrs Ellie are the right people. I know that Mrs Ellie has a granddaughter. Maybe the drawing will stay in her family now."

Emilio Ciricola and all the others present in the room knew that Pasha had told the truth. Ellie finally dared to take the small drawing in her hand and with her eyes full of tears she looked at that immense masterpiece that now belonged to Reginald and herself.

"Thank you, Pasha. We'll take good care of it," she said, because she had understood by now that with Pasha it was better not to stand on ceremony and exaggerate with talkativeness. But she couldn't help expressing immediately an idea which she felt growing from her heart, in total spontaneity.

"Lyuba, tomorrow you and Pasha will fly back to London, because of your business. But then you said that at Christmas time everything is slowed down in business too. So I wonder if maybe you and Pasha would like to come back to spend Christmas and New Year with us. As you know, it will be the first Christmas that Reginald and I spend together as husband and wife, and we have decided to celebrate it at our home with all the dear friends who are present here now. We'd be so happy if you would join us as well." She stopped a little abruptly, because she realized that she hadn't invited Maresciallo Ciricola yet, so also for him it would be a sudden proposal. But in any case they would appreciate his company. According to what they knew he was alone, and spending Christmas on his own, or with another Carabiniere's family, might be a bit depressing for him.

An enigmatic and melancholy smile puckered Lyuba's lips. She looked interrogatively at Pasha, then at William. In conclusion she smiled more openly at Ellie and said,

"It's very sweet of you, because I perceive you are absolutely sincere in your invitation. We'll be delighted to spend Christmas with all of you at your home. We accept with gratitude." She didn't notice or pretended not to notice, the broad smile which lit up the Maresciallo's face.

"Well, I suppose I cannot refuse the invitation at this stage, even though you know I'm allergic to all traditional celebration." William grinned in a funny way. "The only condition is that none of us will be requested to wear a ridiculous Santa's costume and to sing carols...And now it's important that, rather than keeping on playing like children with our toys, I mean the gifts Pasha offered to us, we don't neglect the work connected with our investigation. Themba, we need to speak about what you'll have to do to play your important role. Everything depends on you now...."

CHAPTER TWENTY-SIX

Sabatino Alunni looked with self-congratulation at his own image, reflected in the big mirror behind the counter of the 'Antico Caffé delle Dame', on the main square of Umbertide. He saw an elegant man, with an impressive suntan, whose healthy appearance contrasted with the winter pallor of the other customers on that early December.

It had snowed during the night; just a sprinkling of snow, which had already been swept away from the ground by the passage of cars and pedestrians, but remained as a gracious decoration on the roof tiles.

Sabatino took another sip of his Aperol Spritz and crunched with gluttony a couple of crisps, which he picked up from the small bowl which the bartender had put by his glass of aperitif.

His honeymoon had been as wonderful as every honeymoon should be. Jessica had categorically refused to book at the Seychelles, which he had too hurriedly suggested as destination. She had crinkled her adorable little nose and superciliously commented that only rich, vulgar Italian shopkeepers chose the Seychelles for their holidays by now, but it was irremediably 'out' for people of a certain class. She had taken charge to organize their honeymoon, and she could not have done better. They went to Virgin Islands, to a place he had never heard of before, but which turned to be a kind of smart and exclusive little paradise. That small, remote island had only one five-star hotel which offered all comforts of royal luxury. Small, wildly oscillating roads made large swathes of the island inaccessible for big vision hoteliers, leaving the majority of the coast untouched. They had enjoyed days of total relaxation, fully pampered by the very efficient and professional staff. Every morning, waking up with Jessica at his side, he thought that life couldn't really be better even in his the wildest dream.

Jessica...his true love. Nothing was good enough for her, he thought. He wanted to offer her a gorgeous gift for their first official

Christmas spent together. Jessica loved jewels. Nothing flashy, but something precious and smart, like she was. He had already bought a diamond necklace for her and kept it hidden inside the safe in his office. He imagined that special light in her eyes when she would open the small, silk jewel case. Without realizing it, Sabatino was miming the gesture of opening a box. The bartender and one of the clients gave him a puzzled sidelong glance, but Sabatino didn't pay attention to that; he was concentrating on his own image in the mirror and wondered whether he should have chosen another tie that morning. He noticed with satisfaction that at least the knot was, as always, practically perfect.

Unexpectedly he saw in the mirror the image of another person, a man behind him who stared at him. There was something discomforting in the way this stranger looked at him, because Sabatino hadn't the slightest doubt that he was really the object of such a scanning attitude. He turned round to face the impertinent, prying man and to make clear to him that he didn't like that at all.

The man, an African in his forties, was standing on the threshold of the café and didn't seem to be worried by the fact that Sabatino had reacted to his intrusive attention. There was no offensive or shameless connotation in the black man's eyes. He simply looked at Sabatino with concentrated seriousness, without trying to hide it. The man was very tall, even taller than Sabatino, who was strongly-built, while the African was slender and nearly hieratic. He wore a kind of black long coat, well cut and probably of cashmere, as Sabatino couldn't help noticing, and a purple velvet cap, which would have looked ridiculous on any other man's head, but was elegant on him.

Sabatino took a step forward, but the man suddenly pushed the door and walked out.

A couple of precious minutes were lost to pay the cashier for his aperitif, but when he rushed out to the street, Sabatino saw that the African man was still there, standing on the opposite sidewalk. He apparently didn't care about being caught, but kept on imperturbably and seriously staring at an even more annoyed Sabatino, who—being not a person who could be easily intimidated— walked directly to him and confronted him firmly.

"Do we know each other? I don't think so! Why in the hell are you staring at me like that, what do you want?"

At first the tall African seemed not to hear a word of what the furious Sabatino was saying.

"Damn! I'm speaking to you. Can you understand my language?" Sabatino got closer, and a vein on his forehead started throbbing; he had never been a phlegmatic person.

But the African didn't let himself be overawed. He raised his right hand–Sabatino noticed he wore many golden bracelets–and pointed apparently at Sabatino's left ear. Then he spoke; his voice was grave, nearly solemn, with a light, strange accent, which Sabatino couldn't identify.

"Oh, but I'm not looking at you. I'm looking at the woman at your side..."

What a buffoon, a mad man...Sabatino was losing his temper.

"Are you drunk? What woman? There is nobody at my side!"

"Oh, yes, there is. You cannot see her, but I can. She's right there." And he pointed again at Sabatino's left ear. "A beautiful, tall, fair-haired woman. She wants to tell you something. But of course if you are not interested, it's your problem. I won't disturb you any longer..."

Sabatino felt the distressing impression that his hair stood suddenly on end, but he was not a man who could easily be shocked. He hesitated just a second, but long enough to give to the African time to turn his back to him and go off, without a hurry. Sabatino recovered from his short dismay and reached the other man, who was turning into a side alley.

"Hey, you, wait! What's this comedy? Who are you?"

The tall African, looked at him absent-mindedly as if he were a deserted parcel without known addressee, and kept on walking imperturbably.

Sabatino couldn't help seizing him by the arm to stop him. Usually he would never make such a rude gesture, but something impulsive pushed it to detain the stranger.

The man didn't react, he didn't try to wriggle free either. He remained imperturbable. His eyes seemed to look through Sabatino's body as if he didn't exist. Sabatino let go of the man's arm and felt troubled by a situation which seemed to be out of his control. The African spoke calmly, but determinately.

"I cannot waste my time with you. I have no interest in you. I need to help the lady who walks alongside you. You cannot see her, of course. But I can. I must help her to find her peace. If you don't want to do what is necessary, she won't ever find her peace. But it's not my problem."

Sabatino swallowed his saliva with a certain difficulty. He realized with a worried surprise that he was scared.

The African looked now like an old-fashioned gentleman harassed by a street beggar; too polite to push the intruder out of his way, but unable to hide his calm scorn.

Sabatino was not used to be treated like a nuisance, but he felt that he was in a very stressing condition at that very moment. He mumbled,

"But who are you? A medium?"

The African looked at him with distant and nearly bored eyes.

"You can call me whatever you prefer. Let's say I have a gift..."

Sabatino felt more self-confident for a moment; ah...he had understood whom he had to deal with, a charlatan, a fraud...someone who was used to getting easy money speculating on people's gullibility. But he, Sabatino Alunni, was not a banal dupe. He recovered his normal tone of voice.

"I see. Your little game can stop here now. It was just a stupid way to cheat me. I have perfectly understood the scheme. You collected information about me, knowing I'm a well-off person. You found out that my first wife was dead and you organized your absurd pretence, thinking to impress me and tap me for money..."

But the African stopped him with a large gesture, as if he were driving away pesky flies.

"You didn't understand anything. I told you that I have a gift. If I tried to get money through it, I'd lose it immediately. I don't need your money, as I don't need anybody else's money. My moral duty is helping souls to find their way to reach their final dimension. I do it because it's my fate. I would never ask for a cent. I don't judge anyone. I simply help to pass messages over. It's your right to refuse to help that pour soul whom I see at your side. I cannot force you. So you go your way and I'll go mine."

The tall, black man turned elegantly on himself, flapping his long coat and walked away. Sabatino remained motionless, looking at the other man, who, once he reached the corner with a side alley, stopped again for the necessary time to look back at Sabatino and saying with a serious smile,

"Ah, she's asking me to tell you that she was never on the ship; but you already know that."

Sabatino was thunderstruck and, in spite of the low temperature, he felt sweat running down his back.

He recovered his balance a little too late and, when he arrived at the corner of the sidewalk, in the side alley there was no trace of the disquieting African, as if he had vanished into thin air.

CHAPTER TWENTY-SEVEN

Ellie grinned like a satisfied cat, peeking at Sabatino Alunni in the rear-view mirror. She cheerfully addressed Themba, who was crouched down in the rear of the light van,

"Bow your head, he's still looking around. Ah, he's quite puzzled. It's better that I hide myself too. I wouldn't like him to approach." She crouched on her seat. "Let's wait five minutes, then we can leave. But now you must tell me everything; unfortunately I have seen only the very last scene of the show, when you slipped into the van just a handful of seconds before our man's turning the corner..."

Ellie had been involved as driver, to her great amusement, even though Reginald had been a little anxious about his wife's engagement. But there were not many options. William and Peter could not have an active role because Alunni knew them, and he might recognize them. Reginald was not considered very expert as a driver, while Ellie could easily drive all kinds of vehicles. She had reassured her husband, saying that really, there wouldn't be any risk in that little 'mission'. She had only to drive Themba to Umbertide in the delivery van of the farm, which fortunately had no notable markings, and to wait for him in the agreed place. All had gone very smoothly. But they were only at the beginning.

Themba stretched his long legs with a little moan, which faded into a giggle, when he started telling Ellie all that she had not been in a position to see directly.

"Loredana Sanchini has given me such detailed information about her poor friend Iris, that I almost have the impression that I have met her in person. I didn't expect it could be so much fun for me. At the beginning I felt a little uncomfortable, but then my role became like a second skin for me. Maybe I'm really an African medium, after all... I didn't have a chance to surprise our Sabatino with some specific description yet, but we have decided to take our time to let the situation take its course. It will be Sabatino who will look for me, not the opposite. We'll come back here in a couple of days, and I'll roam about the centre, hoping to be noticed..."

Ellie started to drive securely the small van out of the centre of Umbertide. Then she stopped for the necessary time to allow Themba to take his place in the passenger seat by her, once they were sure that there was no risk of being seen.

"I hope that other two trips to Umbertide will be enough to snare Sabatino." Ellie overtook, maybe a little too unselfconsciously, a big lorry, the driver of which didn't cast a friendly glance at the small van. Themba, found himself thinking that maybe choosing Reginald as driver would have been a more shrewd decision. But he didn't have time to go deeper into his reflection, because Ellie turned into the road down the Apennines, leading them back to Arezzo, merrily jolting her passenger. Ellie was bubbling over with enthusiasm. Obviously she adored the task.

"I hope all will be settled before Christmas. It's quite important for me to organize my first Christmas celebrations with Reginald and all our friends. Of course William will help me with food preparation, but I want to take care of all the rest as carefully as I can. Do you think the two Russians will really come over from London? Lyuba and that Pasha, I mean... I have not heard from them anymore, but I guess they are reliable, in their own way. If they said they would come...they will." Ellie tapped on the steering-wheel and winked lightly at Themba.

"Pasha offered to us the most expensive gift I have ever received. Reginald is still in doubt about what we have to do with it. The drawing is incredibly precious. I cannot be completely sure that it's a real Raffaello, but it's ancient and authentic in any case. Even if it were a work of an apprentice of the Master, it remains of exquisite style and great value. I checked carefully and it's not registered anywhere, exactly as Pasha told us. I still wonder why he decided to give it to us..." Ellie shook her curly hair and fortunately concentrated once again on the road.

Themba made an effort to not peek at the speedometer. There was a little snow covering the side of the road, and he suspected the surface might be icy.

"I think they are really two very lonely people, Pasha and Lyuba. Even though they don't want to be pitied. I'm sorry for Lyuba; she's so obviously in love with William..." Themba smiled sympathetically.

"Ohh..." Ellie goggled with the subtle pleasure of a teenager girl exchanging little secrets with a schoolmate. "Are you...sure? Actually I had that impression myself as well, but Reginald told me I was going too far with my imagination. After all she knows that William and Peter...I don't think he has encouraged her feelings in any way. But it's also true that I have perceived a deep, special communication between him and Lyuba. We don't know exactly what happened when they met in London, but Peter was also there. And then she popped out of the blue a few weeks ago..." As if dragged by her own involvement in those vaguely sentimental thoughts, Ellie energetically put her foot down on the accelerator and passed a phlegmatic car, which, in her opinion blocked her way. Themba closed his eyes instinctively, because the space was really limited, but obviously Ellie was a skilled and confident driver, because she didn't realize her passenger's concern either.

Ellie kept on, following her logically connected reflections,

"I'm not completely sure that our home will be large enough for all the guests we wish to have at Christmas. But it's really important for us to have this informal gathering with all our dear ones. Peter had suggested we might set it at the farm, but it wouldn't be the same. We'll squeeze up a little..."

"But how many people are you going to invite, Ellie?" Themba was amused by her nearly childish enthusiasm.

"Oh, well, you and your family, of course. Then Peter and William. Unfortunately my daughter and my granddaughter won't be able to come over; you know how things work in families...They will spend Christmas with the family of Wendy's dad this year. Next year it will be my turn again. I suppose it's fair..." She sighed imperceptibly, but immediately recovered her joyful tone of voice.

"I thought to invite also Giorgio Cini and his family, after all your Malusi is nearly Paola Cini's official fiancé by now. Then, my Reginald has a liking for the young Luca Cini." She adored teasing Themba a little; of course he had nothing against Paola, who was an adorable girl, but Ellie was aware that the idea of a possible too sudden marriage in the family didn't appeal to him that much.

"We are four and the Cini are five, with William, Peter, you and Reginald we arrive already at thirteen, and I'm sure you have other guests in mind..."

"It's obvious that we'll invite also that so nice Maresciallo Ciricola and the Mayor Sanchini and his wife. Loredana is a wonderful person; I had the chance to know her better when we travelled to Torino together. If Pasha and Lyuba really come over, then we'll be only eighteen. It's not a problem; we have twenty chairs at home, including the ones in my atelier..."

"Well, it means you can invite someone else too. Two guests will have seats and the others might stand, like in a cocktail party; we'll consider them itinerant guests." Themba made a wry smile. He loved Ellie dearly and liked to tease her. "Maybe you could invite all the monks of the monastery of Pieve di Socana. They might entertain us singing carols..."

"Oh, I have thought of that!" Ellie was imperturbable. "But Brother Fulgenzio explained me that they have religious rituals to respect during all of Christmas time and they cannot leave the abbey for a ...uhm...mundane party."

Themba was already passing to a more urgent subject.

"I hope that things will move as quickly as we planned with Sabatino Alunni. I wouldn't imagine myself continuing to roam over the centre of Umbertide, dressed up like a smart charlatan, for many weeks. When are we organizing the second instalment in Umbertide?"

"According to what Peter and William suggested, I think in three or four days..."

Themba leaned on the backrest of his seat and tried to relax, thinking that he wouldn't be obliged to face another rally over that road full of bends for at least a few blessed days.

CHAPTER TWENTY-EIGHT

It was snowing lightly, as if someone were throwing absent-mindedly scattered snowflakes at random, when Sabatino Alunni caught sight of that disquieting, tall African for the second time.

It would have been difficult not to notice him among the crowd of people busy with their Christmas shopping in the central streets of Umbertide. It was not only because his height; there was something peculiar in his attitude, in his way of strolling, which made him different from the other passers-by. He paid no attention to the rich shop windows, sparkling with Christmas decorations. He walked, apparently lost in inner thoughts, taking his time, while little impertinent snowflakes dared to land casually on his long black, elegant coat.

As if he had been summoned, the black man had turned his head and his eyes met Sabatino's ones. There was something troubling in his glance. Sabatino had felt that the man was looking at him without noticing him, but staring once again at something...or someone by him. Suddenly the African lifted his right hand and waved lightly. Sabatino immediately forced his way through the thick crowd of shoppers, but when he reached the corner, where he had seen the African, the man had once again disappeared.

It had happened only five days earlier and now, once again, Sabatino saw the African who seemed, this time, to be waiting for him, just in front of Sabatino's notary's office. He had managed to settle some very important matters with his notary's help, and he felt quite optimistic about the way things were evolving. His surprise in realizing that the African didn't show any intention of disappearing, but was just staring at him without any particularly menacing attitude, prevented Sabatino from speaking first.

"Good morning." The African greeted him politely with his loud and strangely calm voice. "I hope you have realized, by now, that I'm not interested in any material advantage; I don't want to extort money from you. Actually I couldn't care less about you. But, as I have tried to explain, I have a gift, which might also be considered a moral duty. I must help those souls who, for various reasons remain trapped in a kind of grey zone, to get over and to be fully at peace. Let's say that I act as intermediary only. I don't want to know what has happened; it's not my task. But I can see the souls, and I can pass their requests on. They know what they need to be able to pass over. There is a lady, who is always by you, but she cannot communicate with you; she cannot tell you what she needs to go in peace. Did you understand, finally?"

Sabatino felt suddenly a little dizzy, but still he could rely on his self-control. *'I'm not gullible'* he thought.

"I see. But I need to know something more to be sure that really you see this lady and you are not trying to cheat me..."

The African shook his head with patience. "It's a reasonable request. I can understand your doubts. I'll try to ask the lady to give me some details which will persuade you." Then he took on a very concentrated expression and rolled his shining dark eyes. Finally, to Sabatino's great amazement, he started whistling. Initially Sabatino got furious; what a charlatan he had to deal with; what was that stupid story of whistling now? But after a couple of seconds he froze, and not only because of the very low temperature. He recognized the tune.

"How, what...Why are you singing this song?"

"Oh, maybe I'm not in tune, but I'm only trying to whistle as best as I can the song that the lady is singing now. She says you should know it." And the African kept on whistling. In spite of his apparent concerns, he was perfectly in tune.

Sabatino knew that song perfectly. Iris had always considered it their song, because he had kissed her for the first time, after dancing to those notes. Sabatino shivered. He would have probably fainted, if the African had not benevolently held him up.

"So she's really here..." Sabatino mumbled as soon as he recovered his breath.

"Of course! I have already told you that she is always at your side, constantly. She cannot leave if you don't help her." The African spoke to him with the same tone of voice that one might use with a slightly mentally retarded child.

"Does...uhm, does it mean that she has always been with me, since...since..." He stammered lightly, paralysed by the horrifying idea that Iris had been always there, seeing everything he was doing.

"Don't make me repeat always the same things!" the African sounded a little annoyed now. "But you don't need to be so worried. I don't want to know anything about your life or about what happened with her. It's not my task, you see. But I can assure that she has no bad feelings. You see, human passions change after death; there is no sense of revenge, grievance or anger left, if the soul belongs to a person who was good in life. This woman, I see, was a good one, so she's freed from any negative feelings which are reserved as the punishment for those who behaved badly in life. She keeps only good feelings with her. Nevertheless she is still trapped. She needs you to fulfil a few of her wishes, and then she will free to pass over."

"And then she won't be at my side anymore, will she?" Asked Sabatino shyly.

"Exactly, she will be in peace, and she will be in the place where she's destined to be, totally separate from mortal human life." The African reassured him with a large gesture pointing to an indefinite direction, over the roof tiles of the notary's house.

"Well, so please tell me what I can do for her, and I will!"

"Eh, it's not so easy." The African sighed. "It takes me a lot of energy to get in touch with her soul. I cannot do it anymore today. But I can give you my visit card, and you can call me whenever you like. We'll meet in a quiet place where it will be easier for me to connect my energy with hers. I'm worn out now. You cannot imagine how demanding it was for me to perceive the song she wanted me to sing to you..." He removed a refined leather wallet of an unusual purple colour from an inner pocked of his elegant coat; he opened it and handed a visit card to Sabatino. Then he nodded politely to the troubled Mr Alunni and, striding, disappeared into a side street.

Sabatino remained on the sidewalk turning over the visit cards in his hands. It was printed on a very smart, light Bristol board. It didn't look at all like the visit card which one would have expected from an African medium. It was sober and tasteful and read

'Doctor Professor Kunta Nnamani
Spiritual healer'

Then followed a phone number and a website address.

Sabatino went back to his office, even though he could not concentrate on business matters at all. He asked his secretary not to be disturbed for any reason. He swallowed a couple of sips of water and googled the name he read on the visit card.

The search directed him to the personal website, the URL of which was equally indicated on the visit card. There was no other link. Neither was there anything which might connect the mysterious Professor Nnamani with any social network.

He clicked to open the website, which reflected the same style of the visit card. Professional and sober. There was a short, essential biography of Professor Nnamani and a brief explanation of his skills. There were also some testimonials that guaranteed his free and accurate services and testified to the total gratitude of people whom he had helped.

Sabatino ran his fingers through his thick hair. The Professor had assured him that Iris felt only positive vibrations now, and she was free from any negative feeling of revenge or hatred.

For the first time Sabatino felt a very unpleasant, creepy feeling of remorse, which even the thought of his adored Jessica could not make disappear completely.

He had never kept anything hidden from Jessica. But this time, at least for the moment, he would not tell her anything of his meetings with Professor Nnamani.

CHAPTER TWENTY-NINE

There are circumstances which are so totally unpredictable that guessing them cannot be based on any rational reasoning, but just on aleatory randomness.

Lyuba had not gotten in touch with anyone at the farm, since she had left rather suddenly with Pasha about three weeks earlier. William had confined all thoughts about her to a remote corner of his mind, without being fully sure whether he would prefer to get news or not. But he was only moderately surprised when she telephoned him early in the afternoon, on the 23th of December.

William and his staff were tidying up the restaurant which would remain closed until the seventh of January. It was one of his slightly snobbish affectations to oppose the general trends. He had never kept his restaurant opened during Christmas and New Year holidays, refusing categorically to get involved in lavish, festive traditional dinners. William had never been fond of the presumed charms of Christmas traditions and had always avoided carefully celebrating them. This time he had accepted a compromise, because he realized it would be very important for Ellie and Reginald. In spite of his favourite, sarcastic attitude, he was always ready to do everything possible for people he loved.

"Hello, William!" Lyuba's voice sounded as plain as always. "I hope the invitation is still valid, because I'm here, with Pasha of course. We have put up at what appears to be a good hotel in Arezzo. Please, don't say what you are going to say. I know you have many spare guest rooms at the farm, but I thought it would be more suitable for everyone if we keep a certain independence. But of course I'll be happy to be invited for dinner, if it's fine for you. Tasting your recipes is always worth a long journey."

William smiled faintly. He was still unable to guess everything that passed through Lyuba's mind. She could be even more elusive than he could.

"Reginald and Ellie will be happy to know that you decided to come over..."

Lyuba interrupted him.

"Did you have any doubts? You should know I'm a reliable person."

He had the impression that she giggled lightly.

"There is some news about the inquiry we have started, an apparently absurd development, which seems to work fairly well. I'll tell you all details when you are here. Come at any time. As you know we are quite informal among friends."

The phone call ended like that; neither William nor Lyuba wasted time on formal greetings, once the necessary was said.

Peter looked at him from the threshold.

"I never know what to think about Lyuba. I was not completely sure she would really come over. I can hardly imagine her as guest at a typical Christmas celebration at Ellie and Reginald's home." He grinned. "I can imagine more easily Pasha in that role. Ah, by the way, let's give a ring to Emilio. I'm sure our Maresciallo will be happy to join us for dinner too. Mostly after knowing who has just arrived. Then we have to bring him up to date about Themba's great performance."

As if he had perceived that they were speaking of him, Themba appeared carrying a couple of big boxes, in which he intended to store a few little items that he had removed from the restaurant tables.

William teased him with a broad, knowing smile.

"Ah, dear professor Nnamani, you arrive at the right moment, my friend here needs some spiritual healing..."

Themba mocked them, assuming a hieratic expression and rolling impressively his eyes. "I see at your side...I see a cupboard! Well, seriously, I wanted to tell you that, not because he's my son, but really Malusi made a great job with the website. He also placed an invisible site meter, and he told me that our Sabatino has already visited the site five times. Unfortunately he's my only visitor. I regret a little that, once this story ends, also my website will be deleted and the distinguished Doctor Professor Nnamani will disappear forever...alas sic transit gloria mundi!"

Peter shook his head, showing a little concern.

"I hope that this story won't provoke any problem for Emilio, since he's informed of everything. However it cannot be considered a traditional investigation according the usual parameters..."

"Don't worry, Peter. Emilio has not had any active role in that, at least not so far. Then, when he's not on duty he can meet his friends freely." William did his best to be reassuring, but he was aware that Maresciallo Ciricola was taking some risk for their sake.

At that very moment the main theme from 'The Sorcerer's Apprentice' by Paul Dukas started ringing loudly, directly out of one of Themba's pocket. He warned his friends

"Hush, hush, it's Sabatino..."

William and Peter didn't know which ringing tone Themba had chosen for the mobile number that he had settled on only for their tricky purpose, but they found it suitably amusing and had to make an effort to not burst out laughing.

Themba gestured at them, ordering them to leave, if they were not able to stay silent. Then he let the phone ring yet once more and finally answered, speaking with the odd accent he had chosen to adopt for his role.

"Yes, it's me, in person. Of course I know who you are. I felt it. No credit is due. I'm guided by the force of the spirit. Yes, I think you took the right decision. I'm ready to meet you when...Today? I'm not sure..." Themba looked at William, who encouraged him nodding. "Yes, it's possible. I don't think it will take a very long time, but everything depends on my energy and how much of it I'll have to spend to get the communication. It's preferable to be in a quiet place, only the two of us. If I'm distracted by voices or by anything else, my energy fades...I can come directly to your home or to your office...Ah, I see, then maybe I might suggest booking a room in a hotel. Call me back when you have settled everything." Themba interrupted the call and sighed.

"I'm afraid I won't be here for dinner, it seems necessary for me to rush to Umbertide...I hate the idea of disturbing Ellie..."

"Oh, I think that there isn't any need to deprive Ellie of a pleasant dinner with Reginald and the others." Peter took his decision quickly. "I'll drive you immediately to Umbertide. When Sabatino calls again, in case, we'll stop for the necessary time, so he won't realize that we are travelling by car. It will be dark and I'm not obliged to park in front of the meeting place. Sabatino won't notice me. Then, even if he walks by my car, it's quite improbable that he would recognize me; he saw me only once."

William started thinking over at loud voice. "Very few of us will be able to enjoy a quiet dinner. Themba knows exactly what to do, but it means that immediately after he leaves Sabatino, we'll have to keep our dear Mr Alunni under continuous surveillance. We know it's our only chance to find Iris's body. Sabatino will lead us to the place where he hid Iris, but we don't know when he will decide to go there. So we must follow him constantly now. Peter and Themba will be already in Umbertide, but they cannot stay there for a long time; it's too risky, Sabatino might notice them, because he knows Themba too well and our Professor Nnamani is not a person who can go unnoticed. We'll have to organize quickly our 'task force' to relieve Peter and Themba as soon as it's possible. We have to decide the composition of every single small crew. But that will be my business." He tapped on Peter's shoulder with the same determination of a general sending his best officers to the firing line. "Now you and Themba go. Keep me informed. I'll take care of all the rest. Call Malusi, I need him to help me check the availability of a few people. We cannot ask Emilio to be involved in that."

Themba silently thanked his lucky star for rescuing him from another trip with Ellie as driver. Peter was a much more reassuring chauffeur for him. Then he ran to his home to take the clothes he had to wear to play, hopefully for the last time, the role of the great Doctor Professor Nnamani.

Malusi arrived, his eyes sparkling with excitement, ready to be actively involved in the adventure. But he felt definitely disappointed when he realized that William had no intention to send him to spy on Sabatino Alunni. Rather he wanted simply that Malusi contact his girlfriend's father, Giorgio Cini, the photographer of Capacciano.

William felt slightly guilty to ask people to be at his disposal to fulfil such an unusual task, mostly because it was nearly Christmas time and family duties seemed to come first. But Giorgio Cini owed him and Peter something that could not be considered just a big favour. Moreover he had always assured them that it would be his joy to return, at least in part, what they had done for him and his family, when he had been unfairly charged with Fiammetta Innocenti's murder.

It was an emergency situation. William didn't expect that Sabatino Alunni would have contacted the person he considered to be an African spiritualist so soon. But there was no time to regret anything now; things had to be faced promptly. He called Reginald asking him to come over immediately with Ellie and apologizing in advance because dinner wouldn't be what they should expect.

Peter and Themba departed to Umbertide, and Giorgio Cini had just arrived from Capacciano, which was only few kilometres from the farm. Now he was sitting by Malusi, a little puzzled, but listening carefully to what William was explaining to him.

"I cannot force you, Giorgio, of course and, if you refuse I won't blame you. I'm sorry for not informing you earlier about our inquiry, but you knows how things work in Capacciano, even though I would never have doubts about your discretion." William ended his basic explanation leaving to Giorgio the freedom to decide, but being practically sure that he would be in.

Giorgio Cini was in his late forties. He had a broad and friendly expression, rather long light brown hair, and a remarkable nose which gave his face the look of an Italian Renaissance character. He grasped what William would expect from him, but then he summarized it up to be sure that he had clearly understood.

"So I should go to Umbertide to watch and follow a chap, whom I have never seen, but who is very probably a murderer, and I have to keep you informed of all his movements until someone else of your friends comes to relieve me. Of course I can do that. No problems. I have only to call Ilaria to let her know about that in few words."

"You can reassure Ilaria that you won't run any risk." William knew that Ilaria, Giorgio's wife, was very emotional and she had already suffered with so many negative emotions when Giorgio had been arrested two years before. He felt sorry to impose another distress on that so gentle woman. "You won't need to approach the man either; just check where he goes and let me know about that. It will be a matter of a few hours, and then I'll send someone else to relieve you. You see, I cannot find many suitable people for this task in this period and with such a limited time at our disposal. Mayor Sanchini cannot do that, because the man, Sabatino Alunni, knows him well and might recognize him. Then it's better that Sanchini stays out from the plan, because of his official role in the village. What I'm trying to do is to organize small crews of two people each and I cannot ask it-doesn't-matter-who for that. I not only need reliable people, but they must also be clever and have a certain spirit of initiative..."

Giorgio Cine seemed to be proud of being chosen, but honestly he had to state his limits.

"Of course I can do it, William. I can leave immediately and I can also stay there all night long...but, but I have been to Umbertide only once and I have never seen the man I'm supposed to shadow. So I presume I should depend in practice on my crew partner... By the way, whom should I be with?"

William let his arms fall and smiled apologetically.

"The matter is, Giorgio, that I have no idea about the person who can go to Umbertide with you yet..."

Malusi realized it was the right moment to take his chance, and he boldly spoke, as if it were already all stated.

"But it's so obvious. I have never met Sabatino Alunni in person, but I have seen all his photos on the internet, I have made all possible searches about him and I have worked on all the plans of Umbertide and the area where he lives on Google maps and Street Views. I'm informed perfectly about all the details of our plans, and I have my tablet which will allow me to be constantly connected. I'm the one who must go with Giorgio!"

William knew that he hadn't many other options; after all Malusi was right. It was not a dangerous mission, and Giorgio would look after him.

"What could I say? You are of age and we cannot ask for your father's advice, since he's already on his way to Umbertide with Peter. It's better that you and Giorgio leave before your mother suspects anything, or else she would do what she can to prevent you from going. I'll inform her after your departure, heaven help me...So you and Giorgio will be the second crew. I'll call Peter to let him know that they have to keep in touch with you by cell phone."

Malusi was excited and eager to show that he could do his best, mostly because he was together with his girlfriend's father. In any case, Giorgio made immediately clear who was the leader.

"Malusi, go to take a warm coat, gloves and a woollen cap. It will be very cold and we cannot keep the engine running to warm ourselves up. We must be invisible. Then also the cap will be useful to hide your hair, which is a bit too...noticeable. Now we'll pass quickly by my home and we'll take something to eat and a couple of thermos flasks of hot tea and coffee. Hurry up, boy!"

They left exactly as Ellie and Reginald arrived. Once again William brought them up to date about the last, sudden happenings. Ellie looked rather disappointed, even though she tried to conceal her dissatisfaction, hearing that Themba had gone to Umbertide without her. But William immediately asked for their effective cooperation, which was greatly needed.

"It means that Reginald and I will go to Umbertide, to allow Giorgio and Malusi to come back. How long will every shift be? Three, four hours? Oh, William, I'm thrilled. We must absolutely solve also this case. There is already too much unfairness in the world. It's our duty to put order in what we can."

Before William could add a word, the door opened again. With everyone absorbed in their conversation, they hadn't paid attention to a new car engine, mixing its noise with that of Giorgio's car leaving.

Lyuba hesitated on the threshold, and then she came in, followed by Pasha.

"Are we arriving at a bad time? Did something happen?"

Lyuba looked more pale than ever. There was something in her reminiscent of a character of a fantasy film, maybe because she wore a very light blue, long coat, with a fur-lined hood. She could be the Queen of Snow in a fairy tale, one of those characters who can be either good or evil and maybe are both...Pasha, as always, wore all in black, without any headgear. He didn't say a word, but just nodded. William noticed that Pasha's eyes scanned the room, trying to identify the origin of the evident state of general agitation.

William didn't beat about the bush–it wouldn't be worthwhile with Lyuba–and informed the new arrivals about the present situation. After all, they knew everything about the case and Pasha had brought a precious contribution to the enquiry.

Lyuba took off her coat, since it was nicely warm in the room. She did so with a fluid, elegant gesture, a bit dramatic, which struck positively Maresciallo Ciricola, who remained nearly, hypnotized looking at her from the threshold.

William thought that it looked like one of those amusing French theatre plays of the nineteenth century, where different characters arrived unexpectedly on stage, creating funny misunderstandings or coups de theatre.

"Oh, Emilio, welcome! I'm afraid that this evening our dinner will be a little less peaceful than expected. Actually I don't even know if we'll have a real dinner, since I haven't found any time for cooking yet." William invited Emilio to come in and, mostly, to close the entry door, which he had left open, quite absent-mindedly.

Maresciallo Ciricola roused himself from his dreamy surprise and warmly greeted everyone. Ah, if only he had known that Lyuba was there, he would have paid more attention to his clothes. He felt suddenly ashamed of his old trousers, his banal pullover and his worn out boots. Since the Maresciallo's English was still a little basic and William was speaking English with Lyuba and Pasha, who could not master

Italian, Ellie invited him to sit by her on the sofa and informed him of all what was going on.

Lyuba had accepted a glass of Prosecco that William was offering to all the friends in the room and grinned gently.

"Poor William, you must feel very frustrated to be cut off from the action this time. But I perfectly understand that someone must remain here at headquarters to coordinate the operation, and it would be risky if you were recognized by Alunni, while you were shadowing him in his town." She switched to a much more serious tone, after her light mockery. "But we are here at your disposal, Pasha and I. I cannot speak for myself, since I haven't any experience in this field, but, Pasha, you can believe me, Pasha is a professional...Then we might rent a different car every time, so ...I mean it would be more difficult noticing us."

William had to admit that he had immediately thought to give the task to the two Russians as well, but he had preferred to let Lyuba make the first step. Suddenly a whimsical idea crossed his mind and he could not resist to it.

"Lyuba, you are wonderful! I can only accept your help with immense gratitude. But I don't think it would be the best solution for you and Pasha to team together. You see, neither of you can speak Italian and...I'm sure you know it would be a handicap."

Lyuba looked amused too, as if she had guessed William's slight provocation and had decided to defuse it, simply accepting it as if she fully agreed.

"Right you are, William, so who should be the most suitable people to accompany me and Pasha? It's necessary they can speak English, besides Italian, obviously...I'm sure we are thinking of the same two people..."

William admitted that she won on his own field. Lyuba was definitely a very peculiar young lady, but he already knew that ever too well.

"I suppose you might be with Reginald and Ellie with Pasha. There is no real urgency, because Peter, Themba, Malusi and Giorgio Cini are already on their way and there won't be any need to relieve them at least until tomorrow, early in the morning. Now we have only to wait for news. Themba will tell us about the result of his meeting with Sabatino Alunni, and we deeply hope he will push Alunni to do what he believes the spirit of his first wife asks him for. I don't think that, in any case, Sabatino will go to the place where Iris's body is hidden during the day. I presume he will choose to do it at night. Nevertheless, since we are not sure about his intention, we must keep him under constant surveillance day and night."

A general silence followed his words, while everyone was thinking over about what was necessary to do and how. Unexpectedly it was Pasha who spoke, breaking the pause. He pronounced his first words since he had arrived, addressing Reginald

"You can be sure, Mr Reginald, that Mrs Ellie won't run any danger. I'll take good care of her. I could go on my own, of course, but Mr William is right. In case someone noticed us, a couple would look less suspicious, and it's also important that at least one of us can speak Italian properly." As he had spent his entire patrimony of words, he stopped his speech abruptly and looked at Ellie for confirmation.

"I'll be perfectly safe with Pasha." Ellie grinned, crinkling graciously her nose in one of her typical gestures. Ellie liked Pasha, even though she was perfectly aware that the mysterious body guard could be a dangerous person in many circumstances. And it was clear that Pasha liked her in return. Ellie kept on,

"I'm sure that my Reginald will take good care of Lyuba, as well." She hesitated in an unforced, comical way. "Or maybe it will be the opposite. I mean that they will look after each other." Except from the instinctive fondness she felt for Pasha, Ellie didn't like Lyuba that much, and she couldn't honestly admit to herself to be happy to see the young Russian businesswoman as Reginald's teammate. Of course there were no components of female jealousy in this concern. Ellie was not only quite sure of the deep love of her husband, but she knew he would have never been attracted by a woman like the young Russian either. What disturbed her was a confused, irrational feeling, which made her perceive an enormous contrast between her husband's totally transparent life style, based on a nearly exaggerated generosity and sincerity, and the contradictory nature of Lyuba, that Ellie guessed to be full of nuances, not all necessarily good.

Maresciallo Ciricola had remains speechless. He had not expected to find himself in the middle of such a frantic activity at the farm. He had hoped to enjoy a relaxing dinner with a few of his new friends. His professional experience had helped him to understand clearly what William and his crew were trying to organize, and he couldn't deny there were probably good chances that the results would bring to a positive development in the case. Unfortunately his hands were metaphorically tied and he could not help them in any way. Ah, if only he could stand as a candidate in Reginald's place to go with Lyuba to spy on that Mr Alunni...Emilio Ciricola felt frustrated, because he was nearly persuaded that William and the others were right and definitely there was something fishy in all this story of suicide, but his official role, paradoxically, didn't allow him to join a group of amateur detectives, which made its inquiries in an autonomous way.

"You have already understood all, Emilio." William looked directly and frankly at him. "Give us your professional advice. Do you think that we are breaking the law in any way?"

"Well..." Emilio thought over about the question only for a second. "If none of you intrudes into a private property, and if you will only tail that Alunni, without menacing him in any way, well, theoretically, you won't infringe any law. The case of Themba is...uhm...a little more delicate, because he's pretending to be another person. But since this other person doesn't exist in realty, it cannot be considered a case of identity theft. Then, if he doesn't try to extort money from Sabatino Alunni, I'm sure he can consider himself on the safe side..."

"Great! So we have also the blessing of the official authorities now. Thank you, Emilio, for your understanding and for not putting a spoke into our wheel. As soon as we find Iris' body–because we'll find it–we'll retire from the inquiry and we'll pass it to you." William stared at the slightly worried face of Maresciallo Ciricola, who could only nod in assent and added, with an involuntary smile

"If you find the body, I'll get the case officially reopened and Mr Alunni and his new wife will have many things to explain...But let me tell you, William, let me tell you, my friend, that...you are all totally mad!"

William shook his head and laughed, as if he had received a wonderful compliment.

"In a mad world, only the mad are sane. Let me go to see what I can serve to you for dinner now. We'll have so many other practical things to organize soon and a forced starvation won't be of help..."

CHAPTER THIRTY

The most unpleasant thing had been to hide all that from Jessica. He had thought over about the best decision to take and had come to the conclusion that protecting his wife was the right choice. There were no secrets between them, but there were things which Jessica didn't need to know, because it would have been useless to involve her. Whatever might happen—but he was sure that nothing would happen—Jessica wouldn't be responsible for what she ignored. They had not spoken about Iris anymore. Jessica knew what had happened, of course, but he had never told her all the details, what for? She had never asked him what exactly had occurred that night. She was not there either. When they had met, in Savona, he had briefly reassured her that everything had been settled, according to their plans. Jessica trusted him, and he trusted Jessica. He loved her too much to put any unnecessary burden on her shoulders.

Sabatino Alunni hated to feel troubled, because he was proud of his usual self-assurance and self-control. But what had happened to him lately had been very destabilizing. The idea that the spirit of Iris had never left him was not only troubling, but actually scary. He would have liked to have doubts, to consider the African spiritualist a charlatan, a cheat...But he had been obliged to believe in everything that had been revealed to him. The man had not showed any interest for any material advantage. It was Sabatino who had insisted to meet him again; it should have been the opposite, if the African were a crook. Then how could that enigmatic spiritualist know certain things about Iris? Sabatino felt again an invisible hand squeezing his stomach, exactly as he had felt when the African spiritualist had whistled that tune, the song which Iris had considered THEIR song.

Since he had known for sure that the spirit of Iris was still present at his side, he had been unable to make love to Jessica. He had never suffered with any problem of sexual efficiency before, and he was aware that at the basis of his deep relationship with Jessica there was also their mutual physical attraction. He had managed to find a more or less acceptable justification for his lack of ardour in bed claiming to suffer with a terribly painful gastric ulcer. Jessica had been tenderly sympathetic, but the main effect of this excuse was that she had obliged him to follow a draconian diet. Sabatino had always been a big eater, and now he felt constantly starved.

Professor Nnamani, the spiritualist, had assured him that Iris' spirit didn't bear any grudge against him and that she didn't look for any revenge; she only wanted to pass over in peace. But his present situation seemed to be, directly or indirectly, a punishment for him. Luckily there was a way to get rid of Iris' spirit once for all and Professor Nnamani would arrive soon, at least Sabatino hoped so.

Another practical problem to solve had been to find quickly a discreet place where he could meet the spiritualist, who needed calm and silence to communicate with Iris.

The meeting could not be at his home, logically. He had thought of his office, but there were too many people who could see the African there and Jessica had the habit of turning up often. He had excluded the possibility of booking a room at a hotel. He was well-known in town and there would have been gossip, even though unmotivated, about an illicit love affair he might have.

But Sabatino Alunni was a resourceful man; he had the idea to ask his lawyer for the temporary use of his office, which was closed for clients because of the Christmas holiday. He tried to motivate his request speaking vaguely of a very private business contact he must have with a buyer, but the lawyer, who was man of the world, had interrupted him, saying he didn't need to know anything. Mr Alunni could consider himself at home, and the lawyer had given him the key.

Sabatino had immediately called Professor Nnamani, who, at the beginning didn't sound so disposed. But Sabatino had insisted, claiming that it was important to help the poor spirit to pass over; so finally the spiritualist had agreed. It was seven pm, and he was anxiously waiting for his visitor, who had guaranteed his arrival. Sabatino hoped to be able to settle everything and to go back home to Jessica at a reasonable hour. He felt badly because he had to tell her lies. But what else could he do? He had told her that he had still to meet the notary for a signature and then to go to see his doctor to get a prescription. Tablets against the pain provoked by the ulcer. Pains always get more intense during weekends or holidays; everybody knows that.

Professor Nnamani arrived exactly at ten past seven. He didn't apologize for his short delay; he didn't shake hands with Sabatino. He looked around carefully, as if he were studying the disposition of furniture. Then he spoke with his loud voice with that indefinable accent.

"You should sit in front of me, without a table or desk between us. Please, move this armchair and place it there..." He pointed at a precise place before a large, black leather sofa. He didn't make the least gesture to help Sabatino to move the armchair, but sank comfortably into the sofa and gestured at Sabatino to sit in the armchair he had just displaced.

"Can you see...ehm, can you see the lady by me?" Sabatino mumbled, half annoyed and half anxious.

"Yes, she's there, like always. She looks more serene. She wants to tell you something, through me..."

"Wait. Wait a moment..." Sabatino had recovered his balance and had started feeling a pale doubt. "I'd like it if you could reassure me that I really know this spirit, and she really wants to speak to me." Sabatino was satisfied with the way he was handling the conversation; he had asked for proof, without openly putting into discussion the statement of the spiritualist.

Professor Nnamani sighed, as a teacher who has to repeat for the umpteenth time an easy explanation to a dull pupil.

"I have already told you that communicating with this spirit absorbs a lot of my energy, if you make me waste it for nothing, I'm afraid it won't be enough to allow her to tell you everything she wants from you. I don't know how she died, when and why. It doesn't concern me. I'm just a kind of intermediary. I only repeat to you what she wants to tell you, because I can see and hear her, while you cannot. She can see and hear you, obviously. So I don't need to repeat what you have just asked me; she heard it. I don't think it's helpful for her that you don't believe. She doesn't want to do anything bad to you. She's trapped, and she wants only to pass over. Wait, wait, she's telling me something..."

The African rolled impressively his eyes and put his hands on his temples, as if they were throbbing too painfully.

"She says, she says...'*Sabatino you have torn a message I had written and you had taken only a part of it with you. You destroyed the rest and you kept only that fragment*'...I have no idea what it means, but she says you know."

Sabatino had the impression that all his blood was leaving his veins, concentrating into his heart, which was going to explode. Iris was there, without any doubt. He spoke to her directly, without controlling himself anymore.

"Iris, Iris. I'm sorry. Forgive me. Don't destroy all my life. Forgive me. Tell me what I can do to give you peace and to get mine back too!" He started sobbing, covering his face with his hands.

The spiritualist didn't show any particular reaction in front of such a burst of emotions. He simply waited until Sabatino seemed once again in relatively calmer conditions and said,

"Iris, yes, it's her name. Iris wants me to tell you that she cannot leave because the last thing you did to her was not ...well, she says it was not good. She needs a good last gesture to be free to pass over."

Sabatino absurdly felt relieved. Iris would not haunt him forever; she would leave him to live his life, with Jessica. Against his will, he suddenly asked himself if Jessica would be equally generous if he...

If he had only had another option, he wouldn't have done that to Iris. But Jessica had persuaded him that it was necessary; it was necessary for their happiness together. He spoke again directly to Iris, who was there; he knew that for sure by now.

"What would you like me to do for you Iris?"

Professor Nnamani answered slowly. He looked tired, as if he had to make a deep effort to concentrate.

"Iris says that she would like flowers. Yes, she would like that you bring her favourite flowers to her, where she's now. A small bouquet, she says, just a small fresh bouquet. She's smiling, I can see her. She says that you must remember what her favourite flowers are. Freesia..."

"Yes, yes, freesia..." Sabatino nodded in assent. He was not surprised anymore; of course Iris was there. "Purple and white freesia. I do remember. Please, ask her what I have to do with them exactly."

Themba concealed a sigh of relief. Everything had worked perfectly so far. All the information about Iris he had received from Loredana Sanchini and had perfectly memorized, had led to this excellent result. Sabatino was ready to do what they had hoped he would do. Themba tried hard to stay in his role and pretended to be nearly exhausted, as if the effort had been too intense for his psychic skills. He lifted his right hand in one of those hieratic gestures, which had become one of the features of the character he played and whispered,

"Iris says that you should bring her flowers to the place where she is. Then she will be satisfied with this last gesture of kindness, which will efface all the rest, and she will free to pass over and to be in peace forever."

"I'll do it, Iris, I'll do." Sabatino whispered too now. But his pragmatic nature couldn't be totally overwhelmed by his beliefs in spiritualism; so he asked immediately for confirmation. "But how can I be sure that Iris' spirit wont' be trapped in this temporary dimension anymore and she will be really in peace, after bringing her the flowers she loves?"

"Oh, I'm sure you'll feel it by yourself." Themba spoke in a reassuring tone. "In case I might always check it for you. If I cannot see her anymore, it means she's passed over, as I hope for her. It's not the first time I have helped a spirit, and it won't be the last one. I have experience. It's my task, I have told it to you."

Themba stretched his long arms and got on his feet.

"My energy is nearly over now. But I think there is nothing else Iris needs to add now. I have to go."

Sabatino Alunni accompanied him to the door. Then went to look at the window to see what direction he had taken in the street. But he could not see any trace of the African spiritualist, who seemed to be vanished once again.

It was not so important at this stage. In turn Sabatino left the lawyer's office, carefully locking the door. He would give back the spare key to the owner, as soon as possible. The lawyer had said that there was no urgency; his office would be closed until the beginning of January and, then he had another key, obviously,

Sabatino wondered if he could still find a florist who had not closed his shop yet.

CHAPTER THIRTY-ONE

Themba rushed downstairs jumping on the large, marble steps at the highest speed. The office was at the first floor. He had expected that Sabatino might look from the window to watch him, and he had taken his chance in the limited time at his disposal, since Alunni had accompanied him to the door. Finally Themba was able to get into the car where Peter was waiting for him. The two friends hid down among the seats of the SUV until they were sure that Sabatino had left the window. Then Peter started the car and parked again a little further away, checking the movements of Sabatino in the rear-view mirror.

"It's done, Peter, it's done!" Themba sounded both enthusiastic and relieved at once. "He didn't show any serious doubt, and I'll bet he will start immediately to look for freesia... Oh, I had to control myself; I would joyfully have punched him up. He practically confessed his crime in front of me. He was in tears begging his poor wife's forgiveness, the dirty bastard!"

Peter shook his head sympathetically.

"We must be very careful now; we will have to shadow him without giving him any chance to notice us. Luckily it's not late, and there is still a lot of traffic in town. Wait, here he is..."

Sabatino Alunni had come out of the building and was getting into his car, which he had parked nearby. He drove a brand new Jaguar XK coupé of an elegant and sober dark blue; it was not difficult to notice it among the other cars.

Peter followed him keeping a certain distance, without losing sight of the smart Jaguar. As Themba had predicted, Alunni visited a couple of florists, whose shops were still open in the centre, but each time he came out empty-handed.

"They ran out of freesia, evidently." Themba glossed.

During those two short stops, Peter called William to keep him informed and to ask who would come to relieve them and when. William was in full organising mode and Peter was happy to hear him so enthusiastic and positive. He felt the same. His old instincts of a policeman made him feel eager to re-establish justice and to be responsible for doing so.

Sabatino had given up his search for suitable flowers and he seemed to have decided to drive back home.

He lived in a villa, out of the centre of town. There was less traffic now, but at the same time it was easier to trail him, because there were no side streets which he could suddenly turn into. It was obvious that he was heading to his home.

Peter parked his car behind a bend and got out, taking a few steps in a field along the road. He had brought infrared night-vision binoculars and from his position he could clearly see Sabatino Alunni, who had just opened the gate with his remote control and was driving into the courtyard of his home.

It was bitterly cold and, in spite of his suitable outfit, Peter felt frozen. He went back to the SUV, but the situation didn't improve much since the engine was off and the heater was not working.

"I think we can turn on the heater for a while..." Themba probably felt frozen too. "He's home and rather far from us. In case he decides to leave again, we would notice him immediately. It's a quiet road, which apparently leads only to that villa."

"This is our main problem." Peter looked slightly worried. "We cannot get too close; we could be noticed immediately. So we are obliged to stay near the first crossroad only, and remain partially hidden."

"By the way," Themba found a thermos bottle full of hot coffee in a basked with some food that Caterina had wisely and lovingly prepared for them before their sudden departure from the farm. He gratefully took a long sip, then passed it to Peter, "By the way, do you already know who will come to relieve us? The next two of us who will keep watch on Alunni this night, I mean."

"Eh..." Peter gulped down the mouthful of sandwich he had in his hand and grinned. "Eh, yes, William told me. I'm not sure you'll fully approve..."

"Why not?"

"Well, there will be Giorgio Cini. It seems he kindly accepted immediately to help us."

"I'm not surprised. Giorgio is a good chap. Moreover he's so grateful to us for, well, for what we managed to do in that gloomy story about Fiammetta Innocenti's murder. So I think it's good to have Giorgio in. Who will be with him?"

"This is the point, Themba. I'm afraid you won't be enthusiastic to know that with Giorgio there will be...Malusi!"

"Augh! MY Malusi?"

"How many other people named Malusi do you know in Capacciano?" Peter was frankly laughing now. But immediately he realized that it was important to reassure his friend. "Take it easy, Themba. You know better than I that nothing will happen tonight. Alunni didn't manage to buy his flowers; so he will remain at home all night long. Until tomorrow there won't be anything to do with him. The only thing that can happen to Malusi tonight is getting a cold, spending a few hours in a car with Giorgio in this really freezing weather."

Themba had to admit that Peter's remarks were well founded; nevertheless he frowned. "That damned boy should not have done that without asking for my authorization."

"Themba, be reasonable. He could not ask you for anything, while you were here playing the spiritualist. Then, if I remember well, Malusi is of age and he doesn't need his parents' consent to do anything..."

"I see that you have no idea what being a parent means, Peter!" Grumbled Themba. Then he regretted immediately what he had just said. He knew that Peter would have been a very good father.

Time passed slowly and nothing happened as the night progressed. Every now and then a few snowflakes fell lazily, as if they refused to go out into such a cold. Peter's mobile rang suddenly. It was a welcome change for the two watchmen.

It was Malusi who spoke, while Giorgio was driving. "We are approaching the place where you should be now. We should be there in five minutes...Ehm, did you tell my father that...?"

"Of course, Malusi, he's so glad that you are cooperating; you'll see it for yourself." Peter spoke cheerfully, but Malusi was not duped. "You'll prevent him from killing me, won't you?"

"I have explained that you won't run any risk; a boring night will await you and Giorgio. Sabatino won't pop out again until tomorrow."

"Oh, what a pity!" Malusi sounded really disappointed.

Peter could see the headlights of Giorgio's car approaching. So he got out to hand over the watch to them.

CHAPTER THIRTY-TWO

There was a hectic confusion in the big kitchen of the farm. Everyone was speaking and hushing each other at once. William had put his mobile phone in speaker mode, so that everyone in the room could listen to the calls he was receiving from Peter and Giorgio Cini.

Peter and Themba were already on their way back to the farm, while Giorgio and Malusi were ready to spend the night watching over the villa of Sabatino Alunni.

Giorgio had just called to say that everything was quiet, and they didn't expect that Alunni would go out again before the next morning. They were extremely well organized, it seemed. Giorgio had told William that there was no need to send another team to relieve them before the following day. Since they were equipped with sleeping bags, they would have slept on shift; so they could stay there until late in the morning.

"Malusi has elaborated a very clever little trick," said Giorgio "Don't worry, nothing risky, but we need to stay here until Alunni leaves his home tomorrow morning. We'll keep you informed."

William had the clear impression that both Malusi and Giorgio were having fun, even though they also seemed to take their task very seriously.

Reginald, who had accepted without comment to make crew with Lyuba, knew that they would be charged with the task of carrying on Giorgio and Malusi's work. He was trying to get a little more familiar with the rather enigmatic young lady. They were sitting side by side on one of the sofas and were elaborating their strategy.

"This man, Alunni, has never seen either of us, so we can even run the risk of being noticed during the day. We might look like a common couple of tourists, who came to spend Christmas abroad." Lyuba looked even slightly excited and obviously she had taken the leading role. "I cannot tolerate seeing a criminal, a killer free to live normally, safe and sound," she added and her amber eyes narrowed even more. She nervously removed a lock of pale hair from her cheek.

'What a noble soul, what an example of integrity this young woman is!' Maresciallo Ciricola thought, lost in contemplation. Had he been able to read William's mind, he would have been quite surprised...

'Ah, Lyuba, none knows better than I that you cannot tolerate to see a murderer safe and sound...Sabatino Alunni should be particularly worried knowing that you are tracking him. Also for this reason I preferred to separate you from Pasha. If you and your bodyguard were together after Sabatino, I shouldn't be too surprised that a mysterious, fatal accident might befall him...' William grinned to himself.

"I suppose we might pretend to be father and daughter on holiday together, if we have to follow Sabatino Alunni in the centre of the town; no one would suspect us. Maybe he won't be on his own either. After all it will be Christmas Eve, and I don't think he will go to work." Reginald spoke calmly, feeling the need to reassure Lyuba that he wouldn't be a fussy partner. He had the clear impression that the young lady might show a prickly temper in many circumstances. But Lyuba seemed to be in a positive mood and ready to cooperate with him.

"I do have a father, but we don't meet that often. So I'm not sure I can behave like a loving daughter with her dear dad, but I'll do my best. It will be a nice change, at least once in a while." Lyuba spoke in a light tone, but there was no sign of a smile on her lips.

Maresciallo Ciricola had grasped only snatches of the conversation between Reginald and Lyuba, who spoke in English, a language that Emilio Ciricola didn't master as well as he would have liked. But he had understood enough to realize that Lyuba did not have such a close relationship with her father, and he felt a wave of empathy for her. He imagined her solitude and couldn't help comparing it with its own. Sometimes two solitudes can meet and become lighter, sometimes...

The dinner had become a kind of messy party, where everyone took a place at random, not necessarily at the table, which had been transformed into a buffet, covered with various dishes filled with all the food that William had put quickly together. Ellie refilled Pasha's dish with a motherly, friendly care.

"Take some more roast beef, Pasha, and have a good portion of salad as well. Then I suppose we should go to sleep, because tomorrow it will be our turn to go to Umbertide. So it seems we'll have to be there in the afternoon, to relieve my husband and Lyuba...unless Alunni has already led them to the place we are looking for. I'll have all the morning at my disposal to decorate our home. I won't give up the pleasure of organizing this Christmas celebration for any reason. Maybe it will be a little different from what I had expected, but we will have it, and all together I hope. I trust that none of us will be trapped in Umbertide on Christmas day. As for the food, I fully rely on William and Caterina, even though I'd have liked to demonstrate what I can do in a kitchen as well." She winked at Pasha, who incredibly answered. "I'm sure you can cook very well, Mrs Ellie."

Even Lyuba remained surprised by the social attitude of her factotum, but she tried to hide her amused feeling, speaking again to Reginald about practical matters.

"As I have understood, you'll sleep here tonight and I suppose it would be wise to have a few hours of good sleep at least. So I'm leaving soon, but I'll come here early tomorrow morning. Then we'll drive there, to that town, Umbertide. I'll find it easily by GPS. I hope you'll agree to let me be the driver..."

Reginald felt a little ashamed to realize that everyone knew about his very limited talents for driving, but he had to admit it was the truth. He nodded in assent and, just to feel less frustrated, he added,

"No problems for me. I'm a poor driver. But you don't need to worry about provisions. I'll have some food and drinks ready, in case we needed to wait inside the car and everything necessary if we have to follow him walking."

Lyuba understood that she had to leave some freedom of organization to that quiet, polite gentleman. She realized that he was not as naïve and unprepared as he might look. She even gratified him with a pale smile. "I'm sure everything will be perfect then."

When Themba and Peter arrived, Lyuba and Pasha had just left. Ellie and Reginald had decided to wait for their return instead, because they wanted to hear the most recent news. Actually there was no news to add to what Peter had already told them by phone. Reginald persuaded Ellie to have a relatively early night, since the following day would be quite busy. "It will be the most unusual Christmas Eve of my life." Reginald stated. "But also the most important for me," he added, caressing tenderly his wife's cheek.

Finally only William, Peter, Themba and Maresciallo Ciricola remained in the kitchen, sipping together a last cup of coffee.

"Emilio, you know we don't want to be the source of any problem for your professional career." Peter started to give voice to their general concerns. William let him speak, considering him the most adequate person for that delicate task. Emilio listened to him, relieved that finally the conversation was in Italian. He felt torn between two states of mind. The sensible one suggested to him to stay far from the entire matter and to ask his friends not to inform him of their plans, at least not until they could supply him with solid evidence of what they suspected. But his sense of justice and the instincts of a detective made him feel already deeply involved in this unusual inquiry, which he considered to be founded on valid suspicions. He had to confess honestly to himself, that he would have liked taking an active part in it, even though he was sadly aware that it was impossible for him, due to his official position.

"You should tell us frankly," Peter kept on saying, "if we are already violating the laws or whether we are still on the safe side, as we hope."

"So far you are on the edge, but still with one foot solidly grounded on the safe side, if we want to keep on with metaphors." Emilio put down his empty cup. He would have preferred something stronger, but he didn't dare to ask. William seemed to guess his wish– Emilio was no longer surprised by all that William could guess by now– and handed him a glass of Jameson Irish Whiskey adding with a knowing smile

"Consider it a sort of deconstructed Irish Coffee. You drank the coffee first, separated from the whiskey, which you are going to enjoy now. I suppose we can happily do without cream."

Emilio savoured the amber drink; he could not help thinking that it had nearly the same colour of Lyuba's eyes. He immediately drove away that troubling thought to concentrate on the taste of the whiskey which he turned in his mouth, before swallowing. It smelled of peat and rain. It was delicious.

"Personally we are exempted from shadowing our dear Sabatino." William got on his feet lazily, like a big cat. "It means we don't need to have an early night. What do you think, Emilio, if we played some music? It's been a while since the last time we played together. Irish tunes are suitable for a cold winter night, mostly when one is comfortably indoors with the excellent company of a bottle of Jameson. I'll teach you a few old Irish love ballades. You'll love them."

It was an appealing proposal, but, at the same time, Emilio felt slightly uncomfortable about the indirect remark of William. Was it really so evident that he might feel a certain interest for the indecipher-able Lyuba? Definitely very few things escaped William's attention.

CHAPTER THIRTY-THREE

A livid sky had taken the place of the darkness of the night, without the slightest hint of a pink sunrise hue. Lyuba had driven without a word for most of the road, after approving with a nod the items Reginald had prepared for all the possible needs of their task. Malusi had called to let them know where to meet. He said that Sabatino Alunni had come out from his villa at half past seven in the morning and had taken the direction of his office, at the factory. It might sound a bit odd that he had decided to do that on Christmas Eve, but maybe he had something to get there.

Lyuba parked the car immediately behind Giorgio's, by the wall which surrounded the Ciancaleoni factory. Giorgio and Malusi didn't look tired from the whole night spent on surveillance.

"It has been quite boring. Nothing had happened until early this morning, when he showed himself again, driving his flashy car." Malusi summed everything up with a grimace.

"Malusi, try to be objective. He's an evil coxcomb, but he has good taste for cars and his Jaguar is not vulgar at all; it's smart and elegant." Giorgio didn't conceal a sigh of vaguely envious admiration.

"Oh well, it's not important." Malusi was determined to finish his report. "We followed him from a distance and, when we were sure that he was going into the factory courtyard, we parked here, behind the corner of the boundary wall, where he could not see us. There is no traffic at all, so if we heard a car engine, it could be only Sabatino leaving and we...uhm, I mean you two now, won't have problem in shadowing him from distance. But it's not strictly necessary to keep Sabatino's car in sight now." Malusi grinned like a satisfied young leprechaun and invited Giorgio to explain the reasons of his satisfaction, as if he were too modest to tell it by himself.

"Malusi is a little devil. Of course he took a risk and maybe I should have prevented him from doing that, but he took me by surprise. As soon as Alunni parked his car in the courtyard, he rushed into the courtyard too, before I could stop him."

"Oh, but it took me only a couple of minutes." Malusi intervened pretending to be bashful.

Giorgio couldn't help laughing heartily, while Lyuba looked at him with attention, maybe she had already guessed.

"The damned boy had brought one of those devices which are on sale on Internet, I think. Well, in short, he planted a bug in Sabatino's car. Under the number plate, he said."

"Exactly!" Malusi sounded triumphant. "Here, have this. You can follow him on the screen. I have already configured all the data and uploaded a map of the area." And he gave the gadget, smaller than a cigarette box, to Lyuba, who, for the first time, smiled nearly openly.

"It's time to go now. There is always the possibility that when Alunni leaves his office, he might remember having already noticed our car." Giorgio, with an imperative gesture, invited Malusi to take his place in the passenger seat and started, waving at Reginald and Lyuba.

"Good luck and keep in touch!"

They did not have to wait for too long a time. Only thirty minutes later Sabatino Alunni, at the wheel of his car, left the factory and drove toward the centre of Umbertide.

Lyuba's nostrils vibrated as if she were a predator ready to hunt. Reginald, sitting by her, could check that Malusi's device worked perfectly well, so they could take a considerable safe distance from Alunni, without risking to lose him.

In spite of the silence of his partner, Reginald felt like speaking, just to put his thoughts in order.

"I wonder what he had to do so early in his office on Christmas Eve...I would have expected him to spend the whole day with his wife, since he seems to be so fond of her. Uhm...an explanation might be that he had hidden in his office the Christmas presents for her, and he had to go to collect them to take them home. He could always justify his absence like that, if his wife asked him where he had been. But I'm persuaded that he decided also to take his chance to buy the flowers which he's supposed to bring to Iris. Yesterday he couldn't do it because it was too late and the shops were already closed. But if he cannot do it today, then he won't have any chance to find a flower shop open on Christmas and Boxing Day. Everything, literally everything is closed in Italy on these two days."

Lyuba didn't comment, but she had listened carefully. She had guessed that the man, Reginald, in spite of the superficial appearance, was a very clever person.

"Wait, he stopped!" Reginald showed Lyuba the small red dot which was Sabatino's car on the map. It didn't move anymore.

"Fine!" Lyuba started thinking that maybe it was not such a bad idea to make team with the mature Irishman after all. "Let's leave the car and follow him walking." She slipped Malusi's device into one of the pockets of her long, light blue coat and linked arms with Reginald. "Hurry up! Malusi didn't bug his shoes too. We might lose him, if he's not in his car."

But there was no need to be worried, because they could see Sabatino through the large window of a café.

Reginald surprised Lyuba completely (without fully realizing how this result could be considered exceptional) dragging her to the café merrily saying,

"Allow your old dad to offer you a cappuccino. On such an icy morning there is nothing better to do!"

There were no other customers, besides Sabatino, who was sipping a rich cappuccino with a concentrated expression. The bartender looked interrogatively at the couple still on the threshold of his café. Lyuba suddenly looked merry and joyful and she started squeaking like an excited squirrel in front of a heap of acorns.

"Dad, dad, look, fresh croissants! Ask what they are filled with!"

That girl was a born actress. Reginald told himself that he didn't want to be outdone and made an effort to speak Italian much worse than he was able to do in reality and laboriously tried to inquire about the filling of the croissants. The bartender guessed the question rather than understanding it and quickly answered.

"Composta di mele, miele, marmellata di fragole e crema vaniglia."

"Uh?Pardon?" Reginald looked genuinely puzzled, and the bartender opened his arms to show that he could not do more. He couldn't speak English, obviously.

Suddenly Sabatino Alunni's voice resounded clearly in the café.

"These are filled with apples and those with honey. The round ones are filled with strawberry jam and the ones on the left with custard."

'Ah... so he can speak English fairly well, we must be careful.' Thought Reginald. But he smiled gratefully to Sabatino and thanked him.

"Your English is perfect. I'm Brett Marshall, and this is my daughter, Henrietta. Thank you for your help."

"Sabatino Alunni. Nice to meet you." He nodded soberly.

Lyuba, maybe not too enthusiastic about being transformed into Henrietta, reacted quickly to adapt herself to her new name and clung tighter to Reginald, speaking with a chanting voice.

"Dad, I'd like to taste the one with strawberry jam and a big cappuccino, please!" Even the bartender understood when Reginald showed him lifting two fingers that the cappuccino should be for both of them.

When he put the two cups on the counter in front of the couple, Lyuba/Henrietta became garrulous and took out her smartphone from an inner pocket.

"Let's take a selfie, dad. With the cappuccinos and the bartender and the croissants and..."

Reginald understood what she had in mind and followed her.

"But, Henrietta, if I have to hold your phone, I cannot take all that you wish..."

Lyuba, who had become a perfect Henrietta, smiled cheerfully at Sabatino. "Would you be so kind, sir?"

"Ah, of course." Even though he had many other thoughts in his mind, Sabatino had noticed the elegance of the two tourists' clothes, in spite of their casual wear.

Henrietta got closer to him and showed him the settings of her smartphone, which, by the way he already knew perfectly. Then she asked him graciously to take a panoramic picture which showed, all, but really all, the ancient furniture of the historical café included.

He took a couple of snapshots to please the two English tourists, then he finished his cappuccino and left, leaving a handsome tip.

As soon as Alunni get out of the café, Lyuba and Reginald hurried up and paid immediately, in case they had to rush out. But once again they were lucky. Exactly in front of the café there was a florist's shop which was open. Sabatino walked directly into it.

"I checked his pockets, while I was showing him how to take a photo of us with my mobile." Lyuba whispered." And it seems to me he had a small parcel which might be a jewel box. Probably you were right." Reginald made an effort to not wonder where Lyuba had learnt to slip her hands into people's pockets without being noticed.

"What are we going to do now?" Unexpectedly it was Lyuba who asked him to take a decision.

"Uhm, since we have already showed ourselves openly, we can use this to our advantage and continue with the same strategy. It seems to me that the florist sells also little Christmas decorations and candles and even something that from here looks like seasonal garlands. I'm sure that Mr Marshall feels like buying something for his daughter Henrietta. Let's go!" Reginald improvised, but Lyuba seemed to agree.

They crossed the street, arm in arm, and stopped in front of the florist's shop window, looking at the flowers and the other items. Sabatino didn't seem to pay attention to them, but Lyuba and Reginald took the time to play their roles accurately and pretended to discuss what they were contemplating. Then Lyuba nodded twice with a big smile and they entered the shop.

Lyuba started picking up different Christmas candles claiming that they were all so looovely. Reginald kindly reproached her. "Henrietta, you cannot buy all of them; we aren't at home, and we cannot fill our hotel rooms with candles..." In the meanwhile he checked what Sabatino was doing, looking at a big mirror behind the counter, which reflected the entire shop. The shop assistant was packing a huge bouquet of red roses for Alunni, and Reginald felt suddenly worried that they were following a wrong track. Themba had been clear. Sabatino was supposed to buy freesia. But at that very moment Sabatino told the girl who was serving him

"I'd like also a small bunch of freesia, I see you have some there in the vase. But I don't want yellow ones..."

"No problems, sir. I have some lovely violet and white freesia in the back of the shop. We received them this morning, but since we have just opened, I didn't manage to arrange them yet."

"Perfect. It's exactly what I need." Sabatino waited while the shop assistant went to the back room and he couldn't help noticing the other two customers, if he had not seen them yet. He nodded politely.

"Oh, we are following each other it seems!" Lyuba naughty played with the situation, showing her most convincing Henrietta's face. "There are only few people around, probably because it's already the holiday, and it's still so early, but we've got used to waking up very early to take full advantage of our holiday. We have decided to visit a few less conventional places in Tuscany. Of course we have been to the main artistic and well known towns too. But now we want to discover some small Tuscan towns and villages. Umbertide is so charming. Unfortunately we'll leave tomorrow, since we have booked in Arezzo to spend Christmas..."

Sabatino Alunni grinned politely. He had always been sensitive to the charm of classy and elegant young women, even though this one seemed to be quite scatterbrained too. "I'm sorry to disappoint you, miss. But you are not in Tuscany right now. Umbertide is an Umbrian town."

"Oh...But Arezzo is in Tuscany, isn't it?" Henrietta/Lyuba giggled nicely.

"Definitely it is. So you'll spend your Christmas in Tuscany, don't be afraid." Sabatino Alunni turned his back with a last nod of politeness, since the shop assistant was arriving carrying a bunch of freesia.

"Could you pack the freesia in one of those vials, you know, where it's possible to add some water? The matter is that I need them to stay fresh for several hours." He asked.

"Of course, with pleasure!" The young shop assistant reassured him. "In any case it's not warm at all, so you can keep your flowers fresh for a long time, just with a little water in the small glass vial. Should I do the same with the roses?"

"No, it's not necessary for the roses, thank you." Sabatino paid and left, carrying his two bouquets, after a last little nod at the two tourists, who were served by the shop assistant at their turn now and seemed to be undecided as to what to buy.

Reginald and Lyuba became suddenly more determined and they quickly bought a big garland made of fir cones and branches, poinsettia, dried slices of oranges and other elements, which they totally neglected to identify. It was absurdly expensive too.

"It's horrendous!" Lyuba grinned wryly as soon as they walked out from the shop.

"Oh, not so much. I'll offer it to my wife. It will be a souvenir of these highly unusual days." Reginald carried the cumbersome purchase, trudging after Lyuba, who strode out toward the place where they had parked their car.

"We cannot follow him anymore now; we are too noticeable. Maybe we did the wrong thing. Maybe we should have remained hidden from him..." Lyuba sounded vaguely anxious.

Reginald placed the garland in the car boot quite phlegmatically.

"I don't think we did wrong Lyuba. Being at the florist's shop together with Sabatino allowed us to see exactly what he bought. It seems to me that he chose the roses for his wife, his second wife, I mean and the freesia for poor Iris. Since we could hear his short dialogue with the shop assistant, we know for sure that he has no the intention to go right now to the place where, uhm, the poor Iris' body is supposed to be. He cannot stay away from his home for too long a time today. His wife would be suspicious. If he goes directly home now, he can justify his short absence with the roses, which he bought for her. She will be delighted with her loving husband's thoughtfulness. He will leave the bunch of freesia somewhere, maybe at his office. Then he will go to get it later, as soon as he has a chance."

Lyuba curled up on the car seat, relieved by the final passing of the jolly Henrietta. "I wonder why in the world you chose such a silly name, for me. Henrietta, blah..."

Reginald laughed. "I don't know...I said the first name which had crossed my mind and which seemed to be quite opposite to your personality, for the little that I might guess it maybe."

Exactly as they expected, Sabatino Alunni drove straight on home. They parked about 300 metres away from the gate of his villa. He wouldn't leave his home walking for sure, and if he took his car Malusi's technological gadget would show it to them.

"Let's call William and the others now. I'm sure we won't be very busy with any further tailing for a while." Lyuba stretched out her long legs with her typical soft and gracious movement. "Luckily we had time to enjoy a good cappuccino, at least. It's bitterly cold. Who will come to relieve us? I think it will be the shift of your wife and Pasha..." She grinned with a little funny face. "A very odd couple, even more bizarre that you and me..."

Reginald noticed that Lyuba looked much more relaxed than usual and even younger, but he was unable to guess what had contributed to this unexpected change in her.

"I'm not too happy that my wife will be on duty on the evening of Christmas Eve or perhaps even later. She will be tired tomorrow, but for her it's so important to celebrate Christmas at our home. William and Caterina will do everything that needs to be done, but I'd like it if she could fully enjoy the day. If she cannot get enough sleep this night, I'm afraid that..."

Lyuba interrupted him, with a nearly imperceptible hint of envious irony in her plain voice.

"We are out of the game by now. Sabatino knows us too well. The only two 'amateur detectives' left at our disposal are Pasha and your wife. I'm sure they will do a great job and you can be sure that your wife won't be in any danger. Nobody can run a risk with Pasha at their side. The matter would be a bit different if Pasha played for the opposing team..." She smiled again, lost in who knows what strange thoughts. "But what annoys me is that it will be this last team that will win the game... I mean that the credit of finding Iris will go to Pasha and your wife. I'm sure that Sabatino will find his chance to deliver his freesia before tomorrow. Of course he needs an excuse to go out for a short time on his own... What do you think he will invent to justify that to his wife?"

Reginald scratched his head. He felt more comfortable with the young Russian woman now. "I think that he will tell her that he has to go to fetch her Christmas presents, which he has hidden, knowing she would have looked for them all around their home. It's plausible. He will motivate his short absence of this morning with the roses; so he has still the excuse of the presents."

Lyuba smiled again. She looked very young when she smiled, maybe because she rarely did it. "You are very clever, Reginald, in your mock clumsy way..."

"Oh, but I'm really very clumsy. The clumsiest person of the world. You have no idea..."

Suddenly Lyuba became serious again. "William told me of your dearest friend, Julia. I would have liked meeting her..."

"Oh, ehm...She was, she was an extraordinary person. I owe her all my present happiness. If she only could see me now..." Reginald felt suddenly moved and unable to keep on speaking. He took off his glasses and, trying to put them on an imaginary surface, let them fall on the floor of the car under the passenger seat.

Lyuba laughed, gently. "I see what you mean now..." She bent and found the glasses; she picked them up and cleaned them with the edge of her blouse and then gave them back to Reginald. "They didn't get broken. Here they are."

"I have in mind–I might be quite wrong of course–that Sabatino didn't hide Iris' body very far away. Nobody would be so stupid to drive for a long distance carrying a corpse in his car. So there is a good possibility that it won't take too long a time to get to the place from his home. It's nearly obvious that it won't be in the centre of Umbertide. You're right; now I also regret a little that we won't have the chance to follow this last development directly ..." Reginald put on his glasses again, determined to behave more attentively. He took out his cell phone and selected William's number.

CHAPTER THIRTY-FOUR

A thick swarm of snowflakes whirled against the windscreen like crazy bees. *'We'll have a white Christmas.'* Ellie couldn't help thinking with a satisfied little smile, while she was driving with secure smoothness along the sharp bends of the road. Peter had persuaded her to take his SUV, definitely more suitable for driving in these atmospheric conditions. Ellie fully enjoyed the dynamic performance of the vehicle which obeyed her perfectly. The road was practically empty. Who would choose to drive across the Apennines on Christmas Eve with such bad weather?

Pasha, all dressed in black, was comfortably installed in the passenger seat and looked perfectly at ease, following Ellie's rhythms of driving, without showing any sign of the ill-concealed worry which usually characterized Ellie's passengers, her dear Reginald included.

When Peter had given her the keys of the SUV, Ellie had glanced at Pasha and took her chance:

"Do you mind if I drive? I am well acquainted with the road; I have been to Umbertide recently, as you know." And she had smiled graciously, in her typical way, totally deprived of any instinct of female seduction, but so sincere and warmly spontaneous.

To her great relief, Pasha hadn't objected. On the contrary she was nearly sure to notice an amused light in his unfathomable eyes. Pasha was not talkative. Ellie knew it by now, but he had not pronounced a single word, since they had left the farm. She was not able to stand long silences. As she didn't mean to be nagging, she avoided asking him anything personal, but she liked chattering a little while driving, mostly with a person whom she liked and who intrigued her. Pasha fulfilled both features. Ellie decided to be direct, since she guessed it was the best way of approaching him.

"I know you don't like speaking, Pasha. But I hope it won't bother you if I talk. I mean I hope you won't be too bored to listen to me..." Pasha turned his head toward her and imperceptibly nodded. Ellie took it as a sign of benevolent attention and continued.

"I'm sure I'll never forget this Christmas. It will be for sure the most extraordinary Christmas of my life. At the beginning I thought it would be like that only because it's the first one I will spend with my husband at our home. Then I realized it would be even more memorable for the presence of all our friends, you and Lyuba included, of course. And now, even more incredibly, it will be on this Christmas that we, all together, will hopefully unmask a murderer. I'm thrilled. And you know what, Pasha, I have always wondered what feeling the adrenaline might mean. I have read it in many novels, but I have never felt it personally. Now I know. I think it's what I feel now. I'm sure that we, I mean you and I, will find out finally where Sabatino hid poor Iris. Of course each of us has contributed in a remarkable way, but by chance you and I are at the end of the chain and so close to find the solution..." She downshifted skilfully and the SUV turned steadily on the white carpet of snow which was getting ticker and ticker.

It was the same moment that Pasha chose to commit his little mistake. He spoke.

"You are a good driver, Mrs Ellie."

It was just a short sentence, but enough to encourage Ellie on insisting to raise a mutual conversation. She was not a superficial person, in spite of her constant, apparent merriness. She felt deeply and surely that Pasha liked her, and she decided that if there was a person in the world who could push Pasha to be more communicative, well, this person was Ellie Rigby McKenzie.

"I have always liked all kind of engines. I think each of them has a kind of personal language which a good driver must understand. I'm absolutely sure that you are an even better driver than me, Pasha. Would you like us to stop, and we exchange places?"

"Not now. You know the road, I don't. But I'll be glad to accept your offer when we drive back. It sounds like an excellent car..."

It worked, it worked. Pasha had even answered with a rather long and articulated sentence. Ellie felt encouraged.

"It will be my pleasure; you have surely several tricks to teach me to improve my driving ability. But now I suppose we should concentrate on our mission. I won't hide from you that I'm thrilled. Uhm, maybe you are used to... uhm, things like that. But for me it's the first time. My husband and Lyuba have done an excellent job, but now it's time to relieve them. Sabatino Alunni has spoken to them personally twice, and they cannot run the risk of being recognized. I have the impression Lyuba regrets that we are taking her place so soon. I might be totally wrong, but she's such a strong tempered and determined young lady, that she would have liked to be there to follow Alunni until the end..."

Pasha nodded again. Ellie took a peek. He might be considered a handsome man, even though there was something very cold and troubling in him. How old might he be? 40? Like an avalanche it was difficult stopping Ellie, once she was launched toward a certain direction. She went directly to the point.

"How old are you, Pasha? I'm 56, so I could be your mother, I imagine..."

Nearly any other man would have answered with a compliment at this stage. A compliment that would have been sincere, reflecting the truth, since Ellie looked much younger than her age. But Pasha was Pasha. He simply answered the direct question.

"I'm 40."

Ellie felt satisfied that she had guessed right.

"So you are a man of experience, and you know life well. Nonetheless you are still young enough to expect changes. It's a wonderful period in everyone's life. I'm sure you already have your own idea about the way Alunni will proceed...I doubt that he will have any chance of leaving his wife, even with the better excuse, exactly on Christmas Eve, either during the dinner or after it. So I imagine he will try to fulfil his...let's call it task before dinner today. It means without any doubt that you and I will be on watch. It's a big responsibility, but being with you is reassuring; you'll prevent me from committing mistakes due to my inexperience in this...role, and my enthusiasm of newbie. We should arrive at the meeting point with Lyuba and my husband in about 30 minutes. Unfortunately I cannot drive faster today." Ellie apologized with a wink, even though the running speed was remarkable on the snowy road.

"Nothing special, Mrs Ellie. We have only to follow him, avoiding being too noticeable. It depends on where he's going. But there is always the help of the bug that the boy, Malusi, placed on his car. We'll have the receiver that now is in your husband's hand." It was a very long speech and Pasha finished it with a kind of groan, as if he were exhausted after such a titanic verbal effort.

"Do you mind if I put a little music on?" Ellie reached out to the button of the player, ignorant of what they might find in it. Ellie suddenly realised she knew nearly nothing about Peter's musical tastes. She expected some kind of Irish folk music. But, quite amazingly, the interior of the car was invaded by a loud song of Abba.

"So when you're near me, darling can't you hear me
S. O. S.
The love you gave me, nothing else can save me
S. O. S.
When you're gone
How can I even try to go on?
When you're gone
Though I try how can I carry on?"

Ellie looked worriedly at Pasha, ready to switch the music off immediately. But to her great and relieved surprise she noticed that the Russian... was tapping his foot to the music, and she could guess, from the movements of his lips, that he was singing silently the lyrics.

"Do you like Abba, Pasha? But you are a bit too young to remember their songs so well. You were a little child when they were at the top of their popularity..."

Pasha smiled. Well, not a real broad smile, but the most similar expression to a display of joy that might appear on a face like his.

"Things, like fashionable pop music, arrived always with a certain delay in the Soviet Union, Mrs Ellie...I have always been a great admirer of Abba."

"Oh...and so have I! They were one of the leitmotivs of my youth. What is your favourite song?" Ellie hoped in her heart that he wouldn't answer 'Dancing Queen'. It would have been too...too absurd to imagine the obscure and dark bodyguard singing along,

"You are the Dancing Queen, young and sweet, only seventeen
Dancing Queen, feel the beat from the tambourine
You can dance, you can jive, having the time of your life
See that girl, watch that scene, digging the Dancing Queen"

Fortunately Pasha answered, "It's difficult to say. I like so many. But my favourite is probably 'Super Trouper'...I don't know why."

"Blimey! But it's also my favourite song of Abba, Pasha. I'm sure there must be in this compilation, could you see if you can manage to get the menu list of this damned device?"

The ghost of a real smile became slightly more evident on Pasha's lips. In few precise clicks, he found what he was looking for, and Ellie and her passenger arrived on time to Umbertide, at three pm, singing together loudly

"Tonight the
Super Trouper lights are gonna find me
Shining like the sun
(Sup-p-per Troup-p-per)
Smiling, having fun
(Sup-p-per Troup-p-per)
Feeling like a number one"

They necessarily looked still a bit wacky and hilarious when they met Reginald and Lyuba, who were totally unaware of what had made them like that.

They had spoken several times by mobile phone, and it was easy for Ellie to find the car in which Reginald and Lyuba were waiting. They had parked on a lay-by, partially screened by a hedgerow, now completely covered with snow, which looked like the comfortable backrest of a pure white sofa.

The snowfall muffled all sounds. Reginald got out of the car, followed by Lyuba, and hugged Ellie tenderly.

"Are you dressed warmly enough, honey?" Then he tapped on Pasha's forearm in a friendly way, adding, "You'll take good care of her, won't you?"

The road looked like a country one, even though they were not far from the centre of Umbertide. It was a quiet residential area, and there were only the gates leading to a few smart houses, relatively distant from each other.

"Alunni's house is not visible from here; it's right after that bend," Lyuba started explaining pragmatically. "There is no other road, so Alunni is obliged to pass by here when he leaves his house. We can check the movements of his car on this small receiver. As you know, Malusi placed a bug under the edge of his plate." She gave the small device to Pasha, who, before looking at it, gave a glance around the area and said,

"It's better not to stay here. There is no traffic at all, and someone might notice us from a window and wonder what we are doing..."

"Fine. So we'll go back to Capacciano now. Keep us informed." Lyuba nodded imperceptibly as her goodbye. She didn't like formal goodbyes. Reginald kissed Ellie once again and hastened to take his place by Lyuba in their car. One minute later their rear lights disappeared into the swirling snow.

Pasha gestured at Ellie inviting her to sit in the car. He took the wheel, did a U-turn and took the same direction as Reginald and Lyuba. Ellie didn't question him. She had already understood and could only agree with Pasha. But she needed to summarize her thoughts.

"You are right, Pasha. It's much more sensible to park somewhere else, by the main crossroad. In any case if Alunni decides to go anywhere, he'll be obliged to follow the only road, at least until the first crossroad. I have seen a kind of small, open parking lot there, while we were driving to meet Reginald and Lyuba, with a couple of other parked cars. We'll be less noticeable if we wait there. Of course there will be different tracks in the snow, but soon it will be dark, and I suppose that Sabatino doesn't imagine himself being watched and shadowed..."

Pasha didn't comment. Ellie didn't know what he thought either, because no one could guess Pasha's thoughts; but it would probably be not too far from the truth to image that he was pleasantly impressed by the quick mind of his teammate.

"The snow...It's necessary to know the snow deeply to be able to read its language perfectly. Alunni won't notice anything, since also our car is cover with snow now and it will be even more covered while we wait."

Pasha was becoming extremely loquacious.

"But you can read the language of snow, Pasha, can't you?" Ellie encouraged him.

They had arrived to the parking lot, and Pasha skilfully inserted the big SUV between the wall and a shapeless mound of snow which was originally a car.

"I'm Siberian." He added laconically again, as if that could explain everything.

The short afternoon of light was surrendering its place to a long winter night. Pasha and Ellie were patiently waiting in the SUV. And it was nearly completely dark. The car windows had been all covered with snow. Pasha had lit up a small electric torch, which he kept down on the car floor, with an excess of caution, in Ellie's opinion. There wasn't a living soul to be seen around and, in any case, the thick layer of snow which had completely veiled the car would make it impossible for that pale light to be seen from outside.

Pasha had attentively placed a warm blanket on Ellie's legs, although she didn't feel cold. She was well equipped with warm clothes, and the temperature was not too low, maybe just one or two degrees below zero, or else the snowflakes wouldn't be so large. They had drunk warm coffee from a thermos flask, had gluttonously crunched a good quantity of delicious biscuits, and they had even sung softly a couple of Abba's songs in an improbable duet.

Pasha was basically silent, but unexpectedly he liked to sing, Ellie learned. She had tried to make him tell something about himself by all means, always respecting his privacy. But she had not been that successful. So she had decided to try a different strategy and had started telling him about herself. Pasha seemed to listen to her in a very sympathetic way. She could not see his face clearly in that very dim light, but she knew it wouldn't have given her any special hint, since Pasha had always the same impenetrable expression, as if his face were a rubber mask. She had seen something akin to a different, faintly smiling expression only when they spoke about Abba. But she perceived by his posture that he was interested in what she told him about Reginald and about the way they met.

"I would have never expected to fall in love at my age. But it has happened. My husband and I run the risk of being a bit ridiculous, I know. But we are in love with each other like teenagers. I have already told you about his hard life in Ireland and his not too happy youth. He doesn't speak willingly about those years. I can understand his reluctance. He had no family and he decided to become a Catholic priest under the influence of his teachers, all Jesuit priests, who had taken him into their college, which was the only 'home' he had. He has always been very intelligent and skilled. At that time, I was told, they recruited the most talented and intelligent youngsters into the religious schools to make priests or nuns of them. But my Reginald found an alternative family, maybe a little too late. His friendship with Julia Fitzpatrick, Peter's step mother, was a fundamental fact in his life. It took a long for him to question all the former choices of his life, but Reginald found the intellectual strength for that. He's a very brave and intelligent man, you see. Peter and William were extremely supportive. Reginald has always considered Peter like the son he had never had. So he gave up his priesthood and joined Peter and William at the farm, and we met..." Ellie stopped with a small, emotive sigh. She felt always touched when she thought of her story, as if she couldn't fully believe that it's was quite true yet.

Pasha had remained silent and motionless, but suddenly he articulated a few words.

"Know what it means having no family."

Ellie cleverly didn't interrupt him with any questions. She knew that the only way was to let him say what he felt like, without pushing him.

"Mr Orlov, Lyuba's father, engaged me fifteen years ago, to look after Lyuba. This is what I have done at my best. Since then I have always lived with Lyuba and Iraida. Iraida is dead now. I'll keep on working for Lyuba as long as she wants me do so."

Ellie understood that she would draw a blank by insisting. She perceived that Pasha had already been very open to her, measured by his usual behaviour. She guessed that Pasha had not known his parents and, who knows where he had grown up. She felt sorry and worried at the same time. But, in spite of everything, she felt comfortably secure with him; she was not afraid at all.

"You have been always so kind and thoughtful to me, Pasha. I trust you, and I'd like for you to trust me in return."

Reginald phoned to her at that moment, to reassure her that he had safely arrived home, and Lyuba had managed perfectly in the bad conditions of the snowy road. He was at the farm, but he told her that Peter would drive him home, so that he could start arranging things for their Christmas lunch.

'In a few hours it will be Christmas,' Ellie thought with mixed feelings *'I would have never imagined it like that, but, blimey, I love this adventure, it makes me feel so...alive!'*

"William asked me if they have to organize another team to relieve us..." She told hesitantly to Pasha "I wonder if I can be back home before midnight..."

The Russian interrupted her "Here we are; he's leaving his house by car!"

Pasha had been constantly checking the screen of Malusi's small receiver, and now showed Ellie the small illuminated dot which had started blinking.

"Wow!" Ellie felt another wave of adrenaline "What are we going to do now? Maybe he's not alone; maybe he's with his wife. In that case he won't go where we need him to guide us to."

"We'll know soon enough. Stay here Mrs Ellie and don't worry. Let me do it." Pasha warned her quickly and got out of the car.

But Ellie could not accept the idea to remaining inside the SUV; any view from the windows was obstructed by the snow, and she wanted to see what was happening. She also got out of the car and hid herself behind it. It was already dark, and the snow kept on falling even more thickly. Only a pale yellowish light of a street lamp allowed her to view anything. She identified Pasha's silhouette protected by the wall of the parking lot. Only the sound of an approaching car engine broke the silence. Ellie held her breath when the big car of Sabatino Alunni appeared in her field of view and proceeded along the road, past the parking lot.

A handful of seconds later Pasha was again close to her. He didn't comment about the fact that she was not sitting obediently inside the car, and Ellie felt grateful to him.

"He's alone. Let's go."

He quickly cleaned the car windows while Ellie took her place on the passenger seat once again. She gave a look at the car's clock. It was only seven pm. She had thought it was already late at night...

Pasha drove out of the parking lot without hurry.

"We won't miss him. But we cannot stay too close. There is no traffic. He would notice us after a while."

They followed the rear lights of Sabatino's car without difficulty, even though sometimes the falling snow was like a barrier.

Alunni didn't go toward the centre of Umbertide.

"It's obvious!" Ellie exclaimed "He would have never taken his wife's body downtown in the pedestrian area!"

The dark Jaguar coupé turned into a provincial road. 'SP201' Ellie read on a rusty sign that appeared on the side of the road lit by their headlights.

Only the lit up windows of a few scattered houses dotted the uniformly dark fabric of the night. Ellie perceived the glittering of unpretentious Christmas light decorations in small gardens, blurred by layers of snow.

They had been following Alunni's car for about five kilometres. He was obliged to drive slowly, while Pasha could travel much faster with the SUV, more suitable for snowy, hilly roads.

"Where is he going?" Wondered Ellie aloud.

Pasha didn't answer. He had no idea either. Not yet. They went through a hamlet. A handful of small houses with pointed rooftops, which looked like toy-huts out from an iconic crib.

"I don't think he buried Iris's body somewhere in the country-side. It would have taken him too much time to dig a deep enough hole. It's a rural area with many inhabitants, someone would have noticed that...I presume he hid the body in an existing cistern or an old well." Ellie appeared to be in deep thoughts and, after a brief hesitation, she added,

"No, my first idea is wrong. Iris 'body is like the sword of Damocles for Sabatino. If it were found, his entire version of the facts would collapse like a house of cards. No...he must be sure that Iris' body could not be found there where he hid it..."

"Maybe he destroyed the corpse..." mumbled Pasha, a bit worried that he might trouble Ellie with a more detailed description of that.

"Cutting it in pieces and burning it or melting it in acid? Do you really think he could do that? It would have been a very dirty job. I don't think Alunni would have the guts to do that." Ellie wanted to prove to Pasha that she was ready for anything. Actually she felt totally at ease. Maybe she would have a slight emotional breakdown once everything was over, but not now. She couldn't help asking herself if Pasha had ever assisted such a slaughter or if he even...by himself...She looked at the Russian's hands, covered with soft leather gloves, which he kept firmly on the steering-wheel. In spite of these thoughts she had an increasing liking for Pasha.

As if she had read her mind, Pasha suddenly spoke again

"Do you trust me, Mrs Ellie? Don't be scared. I assure you that you won't run any risk. I know what I'm doing. Maybe you'll feel just a little cold. I must keep on driving without the car headlights on. I don't want Alunni to have any suspicions and we need to follow him a bit more closely, because he might stop at any place now." He didn't wait for Ellie's answer. He was sure about it.

He switched off the headlights and opened the side window of the car. Cold air mixed with snowflakes invaded the interior of the car. Pasha kept on driving in nearly complete darkness, looking out of the side windows to get his points of reference.

The lights of a slightly larger village were visible at about 500 metres ahead.

"It must be Montone..." Ellie followed the map on the screen of the small receiver.

Alunni suddenly turned left onto a very small road, which was practically invisible in the total white uniformity of the snowy landscape. His Jaguar proceeded slowly, skidding, even though imperceptibly.

Pasha gave a quick look at the map. He didn't follow Alunni's car along that half hidden road he had taken, but kept on toward the village; he switched on the headlights again and increased the speed of the SUV.

Ellie didn't comment; this way she rose even higher in the scale of Pasha's esteem.

They rapidly crossed the sleepy village, avoiding at the last second a puzzled and numb dog of uncertain pedigree. The animal, grateful to be still alive, found shelter under a small balcony, hoping that someone might open a door for him sooner or later. Once they reached the opposite end of the village, Pasha turned abruptly to the left, and they joined a nearly invisible narrow road which was supposed to be the same one taken by Alunni.

"I see, we are going toward him now. He won't be able to guess we had followed him since Umbertide, even though he may have noticed a car in his rear-view mirror. But I'm sure he didn't pay any attention to us. He's too worried about driving on snow covered ground with his car. Obviously he's not a good driver." Ellie grinned superciliously.

"Here he is!" Pasha nearly whispered, like a hunter who attracts his hunting partner's attention, without scaring the game with an unexpected loud noise.

The Jaguar plodded along a stone wall. Then it stopped. Sabatino Alunni parked with a certain difficulty in a relatively clear space, partially protected by partial roofing. A bus shelter, where he managed to insert at least the front part of his car.

"Slava Bogu!" Pasha switched temporarily to the Russian language to express his relief. "The big idiot parked in a place where there is hope that he will be able to leave from. Considering the way he drives on snow, if he had parked elsewhere, we would have been obliged to help him to get out..." He turned the engine off and took out small binoculars from a bag. Night vision binoculars, exactly like those that the secret agents use. Ellie felt thrilled.

"There is a gate; it looks like a small country cemetery. He has the flowers in his hand..." Pasha informed her succinctly. "We can go now."

He drove fast, without the slightest difficulty. They went beyond the parked Jaguar, which blocked partially the road, but Pasha managed.

"We are doing him a favour." Said Ellie "He can follow the trails of our tyres when he drives back to the provincial road."

Pasha nodded with a flash of his white teeth, which might be called a hint of a smile.

"And now, please Mrs Ellie, don't leave the car; just wait for me. It will take me a few seconds..."

Pasha jumped out of the SUV and, walking like an equilibrist on a tightrope, he didn't step on the freshly fallen snow, but only on the trails of the Jaguar's tyres. He fiddled quickly about the car plate, then came back.

"We can go back to the village, which we have already crossed, and wait there for a little while. Alunni will immediately return to his home now. He's in a hurry, but we are not. We'll come back to look for the place where he left the flowers in this small cemetery."

In a few minutes they were once again in the empty charming village. The dog was still there, under the balcony. Probably he recognized the car, because he took up a defensive attitude. Pasha found a place to park the car without blocking the main road, even though there were no signs of human presence around. Then he nodded apologetically at Ellie and took out a sandwich from the rich supplying of food that Caterina had prepared for them. He walked in the snow, approaching the dog, which looked dubious, but maybe too resigned to leave his temporary shelter. Pasha reached out to caress the animal, then offered him the sandwich, which after a second of hesitation was enthusiastically accepted and gulped down.

"Oh my, none of us had thought of that, except you, Pasha! The bug that Malusi had placed under the plate of Sabatino's car. Of course we had to remove it; we couldn't leave it there."

As his only answer, Pasha handed her the small electronic device.

"That was not a bad idea...To hide a corpse in a cemetery. But, even though it looks like a very small country cemetery, how can we find the exact place that we are looking for?" Ellie kept thinking it over. "Ah, silly me!" she cried joyfully after a second "I'm really stupid, Pasha. We have two perfect hints to follow, the flowers and, even easier...the tracks in the snow. Let's give Sabatino a few more minutes, and then let's explore the cemetery, when we are quite sure he has left."

Ten minutes later they were in front of the cemetery gate once again. The Jaguar of Sabatino had disappeared, but the snow retained the traces of the difficulty he had in making a U-turn.

Ellie and Pasha pushed the gate which squeaked, but offered no resistance. It was even too easy to follow Sabatino's footprints. They were the only visible sign that spoiled the immaculate blanket of snow covering the entire cemetery. The footprints led them to a wall, opposite the entry, where there were four rows of burial niches. Each one of them had carved inscription with the name of the dead person, the date of birth and death, and a photo. A few of them were also adorned with small plastic flowers. Only one niche had the comfort of a rather large bunch of fresh flowers, purple and white freesia.

"We have found Iris...But wait, Pasha, point the light here."

On the marble front of the burial niche adorned with the beautiful freesia there was a photo, nearly faded of a smiling, plump, old man and the carved inscription read

Arturo Pennacci

22-11-1898
30-9-1978

RIP

Ellie remained puzzled. Who was Arturo Pennacci and what had he to do with Iris? This Mr Pennacci died forty years before. How was it possible to imagine that Iris had been buried with him?

Ellie passed her fingers over the small plaque, along the joints. Pasha kept the electric torch with one hand, at her side and with the other hand he touched carefully the edge of that small burial plaque, comparing them with the others.

He exchanged a knowing glance with Ellie.

"So you think exactly like me." She told him with a note of triumph in her voice. "Sabatino had a clever idea, but we were more clever than him. Iris is here. We found her!"

CHAPTER THIRTY-FIVE

It had stopped snowing, but the thick snowflakes, which had fallen all the night long, had transformed the country landscape into a fluffy series of mounds and knolls with smoothed contours, that might hide anything. It was perfect scenery for the most traditional of white Christmas celebrations. The living room of the charming, old house was furnished in an unpretentious, but smart and cosy way. A beautifully decorated Christmas tree dominated a corner of the crowded room. There was even an enormous garland of fir cones, branches and other mixed and coloured elements on the entry door. But it didn't look like any other Christmas he had ever had. He might say it didn't look like Christmas at all.

Maresciallo Ciricola considered with a pinch of self-irony, that everyone present had a feature in common: they were all either tall or very tall. He was the only exception. Even young Luca Cini, the youngest son of Giorgio, the photographer, was tall for his age and with a pang of shame Emilio had to admit that he wasn't taller than the boy either.

'I'm like a garden dwarf that they had moved mercifully indoors to prevent him from being totally covered with snow.' He thought with a melancholy sarcasm. Then he concentrated his glance on Lyuba. She didn't smile so openly like all the others; it was not her style, but she looked relatively relaxed and comfortable. He thought that she was incredibly beautiful in her simple purple outfit, a pair of trousers and a silk blouse of the same colour. Her long, light blond hair was plaited a little less tightly than usual and a few long, free locks danced around her pale face, like silver moonbeams.

In spite of his considerations, Ciricola was happy to be there, and he loved the company. He felt replete and his usual slight melancholy had surrendered to the warmth of the friendly atmosphere, of which he felt to be part. The food was delicious, like always when there was William's touch. But there was nothing connected to the traditional

Christmas menu. "If you expect roasted turkey and panettone, you'll be disappointed, I'm afraid." William had declared with one of his grins, when he and Caterina had started serving the dishes. "Since I could not take any direct part in our investigation, I gave vent to my frustration playing with various recipes. Instead of a traditional display of Christmas dishes, I chose to make a little tribute to the nationality of each of us. It will be a 'fusion menu', with something Irish, something English, something Russian, something African, something Tuscan and, of course something Apulian...especially for you, Emilio."

Ciricola felt moved *("I'm getting too sentimental"* he told himself, without really regretting it), but his feeling changed into a mouth-watering amazement when he tasted the 'Tiella Barese'[6].

"William, I have not tasted such a good tiella for years. It's exactly like my mother did it."

The room was maybe a little too small for eighteen guests, but as Ellie and Reginald had stressed, welcoming them, there were twenty chairs at their home, so even two extra people could have found their place. Emilio tried to imagine his friends (because he considered all of them his real friends by now) seen through a stranger's eyes. They would have looked like the most extravagant bunch of people, unable to match and to get on well with each other. Appearances can be deceptive. Emilio had already learnt that for years, because of his profession, of course. These eighteen people, of ages and backgrounds completely different from each other, were all in a perfect balance of mutual affection and understanding; surely more than many others, coming from the same families, who were celebrating Christmas at their homes in that moment, following all the traditional clichés as a necessary habit, without any really deep joy for the mutual company.

It was true–Emilio couldn't deny the fact–that it was more than simply incongruous choosing as main topic for conversations, on a Christmas gathering, the development of an inquiry about a murder committed two years before, with graphic description of the possible conditions of the corpse and its hideout. But everyone felt genuinely involved. He could only recognize that they had probably solved a case, which the official authorities of police had fully mistaken.

"How is it possible that poor Iris's body was put in the same burial niche of that old man, who died so many years ago?" Mayor Sanchini, after his first strong opposition, had by now embraced the

---

[6] Tiella is the name for a baked dish with rice, potatoes and mussels.

cause that his wife had always supported. He was a proper person and not stupid at all. He had understood and nearly felt ashamed for his initial lack of trust in his beloved wife's insight.

"Pasha and I think that the niche was reopened in order to hide Iris' body there." Ellie reached out a hand to take a serving dish with a big Medovik tort[7], already sliced, and refilled Pasha's plate. She had learnt that Pasha had a sweet tooth. After enjoying all the courses, he had showed a particular interest for desserts, while the other table companions, except Malusi and Luca Cini, had declared to be too full to taste more than a symbolic spoon of them.

"We noticed that the putty or the cement—I don't know what it is exactly— around the gravestone of that Arturo Pennacci, is too clean, too recent, while he was buried there forty years ago." Ellie continued, adding a generous slice of Tuscan castagnaccio[8] to the overflowing plate of Pasha. "Pasha made me notice that it was probably sealed again with a kind of silicone which didn't exist forty years ago. Moreover those burial niches are rather tight. There is just room for a coffin. It would be impossible to put anything else there, let alone the body of a tall woman!"

"So, if we have really found Iris, where has Arturo Pennacci gone?" wondered aloud Reginald.

William had not spoken that much until that moment, busy in warming up the various courses which need it in the kitchen of Ellie and Reginald's home. He was standing up by the Christmas tree, absolutely handsome with his long white apron carelessly tied on his usual jeans. He looked to be in excellent mood and addressed Themba's son,

"Malusi do you think that you won't die with starvation if you stop for a little while to scoff everything edible you can find and make a little search on Internet for us?"

"I'm young and I have to grow up. I need calories and proteins, or else I'll remain short and my girlfriend will leave me. Besides that I must also grow stronger in order to be able to rid my sister of that coxcomb who hangs round her." Malusi, who was already as tall as his very tall father, grinned innocently, gulping down a big mouthful of cake and winked at Saverio Cini, the eldest child of Giorgio. Gianna snorted playfully. She had started feeling a certain interest, quite reciprocated,

---

[7] A favourite Russian honey cake with cooked flour frosting
[8] The castagnaccio is a chestnut flour cake (castagna in Italian means chestnut) with raisins, pine nuts, walnuts and rosemary.

for Saverio, even though they were still in a phase of mutual circum-spection.

"But when the boss calls...I have to answer his orders immedi-ately. What should I find for you, William?"

"Can you consult the archives of local newspapers on line? You should find if in the weeks after Iris' presumed departure on that cruise, there was any discovery of human remains in the countryside near a village called Montone, in Umbria."

"Give me at least ten minutes. I don't think I'll need a longer time. Don't you dare to polish off all the chocolate pastries while I'm away! Reginald, can I go upstairs to your studio? There is too much confusion here to allow me to work properly."

Reginald smiled and nodded and Malusi rushed upstairs with his faithful tablet.

Maresciallo Ciricola had guessed what there was in William's mind and, looking around, he realized that nearly everyone else had had the same idea, after this first indication. He realized that these un-usual amateur detectives had grasped everything. He would like having them in his team, instead of young Carabinieri Maccaluso and Cipriani, who were full of good will, but whose investigative skills were light years behind those of his friends.

"It's absolutely plausible that Alunni emptied Mr Pennacci's burial niche to make room for Iris' body. Pennacci died long time ago; maybe there are none of his close relatives still alive. I bet Alunni searched for information before choosing the niche to utilize. After for-ty years a corpse is surely reduced to a bare skeleton, a bunch of poor, old bones. Alunni put them in a bag and threw everything away as soon as possible. I'm sure he didn't want to drive around with a skeleton in his car boot. But he could reasonably feel on the safe side. Even if the bones were found, nobody could trace them and there would be practi-cally no chance to identify the corpse either. So, very probably he pre-pared the burial niche, getting rid of the body of Mr Pennacci, a few days before killing Iris. In the meanwhile he simply put in place the tombstone, fixing it temporarily, to hide the empty niche. After killing Iris, he went straight on to that little cemetery and hid the body there. Then he sealed again the niche, this time quite properly. A good idea. A cemetery is a perfect place to hide a corpse." Emilio summed up every-thing clearly and precisely. He noticed that Ellie was sitting between Lyuba and Pasha, translating at low voice the Maresciallo's logical analysis. *'Damn!'* Emilio railed silently at himself *'I spoke Italian. Of course Lyuba could not understand a word.'*

"So everything is settled now, Maresciallo, isn't it?" Loredana, the mayor's wife, looked at him, for confirmation. "Now you can perform the necessary action of reopening the case. Finally the killers of my dear Iris will pay for their crime."

The Maresciallo felt terribly sorry to disappoint her, but he was obliged to explain that things were far from being so straight forwardly easy now.

"I'm afraid, uhm, I'm really afraid that it's not so easy. I have already explained that the case is considered closed, and the official inquiry established that it was a suicide. I was never in charge of that investigation. Unfortunately I had nothing to do with it. Therefore I do not have the powers which would allow me to reopen the case without unmistakable evidence..."

Loredana reacted impulsively, nearly shouting, leaving her husband quite upset, since he had never seen her like that.

"But what are you saying, Maresciallo? The evidence is there, you have simply to go to that cemetery, in your official role, open the niche and find Iris' body!"

Emilio felt impotent and frustrated. He had a lump in his throat which nearly prevented him from speaking. There were rules which he could not break.

The old, wooden staircase started creaking, as if for remonstrance, under the heavy thumping of Malusi's steps.

"I've got it, I've got it! I found the article."

Everybody's eyes turned toward him, giving a relieving break to the Maresciallo's distressed embarrassment.

"Here is it. A pensioner walking his dog with his grandchild.

The dog ran away, and they left the main path to look for it. The dog came back with a bone in its mouth, a bone which the dog gave to his master, as they were used to play together like that. You have already guessed the rest. The pensioner realized that it was an unusual bone. In short, he found other human bones and called the police. The investigation and the forensic tests came to the conclusion that the bones belonged to a man, a quite old man, whose death dated back to at least forty years before." Malusi caught his breath. "I found only three articles about this fact. It seems that after a few days the reporters of the local newspaper didn't consider it worthy of interest anymore."

"I think that the normal official procedure in similar cases is like the one we had in Ireland. There is a check of the list of missing people, and the police try to determine the causes of the death. But if the human remains are too old and nothing might connect them to a missing person, the entire matter is dismissed." Peter addressed directly Emilio, who had logically the role of expert.

"Yes, it's what's surely happened. I can only agree with you. We all think that those bones belong to Arturo Pennacci. If it were possible to find one of his relatives and to make a DNA test, I'm persuaded that our hypothesis would be confirmed. But it's difficult to imagine where those poor bones have been placed by now...They might be stored in a police dump, together with other physical evidences, or they might have been incinerated or buried in a common ossuary. In any case I'm persuaded that there is practically no chance of finding them again." Emilio let his arms fall.

Loredana Sanchini was a determined woman and she was not distracted by the last news. She insisted with her direct questions, to Emilio's great uneasiness.

"But Iris was not killed forty years ago and there is no reason for dismissing her murder. You agree with us, Maresciallo, and you are our only hope now. We know where Iris is; we know it for sure. And when her body is found and identified, all the lies that Sabatino and the other woman had told to the police will be revealed..."

Emilio Ciricola wrung his hands. He hated the words that he was now obliged to pronounce.

"It's not so easy, Mrs Loredana. In reality we have no concrete evidence, and there is no justification for violating the tomb of a deceased old man, who had absolutely nothing to do with Iris Ciancaleoni and Sabatino Alunni. He died before Iris' birth. The only way would be finding Mr Pennacci's relatives, if there are still any, and ask them for the permission to peep into his burial niche, just to see if he's still there...You can imagine how absurd this request might sound." He looked at Peter for help; maybe because he considered that, being former policemen, Peter was the most reliable, as for respecting the laws.

"Peter, you had asked me to let you know if your investigation would infringe the law. Well so far you have more or less respected the limits, even though," he gave a slightly reproaching glance to Malusi, who obviously didn't felt guilty at all, "that bug which someone placed under the number plate of Alunni's car..."

"What bug?" Malusi grinned, pretending to look as innocent as a little lamb. "There is no bug there, as far I know..."

"Luckily someone with more common sense than you had the good idea to remove it. But, well, theoretically it was against law and unfortunately everybody, me included, knows that. But at least there is no trace of that anymore. Removing a tombstone to peep into a burial niche is a totally different matter. So I'd like to be sure that none of you and, I repeat, NO ONE is considering the weird idea of doing just that. It would be a crime; even the discovery of Iris' corpse wouldn't justify it in the justices' eyes."

"But I thought that Justice was blind." Malusi tried to joke.

"It's not a joking matter the case, Malusi. You would find yourselves in serious troubles if you tried to do that. And I wouldn't be able to help you. On the contrary, I would be in the unfortunate position of being an accuser. "

"Emilio is quite right." Peter spoke firmly. "But it doesn't mean that we are giving up. We'll follow the longest path, but we'll arrive to our destination. I think that the only option we have is finding Mr Pennacci's family members, gaining their trust, and explaining everything to them to get their authorization to examine the burial niche of their relative. Maybe it will take time, but we'll try."

A frustrating silence descended on the room. Ellie interrupted it with a bit forced, joyful tone

"I'm sure we'll find a solution, but we cannot do anything for that right now, so let's try to enjoy ourselves on this beautiful day. It's time to discover our gifts."

To William's great relief, Ellie had informed everyone that there would not be the usual ritual of presents under the tree, with the relatively disturbing obligation of buying something for everyone. She had asked every guest to bring just a very little item, something simple, but made by their own hands and not destined to anyone else in particular. It could be just a hand written card. Then all the items would be put into a basket, and everybody would take one at random, without choosing explicitly. This way all the friends who gathered at her and Reginald's home would have a token to keep as memory of the lovely day spent together. Nobody knew who had brought what, but it would be fun to try to guess it.

"But what if I take out from the basket, by chance, exactly the item I have made and brought myself?" Asked Paola, Malusi's girlfriend.

"If it's something splendid that you have created, you deserve to keep it for yourself, if it's something horrendous, you deserve it too." Malusi laughed, teasing her.

"If you feel like, we can also try to guess who made every single symbolic gift. It will be a way to check if we really know each other." Ellie was glad because she realized she had cheered up her guests, who had become a little too involved in gloomy thoughts about corpses and murders.

Malusi was the first to pick out a small parcel. They had been all wrapped with the same, plain dark blue paper, nothing to do with the traditional patterns of Christmas. He quickly opened it and found a small jar of jam decorated with a hand written label which wrote 'Bergamot & Red Chili Pepper'.

"It's even too easy! Only William could conceive such a mixture. But, coming from him, I'm sure it's delicious. Only a bit too small for my tastes. I was lucky. Thank you!"

William nodded and on his turn he took out a parcel and opened it. It was a drawing, which showed the main and only square of Capacciano. The style of the yet unknown artist was slightly naïf, but there was surely a pinch of original talent in it. William contemplated it for a while, then he said seriously,

"You know that I'm usually very direct, so you can believe me if I assure the person who made it, that I really like the drawing. I'll get it framed, and I'll hang it on my office wall. Now guessing who the author is needs a bit of reflection. It must be someone living in Capacciano, so I can consider only the Sanchini and the Cini. And I see that the mysterious and talented artist is involuntarily revealing himself by a rightly proud smile. Thank you, Luca!"

The young Luca Cini, who had grown tall quickly and lost weight, changing the appearance of the plump and awkward boy he had at the very beginning of his teens, was rather satisfied , even though he would have preferred that his present were chosen by Reginald, with whom he had always had a deep relationship.

Reginald, on the other hand, chose a parcel containing a warm scarf of a sober Bordeaux wine colour, which he rightly guessed was knitted by Caterina ("I chose a unisex colour, good more or less for everyone.")

Soon everybody had impatiently grabbed a parcel, and they were unwrapping what they had in their hands with amused surprise.

The spirit of the game had been strictly respected, and everybody seemed to appreciate the simplicity of these handcrafted little things, which were infinitely more precious than any expensive thing bought, as a duty to fulfil, in a smart gift shop at the very last moment.

Maresciallo Ciricola noticed that the key ring he had carefully carved into a piece of olive wood and patiently polished was in the hands of Luca Cini, who seemed to appreciate it.

"Who made it?" The young boy asked. "It's so clever, all in one piece and so sweet to touch."

Ciricola didn't answer at once, too occupied to open his own parcel first and then pleasantly shocked by what he found. It was another key ring; so someone had the same idea as he. And he felt nearly sure about the identity of the person who had made the little item he had received. It was a piece of amber that had been pierced to connect it with a thin silver chain with a silver key ring at an extremity. Emilio had no doubt. He looked for Lyuba's attention lifting the amber key ring up, as if it were a stem glass ready for a toast. Lyuba, who was leafing through a small photographic book which she had received from someone, nodded in assent on the Maresciallo's silent answer. Then she approached and added a few words of explanation.

"I didn't violate Ellie's rules. This is handmade. I had this piece of amber with me and I managed to pierce it with a small drill that Pasha found. The silver chain is recycled, I'd say, since I took it from a spare key ring I had in my handbag. Of course you are not obliged to use it." She smiled quickly and slightly, then went toward Reginald, who had just waved at her to call her from the other corner of the room.

Emilio was struck dumb. He felt like an idiot, without fully realizing that, if he had told Lyuba what he felt, that is something about the similitude between the piece of amber and her eyes or any other display of emotional delight and gratitude for the Fate that had chosen him as receiver of THAT gift, Lyuba would not be so positively impressed.

Loredana Sanchini, whose disturbed reaction, when they were discussing the difficulty of reaching a quick solution to the inquiry concerning Iris' death, had flushed her cheeks giving a positive prominence to her usually a bit too plain and dull features, admired the small doily of exquisite workmanship, that she had found in her parcel, asking all the other ladies which of them was the maker. But everyone declared not to know anything about that doily, which was really a little master-piece of crochet. Ellie, who was very curious, had a sudden inspiration. She looked around for Pasha, who was sitting quietly in a corner, apparently absent-minded and imperturbable. She went closer to him and whispered,

"You have a real talent for crocheting, Pasha. I should learn also that from you." It was not a complete bluff, Ellie felt nearly sure she had guessed right.

Pasha looked at her, without changing expression, but Ellie had started to learn how to read something slightly more personal on his expressionless face, and she realized that somehow he was invisibly smiling.

"It's relaxing. I learned it in a place where there were no many other pastimes..." And Ellie knew he wouldn't add another word.

Time had flown away. Night was falling. Little by little the general conversation had come back to the main topic, namely how to break the deadlock of their inquiry. William had supported Peter's proposal about finding the relatives of Arturo Pennacci.

"We'd be glad if you remain for dinner too. We have still some leftovers. I might make some tea," Ellie suggested. Everybody accepted, but Lyuba and Pasha, who claimed they had to go back to Arezzo, but they would come for sure to the farm once again before flying back to London, to say goodbye to them all. While they were collecting their things and wearing their coats, Emilio was the closest to them. The others were listening to William, who was trying to organize the next steps of their detective's work.

"....because unfortunately one thing is absolutely clear, by now, as Emilio stressed. We cannot go to open that burial niche without having official permission..."

Lyuba, cautiously switched to Russian, murmuring something to Pasha,

"Они должны официальное разрешение, но мы не ..."

Although Maresciallo Ciricola couldn't understand a single word of Russian, he was a good detective and knew how to interpret situations. He was sure that he had grasped what Lyuba had in mind and felt worried.

If he had been able to master Russian well enough, he would have had absolute certitude that he had guessed right.

Lyuba's words meant

"They need an official permission, but we don't..."

After the Russians' departure, while Reginald filled the cups of tea for everyone wishing a hot drink. Themba shook his head and told Peter, who was sitting by him.

"I had brought with me the mobile phone with the number I had given to Alunni, because I really expected he would have called Professor Nnamani to be sure that Iris's ghost was satisfied and had left in peace. Maybe I was able to condition him so deeply that he felt free from the embarrassing presence of his late spouse by himself, all in his mind, as if it had really happened. Who knows?"

"I would have expected his phone call too, Themba. But obviously it was not necessary for our Sabatino, or maybe he will call tomorrow. I guess he's celebrating Christmas with his wife and accomplice. It's amazing how criminals feel free to celebrate family holidays without remorse." Peter grimaced with disgust. "It's also possible that Alunni left with his Jessica to an exotic destination. Who knows where he is now...."

CHAPTER THIRTY-SIX

When Sabatino Alunni opened with difficulty his eyes, he had no idea about the place where he was and how he had ended there.

He felt no pain, but neither did he have any clear perception of his own body. *"I must be dead."* He thought and oddly he felt relieved.

He caught a glimpse of a female silhouette bending over him.

"Iris..." he whispered with an uncontrollable relief. He was surely dead and she had forgiven him. Then he lost consciousness again and sank in a dreamless sleep.

"He's waking up!" Shouted Jessica Mandelli Alunni, addressing the indifferent and resigned, plump nurse, who had just come to check the vital parameters of the patient and the condition of his drip feed. "He was trying to say something, I'm sure; he moved his lips. Maybe he was calling me." Jessica took Sabatino's hand in hers. "Saby, Saby, I'm here. How do you feel, darling?"

The nurse turned her back to hide her annoyed and tired puff. She had been on duty since the night of Christmas' Eve and she had still three hours of work before returning home. Every year the same old story; the younger colleagues with children begged her to accept that unfortunate shift at their place.

"You are free from family commitments, Andreina, but we have the children, the entire family is coming over for dinner, my mother-in-law included. How can we manage?"

And every time she accepted and exchanged shift with a colleague, not because of any particular generosity, but only from a sense of resigned tiredness, which freed her from frustrating discussions. Of course the only alternative would have been a solitary Christmas; she often thought that she might take a trip, maybe a cruise, and to enjoy a different kind of celebration for which she might wear a nice evening dress, instead of here nurse's gown, on the 25th of December.

Andreina considered that the young woman in the room had been at least as unlucky as her. The man, the husband of the dark-haired elegant woman, had been brought to the casualty department a little after midnight. A car accident it seems. As he had his documents, it had been easy to inform his wife, who had arrived in haste to the hospital. One of the stretcher bearers of the ambulance, a chap whom Andreina knew well, had told her that the man had driven off the road all by himself, there had been no clash with any other car. His car, it seems, had rolled down the hillside and stopped against a tree. He had been lucky, because the headlights of his car—a beautiful, luxurious Jaguar, but quite crushed and dented now— had remained switched on, and someone had seen them from the road, a small country road with very little traffic. The snow had already completely covered the traces of the accident and the trails of the Jaguar tyres off the road. Had it not been for the headlights still on, the driver of the Jaguar would have remained down there until who knows how long. And then the matter could have been far more serious. It was a very cold night and the driver had banged his head and lost blood from several injuries and gashes. A longer stay outdoors in those conditions would have had far more tragic consequences.

Anyway, his life was not in danger now. He suffered with a concussion of the brain, but the doctors seemed to be optimistic. He had been unconscious for over twenty hours, but he was already showing some signs of reaction.

"Saby, Saby..." the voice was both imploring and peremptory at once, "Saby, Saby..." He didn't want to wake up and leave that comfortable cocoon where he was floating, but the voice insisted. Non it couldn't be Iris; she had never called him Saby. Good grief! It was Jessica. Sabatino decided that he had to be alive, after all. He made an effort to articulate a sentence

"Jessica...Where am I? What's happened?" Now his head was aching badly and he felt unpleasant pains all over his body. He tried cautiously to move one arm. Another, unknown voice, warned him with a reproaching tone,

"Keep calm, Mr Alunni. Everything is fine, but you have a drip, don't move."

Feeling as defenceless as a baby, Sabatino sighed, "Jessica, Jessica what's happened?"

"You had an accident, Saby. I was dead with distress and anguish. You had told me that you would be gone for a very short time, because you had forgotten a special gift for me at your office. It was yesterday afternoon. But then you didn't come back home. I went to look for you to your office, but your car was not there either. It was snowing so heavily. I didn't know what to do. I went home again and I waited. I tried to call you; your mobile was ringing, but you didn't answer. I was afraid that you had been kidnapped. I didn't think of an accident at first. I called the police. Then, I received a phone call from the hospital and I came here immediately. You have been unconscious for so many hours. The police informed me that you were found by someone, somewhere near Montone. You lost the control of the car and had an accident. You could die if none had noticed you, darling. But what in the hell were you doing there?"

Sabatino felt miserable; he had a horrible taste in his mouth and he was quite nauseous. He listened to Jessica's words without fully understanding what she was speaking about. He couldn't remember anything. He mumbled, "I don't know, Jessica. I feel an enormous confusion in my head. Yes, your Christmas present, darling, I'll give it to you on Christmas day. I have it in my overcoat pocket...no, I think it's already home in one of my desk drawers. I'll give it to you on Christmas, with the roses. No, I think I have already given you the bouquet of roses..." He left the sentence on hold. The flowers...he started remembering something.

"But Christmas is today, Saby, today; it's nearly over." Jessica left his hand and gave a slightly worried look at the personal effects of her husband, which had been recovered by the rescue squad.

Sabatino felt lost, and, to great amazement of his wife and the nurse, he started sobbing.

"I cannot remember clearly what's happened, Jessica. I have a terrible headache. I feel so weak. An accident? Did you say that I had an accident? By car? Where is my car now? The Jaguar...Did you see it, Jessica? Is it damaged?"

The idea that his Jaguar might be damaged overwhelmed him and he fainted again.

Doctor Mellini felt dead-beat. He had been on duty for 24 hours, with only short breaks of uncomfortable sleep on the too short sofa of the nurses' room. He looked forward to an invigorating bowl of warm chickpea soup—his wife could prepare it in a masterful way—before relaxing in the comfortable softness of his bed. He made an effort to concentrate and to answer properly the questions of that rather nervous woman, who sounded even a little arrogant ("*It's my imagination, I'm too tired...*" The doctor thought with his usual bonhomie).

He knew who she was. Everybody knew Ciancaleoni family and the whole town had regretted the death of Settimio Ciancaleoni, the factory owner. That woman was not a Ciancaleoni actually. She was only the second wife of the widower of Iris Ciancaleoni. A Milanese she was. Doctor Mellini's wife repeated that Mrs Alunni had not hit it off with the other ladies of the local polite society. "We are too small-town minded for her, probably." She said.

"Doctor, my husband keeps on losing his consciousness. It's necessary to do anything to make him recover his lucidity. Are you quite sure that he has not suffered with any permanent brain damage?"

"Calm down, Mrs Alunni. I have already tried to reassure you in every possible ways. Your husband's life is not in danger and his brain was not irrevocably affected by the consequences of the accident. He suffers for a slight brain concussion. The haematoma will be reabsorbed by itself." Doctor Mellini was infinitely tired of repeating always the same phrases to the patients' relatives, but he understood that for the people involved, every case was unique. He passed his hand across his forehead; he needed badly a hot shower; he wanted to change his cloths for his pyjamas. "Mr Alunni needs to rest, he's under sedation now. He will sleep until tomorrow and then I'm sure he will be completely lucid again. We'll keep him here still for a week, but it's just a routine precaution. You can go home. You need to have a good sleep too. Your presence cannot do anything for him now, but it's important that he can find you at his side, when he wakes up tomorrow."

Jessica nodded, without looking too persuaded. But she realized there was nothing else to do and she felt worn out too. Also she wanted to give a look at Sabatino's desk, at their home. He mentioned a present he had hidden in a drawer there. Unless it was just a fantasy of his banged head...

CHAPTER THIRTY-SEVEN

Lyuba had looked directly into his eyes, when they had shaken hands in a rather formal goodbye. Maresciallo Ciricola had held her gaze, even though those penetrating amber eyes were disquieting to him. Lyuba looked through him, without seeing him, as if he were transparent, but at the same time she seemed to scan his thoughts. Emilio wondered if she had somehow realized that he had noticed the quick conversation she had just had with Pasha and he had probably guessed correct the meaning of it.

"Goodbye, Emilio. I hope we'll meet again once day." She had said with her usual, apparently monotonous tone.

Nearly immediately after the Russians' departure Emilio had found an excuse and had left at his turn. The others had been a bit puzzled, since they had thought that he would stay in their company to finish the lunch leftovers. But no one had insisted, considering that perhaps he had something to arrange at the Carabinieri station, which he had rather neglected for the whole day.

Now Emilio was driving downhill, completely absorbed in frantic consideration. Soon he arrived home. The view of his solitary and slightly gloomy flat had a depressing effect on his mood.

He didn't feel hungry, since the delicious lunch had been huge, but he did feel cold. At random he opened all the cupboards of his basic kitchen and was relieved to find some grounded coffee in a jar. He prepared the reversible coffee percolator, the 'napoletana', and decided to cut a slice from a small panettone which his subordinates had offered to him. It was Christmas, after all.

He put all on a tray and carried it to his tiny living room, which was a little less melancholy than the kitchen. He installed himself on one of the two decrepit armchairs. In that way he faced the massive chest of drawers, the surface of which was covered with framed photos.

He felt a pang of sadness. Among the photos of his family, there was a big picture of his wedding day and other two photos of Rosaria. It was the second Christmas that he spent without her. Without realizing that he was really speaking, not only thinking the words, he addressed his wife's photo, as if she were sitting alive and healthy in front of him.

"Ah, Rosaria, I don't know what's happening to me. You can be absolutely sure that since the day I met you, I had never looked at another woman. You were the love of my life and no one will ever take your place. But I feel so lonely; my life is so empty, and you'll never come back. I don't know what's happening to me, Rosaria. I have met this young Russian. She has impressed me so deeply, even though I barely know her. You and I belonged to the same world, Rosaria. She comes from another planet. She will never turn her eyes down toward me..." Emilio Ciricola was clever and humorous, so he could not help grinning at himself, after pronouncing these words. Actually Lyuba should have to bend a lot to put her eyes at his eyes' level. She was at least fifteen centimetres taller than him. "But I perceive a hidden frailty under her determined manners and, forgive me, Rosaria, I feel the need to protect her. I know, I know, what could do a poor Maresciallo of humble origin for a very rich, cosmopolitan business woman? I have no answer, but I realize she's so lonely and I feel nearly like defending her from herself."

He gave a second, shy look at the framed photo and he had the impression that Rosaria nodded sympathetically. His Rosaria could always understand him.

Emilio took a sip of coffee; it was already cold. The panettone was not bad, but he realized he couldn't eat anything.

He tried to clear his mind, to concentrate better. Maybe he was not as perceptive and subtle as William, but he was also a good detective. He could not be completely sure he had guessed Lyuba's intention, but he was persuaded that he was not too far from the truth. He made an effort to analyse the few data he had in his possession. For a moment he had considered the idea of following Lyuba and Pasha when they left Ellie's home, but he had immediately abandoned that possibility. Pasha was not naïve and he had surely great experience, he would have noticed him quickly and it would have been difficult to justify his presence.

"What do I know for sure?" wondered Emilio. "Pasha is aware of the place where Iris's body is very probably hidden, because he was there with Ellie, when they shadowed Sabatino Alunni. I told them that it's a crime to open someone's burial niche without official authorization. They don't care a damn for legality, when they are motivated by a valid reason. That is even too evident. But it's equally evident that they don't intend to be involved in any difficulty with Italian justice. What would I do in their place?" Emilio scratched his cheeks and incongruously thought that he needed to shave. Nature had gifted him with thick dark hair and a very luxuriantly growing beard, which veiled his cheeks again and again, giving him only a short break between two shavings. But that was not the main task to attend to right now. "What would I do in their place? Well, I'd remove the tombstone from the burial niche, protecting my hands with rubber gloves, to avoid leaving fingerprints and I'd check what is inside, without touching anything. Then either I'd let someone finding Iris's body or rather I'd urge the local police authorities to do so. An anonymous call from a public phone, if there is still one existing. After that I'd hasten to leave the country. Just to be cautious, in case someone might have noticed me around." Emilio felt sure he was on the right path. But how could he know when they would decide to go to the small cemetery of Montone? Logically they wouldn't go there during the day...

"Good grief!" The Maresciallo started in anxiety. "What if they were going there right now?

He thought over about, trying to calm down. No, it couldn't be like that. Lyuba had clearly told William that they would return to the farm to greet everyone there, before leaving. So necessarily their plan had to be to go to the cemetery after being to the farm. And it could not be very late at night, because they had to leave to London or whenever they intended to go, and there were no flights in the middle of the night.

Emilio switched on his old computer and quickly checked the timetable of the flights from Pisa to London–let's hope they are directed to London– the following day. No, that was not the solution he hoped to find. He started perspiring, even though it was rather cold in his flat. There weren't any flights in the late evening. But maybe they had decided to leave by train...

Pasha and Lyuba had rented a car in Arezzo, but logically they could not leave with it. The train was the most probable hypothesis. There were trains to Milan running until rather late.

It was a little like gambling. One couldn't be sure of winning, but sometimes there were good chances, if one was able to consider all factors. Emilio Ciricola didn't like gambling, but he had no choices.

Unfortunately he couldn't rely on many subordinates at his order in that small Carabinieri station. He phoned to young carabiniere
Maccaluso, who was slightly brighter than his colleague Cipriani.

"Maccaluso, you must be at my disposal tomorrow for a very
confidential investigation out of our territory. Inform Cipriani that his
leave is suspended and he must remain on duty at our station, for the
ordinary needs."

Maccaluso seemed puzzled and excited. He didn't dare ask his
Maresciallo for any clarification. He simply said soundly,

"Yes, Sir!"

Emilio tried to drink his leftover coffee; it was cold and tasted
horrible. He felt ill at ease because he was doing everything behind his
friends' back. But he wanted to keep them out of troubles. That would
have been impossible, had William realized what Lyuba had in mind.

Emilio hadn't any clear plan ready yet. He only knew that he also wanted to protect Lyuba from any risk. I would take responsibility
for her on himself, if it became necessary. But he had to be there, to see
what was going to happen.

'I'm putting my entire career on the line' he told himself and,
with a badly repressed anguish, tried to imagine his father's deep distress if it had really happened. He was the only one in his family who
had studied enough to get a degree; he was the pride of his parents.
They dreamed that their son could climb the whole professional ladder
to end at the top of it as general of Carabinieri. At the same time Emilio
felt a kind of adrenalinic emotion which made him consider the hypothesis, not too remote, of contributing in the most effective way to
reopen Iris Ciancaleoni's case and to prove to the frail and strong
Queen of Snow that–like she– he was able to dare and to risk.

CHAPTER THIRTY-EIGHT

Jessica felt hungry. She had not eaten anything decent, besides a couple of antediluvian sandwiches, which she had bought at the cafeteria of the hospital. They were wrapped in an aseptic plastic film and had the embarrassing consistency of cold rubber. She was relieved to be at home again. A hot and relaxing bath would help her to feel much better. The doctor had assured her that Sabatino would sleep until the following morning, and she didn't need to be worried, since the consequences of the accident were not too serious.

After emerging from the scented bath, comfortably wrapped in her soft bathrobe, Jessica felt unbearably starved. She remembered, with an annoyed grimace, that Flordeliza and Joselito, the couple of Philippine servants who took care of the Alunni's household, were on leave for three days–of course, it was Christmas holiday– and the villa was empty. If things had happened as she and Saby had planned, they should have spent Christmas at friends' home. Friends...Jessica didn't know them that well, she had met them only a couple of times, but Saby had insisted, claiming that they had an important social position in town. She had called them quickly from the hospital, to inform them that, obviously, they wouldn't be able to join their party. They had expressed their regret and their sympathy in an apparently warm way, but then she had not received any further call from them, as if they had forgotten that Saby was in hospital, and their absence at the party would be hardly noticed.

Jessica went to the large and smart kitchen, hoping to find something ready to eat in the fridge. Once again she savoured the pleasure of seeing the luxurious furniture and the design of the sophisticated household appliances dominating the kitchen in a triumph of shining steel and precious wood. She was not fully used to live in that kind of rich comfort yet, without any slight financial worries, but she felt she was born for that.

She had been gifted with a natural elegance and a taste for beauty, Sabatino was her perfect match from that point of view.

The villa had remained as it was before...her arrival. Sabatino had fully transformed the master bedroom only, but had told her to feel free to redecorate every room according to her tastes. She didn't feel like making great changes, at least not yet. She liked the style of furniture, everything was remarkably classy.

She never thought of Iris. She had never met that woman and could allow herself to pretend to ignore all that had happened to her in that house. She and Sabatino had discussed carefully all the details related with the role she had to play on the cruise ship, but he had never told her anything about...the rest.

Jessica only knew that, once she had reached and gained the position she had only dreamed of for all her life, she would never give it up. Now she had all that she had always looked for. She had a social position, a man who loved her dearly and a solid fortune, destined to increase even more. She felt quite proud of herself, because she had managed to lead her destiny to exactly where she wanted to arrive. Persuading Sabatino to do what was necessary to do, to be happy together, had not been difficult. The idea had been hers and she was sure that it was absolutely flawless. Everything had followed her expectations smoothly. She had not been in a hurry. They had waited the necessary time, and now all was settled perfectly.

Jessica opened the impressive fridge only to find out that it was miserably empty. A bottle of orange juice and two bottles of champagne stared at her from the bottle racks. There was a solitary jar of yoghurt, lost in that emptiness like a single penguin on an iceberg. She took it out. It was better than nothing. Flordeliza had left everything perfectly immaculate, but she had not thought to buy any stock of food, logically. Sabatino and Jessica were supposed to leave to Prague on the 26th of December to spend a week at a five-star hotel in the romantic Bohemian capital. She swallowed her tears together with the last spoonful of yoghurt, remembering suddenly that the doctor had told her that they would keep Sabatino in hospital a week, just for a precaution. It meant that also the trip to Prague would become impossible. She wondered if she had to call the hotel to cancel the reservation...

She felt terribly lonely in the big, deserted villa. Her smartphone looked like the only link she had with life. She selected the number of the only person she fully trusted and whose advice had always been precious for her: Helios, her astrologist.

Helios answered when she was already worried that he never would. In reality his name was Elio Costantini and he had attained a rather good reputation as astrologist working with a local TV station of Milan. Jessica had found him several years earlier and she had taken the habit to visit him for private consultations. Unfortunately, since her move from Milan to Umbertide, it had become more difficult, but Helios was always ready to support her by phone.

"Jessica, dear..." He spoke in a lively tone; in the background she could hear a confused, merry hum.

"Helios, I apologize for disturbing you today, but I'm in trouble. I need to know how my astral conjunction is today and..."

"But, Jessica, I'm not in my studio now, I don't have the book of ephemerides with me. You can understand that; it's Christmas..." Helios had a certain experience that made him realize it would be difficult to get rid of her, if he were not able to give her at least something reassuring to think about. As one might offer a small bone to an annoying little doggy to be sure that its barking would stop for a while. "Let me see, I can try to perceive something anyway. I feel that something unexpected and troubling has just happened to you..." Elio—or Helios—was very familiar with these tricks which worked a little like the so called 'placebo effect'; when people are fully persuaded of something, they find by themselves all the possible confirmations of what they believe in. It was even too easy; if Jessica had called him on Christmas evening, it meant that something wrong or unpleasant had happened to her. He had no idea about that yet, but it would be Jessica herself to give him all the information, without realizing it, simply following trustfully his inputs.

"You are right, as always, Helios. My husband had an accident..."

"I know, but he's alive and he's not in danger. Saturn had left his sky." Helios was swimming in his element, like a fish in a peaceful sea. It was the usual procedure. If Jessica's husband would have been dead or in danger of dying, she wouldn't have called him and moreover not with that tone of voice. And now it was necessary to hook her with another bait, to make her feel the need of a series of consultations which would have represented a welcome income for the astrologist.

"But there is another presence, Jessica..." If she had been with her husband, Helios thought, she would have been involved in the accident too, and it was not the case. It could only mean that her husband was on his own, or with someone else, when he had the accident. He could hear Jessica's breathing, hung upon his lips.

"It's a woman, Jessica. You must be careful. Your husband loves you, no doubt, but there is this woman who is creating obstacles...I should read the tarots to see clearer in this matter. You might come over one of these days...After New Year, maybe, there is no urgency; I don't feel any immediate danger." He hoped to have reached a satisfying compromise, in order to not miss his consultations and to calm Jessica enough to be sure that she wouldn't spoil his holidays with other inopportune phone calls.

Jessica, who in her life was neither gullible, nor unprepared in life's general matters, was oddly attracted by what she considered Helios's powers. She believed that astrology could determine people's destiny, and she didn't see any contradiction in the parallel use of tarots card to go deeper into the caprices of fate. The matter was that since the first time she asked him for her personalized horoscope, Helios had always predicted to her, exactly, all that had happened. At least Jessica was persuaded that it was like that.

"Could you just tell me something more about this presence, this woman, who could be a menace for me, for my marriage?"

"Jessica dear, I cannot consult the cards right now..." He was at a dinner, and he had left the table, but he looked forward to keeping on enjoying his delicious meal. He decided to tell her something indefinite, generic, at random, just to get rid of her. "It's strange, Jessica, I feel something; it's a presence, a woman who is negative, a blond woman. But everything will end well, don't worry." He thought that there was surely a blond woman among her acquaintances, with whom she didn't get on well, but adding that everything would settle for the best would calm her down and prevent her from any reactions aimed at this imaginary enemy.

Jessica felt only partially reassured, anyway, but the idea that soon Helios would have cleared all the clouds over her future, made her feel better. She told him that she would call again at the beginning of January. The idea of going to Milan, even if only for a few days, was very appealing. She would also do some shopping. Now she didn't need to look at prices tags anymore.

The villa was immersed in a total silence, which might sound disquieting. Only the ticking of the big pendulum clock of Sabatino's office was audible, as amplified, in the corridor. Jessica remembered what Sabatino had mumbled. A present for her was in one drawer of his office desk. He wanted to give it to her on Christmas morning, but...Well, it was still Christmas, at least for a few hours, and she wanted her present, even though the day had been spoilt.

The door of the office was open. She switched on the light and went to sit on the massive chair which was behind the desk. Her bare legs felt the delicate softness of the precious leather. She started opening the drawers on the left. The first one was full of stationeries and papers arranged in a rather orderly fashion. She didn't need to check many other places after that, because what she was looking for was in the second drawer. A small parcel elegantly wrapped with dark green paper displaying the logo of the most famous jeweller' in town. But she didn't remove the parcel from the drawer yet, because she paused for a moment to contemplate the other object, next to it on the bottom of the drawer. A handgun, a dark compact thing which had an anodyne elegant design too. Of course Jessica knew that Sabatino had a pistol. Once he had even taught her how to load it, and she had tried to shoot at some tins, on one occasion when once they had taken a walk along the river in a quite deserted area. However she hadn't expected to find the gun there. She took out both items and put the handgun on the desk while she unwrapped the jewel case. When she held the diamond necklace in her hands, she remained breathless. It was the most beautiful thing she had ever seen. And it was hers now! She immediately wore it. She felt the coldness of the diamonds on the skin of her neck. Everything pure and beautiful is cold, like the perfect crystals of snow, she thought, but diamonds were not ephemeral. There was a large mirror in Sabatino's office. He liked indulging in admiring his image too, rightly proud of his elegance and his perfect style. Jessica stood in front of the mirror that was cased in a precious, old frame and she was pleased by what she saw. The necklaces seemed to be even more shining, transmitting light to her skin, which looked silky. She noticed that she had a small smear of yoghurt on her upper libs. She felt guilty like a child caught doing something awkward, and she cleaned it off with her forefinger. She felt overwhelmed by love for Sabatino, who had chosen for her the most expensive and smartest of presents. She thought that she wanted to be by him, when he opened his eyes, the next morning; so she would have an early night, to be able to arrive at the hospital as soon as possible.

She hesitated, before leaving the office. The handgun was still on the desk where she had put it. She caressed her necklace with the fingertips. She was completely alone in that big villa. Of course there was the alarm system, but... And she had her diamonds to protect now. She took a quick decision; she easily found also a box with the bullets in a third drawer and took them, together with the pistol upstairs to her bedroom.

Jessica had slept with her necklace on. When she went to the bathroom, she realized that her delicate skin had been marked slightly by it. She thought it would have been much more sensible to take the necklace off and to put it into the small safe, which they had behind a shelf. Reluctantly she did so. She felt more starved than the evening before and she told herself that, before going to Sabatino at the hospital, she might stop at a café to have a substantial breakfast.

She chose her outfit with a particular care. She wanted Sabatino to see her as beautiful, when he fully recovered his consciousness. While she was combing her short, brown hair, perfectly styled by the expert hands of her favourite hairdresser, she started thinking again about everything that had happened. Helios' words crossed her mind, like a worrying presage. A blond woman was ready to create problems...Who could she be? And then she realized that she still had no idea about the reasons for which Sabatino was on the place where he had his accident. He had told her that he had to go quickly to look for something he had forgot at his office in the factory. But he had never been there. He had driven along the winding country road up to Montone instead. Of course it was only few kilometres from their home, but the factory was in a totally different direction. What if a blond woman had something to do with that? Often men offer very expensive presents to their wives, when they feel guilty. But they had been married only for two months and he loved her...It was impossible that he already cheated on her. Oh, but there had been those recent problems in their sexual life. Sabatino had always been so passionate, but during the last two weeks he had started claiming he felt unwell, suffering with a gastric ulcer. She had tried to help him by imposing a strict diet on him. In spite of that, his recent activity in bed was reduced to mere sleep. And if it was the negative effect of an envious blonde woman?

Nearly without realizing what she was doing, she took the handgun, which she had kept on the bedtable during the night, and put it into her handbag.

After having breakfast, Jessica felt better and more determined to get answers from Sabatino.

At the hospital the staff shift had changed. Jessica could not find any of the faces she had seen the day before. The doctor on duty looked young and energetic and, once again, he reassured her that all was fine. It was just a matter of time that her husband would wake up. The doctor informed her that it would be necessary to perform other medical tests, but he was practically sure that the patient would be quite lucid and that he could remember everything. Uhm, maybe not the individual details of the accident, but that was a common reaction.

Sabatino opened her eyes again twenty minutes past noon and what he saw was Jessica eating a sandwich in front of him. She put it down immediately and came closer to him.

"Saby, darling, can you hear me?"

Of course he could hear her. He had had a car accident, but he had not become suddenly deaf. Sabatino Alunni felt weak, but he no longer had that deep headache.

"How long have I been here, Jessica?"

"You had your accident in the evening, on Christmas Eve, honey; they took you to the hospital around midnight, and now it's half past noon on the 26th of December. They say you are fine. Let me call the nurse now.

Two nurses came to push Sabatino's wheeled bed to a consulting room where she was not allowed to follow. She waited, finishing her sandwich.

Time had stretched and seemed to be extremely long.

Finally Sabatino was taken back, with bed included, to his room. The young doctor was with him. He smiled at Jessica, assuring her that her husband's condition was very satisfactory, but he had to remain in hospital still a few days.

Sabatino was really quite lucid. He apologetically tapped on Jessica's hand and whispered,

"I'm so sorry, darling. I'm afraid that our trip to Prague must be postponed. But don't worry. As soon as I fully recover, I'll take you there as promised, and if it won't be to celebrate the New Year, we'll find something else to celebrate, only you and I."

The more Jessica felt relieved about her husband's health, the more she felt her irritations grow because he had not given her any explanation about the reasons for being in that place where he had the car accident.

She decided to be diplomatic and clever, without giving him the time to realize in advance what she wanted to know from him. So she started thanking him for the wonderful present, regretting he was not there to give the precious parcel to her on Christmas morning.

"You see, Saby, when you recovered your consciousness temporarily, yesterday, you told me that the present was in your desk drawer and you that wanted me to have it. So I went to look for it. I hope you don't mind; your desk was not locked..."

"Oh, Jessica, my love! Of course I'm not angry at all; you can look into all my drawers, I have no secret from you..."

There he was; he had led himself into the trap. Jessica replied suavely,

"I know, I know. It's exactly because I'm aware that you trust me completely, that I'm rather puzzled because you didn't tell me the truth, pretending to go quickly to the factory, while you went to that village instead. Sabatino–she didn't call him Saby now–why are you doing it to me, why are you hiding things from me?"

What else could he do at this stage? He felt tired and weak and psychologically frail.

"Jessica, my love, I didn't tell you certain things, only because I wanted to protect you. I cannot speak now, try to understand me. It's better that we are completely sure that nobody can hear us. You know why...It's, it's something connected with the cruise ship..."

Jessica sniffed the danger in the air; she immediately understood the subject he was talking about. She was not prepared for that; she was sure that everything had been perfectly arranged by now. And here it is; the fate had made a twist, and old things came back. Sabatino was trapped in that hospital room now. If there was something urgent to resolve, she was the only one who could do it.

Jessica went to the corridor and asked the nurse to not come to the room, claiming her husband was tired due to the medical tests and she would remain to sit by him. Then she closed carefully the door.

"It's important that you tell me everything now, Sabatino." She sounded firm and determined. What else could he do at this stage? He told her exactly what had happened since he met the African psychic.

CHAPTER THIRTY-NINE

Jessica had not interrupter her husband. She had remained sitting by him, holding his hand and trying to control her mixed feelings and her tempestuous thoughts. Only when Sabatino fell silent, she started asking him specific questions, to be sure to grasp every detail.

"But this African psychic, that man...are you sure you had never seen him before?"

Sabatino felt worn out, both physically and psychologically, but he was reassured by the fact that Jessica didn't look angry.

"I'm absolutely sure. He was not a person who could go unnoticed. He's not a charlatan, Jessica. He told me things about Iris that only I know." He hesitated; he felt deeply ill at ease speaking of Iris with Jessica. "No, he didn't ask me for money, for anything. Actually he seemed to be annoyed when I asked him for a meeting. He told me that he had a gift and his task was to help trapped souls to pass over."

"I have heard of that." Jessica was pensive. She had already spoken with Helios of that gift that few psychics had. Her astrologist had told her sincerely that he did not have that capacity. It was another proof of his professional seriousness, Jessica thought.

Oddly Jessica didn't find anything strange in her husband's narration, but she felt an immediately repressed pang of jealousy for that Iris, to whom Sabatino had brought flowers. She wondered if it had not been a mistake ignoring voluntarily everything about her. Perhaps Iris had been more important for Sabatino than what she might imagine. Jessica shook her head; no it was not the case. After all Sabatino had...For the first time Jessica managed to formulate clearly the concept in her head. After all, Sabatino had killed her, because they had decided that together. Jessica realized she didn't know how...she shivered imperceptibly, how he had done that. What Jessica knew for sure was that she could not allow a little mistake to spoil the perfectly oiled mechanism of their plan.

"And, and when you did what she had asked you to do...through that psychic...what did happen exactly?"

Sabatino waved weakly and, to Jessica's worried disappointment, he mildly smiled.

"I felt relieved. I felt that Professor Nnamani had told me the truth. I think that Iris could pass over in peace. She forgave me."

Jessica was troubled, but she tried to maintain a good dose of pragmatism.

"So you really went to leave the flowers there...uhm where she is?"

"Yes, I did; it was the only thing she asked me for..."

"And you feel sure she's not here by your side anymore now..." Jessica shivered a little more intensely, hoping that he wouldn't notice it.

"I feel she left in peace now. I wanted to call professor Nnamani for his confirmation, but I had the accident. I don't think it's necessary, I'm sure that Iris has left and she's in peace now."

Sabatino sounded nearly dreamy, maybe it was only because he felt tired, but Jessica didn't like his ecstatic expression. It was time for Jessica to pass to total pragmatism.

"So you put Iris into someone else's tomb. It was a good idea." She realized she had to encourage him with her approval.

"Yes, I had organized everything in advance. I emptied the place. Nobody would look for her there. Nobody would ever find her."

"Wait...You told me it's a very small country cemetery, but still in use, isn't it? If you put fresh flowers on a burial niche where an old man dead over forty years ago is supposed to be, maybe someone might notice them. Maybe someone might examine the gravestone a little closer and maybe someone might find that..."

"Oh, Jessica, don't worry, darling, it's all so improbable..."

"No, no, Saby, you don't understand. We have been so accurately cautious; we have not neglected a single detail so far, and everything has been well. It means that we cannot neglect anything, even the slightest sign which might lead to us. It's absolutely necessary to go there and remove those flowers."

"But, but, I cannot do it now, darling. Then in a few days they will wither, and the problem will be solved..."

"No, no, the danger, ever so imperceptible, will remain even when the flowers are quite dry. I know you cannot leave the hospital. It doesn't matter; explain everything to me completely. I'll go myself to make those damned flowers disappear once for all."

Sabatino looked at her as if she weren't his beloved wife, but another person, who just looked like her. He couldn't control his painful disappointment in realizing that she could be so merciless against Iris. After all Iris had sacrificed herself for Sabatino and Jessica's happiness, and she had forgiven him. There was nothing wrong if she wanted receive her favourite flowers one last time. At the same moment a red alarm light started flashing in the most logical corner of his head. He had to admit that Jessica was right, even though she might have been more tactful. He started explaining to her accurately where she could find that burial niche.

CHAPTER FORTY

She had chosen a male voice for her GPS. Those female sexy voices which suggested directions were unbearable. They had a kind of alluring and suggestive tone, as if they were promising a close encounter to the driver, once they led him to his destination.

His male, invisible assistant had the impersonal and perfect voice of a good radio announcer, instead. Jessica followed his polite orders as she drove around Umbertide, avoiding the limited traffic area of the centre.

It had stopped snowing since Christmas early morning, the snow had been removed and the streets were clean. Nonetheless she drove slowly and carefully. She identified the place where Sabatino had driven off the road. The traces were still visible on the snowy slope. The Jaguar had been recovered and it was now somewhere in a garage. The policeman who had spoken to her had explained that it was still under police custody, because that was the usual procedure in case of accident. Jessica could scarcely see the tree against which the car had fortunately stopped its fall. It was already dark and the light mist which was coming up from the river seemed to become thicker and thicker. She had not encountered any other car, since she had turned to that small country road. Jessica looked at the illuminated clock of the car. It was only eight pm, but it looked as if it were in the heart of a deep night. She had thought that it would be a good idea to drive to that, uhm, that cemetery at not too late an hour, but when it was already dark and possibly at dinner time. She would be sure not to find anyone there.

Jessica thought that it had been a very long time since she had her last good meal. After Sabatino's car accident she had either eaten sandwiches, which calling average would be an exaggerate compliment, or nothing at all. Her stomach was groaning with scarcely elegant rumbles, which would embarrass her terribly, if somebody were here to hear them.

After a final bend of the road she could see the lights of Montone, veiled by fog. The village had a disquieting appearance, on the top of the rocky hill, still covered with snow. Sabatino had explained clearly to her that the cemetery was about 400 metres from de village. There was a crossroad; one way would lead directly to the village of Montone, the other road, even narrower, was the one she had to take to reach the cemetery.

Jessica turned into the road on the left and she guessed, rather than seeing it clearly, the stone walls which surrounded the cemetery. The fog was really thick now, and it seemed to swing on the bare branches of trees like scraps of a dirty, old veil.

She didn't feel the pangs of hunger anymore, when she parked the car in a clearing by the gate of the wall.

That place was sinister. There was a spooky atmosphere, which she perceived nearly painfully, when she left the protective and warm shelter of her car. She tried to encourage herself, *'C'mon Jessica, it's normal that a cemetery in the fog look sinister. It's only suggestion. In ten minutes all will be over.'*

Jessica stood motionless by her car, without making up her mind to push the rusty gate, which was open and dangled a little from its hinges.

There were no cars in view. But the lack of general noises also allowed her to hear what she would have not heard under normal conditions. She had the impression that there was a car leaving, even though she had not passed by any when she arrived.

Suddenly she felt scared as if she realized only at that moment that she was alone, at night in a deserted place in the middle of the countryside. She wouldn't be able to explain rationally why she did so, but she loaded Sabatino's handgun, which she had in her handbag. She kept her hand on it, irrationally reassured by the simple contact with the metal.

She took a deep breath and opened the gate, which, obviously creaked threateningly.

Jessica felt the irrational certitude that she was not alone. She heard a strange, persistent noise, like a repeated hiss, followed by dull sounds. She was not sure about the direction from which the sounds arrived. The fog also distorted her auditory perceptions, returning sounds from wrong angles. She slipped on a slab of iced, trampled snow and caught hold of a stone cross to keep her balance. She realized with a shiver that she was walking directly on graves. The light from the streetlamp near the entry gate, even though fading in the mist, was enough to allow her to see more or less where she was walking. She had taken an electric torch, but couldn't carry it, because she was clasping the handle of her handbag with her left hand and held herself up, grabbing at random what she could, with the other hand.

Sabatino has told her that she had only to walk through the small cemetery until the opposite external wall, where the burial niches were located.

Jessica zigzagged through the old tombs. The disquieting sound seemed to be closer. She made out the wall; it was only few metres from her. But she became immediately paralyzed by terror seeing that between her and the burial niches a pale, long figure stood up in the fog. It was a female silhouette all draped in a long pale bluish tunic or gown. The tall figure spun round and looked directly at Jessica with her diaphanous, pale face surrounded by light blond hair.

The blond woman... Here she was! The ghost of Iris had come to defend her flowers.

Jessica lost completely her self-control and started shouting,

"Don't come closer, damned soul! Be gone, get out! Go away! I swear it wasn't me. It's Sabatino who killed you!"

The ghost didn't move, but stared at her. Jessica was unable to think over the truism that ghosts cannot be afraid of a handgun, since by definition they are already dead. She seized Sabatino's Beretta 92G and aimed it at the ghost of Iris.

"Go away, or else I'll shoot!"

Suddenly the door of a small funerary chapel, which looked quite derelict, opened and a dark figure jumped out, like a devil from the hell.

It was too much for Jessica; she closed her eyes and pulled the trigger.

The handgun-shot was ear-splitting. Jessica didn't have the time to reopen her eyes; someone or something pushed her down violently from behind and made her slump badly to the ground; she banged her head and everything disappeared.

CHAPTER FORTY-ONE

Young carabiniere Maccaluso was waiting his superior officer, as he had been ordered the previous evening. The service car was ready and, as Maresciallo Ciricola had asked, and he had informed his colleague, carabiniere Cipriani, that he would be on duty at the Carabinieri station for the entire day. But Maccaluso had no idea about the possible mission he would be destined to carry out. Absolutely nothing had happened in Capacciano in the past several days, not even a single car theft.

'I have only the duty to obey orders; it's not my task to speculate further.' He reassured himself when he saw Maresciallo Ciricola approaching.

"Everything is ready, Maresciallo. At your command, sir."

Although Emilio Ciricola had not slept much the previous night, he now felt lucid and determined, because he had taken his decisions.

He took his place in the passenger seat, by Maccaluso.

"I'll let you drive, Maccaluso."

"Where are we going, Maresciallo?"

"To Umbertide."

The young carabiniere drove cautiously along the road leading them through the Apennines. Luckily it was bank holiday, and there was no traffic of heavy lorries.

Maresciallo Ciricola, who was usually friendly and talkative with his subordinates, had not uttered a single word since they had left Capacciano. Maccaluso didn't dare to peep at him either.

It was a gloomy day; the light was dim, even though it was nearly eleven in the morning. After they had passed through the mountain road, they saw the profile of the town, slightly veiled by the mist of the Tiber valley. Maccaluso was obliged to ask the question.

"Where must I go now, Maresciallo?"

Ciricola seemed to rouse himself from a nap, even though Maccaluso knew for sure he had never closed his eyes.

"Let's go to the local Carabinieri station. It should be just on the other side of the Tiber, near the railway station." And he kept silent again.

The Carabinieri station was easy to find, and Maccaluso felt glad he had done so well so far. The station was set in a quite dull and anonymous yellow house, in a quiet street where every house had a different colour, ochre, red, pale green...Maccaluso was sorry to admit that the dirty yellowish paint on the local headquarters of his very dear Corps of Carabinieri was not the most appealing,

"Wait here, Maccaluso."

Maresciallo Ciricola disappeared into the small entry door. Maccaluso remained inside the car without knowing what to do. Then he had the inspiration of taking a cloth out from the glove compartment and started carefully cleaning the windscreen.

More than one hour had passed when Maresciallo Ciricola came out and reached their car once again. He looked to be in a much more jovial mood, nearly excited.

"Do you feel hungry, Maccaluso? I'm starved. Let's go, I invite you to a restaurant for lunch. We have nothing to do for at least three hours. I asked one of our local colleagues to suggest where we might find a good trattoria."

Maccaluso felt rather embarrassed taking his place at the table of that little restaurant, in front of his Maresciallo. He had known Ciricola for only a couple of months, maybe even a shorter time, since the Maresciallo had been transferred to take command of Carabinieri station of Capacciano. He liked the new Maresciallo, but he couldn't say that he felt familiar with him. In any case he was starved and the invitation couldn't be more opportune.

"Choose freely anything you feel like eating, Maccaluso. It's not sure we'll have a chance to have dinner at a normal time this evening." As if to set a good example for him, Ciricola started questioning kindly the rather old and skinny waiter who had come to bring them the menu. "We'd like to know the specialities of the day. Capitano Lo Cascio, whom you know well, has recommended the cooking of your restaurant."

The skinny waiter, who in spite of his absent-minded appearance, sincerely liked his work and appreciated having the Carabinieri as regular patrons (*'It can be always useful to have good relationships with Carabinieri and Police.'* He thought), smiled at the two unknown men in uniform and asked politely if they were two new members of the local Carabinieri corps.

"No, no, we came from Arezzo." Ciricola thought that maybe the name of the town would be more familiar to the waiter than the name of their little village of Capacciano. "We are here on a mission. I'm afraid we'll spend only one day here. What a beautiful town you have. I had never been here before. We'd like tasting your excellent dishes, and I'd be grateful to you if you could suggest to us what we might choose."

"Well, today we made 'vincisgrassi'⁹; then we have 'porchetta'¹⁰ and fried lamb cutlets..."

"Everything sounds delicious. What do you think, Maccaluso? We might taste vincisgrassi and then you can take what appeals you more. For me it will be porchetta! And I think we might even allow ourselves to have a glass of wine, since we'll have sufficient time to sober up before driving again. Then just a glass, it's perfectly licit."

Everything exceeded the level of their expectations. Emilio thought that William would have liked that 'trattoria'. William... Emilio felt suddenly guilty for not informing his friends about his plans, but he was doing so mostly for their sake and, if everything would transpire as he hoped...

Maccaluso had started feeling much more relaxed, and when the skeleton waiter–how could it be possible that the man looked like that, working in a place where they cooked the most deliciously caloric dishes?–brought their two coffees, the Maresciallo made him feel even better by calling him for the first time by his name, Salvatore, instead of his surname.

"You'll wonder, Salvatore, why we have come here. You are a good boy, and I know that, like me, you are a devoted Carabiniere who likes his job. I'd like to give you precise answers, but I can only ask you to trust me, for the moment. Believe me, Salvo, I'm not dragging you in anything less than correct, but it's a very delicate inquiry. The less you know about it, the more your position will be protected, in case things don't turn out in a very good way. I'd take all the responsibility on myself, if that happens...Oh, here is our coffee. Thank you so much!" Ciricola addressed the waiter with a warm smile. "It was all delicious; you can be sure that we'll come to eat here again, next time we have the chance of being in Umbertide. By the way I think that your town is also

---

⁹ A sort of lasagne, baked with parma ham, mushrooms, tomato and cream.
¹⁰ A savoury, fatty, and moist boneless pork roast of Italian culinary tradition.

well known for its artistic ceramic manufactory. I think I even saw a documentary on it."

The waited nodded contentedly.

"I'll bet you have seen a documentary on Ciancaleoni factory. It's an institution in our town. But now they are all dead, the Ciancaleoni, I mean. Settimio died some years ago and more recently also his daughter died. Her widower has taken over the reins of the factory, but I have heard that he had a car accident a few days ago. If I were superstitious, I'd start thinking that the factory is jinxed." And he laughed with a strange gurgling sound.

Emilio pricked up his ears. "But the present manager, the one who had the accident, he's not dead, is he?"

"No, no, I don't think so. I have heard that his car was in much worse condition than him..." Obviously he was quite indifferent to the fate of the man.

Emilio paid the bill, ridiculously cheap and put his hand on Maccaluso's shoulder. "It's time to go, Salvo. I'll explain to you what it's necessary that you know."

It was still daylight, but night would fall early, even though the days were already supposed to become slightly longer, after the winter solstice. They managed to find the village of Montone quite easily, but then they had to roam a little about the country roads to find the place they were looking for. The cemetery was relatively small. The Maresciallo though it looked very much like the one of his native village, although there was never fog there, while now the fog seemed to become thicker minute after minute, as if an invisible paintbrush were painting the air with a watery, dirty colour. He liked snow, but he couldn't get used to fog.

"Remain here in the car, Maccaluso. I need to go on a reconnaissance. If you see any car arriving, any people, by any means, call immediately to my mobile phone and hide yourself. It won't take me long."

Emilio entered the cemetery. He didn't perceive it to be spooky. He had learnt that only living people can pose a danger, but the dead are always harmless. Cemeteries had always conveyed a feeling of melancholy peace to him. The majority of tombs looked neglected, but some of them were cleaned and tidy and had small bunches of flowers or green leaves, now partially covered with frozen snow. The burial niches were at the end of the cemetery, opposite the entry gate.

He noticed immediately the rather big bouquet of freesia, which was still nicely fresh, incongruously placed below the half faded photo of an old, plump man. Arturo Pennacci.

At the two sides of the wall with the burial niches, there were two small funerary chapels, not larger than an average wardrobe. Maresciallo Ciricola tried to push the door of the one on the left, but it was bolted. He was luckier with the other one. The small gate opened and he could enter. It was too dark inside to see all details; there were tomb-stones on the two longer walls, but there was also room enough in the middle, among empty vases and two amazing statues of stone which appeared to be chimeras or sphinxes. He could not identify them for sure.

He knew exactly what to do now. He would wait for the arrival of Lyuba and Pasha. He would allow them to start removing the tomb-stone of poor Mr Pennacci; then he would pop out, to interrupt their work, and he would persuade them to leave. He would be on the safe side, because he wouldn't take any direct, material part in the removal, which would be against the law, a violation of a tomb without authorization. At the same time he would stop Lyuba from going too far and getting into trouble. He had informed the colleagues of Umbertide that he had received interesting information about an old case, and he was following it autonomously, but he would immediately inform them if he found anything confirming the rumours. To his immense relief, they agreed. Of course he would be obliged to adapt a little the reality, but it was for a very good purpose. He would persuade Lyuba and Pasha to return immediately to Arezzo and to forget their trip to the cemetery of Montone. He would tell Carabinieri of Umbertide that there was something strange about that slightly open burial niche, and he hoped they would continue with the investigation. If he could manage to be convincing enough, they would find Iris' body there, and it would be clear that it was the corpse of a woman dead a couple of years before, not the skeleton of a man buried there already for forty years. At that stage he would be free to tell them all that he knew, starting from Loredana Sanchini's documented suspicions. The case would be open again, and the spouses Alunni would be obliged to explain many things.

William, Lyuba and all the others wouldn't be in the risky position of being involved in any crime.

Emilio joined Maccaluso again. The young carabiniere confirmed to him that nothing had happened, absolutely nothing; he had not seen anyone.

"Fine. But we cannot stay here now; we must find another place to park. There is just an unsurfaced path which winds around the outside wall of the cemetery. Do you think you can manage to drive there, without getting bogged down?"

"Yes, Sir! I think so."

"Bravo, Salvatore, bravo! Then go there and park trying to make our car invisible from the main road."

"What must I do then, Maresciallo?"

"Nothing, Maccaluso. Just wait. We'll keep in touch by cell, when we are not together, but I'll be always close."

It was nearly completely dark now. Emilio glanced at his wristwatch. It was six pm.

An intuition, that he didn't waste time to analyse rationally, pushed him to call the farm.

The voice of Peter was warm and calm when he answered. Peter was one of those rare people who, when they speak to you, always give the impression that you are their main interest in that very moment, and they are sincerely glad to have a personal conversation.

"Emilio, what a pleasure!" The Maresciallo heard a confused sound of voices in the background. Peter continued in a slightly apologetic way, "Lyuba and Pasha had just come to visit. They are always welcome, but their arrival was a bit unexpected. So we did not have time to call you, Ellie and the others, asking all of you to join us. Only Reginald and Themba are here now, besides William and myself."

No surprise; they all worked at the farm. Emilio didn't feel excluded, even though he noticed a slight note of regret in Peter's voice and guessed that Peter thought the Maresciallo might like to meet Lyuba again before her departure.

"They are leaving to London, as Lyuba had anticipated, but they dropped in, just to tell us goodbye. Would you like to speak to Lyuba?"

'Is it so obvious that I have feelings for her?' The Maresciallo wondered; he was sure that he had been very discreet, but obviously not enough...

He grinned at himself and told Peter,

"No, it's not the case. My English is still very lame and weak. I can manage to make myself understood in a direct conversation in person. Being a Southern Italian, I have a certain familiarity with gestures and facial expression. That helps, but on the phone...you see. Give them my best friendly regards and wish them a good journey back home from me."

Emilio's brain was quickly elaborating the data like the most effective of personal computers. He knew that he would see Lyuba soon, even though neither Peter nor the young Russian could imagine it yet.

He calculated the time. It might take about one hour for a good driver like Pasha, who already knew the way, to arrive to the cemetery of Montone. He was sure they would leave the farm soon; so his wait wouldn't be very long.

CHAPTER FORTY-TWO

The nearly total darkness enhanced the sounds. From his hideout, Emilio could hear Lyuba's arrival, rather than seeing her. She always moved in a harmonious and silent way, like a feline, like a ballet dancer, like a snow fairy...Emilio couldn't help laughing ironically at himself for his sudden burst of lyricism in such an inopportune position. Actually he was inside the dark and messy small funerary chapel and he felt like a mole, literally and metaphorically. But the sound of steps on the creaking frozen snow seemed to be amplified by the surrounding absolute silence. Finally he perceived the pale glints of light of an electric torch. Lyuba and Pasha were speaking Russian to each other in a very low voice, but they might even shout, and it would have been the same for the Maresciallo, who could only try to guess what they were telling each other. He heard the noise of something metallic which was put down on the stone step of the other funeral chapel. Then he realized that Pasha was leaving.

Initially Emilio felt puzzled. How could Pasha leave Lyuba alone there? Then he thought that he had guessed the right reason. Pasha had great experience in a certain kind of matter. Nobody knew how he had acquired it–and it was probably much better not to know–but he had it. He didn't want to leave their car in sight, parked in front the small cemetery. Someone might notice it. Certainly the Russians didn't want to leave any sign of their passage. Emilio decided he would have done the same. Pasha probably would park somewhere else, maybe near the crossroad, only 200 metres away and then he would come back to help Lyuba.

But Lyuba would never accept a passive role and, without waiting for Pasha's return, she started tinkering and bustling about the tomb-stone, which closed the funerary niche of that unfortunate Arturo Pennacci, with something which might be a small electric drill and a hammer.

All of a sudden, to his enormous embarrassment, Emilio felt irremediably ridiculous. The whole situation was grotesque. What he was supposed to do now? Jumping out like a wind-up clown toy from his box? Of course he had to stop Lyuba before she could really manage to open the burial niche, to prevent her from committing something illegal. But how could he explain everything clearly in English? How could he motivate his presence there and persuade them to leave, guaranteeing them at the same time that their plan would have had an effect? He could hardly say a few basic sentences in English. He felt miserably inadequate. Luckily it seemed that masonry was not exactly one of Lyuba's main talents. She continued her work awkwardly. So far the fight between her and the silicone putty seemed to be quite uneven. But Emilio knew well that Pasha would open the niche in a nanosecond, once he was back. It meant that Emilio had to react immediately.

It was exactly in that moment that things came to a head and the situation escalated.

Someone had entered the cemetery and was approaching. At first Lyuba didn't turn, because she thought it might be Pasha coming back. But Emilio was immediately on the alert. He opened slightly the gate of his hideout, praying that it would not squeak too loudly. His eyes, used to the darkness, could see what was happening because a streetlamp offered a minimal source of pale light, strangely reflected by the fog, which seemed to get thicker at every second. Also Lyuba realized that it couldn't be Pasha; she let her tools fall and spun round.

The newcomer was a woman, much shorter than Lyuba. Emilio thought confusedly that she might be a relative of one of the people buried there, but this idea was immediately cancelled by the behaviour of the woman, who started shouting a few metres from Lyuba. Her voice was piercing and sounded hysterical. The former silence was broken so abruptly that the intensity of her cries seemed to be intolerable.

She shouted in Italian, at Lyuba, who didn't react, quite dumbfounded.

"Don't come closer, damned soul! Be gone, get out! Go away! I swear it wasn't me. It's Sabatino who killed you!"

Emilio grasped it at once. Lyuba didn't react in any way simply because she could not understand a word.

The other woman continued shouting; her voice vibrated on high-pitched tones and produced a very disagreeable effect like the squealing of chalk on a blackboard,

"Go away, or else I'll shoot!"

Unexpectedly she aimed a handgun at Lyuba. Emilio couldn't realize the speed of his whirling and distressed thoughts. He calculated without realizing it that the woman with the gun was too far from him. Since Lyuba was in the middle, he would not have a chance to block her. So he did the only thing he could do. He rushed out from the funeral chapel and flung himself at Lyuba, to protect her with his body.

The handgun-shot was ear-splitting.

Emilio felt a lightning and burning pain in his left shoulder. Something warm and viscous started running along his arm. Lyuba, flattened under his weight, struggled to move slightly and groaned.

He lifted his head, instinctively, to assess the level of danger. But someone had already rendered Jessica harmless. Pasha pushed the handgun away with a kick, even though Jessica had collapsed on the ground, quite unconscious, and it seemed very improbable that she still represented a menace, for the moment.

Pasha came closer to Emilio and delicately helped him to sit on a step of the chapel.

Lyuba, free from the burden, got on her feet again and whispered,

"Emilio, what are you doing here? What's happened? I think you saved my life..."

Then she realized that she had to reformulate her question to have a chance of making Emilio understand anything. She made an effort to speak slowly and simply and to articulate every word. Emilio nodded and manage to ask if she was well.

"Yes, yes...I'm fine. But you are injured; we must take you to hospital, soon."

Pasha bent over him and carefully tried to open the Maresciallo's heavy jacket. Emilio couldn't restrain a moan of pain. The expert eyes of Pasha scanned the wound which was abundantly bleeding. Then he tried to be clear and succinct, which was not difficult for him.

"No danger, Maresciallo, the bullet went through your shoulder, no organ was touched. Do you understand me? No danger, but blood, haemorrhage. You need a hospital. Can you understand me?"

Lyuba had recovered her presence of mind. She took quickly off a silk scarf that she had around her neck and she tried to roll it up tightly around Emilio's wounded shoulder, to reduce the bleeding.

"No, no..." Emilio tried to stop her, but she couldn't understand and looked at him in puzzlement.

Emilio turned to Pasha, nearly imploring him and miraculously Pasha seemed to understand.

"Pasha, time is short. No time. No traces of you and Lyuba. Take her away. You and Lyuba have never been here. Do you understand me? You and Lyuba were never here. My carabiniere, Maccaluso, is here, not far away. He will take me to hospital. I can give you another five minutes to get away, and then I'll call Maccaluso. I spoke to my colleagues, the Carabinieri of Umbertide. They will find Iris here. I have proof now. You must leave. If you don't, you'll be involved. Pasha, take my handcuffs, here. Handcuff the woman. It's Jessica Alunni, isn't it? Pasha, you didn't kill her, did you?"

"No, no, Maresciallo, she's breathing, she just banged her head." Quickly and efficiently Pasha handcuffed Jessica, who was lying on her face. While doing that he noticed a scarf which was partially outside of her coat and used it to bandage Emilio's wound. Then he had a sudden idea; he took the small electric drill and the hammer that Lyuba had used in her vain attempt and pressed Jessica bare fingers on them.

Pasha exchanged a knowing glance with Emilio, who repeated,

"You must go; take Lyuba away; you have never been here. I will do everything necessary. I'll call my Maccaluso now; he will arrive from the right side of the cemetery gate. Did you understand, Pasha? From the right. It's foggy; you go to the left side and hide there. He won't notice you. Then run quickly to your car, I don't know where it is. But quickly and then away."

Pasha nodded. Lyuba kneeled down by the Maresciallo and whispered,

"You are a great man, Emilio." And she repeated hesitating in Italian "Tu uomo molto buono e intelligente. Grazie!" And she kissed him lightly on his forehead.

Pasha seized her by the arm, gently, but firmly, and they ran like the wind into the fog.

Emilio took his mobile phone out of his pocket with his sound arm, hoping not to faint, at least not for a while. He felt dizzy and he had the unpleasant impression of bleeding copiously.

Maccaluso answered immediately.

"Maresciallo I heard a shot. I was so worried, but you told me not to move without your order..."

"Maccaluso, now call immediately the Carabinieri station of Umbertide and tell them to send an ambulance, as soon as possible. I was shot, but it's not my time yet. I'm here by the back wall of the cemetery, where there are the burial niches. I could arrest the woman who shot me, but you should guard her until the arrival of our colleagues. I'm afraid I'm not in condition to do that any longer. Ah, Maccaluso, bring me a blanket."

CHAPTER FORTY-THREE

Glowing embers smouldered peacefully in the fireplace. The room was half-lit; only the reading lamp on the writing table lit up the pages of the book, which William was reading, as he was lying on the couch with his head resting on Peter's knees.

Peter liked playing softly with William's curls, rolling them around his fingers and ruffling his hair a little, until William protested, pretending to be disturbed, while in reality both of them knew he adored it.

"It's pleasant, entertaining and amusing to have all our friends around, but sometimes I really feel the need to spend time only with you." Peter said, scratching lovingly William's scalp.

William nodded and groaned with pleasure.

"Would you like it if we took a little trip, just you and I? The restaurant will be closed until January and Reginald and Themba can manage here at the farm even without our precious presence."

"I'd love it." Peter smiled at the perspective. "Do you have already an idea?" William always had ideas before saying anything.

"Seaside in winter. It's actually the only time of the year when one can go to the seaside in Italy without being trapped among a forest of sun umbrella, deckchairs, beach-kiosks sending every king of pseudo-exotic food and drinks and pedlars who try to persuade you to buy knock-off items and fanciful fakes with a remarkable insistence. We might go to spend a week maybe in Sicily or whenever South. Oh damn! I forgot that there is New Year, in the middle. It would be impossible to find a good hotel which doesn't feature New Years' Eve parties and dances. I cannot make up my mind which is more tragic, a traditional wedding party or a traditional celebration of New Year's Eve..."

"I'm perfectly happy here at home with you." Peter reassured him, smiling silently at the simple idea of William attending a traditional New Year's Eve party maybe on a cruise ship. "We might take a few days off at the beginning of January, when everything is nicely calm after the season holidays."

"Do you know what?" William put the book on the floor and straightened a little. "I have thought over and it seems to me that you and I don't look gay enough. That is quite amazing because we definitely are."

Peter laughed heartily. "But you adore Maria Callas and Italian opera. I have been told that it's a very typical gay feature."

"It's not enough. A lot of straight people love that enormously too. It's not a very distinctive feature. You for example, I have never seen you swaying your hips while walking, and you never squeak with terror when you see a rat. You see what I mean. We should seriously consider the possibility of joining a gay pride parade, as soon as there is one planned somewhere. I might try hard to stand techno-music, and I could wear a pink lace body suit with a lot of feathers emerging luxuriantly from my buttocks."

Peter burst into laugh and then kissed him.

"I'm afraid my attraction for you would drop immediately to dramatically low levels. I claim the right to be my own way, without being accused of voluntary straight-acting. What in the hell did you put into your whiskey glass when I was not looking? You sound more capriciously extravagant than usual."

"I don't know, Peter, maybe it's that if I cannot defeat the stereotypes and the clichés, my only alternative is joining them and..."

William interrupted his own funny soliloquy and pointed at the door. "Do you hear that? A car is arriving..."

Peter got on his feet and went to the entry door to give a look at the courtyard. Actually he could hear the engine of a car, which was parking there. While he was opening the heavy, wooden double door, someone was doing the same from the other side and Lyuba, followed by Pasha nearly fell into Peter's arms.

Peter held her and helped her to the small lounge where William got up in turn and looked at them quite puzzled. He switched on the floor lamp and remained frozen. Lyuba was as pale as death, her hands were soiled with blood, and she had a smear of dry blood on her left cheek as well. She clenched firmly a silk scarf, which appeared drenched with blood, as if she didn't know what to do with it.

Peter was the first to react. He kept on holding Lyuba and asked her with a strangely calm voice,

"Are you injured Lyuba? What's happened?" And he looked at Pasha, who was a few steps behind and appeared to be well, except that his black trench was soiled with mud.

"I'm fine, don't worry. I'm fine." Lyuba whispered with a strange voice.

"But you are covered with blood!" William had approached her, recovering slightly from his initial, paralyzing amazement.

"It's not my blood. It's Emilio's. I'm unhurt. I need to go to the bathroom now, to clean myself. Forgive me. Pasha will start explaining to you. I'll be back soon." She wriggled out from Peter's thoughtful hold and quickly crossed the corridor to get upstairs.

Peter and William looked at Pasha interrogatively, and the Russian realized that his usual lack of verbal communication would be quite misplaced in the present circumstance; so he took a deep breath and started,

"Lyuba and I are well, but Maresciallo Ciricola was shot. Nothing serious, his life is not in danger. I examined his wound; the bullet crossed his shoulder and left from the other side. He lost a lot of blood, I'm afraid. But I'm quite sure that no vital organ was touched. Miss Lyuba is covered with blood, because she tried to staunch his haemorrhage with her scarf and mostly because the Maresciallo was lying on her. He had pushed her down to save her life from the woman who fired the shot. I arrived at that very moment. I made the mistake of leaving Miss Lyuba alone for a handful of minutes, just enough the time for me to hide our car. I didn't imagine that there would be other people. I failed in my task. It was a big mistake. Luckily Maresciallo Ciricola was there too. Maresciallo Ciricola is a great man. Very intelligent and very brave.

"Of course we would never have left him there on his own and injured, but he told us that one of his Carabinieri was there, that the local police were informed and that we had to leave immediately, before any of them could notice us. He was right. Miss Lyuba could not remain there. So I drove her straight on to your home. We had no other place to go. We had already checked out at our hotel. Then we had to inform you of everything."

Pasha was silent again, satisfied with his report, which probably appeared short but fully accurate to him. But William lost his temper and approached Pasha nearly threateningly. Instantly the Russian put himself automatically on the alert, ready to block any attack by any means, but immediately after that he realized that he was facing William, who wasn't a hostile stranger, but a friend. So he let his arms fall down by his body and waited.

"What the fuck are you babbling, Pasha? This afternoon you were here with Lyuba, to greet us, you claimed. You were supposed to leave to London. And now you appear again, at night, covered with blood and telling us that our friend Emilio was somewhere with you, and someone shot him." William was shouting and Peter felt troubled. He had never heard William shouting like that.

Pasha was motionless. For a moment Peter was seriously worried that William might punch him and then who knows what might happen...Then the Russian spoke again,

"You are right to be angry, William. My report was not as efficient as I hoped. But I'm not good with words. I apologize. Lyuba will explain everything to you much better. We were at the cemetery, where Mrs Ellie and I had identified the place where that poor woman's corpse is surely hidden. Lyuba wanted to do for you what you were not allowed to do, that is opening the burial niche. We had thought to go there, to take out the body of the woman and then to leave unnoticed. Someone would have found it, and the case would be reopened.

"But then that woman, Jessica, arrived. She saw Lyuba and started shouting at her in Italian. Then she took out a handgun and tried to kill Lyuba. I saw her too late, when I was coming back after hiding our car. Fortunately Maresciallo Ciricola was there. We didn't know it. I think I have understood everything only now. He jumped out and pushed Lyuba down on the ground, and he took the bullet that was destined for her.

"At that point we managed to understand each other. He's a man of action, like me. I understood what he wanted me to do. He was right. I rendered Jessica harmless. The Maresciallo made me understand that I should handcuff her. I think he will declare that he was alone there. Jessica didn't see me; she saw only Lyuba. She banged her head; I took her from behind. In any case it will be her word against the Maresciallo's. The case will be reopened. The Maresciallo found the right thing to do. I would have never left him alone, but he was right, and I was responsible for Miss Lyuba."

William calmed down immediately, but he was still very worried about Emilio.

"I must go to get news of Emilio. He has no family, no friends here, besides us."

Lyuba reappeared, she had combed her hair, and she had cleaned her face and her hands, but on the sleeve of her pullover there were still a few dark spots. She seemed to have recovered her spirits. She had heard William's last words and she said,

"I'm relieved if you can manage to get news about Emilio's condition. It was all so sudden. I know you are annoyed with us for our initiative. But we wanted to be of help. You know I cannot tolerate injustice, and the idea of two murderers who could enjoy life freely really made me feel sick, mostly because you and all the other friends had collected evidence of their crime. I won't leave until I can go to see Emilio to thank him for saving my life and for everything. I want to stay at least a few days with him, supporting him. Nothing will be enough to thank him, but I can at least offer him a friendly presence. If you and Peter would be so generous and kind to let us stay here for a few extra days, it would be perfect. I think it might sound slightly suspicious if, after checking out, we check in immediately again at the hotel or if we chose another one with the risk of being noticed. After all we have to give our documents to be registered in any hotel...."

"No problem, Lyuba, you are at your home here. Now take all your time and tell Peter all details. Pasha has made an appreciable effort to explain to us what happened, but maybe you can do it in an even clearer way. As for me, I'm going to the Carabinieri station in Capacciano and, as soon as I know where Emilio is hospitalized, I'll go immediately to see him. Then I'll call you to keep you informed." William quickly put on his sheepskin coat and a woollen scarf, seized his cars keys and left.

"Let's go to the kitchen. It's comfortably warm there. I'll make tea for everyone." Peter remembered that the Russians preferred tea. "Then if you feel like, you can eat something. I can understand that you must be tired, Lyuba, but I'd be grateful if you could tell me everything, before going to sleep."

And Lyuba did so.

CHAPTER FORTY-FOUR

When the young carabiniere Maccaluso, who had spent a few difficult hours sitting on a very uncomfortable metal chair in the corridor of the ward, saw the familiar face of Mr. Collins, one of the owners of the farm, he felt like a shepherd boy to whom the Virgin Mary had just appeared.

Of course the colleagues of Umbertide had been polite with him, but they had no time to be supportive. They merely paid attention to him, after the careful interrogation that he had to undergo. They had taken custody of the woman who had shot Maresciallo Ciricola. Maccaluso had told them that he had found her already handcuffed. The Maresciallo had done that by himself, when he had managed to render her harmless. Maccaluso had explained that the Maresciallo was practically lying on the woman, whom he had pinioned on the ground.

Capitano Lo Cascio had realized that Maccaluso could not add much more, since he had not been present to witness the facts. The Capitano had told him that his presence was no longer necessary and that he was free to go back to Capacciano, if he wanted. But how could he leave the Maresciallo on his own in that hospital?

"Mr William, it's good that you are here. How did you know that..." The young carabiniere felt relieved. He didn't know what to do, but he knew that he was less alone now.

"Maccaluso," William realized he didn't know the young man's first name either "Where is Emilio? What did the doctors say?"

"Ah, Mr William, it was awful. The Maresciallo is under sedation now; the doctors gave him a blood transfusion. But he will be fine, thank God. I was useless; I couldn't give him blood either. The doctor told me that my blood group was not compatible. The Maresciallo was so brave; he didn't lose consciousness for a single second. The colleagues of the Carabinieri station here in Umbertide were impressed." He lowered his voice, "I'm not completely sure that I can tell you that, but you are such a good friend of my Maresciallo...One of the colleagues let slip that they found a body of a woman inside a niche, at the cemetery, while it was supposed to be the tomb of an old man, dead many years ago. Maresciallo Ciricola told them what to do. It seems that the corpse was that of a murdered woman. I have also heard that the husband of the woman, who shot poor Maresciallo, is hospitalized here; he had a car accident. He's under surveillance in his hospital room now. He's suspected of being a murderer. But they are just rumours so far..."

William smiled. "It's not a matter of rumours, Maccaluso. It's really like that. We are all grateful to Emilio for what he has done to establish the truth. You look worn out, by the way I don't know your first name, and it seems to me quite absurd calling you 'Maccaluso' in these circumstances."

"Salvatore, my name is Salvatore. My friends call me Salvo...Yes, I'm quite tired. But I can stay here as long as necessary. No problem."

William tapped friendly on the young carabiniere's shoulder.

"If you feel like driving back home you can go, Salvo. I'll stay here with Emilio until he wakes up. If you give me your cell phone number, I'll call you to give you news."

Maccaluso found the energy to smile faintly.

"Yes, I can drive. Then I do think I should go back to our headquarters in Capacciano. Beppe, uhm, I mean carabiniere Cipriani, is alone there. If you think you don't need me here, Mr William, then I will drive back home, and I'll wait for your phone call."

Maccaluso was so used to take orders, that, without realizing it, he had conferred the authority to William.

"Go, go, Salvo and drive carefully on the road. Then try to have a good sleep. You need it. I'll stay here. Don't worry." William had to make an effort to repress a grin, when young carabiniere Maccaluso automatically offered him a military salute before walking away along the corridor.

A couple of nurses came out from a room. They looked at William in a rather inquisitive way. But a more attentive, second glance replaced their slightly puzzled suspicion with a genuine admiration. The tall man with the dark curls was definitely the most handsome person they had ever seen. He approached them and smiled. His smile was not the usual arrogant display of self-congratulation of a man who is conscious of his power of seduction. He smiled with a genuine empathy in a spontaneous and kind way.

"I'm looking for Maresciallo Ciricola, the carabiniere who was shot...I'm one of his dearest friends, and I have just come from Arezzo to see him."

"Oh, yes, sure. He's sleeping now, but you can see him. It's good he can have a friend by him. If there is any need you can call us. We are on duty for the whole night." The older of the nurses, a slightly plump woman in her forties pointed at a door.

"I'm sure that my friend Emilio is in very good hands. Thank you for taking care of him so professionally and so kindly." William felt unpleasantly sycophantic, but he had to gain the nurses to his cause to get their authorization to stay with Emilio. He knew that usually the work of nurses is not always recognized to be of proper value by the relatives of patients.

Emilio was sleeping in his bed, with a huge bandaging over entire his shoulder and all the usual little tubes which connected him to the drip and to the monitor. He was snoring a little and looked calm.

William left the room again and tried to find a corner where he could use his cell phone without disturbing the night stillness of the ward and the other patients. A few metres further he found a kind of small waiting room, with a drinks machine. A middle-aged carabiniere was rummaging in his pockets to find coins. When he saw William, he nodded to greet him and added with an apologetic note,

"The machine accepts only coins. One has never coins enough when one needs them. I'd like to take a cup of coffee also to my colleagues, but I cannot even find enough coins for myself."

"I have small change, how many coins would you need?" William emptied his pockets and put a handful of coins on the tablets by the machine.

The carabiniere gave him the equivalent in banknotes and started following the instructions written on the machine.

"Every machine is different; they were made to make people confused. The only thing they have in common is that the quality of the coffee is equally miserable." He looked tired, but he had a meek expression on his badly shaved face. He fiddled with the various buttons, and he managed to arrange three small plastic cups of coffee on the side table, but when he tried to get the forth cup, the machine balked and refused stubbornly to give him a further coffee, but kept the coins he had properly and duly inserted into the slot.

"Damn!" The man started punching lightly the machine front, without any apparent result.

"Please, let me try..." William smiled again and took out his Swiss Army knife and inserted one of the small tools into the seam around the slot, and moved it carefully, and then he bent over and looked inside the section where the coffee was supposed to ooze and gave it a quick, precise tap. The machine grunted and started working again.

"Amazing! Thank you so much." The carabiniere took his coffee with a glance of admiration at William, but then he looked again at the machine, which didn't seem to intend to stop working, once it had started again and was keeping on producing cups of coffee, even though no one had introduced any further coins.

"Ah, this is crazy! How can we stop it now?" An open smile appeared on his worn out face.

"The only way I know at this stage is a drastic one..." William unplugged the cable. Then he connected it again and the machine remained wisely steady with all its lights on.

"You have even more coffee than needed now and, in any case, you cannot carry all the cups at once. Let me help you. Ah, by the way, my name is William Collins. I came from Capacciano. I'm a dear friend of Maresciallo Ciricola, and I'm here to take care of him, to support him and to offer him a friendly presence when he wakes up. We are all worried for him at our village..." He added.

"Nice to meet you. I'm Vice Brigadiere Giovanni Tiveron of the Carabinieri of Umbertide. I suppose you are already informed, since you are a friend of Maresciallo Ciricola." Vice Brigadiere Tiveron wringed William's hand.

"I had been at the Carabinieri Station of our village, Capacciano before coming here and, as soon I arrived I spoke to carabiniere Maccaluso, whom I also know well personally."

The two men set off for the lift, carrying as many of cups of coffee as they could. "We have to go to the second floor." Explained Tiveron. "My colleagues and I are on duty to keep under surveillance two arrested people, who are both hospitalized. But they are probably better than you and me...What can one do? We can only follow the orders."

William decided it was the suitable moment to play his cards.

"I'm informed about the unofficial investigation that Emilio—Maresciallo Ciricola, I mean—was conducting. We have tried to help him in all possible ways. Our Mayor's wife was the best friend of Iris

Ciancaleoni, and she has never believed that Iris could have committed suicide..."

"Oh, but it means that you are one of the people mentioned by Maresciallo Ciricola. Our superior officer, Capitano Lo Cascio, needs to ask you several questions. He thought to call you at a more appropriate hour, but you are already here...We found a corpse, exactly where Maresciallo Ciricola told us to look for it. I was there; it was only few hours ago. The body was somehow mummified. It happens when a corpse is sealed in a burial niche, without air. It was still easy to realize that it was not the body of an eighty years old man who died forty years before. It was a woman, apparently young, with long blond hair. Then the forensic experts arrived and took the body away, for identification.

"Maresciallo Ciricola was already in the ambulance, but he still spoke to Capitano Lo Cascio, who came here to the hospital with him. I don't know what they told each other, of course, but I was ordered to organize a strict guard watch here. The woman, who shot Maresciallo Ciricola, was arrested, but she needed medical attention, because she banged her head. Her husband was already hospitalized here, but he has been remanded into custody also..."

They arrived at the other ward, at the second floor. Three other Carabinieri were there. William helped to deliver coffee to everyone.

"I'm sorry, but you'll understand you cannot stay here now..." Tiveron sounded ill at ease.

"Of course! Don't worry. I'll go back to Emilio's room. I won't move from there. Tell your Capitano where he can find me, if he needs to ask me anything."

William went straight on to the stairway, neglecting the lift. On the landing between two floors he stopped and took out his cell phone. He read on the display that it was already four in the morning, but he knew that Peter was waiting for news.

CHAPTER FORTY-FIVE

Silence doesn't mean to be quiet but to observe what's going on. Silence is a secret weapon that few can master because the noise of the world is more appealing.

Peter found Pasha and Lyuba in the kitchen. Morning hadn't broken yet. Pasha was wearing, as usual, a white shirt with a black suit and a narrow, black tie. He looked impeccable, nearly aseptic, in his apparent–or real–total lack of emotions. He was sipping slowly a cup of tea, and he barely lifted his eyes when Peter entered the room. He didn't say a word. Peter wondered if he had spent the night there, on that chair.

Lyuba was not in a talkative mood either, but she greeted him with a question. "Did you get any news, Peter?" She had somewhat dark bags under her eyes, which seemed to be narrower.

Peter sat down on the edge of the massive wooden table and told them everything that he knew.

"...William will call again when Emilio wakes up. It seems that later he will have to meet a certain Capitano Lo Cascio. Emilio told everything to the Carabinieri of Umbertide, omitting only the presence of both of you in the cemetery. Jessica and Sabatino were arrested." He concluded.

The door suddenly was flung open, and Themba made a noisy and colourful entry. He remained astonished seeing Pasha and Lyuba, whom he thought would be already back in London.

"I see..." Peter sighed, "I must start over my whole report once again!"

While speaking he could read a different expression on Themba's face. Finally Themba said,

"What a night! Now I understand why Sabatino didn't call me. Poor Emilio, he has been remarkable."

"Indeed." Peter nodded in assent. "And now I have to inform all the others. I'll go personally to Capacciano to speak to Loredana

Sanchini and the mayor. Loredana is the one who has the right to know the developments of the inquiry more than anybody else. Everything started from her motivated suspicions. She'll be relieved to know that Iris' body was found and that her murderers will pay for their crime."

Pasha gave a side glance at Lyuba and, at long last, he spoke.

"If you don't need me for a couple of hours, I'd like to go to Mr Reginald and Mrs Ellie's home to bring them up to date."

"Sure, Pasha, sure. But later I need to go to Umbertide to visit Emilio at the hospital..."

Lyuba looked infinitely tired. Peter felt terribly sorry, thinking of what he was going to tell her. He had thought of that since he had spoken with William. That thought had taken a more and more precise shape in his mind and he felt persuaded that it was his task to tell Lyuba about that. He hoped to be able to find the suitable words.

A pale daylight had started filtering little by little through the windows. Themba rushed home to give the extraordinary news to Caterina and the twins.

Pasha took his car keys and left silently. He had to preserve all of his potential ability to speak to inform exhaustively Reginald and Ellie. Peter thought that the affection that Lyuba's bodyguard seemed to have developed for Reginald and Ellie was much less surprising than what one might at first consider. Reginald and Ellie were gifted with a natural empathy and a spontaneity which made everyone feel comfortable with them. They were intelligent and humorous, and they were of reassuring age, which prevented them from any risk of competition with younger people. Probably Pasha was used to being lonely. It was a voluntary choice. Who knows what there was in his past and maybe also in his present. Maybe the warm and merry temper of Ellie and the wise joviality of Reginald had appealed him because they were uncommon in his life.

Reginald was not only Peter's dearest friend, but he had always had a special role in his life, a little like the father he had never had. For Peter it was not surprising imagining that Pasha might find something vaguely motherly in Ellie.

Peter felt even saddened by the conversation he was going to have with Lyuba. He had been so lucky in his life. He had everything that Lyuba did not have. Friends, a serene life...and William.

They were on their own, now in the kitchen. Only Peter and Lyuba, who had let her tea cool down in the cup.

"Lyuba, we must talk, you and I. It's not easy to find the opportunity for a private conversation here at the farm. Mostly in this period, with all what has happened..." Peter was still sitting on the edge of the old, wooden table and he felt incongruously like one of those modern teachers, who think that lecturing in a less formal way, sitting uninhibitedly on the desk, might convey more easily complicated or simply boring concepts to their students.

Lyuba curled up on the sofa, opposite him; her trousers clung to her long legs.

"I was sure you would look for an opportunity." There was a suspicion of sarcasm in Lyuba's words, or a light reaction of self-defence. "I suppose you'd intend to speak about William and my relationship with him, even though there is nothing I could define like that."

Peter realized he had an advantage on her, because she didn't guess what he meant to tell. She would be more spontaneous in her reactions for that.

"We are two strangers, since we have never spoken to each other in a slightly more personal way, Lyuba. But often staying aside, rather than being directly involved, allows us to develop a kind of unbiased observation that can make us understand certain details, which might be missed in a conversation. I have no well-founded reason for discussing with you about William. I'm aware that he can communicate easily with you, and I think you and William have a few features in common. I noticed immediately, the first time we met, in London, that you had deep feelings for him. I'm in love with William, so I can easily detect the same symptoms, if I can call them that, in another person. Believe it or not, I have never been jealous of you. It's not because I think you could not interest William in a more complete way. On the contrary, I'm persuaded he could be attracted by you even physically. I'm not jealous of you, Lyuba, because William is in love with me, and I deeply trust what we have built up together. I know it's what William wants too. You cannot imagine what William was like when we met, and I won't speak to you about that. But he has found in our relationship what he was looking for. I won't poison his trust with my jealousy. If one day he stops loving me, there will be reasons which I'll try to accept and respect. But now it's not that time, and there is no reason for that, which might worry me. So I don't need to speak to you about William. But I need to speak to you about Emilio."

Lyuba shook her head; she was taken by surprise. She expected that Peter wanted to warn her to keep out of William's way. She felt annoyed with herself, because she had made a wrong evaluation.

"Emilio? But you said that he is relatively well, and William confirmed that his life is not in danger. I intend to go to visit him and to stay with him as soon Pasha comes back to drive me there. He's such a clever and generous man. He saved my life. That psychopathic, stupid woman would have killed me. And it's not only that. In spite of his wound, Emilio still had the lucidity to arrange everything to leave me and Pasha out from the whole story. Actually it could have been embarrassing to justify our role to the Italian authorities, and my professional position would be delicate if I were involved in...in matters like that in a foreign country."

Lyuba spoke quickly; her words had the intensity of a swollen river, as if she wanted to overwhelm Peter's concentration. But he didn't lose the thread.

"I know, Lyuba, that you have no obligation to be sincere with me. But I'm sure you are basically a very sincere person. I have only a simple and fundamental question for you. Do you think that, one day, there would be at least a slight chance that you fall in love with Emilio Ciricola?"

Lyuba looked at him with a pinch of hostile amazement, what an inane question. Then she thought over. Lyuba was intelligent and, as Peter had rightly stressed, basically sincere.

"What does it matter? Nonsense. Never say never, of course. But no, I don't think I might fall in love with Emilio. I have a deep admiration for him, he's pleasant, but..."

"Exactly, Lyuba. You see, Emilio is rich in qualities, but he does not have what would be essential to make a woman like you fall in love with him. Emilio comes from a very modest family of Southern Italy; a background which is alien for you. You studied in the most exclusive Swiss college. It's not because financial status; it's much more than this. Emilio has fought all his life to get what he has achieved. He lost his wife, whom he loved immensely, only one year ago. He has lived in grief since then, ignoring any other women. Then he met you. I don't intend to analyse what he had felt and why, but he is falling seriously in love with you. We have to protect him from a disappointment, because he would suffer too much and the only way is not to allow him to nourish illusions. If he found you by his bed and if you remained close to him for several days he would start thinking that maybe you could love him, and he would start basing his renewed sentimental life on that expectation." Peter read in Lyuba's face that she had understood, even though she was not ready to admit it yet.

"But I have never given him any reason for illusions..."

"Maybe you didn't, consciously. It would be so far from your mind. But now, Lyuba, now, if you nurse him as a devoted fiancée..."

"It would be only as a friend, not as a fiancée. I need to show my gratitude and..." Lyuba protested feebly, but only not to give Peter the satisfaction of agreeing with him.

Peter kept on implacably, but with sympathy.

"This is the point, Lyuba, in that you remind me of William as he was when I met him. You need to show your gratitude. You'd do it for yourself, without thinking what is better for the person who deserves your gratitude."

"So what should I do?" Lyuba asked, even though she knew that well by herself.

"Do what you are thinking of at this moment. That is the best for Emilio, not for your ego. Go back to London as you had planned."

Lyuba nervously changed the position of her legs. She hated to admit that Peter was quite right indeed and that, despite the fact that he would never be her ally in anything, she couldn't help respecting him. It was necessary to be somehow special to be loved by William. That was sure. She wouldn't show him her frailty. She wouldn't confess that the idea of finding herself in her big, empty house of London, without Iraida, without anyone, would sound unbearable. But she was used to being alone, even among people. Being the boss anywhere is lonely. Being a female boss in a world of mostly men is especially so. Her father, besides giving her financial support and a high level education, had given her only one advice,

'If you want, you can make your own destiny, Lyuba. But when you realize that fate is invincible, don't take it into your head to change it and in that manner to prepare your own defeat. Choose to follow another path and go farther.'

"But Emilio will ask for me..."

"Of course he will, and we'll tell him that you are fine and very grateful to him and you are back at your business. He'll accept the idea that his crush on you is destined to remain a dream. He'll get over it, and he won't suffer more than a little."

Lyuba looked tired, but also very young in that moment, something similar to a melancholy smile appeared on her lips.

"I'd like to be able to detest you, Peter. But unfortunately I cannot. Absurdly I have a liking for you, and I dare to imagine that it would be good to be your friend. Promise to me that you'll take good care of William, because something tells me that there are very few chances that I might meet him and all restof you again."

Peter would never be able to explain why he did that, but impulsively he went to sit by Lyuba and hugged her. She didn't reject his embrace, but for a few seconds she remained pressed against his chest with a strange feeling of relief.

Peter's cell phone chose that moment to ring.

William told him joyfully that Emilio had woken up and was happy to find him by his bed. The doctors said he was fine and in few days he could come back home. William had met Capitano Lo Cascio, and now he had a much clearer idea about what's happened. Iris's body had been officially identified. Sabatino and Jessica were under arrest, and they had already undergone a strict interrogation. It seemed that Sabatino had started confessing to having murdered his first wife. Emilio had given the colleagues of Umbertide all the collected data on the case. He had spoken about all his friends' roles in the enquiry, Loredana's suspicions, the trip to Torino, Themba who played the psychic and the shadowing of Alunni. Emilio had only neglected to mention the contribution of Lyuba and Pasha, for obvious reasons.

Lyuba could only hear the pleasantly excited sound of William's voice from the cell phone, without grasping the single words.

William informed Peter of his conversation with Capitano Lo Cascio, when he had confirmed Emilio's version. The Capitano had sounded frankly amused by their spirit of enterprise. Emilio would have surely received an official commendation and maybe even advancement.

"Come to see Emilio, when you can. He would be happy. Then I must confess I'm feeling a littlc tired after a sleepless night, and I'd like coming back home to take a shower and to get a few hours of sleep, when you arrive here to relieve me. We must not leave Emilio on his own. He must feel that we are his family. What are you doing now?"

"I'm here, only with Lyuba. Then I think to go to inform Loredana and the Mayor. They have the right to know all the news from us, not from the media. Pasha's gone to see Ellie and Reginald for the same reason."

William changed tone.

"Let me speak with Lyuba. I have something to tell her."

Peter handed his cell to Lyuba and smiled in a friendly way, creating in a second a kind of sympathetic intimacy with her. Then he left the kitchen to give her the freedom to speak to William privately. Lyuba was not too surprised. It was a confirmation of Peter's nature, which she was starting to discover.

William came immediately to the point. "Lyuba, I know I'll sound hard to you, but I'm equally sure you'll understand. It's Emilio. I know you would like to come here and to stay with him because he...he did what he did for you and Pasha. But I know you can't give him what he would like receiving from you and...He had already suffered so much in his life..."

Lyuba interrupted him with a snigger full of sadness.

"You and Peter are really a perfect match. Don't worry. I have understood. You both showed me that it would be unfair to give any illusions to Emilio. I know what it means to be in love with a person unable to reciprocate." She sniggered again.

"So I guess that Peter thought the same, and he has spoken to you. I assure that we didn't make any prior agreement. We didn't speak about that between us either. So what are you going to do now, Lyuba?" William wondered with curiosity what words Peter had found to convince Lyuba so easily.

"I'll go back to London first, as planned. But I won't be able to remain there. I need a change of atmosphere, to turn a page. Don't worry about me, William. There is a person I know, a very good acquaintance who lives in San Francisco Bay area, in Oakland. He has proposed that I join his business, to invest in real estate. I had never taken a decision about that, because I didn't want to leave Europe. But things change. Future is a fluid dimension; there is nothing static. Maybe it's a good idea to put an ocean between us." Lyuba spoke calmly, slightly ironically.

"Oceans might not be big enough." Also William spoke with a tenderly ironic note in his voice. "I need to ask you for a promise now, something very serious, Lyuba. Please, give me your word that nothing unexpected will happen to Sabatino Alunni and his wife Jessica. You know what I mean. I deeply hope that there won't be any sniper appearing from nowhere to shoot them. Let justice do its work, Lyuba."

William tried to be persuasive and convincing, without sounding commanding. Being peremptory with Lyuba would have the opposite effect.

"You should ask Mrs Sanchini for this promise, not me. Iris was her best friend, not mine." Lyuba stretched her legs and clenched the mobile phone, as if it were the last link she would have with William.

"Good to know that. Tell your friend in Oakland to treat you well Lyuba, you deserve it."

"I'm sure he will. Then goodbye, William."

"Goodbye, Lyuba".

Acknowledgments

I'm extremely grateful to W.B. who not only has patiently and effectively helped me to make this book readable, but has also constantly encouraged me with his positive and sympathetic remarks.

My characters are equally thankful to him, because he has made them feel real, which is something that all the characters of a novel would like to be.

Thank you to all my editors who have collaborated in effective way, each one of them according to their possibilities, but always with sincere enthusiasm.

And most of all, thank you to my wise, generous and clever husband for everything he has done, he does and he will do.